"**H**ad enough?" sneered the dwarf, his stance ready for whichever way this went.

"In your dreams!" shouted the big man as he simultaneously surged to his feet and launched himself at the dwarf.

Again the barbarian was ready for him. He easily side-stepped the attack and again stuck out a leg to trip the bigger man. As he did so, he clasped both hands together and brought them down on Grouthuum's exposed neck as he went by. The resultant blow caused the fighter to land face first in a heap on the floor.

Again the bigger man pushed himself to all fours, even more slowly this time, however. He shook his head and looked up bleary-eyed, trying to find his opponent.

"Stay down," said the dwarf, "and I'll buy you an ale for your effort." He smiled to remove any hint of ill intent from his demeanor. "Come at me again, and I'll stop playing nice!"

THE LIBRARY OF ANTIQUITY

VANCE PUMPHREY

LEAPING WIZARD PRESS

The Library of Antiquity

Book Two in the Valdaar's Fist Series

Copyright © 2015 by Vance Pumphrey

Cover Art © 2015 Joe Calkins
Sword Logo Design © 2015 Joe Calkins

Published by Leaping Wizard Press

ISBN-10: 0988740559
ISBN-13: 978-0-9887405-5-6

This book is also available in digital formats.

Discover other titles by the author at
VancePumphrey.com

I'm dedicating this book to the U.S. Navy.
They took a skinny 17-year-old and filled him out in more ways than one.
I tested their resolve on more than one occasion, and they tested mine.
Together we managed to produce a pretty decent product over my 18-year career.
Without the Navy, I probably would have never gotten involved
in the realm of Fantasy, and therefore never would have put together
the material to write these books.
While the U.S. Navy can be a rough life,
the friendships made there will stand the test of time.
Thank you...

The Library of Antiquity

What has Gone Before

Forged by mortals. ... Enchanted by Drow. ...
Wielded by a God. .... Lost by man...

Or was it?

If you have not read *Dragma's Keep*, then I would suggest you do so! Beg, borrow or _____ a copy and read it. (I have chosen to omit the third part of that particular saying on the advice of counsel. They fear some might take that option literally and point back to this austere tome as proof they were told it was OK.) Actually, I would prefer you buy your own copy. You will not be disappointed.

The Library of Antiquity is the second book in a series known as Valdaar's Fist. However, in the event that it has been some time since you read the first book, or if your memory is as spotty as mine, here is a synopsis of what has gone before.

Sordaak, a mage by trade, was having a little fun in a local drinking establishment where Savinhand, a rogue by trade, was busy fleecing the locals by way of a not-too-friendly game of chance. The scene turned ugly and one—or more—of the locals got themselves dead by way of our aforementioned heroes. They made a hasty retreat, most of the local farmers' coin in their pockets.

Previously unknown to one another, they teamed up and made a run for it, ending up at the local livery where Savin (also known as "Thumbs") had a horse and some pack mules. Sordaak did not own a horse but looked around and appropriated one he liked. (His version of the story: He intended to return it after all the hubbub died down.)

They rode fast and hard out of town, during which Savin knocked a lantern over. That ended up burning half the village, thereby ensuring they would not be immediately followed—but also ensuring they would never again be welcome in said town (Brasheer, if it matters!).

They made their way to visit some of Sordaak's friends, where they intended to hide out until a plan was formulated. Sordaak had been in town recruiting party members for an assault on Dragma's Keep and was trying to decide whether this rogue would make a suitable asset when the owner of the appropriated horse made a sudden appearance. This owner was intent on meting out justice by the tried-and-true method of discouraging said activity by separating the culprit's head from his or her shoulders.

However, ever quick of wit, Sordaak spun a compelling tale and convinced the way-oversized fighter—actually Paladin, Thrinndor by name—that he knew where this Dragma's Keep was and even persuaded him to join the foray. (Did I mention this mage was a good fast-talker? Paladins are notoriously hard to sway from a given task, particularly when it involves theft of something that belongs to them, as they generally don't own much.)

Thrinndor went to town for supplies (fortunately, the sundries shop was spared from the previous night's bonfire) and returned with a longtime companion of his—Vorgath by name, barbarian by trade. He is of the race of dwarves and very old...at least by human standards.

Unable to find a healer (cleric), they decided to make the attempt without one. But first Sordaak had to make the call for his familiar.

He did so and was answered by a Quasit—a small demon that very, very rarely answers this call, and only then to the most powerful or soon to be most powerful of mages. (Does that not portend some good things for our hero?). It had been many centuries since the calling had been answered such.

But then I digress. If you are not familiar with this familiar, then go back and read (or re-read) Book One!

So our troop got on the road. Sordaak—through Thrinndor's trip to town—had arranged for the current occupants of the entrance to the Keep to be away "on business." Or at least most of them (rumored to exceed 200 orcs!). There was a small contingent left behind, and thus the members of the party had to fight their way in.

The rogue was seriously injured in the ensuing battle, and only by way of the use of one of their precious healing potions and a brief rest were they able to continue.

But continue they did. Several more battles ensued, and only the wiliness of the wizard, craftiness of the rogue and the strength of the two fighter types enabled them to keep body and soul together.

However, their supply of healing potions was dwindling rapidly, and there had not been a large amount to start with. They happened upon the room they had determined must be the study/library they were looking for (Sordaak had reluctantly revealed he had a map). Locked within the room was a couple of huge, armed Minotaurs who took exception to being disturbed and let our heroes know as much by immediately attacking.

In the ensuing battle more than one of the party was seriously injured (I don't really remember who or how bad—maybe I should go back and read Book One, huh?). They also discovered a young woman, unconscious and emaciated, hanging by her wrists from the ceiling. They cut her free and were able to revive her.

Her name was Cyrillis, and she was revealed to be a healer by trade! In fact, she was a Cleric of the Order of Valdaar. It just so happens that Thrinndor was a paladin of the Paladinhood of Valdaar. She had also recently come into possession of Kurril, one of the ancient artifacts of power thought to have been destroyed in the Final Conflict that saw the death of their god, Valdaar.

So now the party was complete. After eating, resting and some exchange of information, they were ready to proceed. Much searching revealed the secret door they knew had to be in the chamber. Sordaak magik'd it open, and they were now certain they had found their way into the Keep proper.

The resulting passage led to an underground (by now they were far underground, indeed) lake, illuminated by some strange lichen none of them had encountered before. Here they rested and told tales (some of them even true, I'm certain!).

Refreshed, they followed a path that abruptly ended at a sheer cliff. After determining they could not go over, Thrinndor attempted to go under (through the water, of course). He found a passage that led to another chamber, but a brief underwater swim was required.

Soon, dripping wet, all stood on an embankment on the other side. It was an embankment that had obviously been carved—or at least finished—by the hands of man (Dwarfs, probably, Vorgath announced)! There they discovered a single set of doors.

While Savin was doing his required due diligence by checking for traps and locks, Cyrillis screamed for help when she was attacked by a monster from the deep pool through which they had just swam. An octopus—a giant octopus.

Our heroes came to her rescue (of course!) and after a vicious struggle, the good guys prevailed. But not without a cost. Again, several in the party were hurt, and Cyrillis' recently restored healing skills were put to the test.

Weary and running low on food and other supplies, they decided to press on lest they die from lack sustenance in the not-so-distant future.

They made their way through the doors only to encounter a party of orcs that had heard them enter. Yet another battle ensued and our heroes again prevailed, this time without much damage to themselves. They managed to capture one of the creatures for interrogation. But it was unable to provide much useful information; just that he was part of a much larger group.

Great! Now what?

Well, they had not much choice at this juncture. Turning back was not an option, so they continued.

Not long after that, they ran into another band of orcs. This time, however, they were accompanied by at least one human!

And an assassin!

An even bigger battle followed. But such was the strength of the good guys that the ranks of the orcs were quickly decimated. However, a small contingent—including the human (later to be determined to be a powerful mage)—broke from the main group and ran.

Thrinndor was gravely injured by an attack from the previously mentioned assassin, and only quick work by the healer saved his life. However, these necessary actions allowed their adversaries to escape and left the party little hope of catching them.

After another much needed rest, during which they learned more about each other, they ventured deeper into the Keep.

Soon they came to a huge chamber that was obviously a temple. Sordaak produced yet another map, and they determined that in order to continue they must solve a puzzle.

While the mage worked on the puzzle, the thief scouted around and encountered another assassin—much to his chagrin and almost to his demise. When he was discovered missing, the rest of the party went looking for him. They found him not breathing in an antechamber in an adjacent hall.

Once again only quick work by our healer, this time augmented by assistance from someone—or something—in the afterlife, returned his life-force to his body.

After admonishing the rogue, the caster decided they should look around, saying certainly a group of the size they had encountered must have had some supplies. He was right, and they were able to replenish their store of food, wine and water.

Once again Sordaak set about trying to figure out the puzzle, and—with a little help from the dwarf (they are said to be good at both making and solving puzzles, after all)—soon was able to do so.

Once solved, it turned out the chamber they were in (yes, the whole damn thing!) lowered more than twenty feet, revealing more hallways branching out from the regularly spaced doors circling the walls of the temple.

Searching these finally led them to an ornate set of doors. These were heavily trapped and barred. Only after an exhaustive search, and subsequent removal of said traps, were they able to continue. A smaller chamber was on the other side—a chamber of summoning! They were beset by a huge fire elemental that truly tested their skills.

However, prevail they did. As they healed up, they wondered what could possibly be next.

Our heroes did not have to wait long to find out. An apparition appeared on a raised dais, and they once again made ready to do battle. But the apparition allayed their fears and introduced himself as Dragma!

He wove for them a tale and told them what to expect next. It was here we discovered that Thrinndor was of the lineage of Valdaar. Yes, descendant of a god!

Dragma told them they must stay the course and find the remaining artifacts of power from Valdaar's reign. For only through these could the god be returned to our plane! Some of this story was known to the paladin, for the blade known as Valdaar's Fist was the reason he was here!

After warning our weary party that there was probably a trap waiting for them once they exited the Keep, he showed them the way to the treasure chamber by raising the dais to reveal a stairway that wound down beneath it. Dragma, released finally from the geas that had held him for centuries, faded out of existence, bidding our heroes farewell.

Buoyed by the promise of treasure, the party descended the winding staircase to the chamber below.

In the chests they discovered Flinthgoor, Foe-Cleaver and Death-Dealer—the ancient greataxe once wielded by Valdaar's General of the Armies. Vorgath laid claim to this weapon.

They also found the fabled Dragma Jewels, Dragma's spell book, much coin and many gems—but nothing else, save the shield Thrinndor believed was once used by the god himself.

Neither of the other two artifacts of power—Valdaar's Fist nor Pendromar, Demon's Breath (Dragma's staff of power)—was among the horde.

When Sordaak claimed a ring from among the treasure, mistakenly thought to be part of Dragma's Jewels, he revealed that he too was a direct descendant of one Valdaar's Council—yes, the powerful Dragma himself!

A rest period was called and Thrinndor was convinced to perform The Telling—the complete story of the final battle that saw the imprisonment of their god, passed down only by word of mouth for thousands of years. The story of which only the Paladinhood of Valdaar knew, yet seldom spoke.

After the rest, they made preparations for what they were told waited for them on the other side of a portal that opened for them when they were ready.

As they stepped through, they were indeed met by a small army of orcs and, of course, the mage they had only briefly encountered earlier.

Although our heroes once again prevailed, they were sorely tested. None escaped injury, and to some the wounds were indeed grave. But prevail they did. In the end, Sordaak discovered it had been his master with whom they battled. Now he was going to have to find a new mentor.

The group rested and tended to wounds.

During this time, Sordaak revealed to the group a theory he had—the theory that Cyrillis must be the one remaining human piece to the puzzle. She must be from the lineage of Angra-Kahn! As she had no idea who her parents were, she could not verify, nor discount as false, this theory.

So the group decided that each must meet with his or her masters—except for Sordaak, of course, who would have to find a new one. They each had training to do, and Cyrillis was compelled to do research into her past. Thrinndor agreed to help her once he had finished with his own training.

They decided to meet in Farreach in five weeks' time and there figure out just how it was they were going to continue their quest to find the remaining artifacts of power and return Valdaar to his rightful place in this plane.

So without further ado, I launch into the second book of the Valdaar's Fist series: *The Library of Antiquity*.

Chapter One

Farreach

Vorgath glanced around the inn, his manner disdainful. The others who occupied chairs or benches had little—in some cases no—desire to do any more than what there were doing. Eat, sleep, work, drink…

Die.

They were content.

Seeing that contentment in others reinforced the dwarf's belief there was more out there, anywhere. To occupy a seat in a bar as one's only source of relief, that was sheer ignorance.

Mind you, Vorgath thought absentmindedly, hoisting an occasional pint, or two, in honor of whatever was a nice distraction. He had no problem with that, just with the mindless "whatever."

He paused to consider the last month as he brought the brew to his lips and took a long draught. He figured he would get to Farreach before the others, and even briefly considered stopping to visit with Sordaak. He had quickly dismissed that as a bad idea. Those wiggle-finger folk don't usually appreciate distractions when studying.

Studying! He snorted loudly, attracting the attention of a couple of nearby patrons, but he ignored them. Soon they went back to whatever it was they had been idly chatting about.

Although he deemed himself of above-average intelligence, that studying crap made his head hurt. Besides, he thought to himself as he again brought the flagon to his mouth, it got in the way of beer drinking!

After leaving the aforementioned wiggle-finger with Rheagamon—and verifying they would not kill one another (there was always some possibility of that when these egghead types got together!)—Vorgath had made his way back to the Silver Hills in short order without incident.

The Dragaar Clan to which he belonged was glad to see him. He had been away for several years this time—close to ten, they reminded him. Such absences were not uncommon, but they had been growing longer each time, his father told him.

They were always anxious to hear the goings-on of the world beyond the self-imposed boundaries of the one in which they lived. And Vorgath always took time to remind them what a wide, wonderful world it was.

But, alas, it was always the same. They had found a new vein of some interesting precious metal—silver this time—and were busy working that.

Whatever.

Vorgath performed the tasks required of him methodically: storytelling, story listening, some brief and minimal training on the lore of metals, some almost useless (to him, anyway) training involving the Dwarven Axe. He preferred the greataxe, and no amount of discussion was going to change his mind.

For now.

He was mildly intrigued by the discussion that, with considerable additional training, he could learn to wield two such axes effectively and even drop into a defensive posture if the situation required (a notion at which he snorted when it was brought up!).

Anyway, he was in a hurry to get to his barbarian trainer in Pothgaard to learn more in the control of the Barbarian Rage and to see what they knew of Flinthgoor—his new greataxe. The dwarves knew nothing of it but marveled at its construction. The elders said the alloy was one they had never seen. They wanted Vorgath to stay so they could study it, but he knew that could take years and he certainly had no time for that!

He made a deposit in the Dwarven Bank. He liked the security it gave but was always less than pleased at the ten percent he was charged for that security. However, he considered it a necessary evil. He couldn't carry that much loot with him, and he couldn't very well bury it in a hole in the ground. Holes had a way of getting discovered.

He had accumulated a very tidy sum—as well as a few enchanted items he could not currently use, but did not want to sell or discard—stashed away now. If ever he decided to settle down, he would be able to afford whatever he wished.

But what he wished for now was more adventure!

A dragon! Now that was a worthy adventure!

The elders—his father was one—again pushed for him to settle down and get married. Have sons, many fine sons! One would do, many would be better!

To that end, it was arranged for him to meet many of the clan's eligible women. However, since he was considered a wanderer—a barbarian, even— many of the eligible daughters' fathers secretly found other places for their daughters to be when their time came.

That was fine with Vorgath. He was not settling down anytime this century! And maybe not the next! Places to see, people to do, and dragons to kill!

He would settle down when the time came and when he found the right woman. None of these complacent dwarven women would ever draw a second glance from him.

His wife must be…. Hell, he thought, that adventure is for another day. Maybe after his second, or third, dragon. Maybe…

He was "home" only for two days, much to his father's chagrin. But there was just too much to do to sit around and grow thick in the middle—not that there was anything wrong with a dwarf who was thick in the middle. That was standard after the first hundred years or so, after all. But life as a fighter-type required a different physique.

So without so much as a glance behind him, he slung his now much lighter pack over his shoulder and set foot on the path toward Farreach. From there he would purchase passage to Pothgaard, home of the barbarians.

His weapons were now arranged such that Flinthgoor was closest at hand, but others were at the ready should they be needed.

They shouldn't be, he had thought as he trudged down the road, patting the haft of the greataxe as it protruded from under his cloak. But, he admitted regretfully, there were a few critters for which this blade was not suited: Ochres, Slimes and Jellies, just to name a few. Oh, and of course, Rusties—they eat metal. The blade gleamed at him as he cocked an eye toward it. Maybe not this alloy, he smiled smugly, but it would not do to find out otherwise.

No, the club for the Rusties.

He started whistling a favorite shanty as he picked up the pace. He wanted to get to Farreach by midmorning tomorrow.

He overslept, and thus did not make it in to town until shortly after noon, but he was still able to book passage to Pothgaard, leaving at first light the next morning.

In Pothgaard, he chased down his mentor—an old barbarian named Kragaar, if it matters—and they spent the better part of two days catching up. Which is to say much ale was consumed and many tales swapped; some of them even true!

The last few years had not been kind to his mentor, Vorgath noted. Still, any barbarian who lived as long as Kragaar had must be a good one, because advanced years among this fighter class was definitely a rarity.

Still, by the looks of the old human, Vorgath was going to have to find himself a new mentor his next visit.

The old man marveled at the dwarf's tales from the Keep, and his eyes misted over when he was allowed to inspect Flinthgoor. "Oh that I was still young enough to wield such a weapon!" he had said.

In all, Vorgath spent twenty-five (or so) days studying his craft. He learned how better to control the battle rage, increasing his strength and stamina at the same time. He spent many hours honing his skills with his new greataxe, even learning how to use it in defense should the need ever arise. Vorgath doubted it, but he bowed to the will of his master and learned it just the same.

Finally it was time for him to go. They clasped forearms one last time and Vorgath felt his eyes burning as he looked into those of his master, most likely for the last time.

Kragaar also sensed this and promised to arrange for a new mentor for his pupil before the dwarf's next visit.

Vorgath said nothing—in truth, he did not trust his voice to speak aloud for fear of cracking with emotion. Instead, he merely nodded, spun on his heel and quickly ascended the ramp to the boat that was to take him back to Farreach.

Without a word to the ship's master, he disappeared below decks and made his way to what passed as the vessel's tavern, sat down and worked steadily at washing the memories away.

*

Vorgath shook his head, clearing it of the unwanted memories, and smiled as he brushed the back of his hand across his mouth, wiping away the foam left there by this most recent distraction placed before him by a sullen barmaid.

Obviously she had been doing this too long without hope of relief.

Deciding she needed a distraction, Vorgath reached out and pinched her none-too-gently in a location generally deemed inappropriate, but one she was certainly accustomed to, he figured.

She let out a startled yelp and spun quickly on a leather booted heel, leveling an open-handed slap at where the face of most normal-sized offending patrons of the establishment would be. But it passed harmlessly over the head of the dwarf.

He grinned hugely and deftly grabbed her wrist as it whiffed by and pulled her arm down. Startled, she lost her balance and took an involuntary step toward the barbarian.

Smiling even bigger now, Vorgath spun on his stool and continued pulling her toward him. Off-balance to where she was about to fall to the floor, the fighter wrapped his other hand around her waist, catching her as she landed rather unceremoniously in his lap. Her empty tray clattered to the floor at their feet.

Still too surprised to offer any real resistance, she didn't know what to do when Vorgath reached up, put his hand on the side of her head and pushed it down toward his waiting lips and planted a kiss on her that he was sure she would not soon forget.

Finally regaining some semblance of control, she jerked back and swung another slap at Vorgath's exposed cheek. This time she connected with a resounding smack. She surged to her feet, straightening her tunic with her free hand as she did so. "Well, I never!" she said quickly, her face turning a deep crimson.

"Now," said the dwarf, "I seriously doubt that." He was still grinning from ear-to-ear as he rubbed the side of his stinging face. "Certainly, I cannot be the first to make the attempt to brighten your day!"

"Of course not," she said quickly—too quickly. Realizing the corner she had painted for herself, she quickly turned on her heel and marched off toward the kitchen.

Still smiling, Vorgath turned his attention back to the ale sitting on the table before him. "Too bad," he said as he clucked his tongue to add to the tone of disappointment he was trying to convey. He allowed his eyes to follow her toward the door. "Ah, well," he said to her retreating form, "a little skinny for my taste, anyway!" He turned and winked at the farmer nearest to him at the bar.

"Hmph!" was all the denizens heard as the curtain closed behind the barmaid, taking her from their sight.

There was a moment of stunned silence—the entire episode had only taken maybe ten or fifteen seconds—and then the room burst out in laughter.

After a bit, the laughter died down and most of the tavern's patrons turned back to their own drinks.

Most, but not all. A previously unnoticed man seated at the far end of the slab of wood serving as a bar picked up his flagon, stood and made his way to the table where Vorgath sat. When opposite the dwarf, he said without preamble, "For that I'd like to buy you a beer."

Vorgath looked up from his half-full flagon to meet the eyes of this man who stood before him. What he saw caused him to do a double-take. The man's eyes were deep brown, almost black. They were set in a nondescript but somehow handsome face. He was not tall, but not short, either. His clothing was some sort of animal skin, but not hardened like armor. Instead they appeared supple from extended wear. The extra-long outer garment served to cover the hilt of more than one weapon, Vorgath was certain.

The barbarian took a second to glance over to where the man had come from, not sure how he had missed him and more than a little irritated for having done so. He was not accustomed to missing someone such as this in even a crowded room—and this room was not crowded.

"I don't recall ever having turned down a free beer," the dwarf said amiably. However, his senses were now on high alert. Something about this man bothered him. "Sit down if you're of a mind to," he said as he waved a hand at the bench across from him.

"I don't mind if I do," the man said as he hooked a toe under a leg of the bench, pulled it away from the table and slid easily onto the now open seat. His movements were graceful, almost like those of a cat.

Once seated, he raised a hand to signal the barkeep. "Two pints of your coldest ale, if you please, kind sir," he said. The barkeep merely nodded and then turned to remove two clean flagons from the shelf.

"I'm Breunne," the man said as he stuck his right hand out by way of greeting.
Reflexively, Vorgath reached out and they clasped forearms in the standard way.

The barbarian sensed rather than felt a coiled strength in both the man's grasp and forearm, without any obvious effort on the man's part to convey that strength.

They both released at the appropriate moment. "Vorgath," the dwarf said without elaborating. He was unsure what exactly was happening, and he was uneasy about it. Still, he could sense no danger, and he had long ago learned to trust his senses.

Both men were silent as two fresh flagons were set before them. The barkeep stood and waited impatiently for the men to finish their previous libations.

While Vorgath downed his, the barkeep said in a low voice. "I'd get out of town if I were you, dwarf." He turned his eyes to look through the curtain through which his barmaid had recently passed. "Her man don't take kindly to someone messing with his woman."

Vorgath put his empty flagon down with a bit more force than was necessary, resulting in a rather loud thud. "Bah," he said as he raised his eyes to meet those of the barkeep. "First of all, you are not me!" He paused to make sure he had the man's undivided attention. He needn't have bothered; the barkeep and several of the closest patrons were now looking directly at the dwarf. "Second, I was only having a bit of fun." His tone was even, and his smile did not touch his eyes. "Last…"—his tone was now decidedly menacing—"…if her man ain't man enough to take her off the open market, then he ain't someone I should have to worry about." He turned his attention to the man seated across from him, effectively dismissing the barkeep.

Unsure what to do, the barkeep made a move to go but stopped. He said, "Just the same, dwarf…" His tone left little doubt how he felt about the race—or maybe it was this dwarf in particular. "When Grouthuum hears of this, he will certainly have something to say about it!"

"Grouph-who?" Vorgath deliberately mispronounced the name. "You say that like I am supposed to have heard of him, and maybe even like I should be trembling in my boots." He slowly turned his eyes, now mere slits between his forehead and cheeks. "Nope and nope," he said as he turned back to his drink. "Now do as you were told and go away. You're starting to get on my last nerve—and that ain't a good place to be!"

One of the men sitting by the door got to his feet and pushed his way through the curtain out into the street beyond. The receding patter of unsteady feet could be heard as the man tried to run down the dirt street.

The barkeep, his back stiff at being dismissed so, made his way back to his bar. "Just you wait!" he said from the relative protection the bar provided.

"Grouthuum will certainly teach you some manners!" It was his turn to sound menacing. "Don't say I didn't try to warn you!"

"Whatever!" said the dwarf as he waved his right hand dismissively. "I ain't killed nobody yet today." He looked up suddenly at the man across the table from him. "Hell, I ain't killed nobody yet this week." He looked at the barkeep. "Key word there is yet!"

Again he turned his attention back to Breunne while clearly talking to the barkeep. "Now shut it and bring the ales when requested, or I'll have to end that unprecedented streak with you!"

The barkeep glared at this impudent dwarf. His mouth worked but no sound came out. Finally, he turned and began slamming dishes around in his anger.

Vorgath grinned at the man across from him, winked and put his flagon to his mouth and took a long pull.

Breunne did likewise. As he returned his drink to the table, his eyes were twinkling. "You certainly know how to liven things up, my friend!"

Just then, the curtain leading to the street was brushed aside and a bear of a man stepped through into the dim light of the tavern. He paused briefly as his eyes adjusted, casting his head from side to side, obviously looking for something—or someone.

"Not yet," said the dwarf, "but things are beginning to look up!" He reached out, grasped his flagon and again took a long pull from it.

The big man jabbed a finger in the direction of the two seated at the table. "You!" he bellowed into the suddenly quiet room.

"Now you're gonna get it," sneered the barkeep.

Vorgath didn't acknowledge either man. Instead, he took yet another pull from his drink, this time emptying it. "Barkeep!" he bellowed. "Another round for me and my new friend here!" Again he winked at his companion. "And make it quick!"

"What?" cried the incredulous barkeep.

"Are you deaf and stupid?" asked Vorgath. "I said bring us another round!" He shrugged in mock exasperation. "And hurry!" he added. Next he coughed a couple of times while rubbing his throat. "We're parched over here!"

During this show the big man from the street had not moved. He was obviously not used to being ignored. "You!" he repeated, this time taking a noisy step in the direction of the dwarf.

Vorgath turned tiredly toward the newcomer. "Are you talking to me?" he said, his tone sounding almost hopeful.

The big man glowered at Vorgath. "Did you make a move on my woman?"

Out of the corner of his eye Vorgath saw the curtain to the kitchen part and the barmaid stepped back into the room. She folded her arms across her chest, her smile indicating an obvious inability to wait for what was to come.

The barbarian hooked a thumb in her direction and said, "If you mean her, then yes. She was having a bad day and I tried to brighten it somewhat." He grinned broadly before continuing. "If you are indeed her man, you're not doing a very good job of keeping her happy!"

"What?" shouted the big man. "Why you..." He took another step toward the seated barbarian.

"Sit down," said the dwarf amicably. "Have an ale on me and we'll discuss womenfolk and their general needs." He patted the bench next to him invitingly.

The big man stopped abruptly. "What?" he shouted as he puffed his chest out. "I don't need no lesson on women from no stinking dwarf!"

Vorgath allowed a pained expression to cross his face. "Now there you go, gettin' all personal an' shit!" He raised his left arm and took a sniff up underneath. "Why, I had a bath..." He turned to Breunne and asked. "What day is it?"

"Thursday," replied his newfound friend, unable to keep the smile off of his face.

"Thank you," Vorgath replied with a formal nod of his head. He returned his attention to the flabbergasted bear of a man. "Let me see," he said as he turned his eyes to the ceiling and began counting on his fingers. "I had a bath on Monday, I think..." He furrowed his forehead, apparently in deep thought. "Today is Thursday, so that makes..." He again worked his fingers. "...three days." The dwarf lowered his eyes and smiled at the big. "See there," he said in his best demeaning voice, "I shouldn't really start stinking for at least another week!" His smile broadened. "Unless, that is, I break out in a sweat." He narrowed his eyes. "But, I don't see that happening anytime soon!"

Crimson started crawling its way up the neck of the big man. He was sure he was being made fun of but not exactly sure just how. No one had ever accused Grouthuum of being overly bright, but most never said anything about it for fear of setting off his somewhat short temper.

Vorgath started to turn back to his ale but stopped and again patted the bench next to him. "Now, are you going to sit down or am I going to have to whup your ass in front of all these good townsfolk and your girlfriend?" He arched an eyebrow to complete the question.

There was a second or two of silence while the taunt sank in, but sink in it eventually did. With a roar Grouthuum lowered his head and launched himself at this not very bright dwarf sitting only a few feet away. He obviously intended to end this fight before it really got started.

Vorgath had different ideas. Anticipating the attack, he kicked out with both feet and threw his weight backward. At the same time he brought his balled-up left fist—the side that had been toward the rather loud buffoon—up to meet his right cheek with a thud. Grouthuum's head snapped back as his cheek split open in a shower of blood.

The big man's momentum carried him forward, however, and he crashed into the dwarf and table simultaneously.

Quick as a cat, Breunne's hands shot out and grabbed both half-empty flagons before they could spill, a knowing smile on his face as he took a pull on the ale that was his. He stood and stepped back as the table splintered under the weight of the big man and crashed to the floor.

Vorgath had underestimated the quickness of the big man and failed to completely escape the oncoming bull rush. Grouthuum's right arm caught him as he flung back, knocking him sideways off of the bench, where he also tumbled to the floor.

Both men rolled away from the other and sprang to their feet quickly, each in a crouch and ready for action.

Grouthuum, grinning madly, brought his right hand to his cheek and paused to inspect the blood on it when he drew it away. "You'll pay for that, little man." He smiled wickedly.

Breunne finished off his ale and was eyeing the half empty flask in his other hand—Vorgath's—when the dwarf, without even a glance in his direction said, "Don't even think about it!" Now it was his turn to grin. "This won't take long. Go ahead and order another round."

As Vorgath turned his head to emphasize the point, Grouthuum launched himself again at the barbarian, sensing an opening.

Again anticipating the move—actually, he had planned it that way—the dwarf stepped to the side and stuck out his left foot to trip the big man on the way by. But again he did not anticipate Grouthuum's ability to adjust quickly and was instead again knocked to the floor by the oncoming fighter.

There was a brief tussle as both attempted to gain an advantage by grappling whatever anatomy was in front of them, but both failed and they again rolled hard in opposite directions and surged to their feet, with Vorgath, either by happenstance or design, standing next to Breunne. He snatched his ale from him and quickly quaffed the remainder.

Wiping his hand across his mouth he said, "That other round here yet?" His eyes never left his opponent. "This may take slightly longer than I thought!" He watched in amusement as Grouthuum grabbed a flagon of ale from a man standing at the bar, knocking him to the floor in the process, and downed it.

"Hey!" groused the man as he surged back to his feet, bumping into another patron who spilled his ale all over the two of them.

"Dammit!" shouted this second man, and he brought the flagon down on the offender's head with a thud.

A general melee ensued, as everyone with a mind to found an excuse to punch, kick, bite or claw whoever stood next to him. (There was most certainly a lack of excitement in this town!)

Grouthuum eyed with amusement what he had started but remained focused on Vorgath. "Don't you try to escape, little man!" His smile never touched his eyes.

OK, thought the dwarf, this had already taken longer than he had anticipated. But he loved a good fight, and this one was turning out to be way better than anticipated. "Escape?" Vorgath spat on the floor in disgust. He noticed the phlegm was tainted pink. He must have taken a shot to the mouth he didn't remember. He shrugged. "I figgered you started that ruckus so you could sneak out unnoticed!"

"Shit, you say!" shouted the big man, wiping the blood dripping off of his chin. "You ain't gettin' off that easy!"

Vorgath allowed his shoulders to droop in mock disappointment. "Very well then," he said tiredly, "come on and get your ass-whuppin." He could see the bartender handing another pair of ales to his new friend. "Before my ale gets warm!"

Grouthuum growled deep within his barrel chest, not unlike a bear. He started toward the dwarf, slowly and deliberately this time.

As he got close, he lifted a booted foot and shoved a chair that was in his way, sending it skittering across the wooden plank floor until it crashed into another.

Vorgath was ready for the move. As the big fighter's right leg extended from the kick, the barbarian dove at the remaining plant leg. He connected with a thud—it was like trying to tackle a tree trunk!

It was enough, however, to knock a surprised Grouthuum off balance and he tumbled over the dwarf at his feet.

Vorgath was quicker to regain his footing and he landed a haymaker to the right side of the bigger man's head. Grouthuum's head snapped around and he collapsed to the floor, hard.

The big man pushed himself to all fours, more slowly this time, shaking his head slowly from side to side in an attempt to get the buzzing to stop.

"Had enough?" sneered the dwarf, his stance ready for whichever way this went.

"In your dreams!" shouted the big man as he simultaneously surged to his feet and launched himself at the dwarf.

Again the barbarian was ready for him. He easily side-stepped the attack and again stuck out a leg to trip the bigger man. As he did so, he clasped both hands together and brought them down on Grouthuum's exposed neck as he went by. The resultant blow caused the fighter to land face first in a heap on the floor.

Again the bigger man pushed himself to all fours, even more slowly this time, however. He shook his head and looked up bleary-eyed, trying to find his opponent.

"Stay down," said the dwarf, "and I'll buy you an ale for your effort." He smiled to remove any hint of ill intent from his demeanor. "Come at me again, and I'll stop playing nice!" He extended a hand to Grouthuum to assist him to his feet.

The bigger man eyed the hand warily and it crossed his mind to grab and pull—but only briefly.

Something must have shown to Vorgath. "I wouldn't," said the dwarf menacingly, no longer smiling.

All fighting in the room had stopped as the room waited tensely for a response.

Abruptly, Grouthuum allowed his shoulders to sag as he started to laugh. "No," he said as he spat out a tooth that had become dislodged during the fight. "I wouldn't, either!" He grasped the proffered hand and allowed himself to be helped to his feet, where he leaned unsteadily on the dwarf who was just barely over half his size. "But I would take that ale!" He smiled a big toothy grin—albeit one slightly less toothy than it would have been a few minutes before.

Spotting his Breunne standing not too far away, Vorgath raised an eyebrow in question.

Breunne merely shook his head and shrugged. "You took too long," he said by way of explanation as he turned the flagons in his hands upside down, showing they were empty.

Vorgath smiled and shook his head sadly. He then raised his head and shouted. "Wench! Three cold ales!" He turned to Grouthuum and winked. "And hurry! My friends and I are dying of thirst over here!"

Together, the two half walked, half stumbled to a table that had somehow escaped the almost total destruction inflicted upon the tavern. Righting it, they drug some chairs in place and plopped unceremoniously into them as the barmaid set three ales on the table. Breunne sauntered over and settled into a chair opposite them.

Both the dwarf and his former opponent hoisted their flagons at the same time, tipped their heads back and took a long pull.

"Damn!" said Grouthuum as he set his drink down on the table with a thud and rubbed his jaw with left hand. "You hit hard!" His eyes locked with those of his former opponent. "I ain't never been bested bare-knuckles!"

Vorgath also rubbed his jaw. "You ain't no lightweight yourself!" He smiled. "I've got about a hundred years or so experience on you, young fella. You did just fine." He shook his head wistfully. "That was the best fight I've had in over a month! Thank you!"

"Damn!" repeated Grouthuum. "I've never been thanked for a fight before!" He shook his head in wonder as he took another pull from his ale.

Vorgath snorted loudly, "That's because most don't thank you for whuppin' their ass, I shouldn't think!"

Grouthuum bellowed in laughter. When he was able he said, "There is that!"

The bartender, who had been surveying the damage, spoke from the relative safety of his bar. "What I want to know is who is going to pay for all this?" His tone was belligerent.

There immediately ensued a lot of finger pointing and innocent looks at the ceiling—including those at the table where the three sat.

Vorgath exaggerated a roll of his eyes. "Very well," he stated as he pulled the string on a small pouch tied as his belt. He dumped the contents, a few coins, into his left hand. "I can see none of you dirt farmers and sheep herders—"

"Hey!" came several indignant voiced scattered around the room.

"——can afford to pay for this." Vorgath ignored them as he selected several of the coins and slapped them hard onto the edge of the table. "And there's probably some truth to the notion I may be responsible for said damage." He smiled.

The startled barkeep scurried around the end of his bar, quickly approached the table and snatched up the coins. He put one to his teeth and bit hard as those at the table watched with interest. His eyebrow shot up in surprise as he was unable to even mark the coin with his experienced bite.

"That's five plat," said the dwarf matter-of-factly, "which should be more than enough to buy this entire establishment!"

Not sure whether a protest was in order or not, the barkeep hesitated. It was indeed more than enough to cover all damage and leave a considerable sum for...

Vorgath shook out another platinum coin and flipped it to the barkeep, who caught it deftly. He said, "And that should buy a round for the entire place and keep the three of us swimming in ale through the night!"

Chapter Two

Thrinndor & Cyrillis

Thrinndor's mind turned to the events of the past month. Yes, he reflected, it had only been a month—but one that been very busy for him.

He and Cyrillis had taken two and a half days to get back to where the horses had been staked. Something had spooked them, because they had bolted from the place where they had been left. But he knew they were around, and he used that innate connection between himself and his steed to quickly locate him.

Most of the pack animals were still with him—but all but one of the mounts had scattered. He could not tell where and did not have the time to look.

He and Cyrillis had paused to rest the remainder of that day. It was getting late anyway.

The morning of the next day they mounted up early and rode hard—the horses were eager to be on the move after all the inactivity. The pack animals… not so much. But, as they were hitched together with the steeds, they had little choice in the matter and followed along.

Thus, they made good time and were outside Horbalt by the end of the second day. Not wanting to be seen in the vicinity just yet, Thrinndor had bade the cleric farewell, with the promise to meet her in Horbalt in one week's time.

He had ridden through the night, trusting his steed to pick his way along the much-traveled road toward Brasheer, only a half-day's hard ride from his destination: Khavhall, Paladin home.

He arrived there late on the sixth day following his departure from the main part of their group. Physically, he was fully healed, but mentally he needed work. He required communion with his god and companionship with others of his order.

That first day back had been mostly the companionship thing. His mother was understandably happy to see him. She had visibly aged since he last saw her—little more than a year ago—and that bothered him.

She was yet a beautiful woman, even in her advancing years. But her eyes were not as good and the stiffness of age had settled in her joints. She could no longer work with the younger members of the sect, and that bothered her.

Only news of her son kept body and soul together, she had informed him. In response, he had promised he would provide such news more often. But she had quickly grasped the front of his tunic, drew her face within inches of him and said sternly, "Do not!" She had looked deep into his eyes and commanded his attention. "Your work in finding Valdaar's blade must be above all else." She had paused for a moment. "Promise me this."

Her demeanor left no room for discussion.

He vowed as requested.

One last thing she had asked of him. He must father a child. Their line must continue.

On that he could not promise—he would not father a child with a woman not his mate, in that he was adamant. But he had said that he would work on it…

After that, he got serious in his training. There was not much this time around. But next time, next rank, his training requirements would be extensive.

He was told he was nearing the time when he would be trained as Lord—and thereby expected to assume his role as leader of the Paladinhood. He was not ready for that, yet.

Not until he held Valdaar's Fist.

Only then would he feel comfortable settling down to rule. But even then, only if his god required it of him. Otherwise, there was still too much of the Land to see. Too many important people he had not met.

And thus he was back in the saddle on the morning of the fourth day following his riding through the gates of his mother's keep. He was anxious to see what Cyrillis had been able to find out.

And, he had to concede, there might have been a bit more to his wanting to see her. But, he had admonished himself, he had not time for that. Yet.

He decided he needed to go in disguise when he went in to see Cyrillis—as a regular man. No armor. No weapons, save those a "normal" man might have.

He rode into Horbalt a full day ahead of when he said he would meet the Cleric. He wanted to do some scouting in advance. He wanted the chance to ask questions.

He felt naked without his equipment, fully out in the open for all to see. It was not something he was accustomed to. He had worn armor of one sort or another since he was old enough to hold a shield and see out of the eye-slits in whatever helm his mother had plopped on his head.

People certainly had reacted differently to him without his armor. Black armor tended to bring out the good in people, and he was usually shunned.

Now his good looks and natural charisma made him uncomfortably popular. He could not walk down the street without at least one person stopping him to talk. Weather. Crops. Recent Orc activity. All manner of mundane conversations.

He was beginning to question his own decision to try this incognito thing, but then he discovered what everyone else seemed to already know: To find information, one hung out at the local tavern, or taverns.

He had not had much use for drinking until now. He quickly discovered that buying drinks for others and—almost as important—allowing them to buy drinks for him really served to loosen one's tongue.

Knowing the effect of drink on the mind and tongue, however, he spent considerable effort drinking as little as possible. He decided that must involve some sort of art form—one he quickly mastered.

In this way he had been able to subtly inquire about the temple dedicated to Set—where Cyrillis presumably still was—just a few miles outside of town.

But there was not much to find out. Just the usual: Most of the town was afraid of this dark temple. Yet the locals grudgingly welcomed the modest income the town enjoyed from its proximity. The temple needed supplies and brought in visitors. Most of the time they were glad to take the dark consortium's coin but just as glad when they left their humble community behind.

They tolerated the occasional missing farm animal—not really wanting to know what happened to it, and certainly not wanting to go to temple and ask. Over the years more than one foolhardy soul had gone out there to get some purportedly prized hog or goat back, never to be seen again.

Without any formal decree, the temple was more or less placed off-limits to locals and adventurers alike. Although it was a loose decree when it came to adventurers, mostly just a verbal warning and the situational derision as required for those who claimed they were going to go clean out that den of evil. Most were also never heard from again.

However, once in a while one of these adventurers could be seen riding back through town, but they never stopped to explain how their sojourn went. They just rode on through, with the occasional turn to look worriedly over their shoulder.

Pry as he might, Thrinndor could find no one who had actually been out to the temple. "What? Are you nuts?" was the most common response. "We leave them be, and they leave us be...mostly." This last was usually accompanied by a nervous checking behind them to see who might be listening.

His even more discreet inquiries as to servants of Valdaar were usually met with blank stares. Most of the locals had not even heard of the god, and those that did just scoffed and proclaimed, "Why would anyone want to serve a dead god?"

Most.

There had been one, however, who feigned the same disinterested dismissal. But the paladin had sensed the man's sudden unease. He had gently tried to probe further with this individual, but the man had said he had business to attend to, got to his feet and left quickly.

After he had gone, Thrinndor had gently plied some of the locals about the man. He was informed that the man was not a local. He had been coming around for the past couple of years. He sometimes stayed for a day or two, sometimes for weeks at a time. He rode into town, stayed at one of the local boarding houses, ate wherever he could buy a meal, drank with the locals and mostly just listened.

None the paladin talked to even knew the man's name—a fact they themselves found odd when asked, but obviously not odd enough to do anything about it. They just shrugged it off and went back to the ale the handsome young man had provided.

Thrinndor decided he needed to talk with this man some more. But he soon discovered that the man had ridden out of town shortly after they had talked. The paladin wanted to ride out after him but dared not as Cyrillis was due to meet him in town this day. He did not want to cause her undue concern by being late.

So he contented himself with familiarizing himself with the tracks of the man's mount and noting the direction he had gone off in. He had gone the way Thrinndor had come in. He had allowed himself a brief walk out that direction to verify a suspicion. Sure enough, the man had left the trail not far out of town and circled the town!

When the man finally settled on a path, he had been headed directly to the temple! Interesting, the paladin thought. He was about to go back to town to get his mount to follow but ruefully decided against it. Again, he imprinted on his memory the tracks of this man's mount and then turned back and walked slowly to town.

He had spent the rest of the day going from inn to inn, boarding house to boarding house and visiting the other businesses in town. He and Cyrillis had not set upon a specific place to meet up, and he now regretted that omission on his part. There was no telling exactly where or even when she would show up. Yet the town was small, and there were no more than eight or ten likely candidates.

So he made the circuit at regular intervals, always leaving word that if a pretty woman came looking for him, they should find him immediately. He bought another round to ensure they would remember to do so. They would, he had been assured.

An hour after the sun had set and still no sign of her, he had started to worry. He was fairly certain she would not willingly travel alone at night. And he was also fairly certain she would not be late if she could avoid it. He, of course, did not know this, yet he thought this to be a reasonable assumption.

He was now regretting not following the man in the direction he figured he also now needed to go. Yet the paladin did not know the area well enough to travel at night, and Horbalt's proximity to the Badlands made that a bad idea anyway. Riding at night to Khavhall was different. That was home. No, he must wait until tomorrow.

He had made one last round, finding most of the businesses other than the inns were now closed, however, and that made for a short trip. He had left word where he could be found and then went to his room and turned in early. He wanted to leave well before first light to retrieve his gear, which was now regrettably along the path he had come and not in the direction he needed to go.

Yet he knew he must also not leave before giving Cyrillis a chance to get to town; maybe she had just gotten the days mixed up, or had needed more time. Either way, he knew he could not leave before noon. But he did not want to have to ride out in the wrong direction once he was sure she would not be coming in. So he needed to stage his gear on the road to the temple; it was as simple as that.

When she had not shown up by the noon deadline he had set, the paladin had left word that the cleric should wait for him here if she showed.

He then had mounted his already prepared steed and rode out of town toward the temple at a rapid pace. His horse was rested and eager for the trail. He let him run once they were clear of town. The temple was no more than a half-day's normal ride to the east. He figured to make it in two or three hours.

He had stopped briefly to retrieve his staged gear, adorning only what he could not while riding. Thus he was back in the saddle after only a few minutes, attaching his breast plate as his horse once again hit the trail running.

And so it had only been barely mid-afternoon when he spotted the temple a half-mile or so off of the main road. He slowed his mount to a canter, deciding it prudent to not appear to be in a big hurry.

As he approached the entrance, two men in the dark robes he knew to be worn by The Minions of Set turned to acknowledge his presence.

Thrinndor had dismounted and tied his horse to a rail intended for that purpose. His mount had immediately dipped his muzzle into the nearby trough and drank deep.

"What is your purpose?" asked one of the minions.

The paladin had had plenty of time to plan a course of action once he got here, so he decided to jump right in. "I am seeking a young woman who would have arrived here about a week ago. Pretty blonde, medium build, in her early twenties; have you seen her?"

The two turned and spoke quietly to one another. Try as he might, Thrinndor could not make out what was said, although he was fairly certain they spoke in a language he did not recognize.

As one, they both turned their attention back to him. "Please remove your helm that we may know you." The same minion spoke who had initially greeted the paladin.

Thrinndor considered the request briefly and then did as requested; he could see no reason not to. He could detect no animosity from the two.

"Will you not give the same courtesy?" he asked, deciding not to press too hard on the missing cleric at the moment, though he sorely wanted to.

The other priest spoke for the first time. "We must remain covered when out of doors." There was a pause. "Would you please to come inside so we can meet your request?"

Thrinndor hesitated only slightly, unsure as to what waited for him inside, but he did know Cyrillis was not waiting for him out here. "Of course," he said amicably.

The two priests turned as one and went through the open doorway side-by-side into the dimness beyond. The paladin followed without hesitation.

Once inside, Thrinndor quickly surveyed his surroundings as his eyes adjusted to the gloom. They passed through a small entry chamber, no more than fifteen feet square, and through another set of double doors to the temple proper.

The temple was of modest dimensions—to be expected for such a remote location—perhaps fifty or sixty feet wide by just over a hundred feet in length. There were regularly spaced benches for those of the order to congregate. Heavy curtains lined both side walls, blocking out any light from the windows Thrinndor had seen from the outside as he approached. The whole was dimly lit by sconces regularly spaced throughout the chamber.

Ahead the paladin could see a raised dais, with an altar of sorts and two ornate chairs—thrones almost, he thought to himself. They never got that far, however, as the two priests stopped and again turned as one to face him.

Simultaneously they reached up and pushed back their hoods until they fell behind their heads, bunching up there.

The two were identical in every way: same dark hair, cut the same way, clean-shaven with the same piercing green eyes. They both even had the same non-committal expression on their faces. Twins.

Interesting, the paladin mused.

"Now how may we be of service to you?" asked the man on the left, the other nodding his agreement to the question.

"The girl," Thrinndor said, outwardly remaining calm, inwardly wanting to shout. "Have you seen her?"

Without hesitation the one on the right said, "Yes. She is here."

Startled at this news coming so quickly and relieved at having found her, the paladin asked quickly, "May I see her?"

The priests turned toward one another, but this time they said nothing. Instead, they somehow seemed to communicate without speaking. They turned back to peer at the paladin. "What is your purpose with her?"

Thrinndor had to force down his rising anger so he could reply calmly. "I had arranged to meet with her in town yesterday," he began. "And I grew worried when she did not appear as scheduled."

The priest on the right hesitated only a moment. "She made no mention of such an appointment," he said. "She is busy."

Startled, the paladin's voice rose slightly. "Busy?" He looked from one to the other. "In what way is she too busy to keep scheduled appointments?"

This time there was a noticeable hesitation before the priest on the left said, "She and those of her order are making preparations to depart." Neither man moved.

"Depart?" asked Thrinndor, an edge creeping into his voice. "What do you mean?"

Again the two faced one another and silently communicated. The paladin detected slight eyebrow movements but nothing more. When again they faced him, the priest on the left said, "We have tolerated those of her order long enough."

The minion on the right continued for him. "Our order is growing, and we now require the space allocated to those of her order."

"They will be out by the time the sun settles in the west, or what remains will be forfeit," the one on the left said.

"To us," right finished.

Thrinndor's eyes darted from one to the other. He again fought down his urge to shout at them. "Where are they going?" he said.

"That is not our concern."

The paladin's mind raced as he tried to make sense of what he was being told, unasked questions dying on his lips. Deciding he would not get answers from these two, he again asked, "May I see her?"

"You may," said left.

"However," continued the one on the right without pause, "it would not be wise to inhibit her preparations for departure."

"Inhibit?" Thrinndor's voice was now rising higher than he had wanted, and with no small effort, he visibly forced back his ire.

"Calm yourself, young man," said left, "or we will have you removed."

Thrinndor considered throwing down the usual gauntlet at this point along the lines of, 'You can try' but noting activity along the side walls and behind the dais he had not seen before, he forced that down as well. He closed his eyes and took in a deep breath, releasing it slowly as he again opened his eyes. In a voice more calm than he felt, he said, "Take me to her, please." To forestall further discussion, he added quickly, "I will aid them in their preparations if it is as you say."

"You doubt us?" left said without emotion.

Thrinndor's eyes went from one twin to the other. "Of course not," he stated. "However, I require from my friend her account of what has happened since last I saw her."

The brothers again communicated and then simultaneously turned to walk toward the raised dais.

"Very well," said right.

"Follow us," said left.

Thrinndor moved to follow, his right hand resting on the haft of his sword. He hoped it would not come to that, but it was prudent to be prepared, he thought.

Abruptly, both priests stopped and turned slowly. The paladin could detect no malice in their actions, but kept his hand on his sword just in case.

"Would you draw your weapon in this place?" asked right.

"A place dedicated to the servitude of our god?" asked left.

Taken aback by the sudden turn, Thrinndor hesitated before answering. "Your god is not my god," he said, also without malice.

"True," said right.

"Yet you are a man of faith," said left. It was not a question.

Right continued, "You are of the Paladinhood of Valdaar." Again, it was not a question.

"You are a Holy man," said left.

Both said in unison, "Would you draw your weapon in this our temple to our god?"

Stunned, Thrinndor took a step back where he regained his balance. His hand did not waver from its place on his sword. Somehow, he knew to deny their claims would result in...what? He knew they would not believe him. That, and as a Paladin of Valdaar he could not deny the claims if they were true. He could not lie. That was a basic tenant of who he was. "How do you know this?" he asked finally.

The two communicated in their peculiar way and the minion on the right answered by saying, "Do you not know us to be Minions of Set?"

The priest on the left continued the thought, "So it is that we also recognize you as a servant of Valdaar."

Again in unison they finished the statement. "It is just so."

They waited for him to speak. When he did not, right spoke again. "Will you draw your weapon in this place?"

Knowing the question was coming again, this time the paladin was ready for it. "No," he said. "Not unless I—or my friend—is attacked directly." His eyes bored into those of first the priest on the right, and then shifted to those of the priest on the left.

The priest on the right said, "You will not be attacked," as if discussing the weather.

Left finished. "However, if you do attempt to draw you weapon in this place, you will be prevented."

With that, both turned and again moved toward the dais.

Thrinndor wanted to argue the point further, but he was soon standing alone in the temple to another god. He thought better about the argument and hurried to catch up.

The two brothers marched in step to the base of the dais and without hesitation ascended the steps up to the platform. Once there, they circled the altar to the left and approached a set of heavy draperies along the back wall. These they parted, revealing a single door. Opening it, they stepped through; the minion who he only knew as 'left' first, and resumed their march down a long hallway with regularly spaced doors on either side. They did not appear to be hurrying, yet Thrinndor had to take large steps just to keep up, and he was taller than most.

They reached the end of the hallway, which branched both right and left. The passages looked identical to the paladin, but the priests without hesitation took the left one. Seeing a set of double doors a short distance down this passage, Thrinndor sensed they had reached their destination.

Indeed, both men stopped at the door. The priest on the left rapped solidly on the door with a staff that Thrinndor had not noticed before. Checking quickly, he saw that both priests had staffs in their hands. How had he missed that?

He didn't have time to sort it out, however, as the door on the right opened to reveal an old man garbed in priest robes similar to, but certainly different from, those worn by the twins.

"Yes?" the old man said. He was clearly not happy to see the two men who stood before him. "You said we had until—"

"You have a visitor," the minion on the left interrupted.

"Who –?" began the old man, but he was again interrupted, this time by a woman's voice.

"Thrinndor!" said a delighted Cyrillis as she shoved her way past the old man and pushed through the two priests who had been standing side-by-side in the doorway. She took the two remaining steps in a rush and threw her arms around the big fighter's neck and hugged him tightly.

"I am so happy to see you!" Her voice was muffled, as her face was semi-buried in his shoulder. As he was about to respond, Cyrillis spoke again, but just loud enough for him to hear. She was whispering in his ear, obviously not wanting anyone else to hear. "Say nothing of substance. These walls have ears." Again before he could respond, she pushed back but kept her arms around his neck. "Did you not miss me?" she asked teasingly, her lower lip protruding.

Thrinndor's confused eyes locked with those of the cleric, and she winked. She was acting for the sake of—what? He had no idea. He decided he should play along, however. Besides, it was not an altogether unattractive act. "Of course I did," he replied, suppressing the doubt in his voice and replacing it with the surprise he genuinely felt. That at least was not hard. "You just caught me by surprise, that is all." He briefly considered returning her wink to let her know he had heard and understood, but the twins were studying his eyes with obvious distrust clouding theirs.

"Good," she said, delight playfully running in her tone.

She then released him, grabbed his hand and started toward the doors she had so recently rushed through. She again pushed her way through the two Minions of Set, a happy smile plastered on her face, pulling the paladin along behind her.

Once they were in clear of the door, right tried to follow, but Cyrillis gave him a stern look and slammed the door in his face.

As she turned to look at the paladin, he said, "What—?"

"Shhhh," she said quickly, holding her fingers to her lips. For emphasis, she waved her arm around her, indicating the walls of the chamber and then pointing to her ears.

This time he did wink, nodding compliance.

Let me do the talking, she mouthed.

Again, Thrinndor nodded.

The paladin looked around, briefly. The chamber was not near as large as the temple he had recently passed through, yet it was obviously a temple as well. Perhaps it was the first temple built on the site, or maybe one used for special events. Everywhere there were signs of preparation for a hasty departure. He raised a questioning eyebrow.

Now loud enough for anyone listening to hear, Cyrillis said, "We are being forced to move." She frowned.

"The obvious question is why," said Thrinndor, pleased at finally finding something he could talk about.

Cyrillis took in a deep breath and shook her head to indicate either what she was about to say wasn't exactly true, or it wasn't the whole truth. "We do not know," she said with a shrug. "They came in this morning and informed us we had until the end of the day to vacate the premises." Her eyes searched those of the paladin. "Our presence would be no longer tolerated."

"I am certain there is more to it than that." He arched his eyebrow to indicate he was available to find out just what that was, should she want.

She shook her head. "We agree, but we are not in a position to challenge them at the moment." Her tone took on a forlorn quality.

This was not wasted on the paladin. "Where shall you go?"

"We do not know!" She was almost pleading for him to understand, and Thrinndor could see she indeed did not know but was not nearly as worried about it as she was leading him to believe.

"Maybe I can help—" he began with the others in the room looking on, obviously confused about the conversation.

"Us pack?" she cut in hurriedly, holding up her hands to forestall him from continuing the thought. She also shook her head as she continued, "That would be wonderful!" She winked at him. "We could use your strength with a few of these items. You must forgive my manners," she went on before he could speak. "Allow me to introduce my colleagues." Again she winked. "There are only the four of us." She pointed to the old man who had answered the door. "Magrinnist you have already met."

The elder man bowed and said, "Pleased to make your acquaintance, young man. Albeit I would wish it were under different circumstances."

Cyrillis went on with the introductions, indicating a young woman—scarcely more than a child in her mid-to-late teens—who had been standing silently taking in the whole scene, "This is Kiarrah." The girl bowed lightly at the waist, her smile forced. "She is an adept of the order." Cyrillis smiled at the girl. "She is a quick study and is progressing through the ranks rapidly."

The girl smiled nervously in response, but her face glowed light pink at the compliment.

"And this is Jacinth," Cyrillis said, turning to indicate a woman in her later years—probably seventy or eighty, Thrinndor decided.

As she too bowed at the waist, he suddenly remembered what Cyrillis had said about a young woman of that name. "What?" he asked, standing suddenly from the bow he was in the process of returning. "I thought—"

"She was dead?" Cyrillis was getting used to breaking in when he said too much. "Hardly, as you can see she is very much alive!"

"I do not know about 'very much,'" the old woman said with a sardonic smile playing on her wrinkled face, "but certainly body and soul are still one!"

"Ha!" returned Cyrillis. "Fit as a bard's lute and ready for adventure!"

"I will leave the adventuring to you young folks, if you do not mind," Jacinth said as she turned back to the shelf she had been emptying. "For now, I must be content with readying for a move from the only place I have ever known."

Thrinndor looked at Cyrillis who returned the look with a shake of her head, also pressing a finger to her lips to ensure he did not carry forward with this thought.

The old woman looked up at the ceiling. "Well," she said as her eyes took on a faraway look, "I seem to remember another place...maybe even two..."

Thrinndor could see that Cyrillis held her breath, waiting for what might come next, so he quickly stepped in and put his arm around Jacinth's shoulder and squeezed lightly. "That is all right," he crooned softly, "you will have plenty of time to sit and remember once you are settled at your new home."

"Hmmm?" she said as her eyes regained focus. "Home? Yes, that will be nice." She looked at Thrinndor as if seeing him for the first time. "I do not believe we have met. What is your name, young man?"

"Thrinndor," he replied as Cyrillis finally let out her breath. She moved over next to the woman and also put her arm on a shoulder.

"The quicker we get ready to leave, the quicker we can get on the road to your new home and the quicker we can get you settled there!" Cyrillis said softly.

"Oh, yes," said the woman, "then we must hurry and pack." Without another word, she went back to removing books and other items and placing them in bags at her feet set there for the purpose.

Cyrillis grasped the paladin's hand and pulled him aside while Jacinth hummed happily as she went about her task. She pulled him toward her and whispered in his ear. "We will discuss this later."

Thrinndor nodded and said loudly, "Show me what I can do to help."

Cyrillis took him to another door that led to a small fenced-in area that held two wagon animals and a couple of horses, one of which was the mount Cyrillis had ridden when last he saw her. The wagon was staged just to the right of the door. "These are ours—or rather," she corrected herself, "they are ours to use." She frowned her displeasure. "They must be returned here when our move is complete."

Thrinndor nodded and dropped his voice so it was barely audible. "Can we talk?" He did not look at her and made an effort not to move his lips.

As he turned to see her reaction, she just shook her head minutely. "Come on," she said listlessly, "we need to get to work." She then looked up at the early afternoon sun. "They have given us until sundown to be out of here." Her face showed concern. This time, the concern matched that in her voice. "And that is only a few short hours off."

Chapter Three

Respite

With Thrinndor's help, the wagon was quickly loaded. He had explained that he did not want to travel at night, so they needed to depart as quickly as possible and get to town before darkness set fully.

The goodbyes had been brief enough—none of Cyrillis' order was leaving family or friends behind.

Still, it was a big change for them, and the older two turned and looked back more than once as they set out on the path to town. Jacinth and Magrinnist rode in the wagon as Kiarrah, Cyrillis, and Thrinndor led with the horses.

The way Cyrillis sat the saddle forbade discussion, causing Thrinndor to wonder just what was going on. She set a tough pace, one that certainly precluded idle chatter.

As such, they reached town just as the last of the light was waning in the west. Thrinndor arranged for rooms for them all, no easy task in this small town. But he had become familiar with several of those that put up boarders and managed to arrange for all to stay at the same place.

When he was washing up in an urn provided for the task, Thrinndor turned at a light knock on his door.

He opened it to see Cyrillis standing there in her priestly robes but no armor. She held a finger to her lips when she saw him and motioned for him to follow. She also indicated that he should leave his armor.

Feeling naked without his stuff, he grabbed his sword, still sheathed, and followed her rapidly receding figure down the hall.

They went down the back stairs and after checking to see that no one was out in the alley they slipped silently out of the back door and into the darkness beyond.

Neither of the moons was up tonight—a fairly rare occurrence, Thrinndor mused. His eyes adjusted quickly to the starlight on this cloudless night, providing ample illumination for them to walk along the path she chose.

The healer must know where she's going, he thought, because Cyrillis did not hesitate as she covered ground quickly. Soon they were on the outskirts of town, and still she pressed on along a path that would have been dim in the daylight.

The path skirted the trees on the edge of town and wound its way down to a narrow creek. Cyrillis stepped lightly on some stones, crossing easily.

On the other side, she lithely scaled the ten-foot embankment and once again set foot to the path. The night air had a chill, and she pulled her cloak tightly about her shoulders as she tread along.

Finally they came upon a tiny stone structure in a small glade next to the creek. The water rustled lightly over a stone bed here, masking their footsteps as they approached.

Thrinndor could see the structure was actually a small cabin, and old. Very old. Even in the starlight he could see that rain, wind and sun had worn the stones over what must have been many hundreds of years.

Cyrillis opened the door and peeked inside. She must have been satisfied because she backed out, closing the door as she did. She looked around briefly, brushed a wayward lock of blonde hair back out of her face, and sat down on a log bench just to the right of the door.

"Now we may talk," she said with a sigh. It had been a brisk walk. "However, we do not want to be gone long. We must not allow anyone to notice our absence."

Thrinndor had several questions roiling about in his head. Finally, he settled on one. "How did you know of this place?" he asked as he sat on the bench beside her. There was ample room for both.

"I discovered it when I was in study at the temple," she replied. "We did not often come to town, but when we did, the others had things to do." She looked at him. "I did not." She shrugged. "I needed a quiet place, and this fit the description."

"Indeed," responded the paladin. He liked the feel of the place. Quiet. Old. The smell of pine and other things that grew. It just felt…right.

"It is old," she said. "Very old."

"I can see that," said Thrinndor as he rubbed his hand over the worn stone of the doorway.

Not knowing how to ask the many other questions that remained, or which to ask first, he lumped them all together. "What is going on?"

The cleric took in a deep breath and then let it out slowly. "I do not know," she said finally. When he took in a breath to reply she held up a hand to forestall him. "Wait. Let me talk. It will go quicker this way."

Thrinndor let the breath back out and nodded.

Cyrillis thought for a moment, trying to figure out where to start. Finally she said, "Everything is different." Knowing this did not help much, she went on. "When I left the temple to go in search of answers to my questions not much more than a month ago, there were several others of my order still studying and worshiping there." She thought for a moment, counting in her head. "Four, to be more precise: A man and his wife in their middle years. They have a son—perhaps twelve years of age or so." She shook her head. "There was another man, also in his middle years." She looked up at the paladin, trying to penetrate the darkness that hid his eyes. "Neither Jacinth nor Kiarrah were there when I left."

She paused to think about what to say next, and Thrinndor took the opportunity to say, "I thought you said Jacinth was a young woman."

"She is," the cleric began, "or was." Flustered, she continued, "I do not know!" She again tried to penetrate the dark pools that were his eyes. "It makes no sense! When I knew her as a child, she was no older than her late teens—and when she left she was certainly not past her early twenties." Exasperation crept into her voice. "But that was no more than four or five years ago!"

Thrinndor considered this and said, "Perhaps this is a different woman?"

"No," Cyrillis said. "I, too, considered that." Her voice grew quiet as she continued. "I questioned her. While this Jacinth is obviously having problems with her memory, she does know me. However, she remembers me as I was when I was but a child." Her eyes searched the dark grass at her feet for answers. Finding none, she went on. "She remembers nothing of our last few years together. Nothing as to why she left—nor does she even remember leaving. And nothing that transpired after her leaving before arriving at the temple." Her voice diminished to a whisper. "Nothing."

Thrinndor listened to the water rushing over the rocks in the stream. Finally he said, "We will have to investigate that further at another time." When still she said nothing, he asked, "What became of the others of your order?"

The change in subject caught her off-guard. "What? Oh," she said as her mind grasped what he asked. "That is not certain." Even more doubt crept into her voice. "The elders told me that one day after my departure Kridmaar—the unmarried priest—said he needed to make sure I was all right, and left." A sharp look from Thrinndor caused her to add quickly. "He fancied me." The paladin was certain she was blushing despite her face being veiled by the darkness. "While that may explain his departure, he was no adventurer."

Her voice grew stern, "He was a fool!" she said. "I had informed him on more than one instance I was meant for no man." Again her voice grew quiet. "Yet he persisted."

The silence hung in the air like a bane. When Thrinndor could stand no more he nudged her gently, "And the man, wife and child?"

"Huh?" she asked, shaking her head to clear whatever scene had been playing itself out there. "Oh, yes, Correlle and Brequarre," she went on quickly. "That is even more bizarre." Her face twisted in thought. "The elders told me that all went to bed one night and then the next morning, the three of them were gone!"

"What?" asked the paladin.

"No sign of hasty departure," Cyrillis added. "All of their belongings—which were not much as you might imagine—were missing as well." Sorrow crept its way into her tone. "Nor was there any sign of foul play."

"Had they been there long?" At her quizzical look, he added. "At the temple, I mean."

"All their lives. Their son, Drummarre, was born there. He was indeed his father's son," she said with a hint of pride to her voice, "and said to be one of the quickest studies to serve our lord in many a year."

"Any theories?"

"None," Cyrillis said simply with a shrug. "Their disappearance makes even less sense. Their only goal was to train their son—and any who cared to learn—in the healing ways of our Lord."

Again silence filled the air.

"Kiarrah?" he prodded.

"Almost as bizarre," she said with an insecure sigh. "Kiarrah showed up, by herself, one day about a week after I left. She gave no explanation, just professing the desire to be cleric of Valdaar."

Thrinndor was trying to digest all that he had been told when Cyrillis said abruptly, "I do not trust her."

"Please explain."

"I cannot," she said forlornly. "Yet, I feel thus." Her eyes searched his face. "I sense in her no deception. Yet…" She looked away. "Her appearance at that time is simply too much of a coincidence." She hesitated.

"And?" Thrinndor asked.

"She is too good," the cleric said.

"She is but a child," said the paladin.

"She is not a child!" The vehemence in her voice startled the paladin. "She is too quick a study! No one is that good!" Thrinndor could sense her eyes flashing. "I had prior training, and I was not as quick a study!"

"You think her a spy?"

"Yes!" she snapped. Then she countered herself. "No. I do not know!" Now her voice was almost a wail.

The paladin decided it best not to say anything more. Besides, he was at a loss for words.

They sat in silence for a bit, listening to the rustle of the water over the stones in the brook. Finally, she said, "I am sorry. I do not mean to be so emotional."

Sensing her unusual frailty, Thrinndor chose his words carefully. "In light of what you have been through," he said, "you certainly have a right to such emotion."

"Thank you." Her voice was barely audible above the noise of the creek rushing past.

"However—" he went on, a little more authority in his tone.

She cut him off by standing before he could continue. "We must get back."

He did not move. He grasped her hand and pulled her back to the bench. "We have not been gone that long," he insisted. "And we have yet to discuss your family line."

She did not struggle but also did not immediately say anything. Instead, she pulled her cloak more tightly about her shoulders. "You are right," she said finally. "But we must not tarry much longer. I do not want anyone to believe we are being secretive."

"Nor do I," he said.

"Besides, there is not much to discuss." She shrugged under her cloak. "The elders knew only that my parents were the elders before they were slain. I was known to be a 'special' child and 'reserved'—no more than that."

"You have said that before," Thrinndor said. "What is meant by 'reserved'?"

Her shoulders slumped. "I know not," she said quietly. Before the paladin could say anything she added, "We know only that I may give myself to no man until released to do so by Valdaar himself."

"But," began the paladin, "direct communication with him is impo—unlikely."

"I know," she said forlornly. Then, however, a note of defiance crept in. "Yet somehow his will is made known." Her eyes flashed in the darkness. "It was so with my mother, I am told. She, too, was 'reserved.'"

Thrinndor shifted uncomfortably on the bench, and not just because his backside was complaining about the hardness of it. This was not how he had envisioned the conversation going when it began.

"Very well," he said meekly. Then deciding there was trouble ahead with that train of thought, he went back to the original line. "Could there be any records back at the temple that might help us trace your history?"

After a moment's thought, she sighed. "I know not. I inquired about that very thing a couple of days ago and was told there were no such records." Frustration crept back in her voice. "Yet I know the Minions of Set keep detailed records!"

He pondered that for a few heartbeats. "Do you think your sudden eviction could possibly have anything to do with your inquiry?"

"That has crossed my mind as well," she said, her tone heavy. "But why?"

"That is one of the questions we must ask them," he said ominously. "But only after we get your people settled." He abruptly changed the subject. "Do you know where you will go?"

She thought about the change in topic for a moment and replied, "No."

"I do," he said quickly, finally finding something he had been prepared to talk about bolstered his confidence. "You—those of your order, at least—will be welcome at Khavhall."

"Paladinhood Home?" she asked. "Are you certain?"

"Yes," he said as if the matter was settled. "My mother would certainly welcome others who serve our Lord Valdaar. There are too few remaining. We must band together!"

"That certainly makes sense," she said guardedly. "Is there a temple at which we may worship?"

"Yes," he replied again. "It is but a small one. However, I am certain it will serve the purpose."

"Very well," she said, hesitantly. "If you think we will be welcome."

"I am certain of it," he said. "I will hear no more discussion in the matter!" He was secretly pleased at being able to assert himself at last.

Silence enveloped them again. After a few moments Cyrillis stood, repeating, "We must get back."

This time he did not argue and got to his feet and rose beside her. They stood there like that for a few moments, each trying to read the other's thoughts.

With a huff, Cyrillis started off back the way they had come, not looking back to see if he was following. If anything, she set an even harder pace on the way back, precluding further conversation. Thrinndor had no idea what else to say anyway, so he remained silent.

When they stopped at her door they did not say anything, but both were obviously reluctant to depart. Finally, Thrinndor looked into her eyes and said softly, "Thank you."

Not knowing how to reply to that, Cyrillis said, "You are welcome." Quickly she added, "And thank you for listening." Not sure what else to say, Cyrillis made the point moot by stepping into her room and closing the door behind her.

Thrinndor stood staring at the door for a moment and then walked as silently as he could down the hall back to his room and went inside. Once there, he made ready for bed and fell in the one made for him, suddenly exhausted by the events of the day.

*

Thrinndor did as promised and took the group the next day to Paladinhood Home. It took a little longer than when he rode alone, but the group traveled well and made it before the evening meal.

After first meeting to discuss the matter with his mother, he showed the Order to their new home.

Once the excitement died down, Cyrillis pulled the paladin aside—their first opportunity to talk since the night before—and asked, "What did you mean last night when you said 'That is one of the questions we must ask them'?"

He looked at her and said, "Just that." She took in a sharp breath to reply, but he held up a hand to ask her to allow him to explain. "You and I are going to go ask them a few questions."

"When?" she said, curiosity getting the better of her.

"First light."

She was silent for a few moments while her eyes searched his. "And if they do not want to provide answers?"

He shrugged and smiled. "Then I will be more insistent." He locked eyes with the cleric. "We will gain access to their documents." She felt an involuntary shudder pass through her, and he went on. "I will of course start with diplomacy, but should that fail..." He placed his right hand on the pommel of the sword protruding from its sheath at his belt. "...we will have what information they have." He looked around the room, ensuring none was trying to listen in on their conversation. Seeing no one, he continued, "I sense they are hiding something." He turned to again look into her eyes. "Their eviction of your Order after all the years they had been there—I think the timing bears a deeper investigation."

Her eyes tried to determine the depth of his resolve. "As do I," she agreed. "However, do not underestimate them." She put her hand on his as it still rested on the haft of his sword. "The brothers are strong in their service to their god." She paused as her eyes searched the room for Kiarrah. She was facing away and laughing joyfully at something Magrinnist had said. "I feel they will not give of the information willingly, and they will certainly prove a formidable opponent."

Thrinndor nodded. "Of that I have no doubt. Yet I am certain they have information we must have." His eyes followed where the clerics were probing. "Mayhap you have misjudged her. She seems very sincere, and I sense no deception in her."

Cyrillis' eyes did not leave the back of the teen. "Perhaps."

After a few moments the paladin said, "We should get some rest. We must leave early tomorrow and ride hard to get there ere night falls."

The cleric nodded and without looking at him again, walked over to join the elders and Kiarrah.

Thrinndor stood there and watched her as she easily joined the conversation. He shook his head as he turned and went to his personal chambers.

Chapter Four

Set and Match

In the morning, Thrinndor bade his mother to inquire quietly about the missing clerics. She assured him they would do so.

The ride back to the temple was uneventful. Thrinndor decided they would use the cover of returning the wagons to the brothers as their guise. The time-consuming ride with an empty wagon played into their hands, as he had decided it would be better if they approached in the morning. The paladin found a place to set up camp a few miles away.

From a discreet distance, they scouted the temple as the sun set. Thrinndor counted at least nine sets of robes, including the twins and two women.

These last bothered the paladin the most. While he had no problem dealing as necessary with Minions of Set, he disliked having to fight—and possibly kill—women.

He hoped it would not come to that.

Satisfied that he knew the comings and goings of the denizens of the temple, he and Cyrillis went back to where they had set up camp.

As sneaking in was not his style, the next morning he and Cyrillis rode up to the main entrance much as he had only two days earlier. It seemed longer.

Again one of the brothers was waiting for him as they approached. The second came through the door when they rode up. As before, the brothers' faces were hidden in the deep shadows of their hooded cloaks.

"We thought we were rid of you," said the brother who had just arrived. There was no attempt at civility in his tone.

Momentarily taken aback, Thrinndor blinked in the early morning sun. Quickly regaining his composure he said, "We have some questions for you." He made no move to dismount.

"Ask," replied the one who had been waiting for them.

"However," said the one who spoke first, "consider that we may not provide answers."

His brother nodded. "Or that the answers provided may not be the ones you seek."

"We will just have to see about that." The paladin in him was starting to get pissed off. He started to dismount, but Cyrillis put her hand on his arm and applied just enough pressure to cause him to pause.

He turned to face her, but she ignored him and said, "Forgive our intrusion into your place of worship." Her tone was soothing yet deliberate. "And forgive this one who does not understand what it means to serve as we do." She dipped her head in deference to them.

Hidden by his helm, Thrinndor's right eyebrow inched incrementally higher. This had not been part of the plan. What in the name of the Seven Hells was she up to? He decided to play along and growled a low, menacing rumble deep within his chest but said nothing.

Ignoring him, she removed her hand from his arm and lithely dismounted. She immediately dropped into a sweeping bow before the twins, who now stood side by side. Kurril held out prominently in front of her as she bowed.

They said nothing, but she certainly had their attention. Thrinndor decided they were probably as thrown off by her actions as he was.

He followed suit and dismounted noisily, making sure the haft of his sword was free—and visible—as he did so.

"What is it you seek?" Thrinndor was not certain, but he thought the one on the left's tone had softened perceptibly. He was certain, however, that they were making a show of ignoring him. Good, he thought. Maybe she had a plan after all.

"Well," she began, her voice dripping with sweetness, "I was wondering whether you might be able to help me settle a matter within my order." She batted her eyes at the minion on the left.

Nice touch, the paladin thought.

"What might that be?" the one on the right asked.

Yes, his demeanor was certainly less suspicious. Amazing what an attractive woman, a sweet voice and some eye-batting did for the male demeanor. Even a priest of Set's demeanor, apparently.

"I am interested in the open leadership position in my order," she began coyly, "but I have been told that I must prove my worthiness by showing the appropriate lineage." She allowed a twinge of regret to creep into her voice.

"Bah!" snorted left.

"Leadership worthiness can be only shown though dedication to your God and prowess in battle!" said right.

"Alas," Cyrillis said, "were it to be so." Thrinndor was certain she was about to shed a tear—she was good! "I fear my order will deny my request without proof of lineage."

"Well," said left, "your order certainly could use an upgrade at leadership." He appeared to ponder her plight.

"Be that as it may," said right, "what is it you would ask of us?" His suspicion was obvious.

Cyrillis looked up at him, brushing an imagined tear from her hopeful eyes. "I understand you keep such records," she said, unable to keep the hope out of her voice. "Is it possible you might be able to prove my heritage?" More eye-batting. "Please?"

Damn, she was good. Thrinndor knew he would be able to deny her nothing at this point.

The twins turned to face on another; they were obviously communicating in their peculiar manner.

Thrinndor decided then and there that he must research how they did that. He found himself holding his breath as they communed, hoping this plan of hers would work. He found he did not want to kill the two, although their service to their god was an abomination to him.

When they turned to face the healer once again, right spoke for them. "Yes," he said. "We may have the information you require."

"But he," left said, indicating the paladin, "must remain out here. He and his weapons will not again be permitted within these hallowed walls."

Thrinndor was certain the walls were not all that hallowed and was about to say as much when Cyrillis spoke. "That is acceptable," she said as she told the paladin with her eyes to trust her and that she would be fine. "Thrinndor came along only to ensure I got this far safely." She looked at the twins, her gaze impassive. "And to make sure I return safely."

She left that out there for them to ponder. The brothers communicated with one another, and then the minion on the left said, "Very well." He then turned and started up the steps. "Follow us."

Cyrillis started after the two, then turned and said to Thrinndor loud enough for all to hear, "This could take a while." She locked eyes with the paladin. "Would you please see to our horses?"

Thrinndor picked up on the code in her voice. She really wanted him out back in the stable area for a reason and presumably out of sight. She also was indicating it should not really take all that long. "As you wish," he said with a formal bow, showing her he understood. "Let me know if you require anything further." He winked. "I will be within a shout if you need my assistance."

"Oh," she said with a hurried look over her shoulder at the still receding brothers, "that should not be necessary." As she turned back to the paladin, however, she nodded imperceptibly and winked. "I am sure I will be all right in the hands of Gravinalt and Flavinalt."

With that, she went up the steps and disappeared through the open doors of the temple.

Finally! Thrinndor now had names to go with the faces. Gravinalt and Flavinalt. Cute. Now, which was which?

However, the paladin did not like this—it was not what they had planned. He had to admit, though, it would probably work better than squeezing the throat of one or both of the brothers until the required information popped out.

Probably.

He scooped up the reins of her horse with a shrug and led both of their animals and those that had been loaned them by the Minions along the path that skirted the main building and led around back to the livery. He released the borrowed animals first and returned the wagon to its place next to the stable. Next, he took extra care with his and Cyrillis' horses, noting that the livery was sparsely supplied with goods for the task. All the while he took care not to wander more than a stone's throw from the side entrance he knew would take him into the temple should the need arise.

He did not have long to wait. As he added water to the trough in front of their horses, his hyper-attuned hearing picked up a muffled shout from inside the temple.

A female shout.

Thrinndor hit the path running toward the door he had been watching, sword and shield in hand.

As he pushed the door open and stepped inside, he spotted sunlight as it glinted off of something metal in the corner of his eye, and he ducked barely in time to avoid a blow to the head.

A trap! They were waiting for him!

The mace grazed harmlessly off of a hastily raised shield. Thrinndor slashed at where the body should be at the end of the arm swinging the mace.

Some resistance and a stifled cry informed the paladin his hasty swing had at least done some damage, and the sound of steps coming up behind him told him he was up against multiple assailants.

"Cyrillis!" he shouted as he dove to the floor to escape whoever was trying to get in behind him. He slashed his sword in a sweeping arc as he surged to a crouch and felt another satisfying crunch as his blade hit bone in the leg of one of his assailants.

A scream of pain ripped the air as a body collapsed to the floor, writhing as it cursed. He heard the rapidly receding footsteps as his first attacker fled down the dim passage.

"Fools!" a shout split the air. Thrinndor recognized the voice—one of the brothers! He was not far away.

"When you want something done..." he heard the other say.

"You must do it yourself!" Thrinndor shouted as he sprinted down the hall and dove through the door from which he had heard the voices.

He rolled forward twice before surging to his feet. It was a standard maneuver he'd worked on during his recent training that in theory was designed to throw off the aim of an adversary.

In theory…

The twins had obviously been expecting such a maneuver because as he rolled he spotted one of the brothers to his left, staff at the ready, and the other standing behind the altar he had seen a couple of days ago, a long curved knife in his hand, pressed against the throat of a bound and gagged prone figure.

Cyrillis!

"As we have said before," said the one holding the staff.

"You will be prevented," said the other.

"Guards!" they shouted in unison.

Thrinndor heard the sound of several pairs of feet approaching rapidly from more than one corridor. He knew he had only a few seconds in which to act.

"Put down your weapon," said the brother holding the staff.

"Or she becomes the latest sacrifice to Set!" sneered the other. He was smiling. It was not a smile, however, that endeared one to others.

Cyrillis, her eyes bulging in fear, shook her head. He could not be sure whether she meant for him to comply, or whether she was telling him not to try anything heroic.

Thrinndor hesitated and allowed his shoulders to slump. "Very well," he said as he bent over to place his sword and shield on the floor. He tilted the shield slightly and pulled the trigger, releasing the bolt from the crossbow affixed to the back of it.

He briefly hoped his aim was true, but just as quickly the response came to him that it probably did not matter. If he surrendered easily, they were probably both dead. If he did not, they had a chance to live.

So he chose what he figured was their one chance to survive.

His aim was indeed true. The speeding bolt pierced the cleric holding the knife just below his larynx. The resulting scream was really no more than a muffled, bubbling sound as bright red blood instead of sound came out of his mouth. He dropped the dagger and both hands clawed at the bolt as he stumbled back a step.

"Flavinalt!" shouted the remaining twin. His attention was momentarily distracted as he prepared a healing spell to aid his brother.

The paladin seized this opportunity to fling his shield saucer style at who he now knew to be Gravinalt just as the guards burst into the room. The shield connected solidly on the side of the priest's head. His aim was getting better, Thrinndor reflected briefly.

While the shield did little damage, it accomplished what he wanted: It kept one brother from aiding the other.

His left hand free of the shield, he used it to grasp the haft of his now flaming bastard sword and swung it in a vicious arc, screaming at the top of his lungs in his best Vorgath impersonation as the blade whipped through the air.

The yell had the desired effect, he noted—he would have to inform the barbarian of that the next time he saw him—as it momentarily confused the guards and they hesitated slightly as they bore down on him.

It was enough. His hurried swing first glanced harmlessly off of the nearest guard's shield, but that only served to deflect his blade higher. His sword's momentum swept it further along where the next guard was not so fortunate. Unable to react in time, he was caught just above the bridge of the nose by the flaming blade, biting deep into his skull. He was dead instantly.

However, Thrinndor's swing exposed his back to the other two arriving guards, and one of them recovered quickly enough to shove his pole-axe—the weapon favored by the guards of the Minions of Set, and thus wielded by all four assailants—into an unprotected area just under the paladin's left arm.

Fortunately, the blade failed to penetrate deep as it scraped the skin along his rib cage. However, it left a long nasty gash that produced a lot of blood.

The paladin howled in pain and dropped one knee to the floor as he spun to face these new guards. As he turned, he again whipped his blade around blindly, this time connecting with one of the guard's legs just above the knee. Thrinndor felt the blade pause only momentarily as it met bone, passing clear through one leg to slice into the other.

The guard screamed in pain as he toppled over, his hands attempting to staunch the flow of blood from the remaining stump of his right leg.

Thrinndor surged back to his feet as the remaining two guards—their numbers suddenly reduced by half—backed off a step, unsure whether to continue the fight or run. He used the momentary respite to locate the cleric with the bump on his head.

He was fortunate he did, because this brother's face was contorted in rage and he was waving his arms in preparation for a spell.

Instinct kicked in and the paladin dove headlong toward the cleric, but the distance was too great. The air erupted behind Thrinndor and knocked him farther along than he had intended.

Flame strike!

Momentarily stunned and singed from the blast, the paladin rose slowly to his hands and knees. He had lost track of the cleric, and that was not good.

His momentum and the blast from the spell had taken the fighter almost to the feet of the brother, where in continued rage the cleric brought his staff down hard on the back of the prone paladin's head, screaming at the remaining guards to finish him.

Thrinndor's helm deflected most of the blow, but his ears were ringing as he stumbled to his feet. He staggered to his left, away from the two guards who were obviously more afraid of this cleric's wrath than the injured paladin. They stepped in—more cautiously this time, their pole-axes at the ready.

Somewhere, the fighter had lost his weapon. No matter, his buzzing head told him, without a shield his two-handed sword was the better choice.

With the deftness of much practice, he swept the blade off the hook that secured it to his back, bringing the huge blade around for the attackers to see.

He waved it out in front menacingly. One of the guards grew wide-eyed, and backed away slowly. The other pressed his attack.

Unfortunately for the guard, he was no match for the paladin. Finesse was not Thrinndor's normal skill set when it came to battle, but with a two-handed broad sword in his hands, it was even less so. And he was more than strong enough to make that work to his advantage. Two all-out slashes with the sword later, the less intelligent of the two guards lay dead at his feet.

He looked around for the remaining guard. If this man had feared for his life before, he was terrified now. He ducked through the nearest curtain along the wall and was gone.

Seeing this fleeing guard was now no threat, Thrinndor turned his attention to the clerics. He quickly realized he should have paid more attention to them— or at least the one that remained alive. Flavinalt lay where he had fallen, his eyes glazed over in death.

However, Gravinalt was staring insolently at the paladin. In his right hand was the same long, curved dagger his brother had held. It was again pressed to the throat of Cyrillis. The priest's other hand had a handful of her hair, drawing her head back and exposing her throat.

"Worry not for my brother. I will deal with him once I finish with you," the Minion of Set said, his voice low and menacing. "He will yet live again." His eyes showed…pride? "That will be easy enough for me. Now, put down your weapon. This time with no trickery or you will watch her die!"

Thrinndor took a menacing step toward them, but the minion pressed his blade hard enough against her light skin that it drew blood.

"I said," Gravinalt screamed, "put down your weapon!"

Cyrillis' eyes were wide in fear, yet she jerked them side to side, telling the paladin not to comply. Then she made an effort to look down to where her hands were bound at her midsection.

Without allowing his eyes to follow her motion for fear of alerting this madman, he heightened his perception in that direction and he could tell she was working her hands free!

However, she needed more time. He needed to stall.

"Very well," Thrinndor said as he allowed his shoulders to droop in defeat. "What will you do with us?" His tone was abject.

The minion smiled in triumph. "Put down your weapon…" He was pretty good at sneering and talking at the same time. "…and we will talk about it." He jerked on the prone cleric's hair to show he was serious.

"But," began the paladin.

"Enough!" shouted the minion. "Drop your weapon now, or she—"

He never finished the sentence. Cyrillis' now free hands shot up, grasped his hair and jerked his head down toward where she lay. At the same time Cyrillis twisted away from the minion, attempting to pull him off balance as she tumbled off of the altar.

Attempted. She was nowhere near the man's size, and she only succeeded in knocking him off balance. Unfortunately this had the unforeseen effect of causing him to press down harder with the blade in his left hand.

She screamed in pain.

He screamed in fury.

Thrinndor screamed because it seemed the thing to do at the time. He took the two steps required to reach the altar in the time it took to blink an eye, his sword instantly poised for the strike to end this.

Yet he could not swing the mammoth blade for fear of hitting Cyrillis. He hesitated briefly then grasped Gravinalt with his free hand by the tunic and lifted him clear of the altar.

Cyrillis' eyes were wide in fear as she felt her life blood flowing from the widened gash in her neck. Her hands attempted in vain to close the wound, but no spells came to her lips as she laid her head back to the cold stone beneath her, frothy blood bubbling at the corner of her mouth.

He knew he had little time to save her, but Thrinndor also knew that he first had to deal with this minion once and for all.

Using his enormous strength, he flung the screaming man into the air and then with both hands on his sword he swung as hard as he could at the falling minion. His blade caught Gravinalt in his unprotected right side and sliced deep. Such was the momentum of the swing that it folded the falling cleric around the blade and flung him several feet into the wall behind the altar. He hit with a thud, slid down the wall to the stone floor and lay still.

Thrinndor dropped the blade with a loud clatter and turned to face Cyrillis. There was a lot of blood from the slash in her neck, and it pooled in the altar beneath her. There was also a trickle of the deep red fluid running from her mouth.

Her eyes were calm with the knowledge of being on the door of the afterlife. Her lips moved in an effort to speak, but only more blood came forth.

"Shhhh," said the paladin, tears in his eyes. "Try to speak not! Let me work my—"

Cyrillis' eyes were growing weary in death, but she shook her head side to side, knowing the wound was indeed mortal.

"Do not move!" said the paladin, his voice harsher than he intended. "You will not die! Not while I yet live!" He was almost shouting.

He reached out and with both hands pulled the skin together and poured the powers of healing granted to him by Valdaar by way of the Paladinhood into her torn flesh.

The skin closed—seemingly of its own accord—and the bleeding stopped. She had slipped into unconsciousness, however, and did not move. Seeing this, Thrinndor worked his hands gently along the scar still visible on her lovely neck and again poured his remaining healing power into her.

The scar visibly lightened, yet her eyes remained closed. Thrinndor checked for a heartbeat and found one, weak and inconsistent. She had lost a lot of blood.

Knowing he had to get her out of there, the paladin gently lifted her off of the altar and stumbled toward the door. He had forgotten about his own wound. He too had lost a lot of blood. He was feeling it now.

"Wait!" said a weak voice behind him.

Thrinndor turned to see Gravinalt trying to regain his feet. Unable to do so, he muttered a few words, made a gesture and became visibly stronger.

Knowing he didn't have the strength for yet another battle with this minion if he was allowed to regain full capacity, Thrinndor set Cyrillis gently on the cold stone floor next to where he had dropped his sword.

Picking it up, he shouted if for no other reason but to distract and took the three steps between himself and the priest in a rush, swinging the blade as he did.

Yet such was his own state that the minion was able to twist aside and cause his sword to whisk harmlessly by. In so doing, the paladin lost his grip on the blade. His sword flew out of his hand and clattered noisily to the floor some distance away.

Gravinalt sneered as he readied yet another spell, releasing its energy into the paladin as he stumbled closer.

He'd chosen the wrong spell! Thrinndor could feel the energy of the spell designed to beset him with disease or poison. However, he as a paladin was immune to both!

With the cleric bewildered by his failure, Thrinndor seized the opportunity. He swung his right fist with all of his remaining strength in a roundhouse that connected solidly with the jaw of the minion.

The cleric's head whipped around and he hit the wall again with a solid thud.

Still he refused to go down!

Thrinndor followed the first punch with a second to the solar plexus, causing the minion to double over in pain as the air left his lungs in a whoosh.

The paladin grabbed what he could immediately get his hands on and lifted the man and then dumped him unceremoniously onto the recently vacated altar.

Spying the dagger lying nearby on the floor—its blade still gleaming with the moisture of Cyrillis' blood—Thrinndor scooped it up, straightened and plunged it into the chest of the minion until the haft was pressed against Gravinalt's tunic.

The minion's eyes widened in surprise and his mouth worked, but no sound but a hoarse whisper came forth.

"May this 'sacrifice' be worthy to your god!" Thrinndor said, his own voice gasping as his overworked body fought for air.

Finding his voice at last, Gravinalt wheezed out, "You would desecrate this holy place so?" There was much pain in his eyes, not all of it from poundings on his human form.

"This is no 'holy' place," sneered the paladin. "And I have yet begun to desecrate!" With those words, Thrinndor picked up his sword and walked along the walls, destroying the sconces with his blade and sending the flammable oils flying all over the walls and, more important, the curtains hanging on those walls.

Flames immediately leapt up the ancient, dry draperies, spreading quickly to nearby tapestries until the entire room seemed to be burning.

"No!" came a wail from the altar, Gravinalt's voice already weak in impending death. "This cannot be!"

"I assure you it is!" said the paladin as he once again stood at the side of the minion lying on that altar. He looked deep into the wide eyes of the twin. "This place will no longer be an abomination to man." He looked at the burning walls. "I will see the land returned to the locals and a shrine built here to those that were slain here in a false god's name!" But his words were now wasted on the dead man's empty gaze.

Thrinndor quickly retrieved his sword, slung it over his back, picked up Cyrillis and stumbled toward the exit. It seemed much farther away now as the chamber filled with smoke.

He burst through the door into the bright afternoon sunlight, his lungs gasping for clean, smoke-free air, and he fell to his knees at the bottom of the steps. Cyrillis tumbled from his grasp, rolled a short distance and lay still.

He fell to his hands and knees, spilled forward onto the ground and rolled over onto his back, all the while his air starved lungs heaving.

"Kurril." Cyrillis' voice came to him in a whisper.

"What?" he gasped as he struggled to rise.

"Kurril," she repeated as she tried to raise her head.

The staff! "Where?" he asked quickly. But realizing she was already again unconscious, he eased her back to the hard-packed dirt.

Knowing her staff must not be lost gave him newfound energy as he struggled to his feet. He hastily wrapped a cloth around his head, making sure his nose was well covered, and sprinted up the steps leading into the temple three at a time. As he entered the temple, he cast fire resistance on himself, hoping that would allow him safer passage.

He had not seen it in the chamber during the recent ordeal, so where could it be?

Thrinndor ran through the temple and brushed aside a curtain engulfed in flames to enter the hallway he knew to be back there. The flames had already reached this far, and he knew he had not much time left.

He searched several rooms before coming upon what must have been their library—or records room. He spotted the staff leaning against one of the heavily laden bookcases, but the table between it and him was already ablaze!

He kicked the table aside, and it crashed into yet another book case and immediately the dry parchment shelved there exploded into flames as well.

Stunned, he stumbled forward and grasped the staff and just as quickly jerked his hand back with a yelp. The staff had shocked him! Badly!

He briefly looked down at his charred hand, remembering that none but the owner of the staff may touch it.

Damn!

He whipped the cloak off of his shoulders, wrapped his left hand in it and then reached for the staff. It did not shock him this time.

He then spun and bolted for the door. Once in the hallway, momentarily disoriented, he finally turned to his left and ran with all of his remaining strength toward where he remembered there being the door out to the livery.

He hoped…

Yes! He could see down the passage ahead of him. He brushed aside flaming tapestries and curtains as he reached the door.

Locked! It was locked!

He threw his shoulder into it, but the solid door did not budge. He tried a second time, getting the same result.

He was out of time. The flames were licking at his leggings, and the hem of his cloak had begun to smolder.

Quickly, he whipped the staff around and smashed at the locking mechanism with it. In so doing, his hand slipped off of the cloak and onto the bare wood.

He again screamed. Then, ignoring the pain, he raised the hardened wood and again smashed the staff's heel against the mechanism.

This time it broke free and he kicked the door open and burst through into the bright sunlight beyond.

He stumbled down the steps and onto the path that led to the livery. He fell to his knees and pitched forward onto his face as everything blacked out around him.

*

Moments later he came to as a cold, wet, soft…thing pushed against his right cheek. He could feel the heat of the burning building on his left side.

"Wha—" he croaked as he tried to push himself back to a sitting position. "Ah!" he screamed as he put pressure on his hands. He looked down at them to see they were badly scorched.

Rolling to his back, the paladin struggled to his feet to see his horse standing over him. The cold, wet feeling that had awakened him? His mount's nose!

Again wrapping his hands in the smoldering cloak, he picked up the staff with one hand and grasped the mane of his horse with the other. Unable to pull himself up, he clucked his tongue and the horse started toward the livery, dragging the stumbling paladin along with him.

Once there, already feeling better from the curative effects of the fresh air, he went about and methodically released any pent-up animals, giving them a good whack with a rope as they ran from the stable and away from the approaching flames.

Then, gathering Cyrillis' mount—the staff affixed securely to her saddle—two pack animals and his own mount he exited the barn as the roof was starting to smolder from embers cast high in the sky by the burning roof of the temple.

As he looked back at the compound from the relative safety of the front, he could see that the entire group of buildings was doomed. The recent dry conditions coupled with the wood that was, at a minimum, decades old spelled their end.

He shrugged his acknowledgment that it was probably a good thing, at least for the nearby community, the loss of the generated commerce notwithstanding.

Still, he mourned the deaths of so many for a reason he was unable to discern. However, they had brought the fight to him. He had not come here to kill them, he reasoned.

He found the healer as he had left her, lying on the hard-packed earth a short, but safe, distance from what had been the entrance to the temple.

She remained unconscious, her breathing labored. He shook his head wearily as he checked her over, not sure if she had even been conscious to warn him of the staff's peril. He felt reasonably certain that mere fire could not damage the artifact. Still, that was not a certainty, and he was glad he had been able to retrieve it.

He looked momentarily at his hands. They were badly burnt from his mishandling of the boon—but they would heal, he decided.

With a crash that startled him, the roof of the temple caved in. He decided quickly that they must get back to their camp. The paladin was loath to move her, yet he knew they could not stay here. There was at least one, and possibly two, minion that yet lived, and he was in no shape for a fight.

As gently as he could, he lifted Cyrillis into the saddle of his own mount, trusting his horse to walk steadily so she would remain there.

After shifting the staff so that he would not come in contact with it, he climbed wearily into the saddle of her horse. He gathered the reins and led the processional back down the path by which they had come no more than a few hours earlier.

Chapter Five

Breunne

Vorgath spluttered angrily at the intrusion into his slumber. At least he thought it was slumber. It might have been more of a comatose state, however…

Wiping the water thrown on him out of his eyes, he sat up quickly—too quickly as it turned out. He allowed his head to slump slowly back from whence it came. The floor.

Now someone was nudging him none too gently in the side with the toe of a boot. If his head hadn't hurt so much, he probably would have done something about that. Probably.

"Wake up, old one." The voice seemed to be aimed at him, but of that he couldn't be certain. Not until he opened his eyes, anyway, and that was still some time off.

The voice also sounded vaguely familiar, yet he couldn't place it.

"I wouldn't do that, were I you," said yet another voice, also familiar—more recent, he thought.

There was a pause in the action, during which the barbarian succumbed to the pounding in his head and drifted back into oblivion. Maybe these fools would just go away.

Cyrillis wrinkled her nose in distaste as she surveyed the room. And a mess it was. Broken tables and bits of chairs littered the floor. Bodies lay strewn among the wreckage. She used her senses to verify all lived. They did, although more than one was going to regret that status when he regained consciousness. The place stank of stale beer, unwashed bodies, and urine.

Being in the tavern made her stomach churn. However, Cyrillis forced down the bile in the event she was needed, and she was fairly certain that would be the case.

The cleric watched as Thrinndor eyed the man who had spoken, again nudging the dwarf with the toe of his boot. "I will be fine," said the paladin. "Vorgath and I go back a few years."

"All the same," said the stranger, "he's had a pretty wild night."

"So it would seem," said the paladin as he looked back down at his friend. Not getting the results he wanted, Thrinndor reached down and grabbed a handful of tunic and lifted the upper torso of the dwarf clear of the floor. He then picked up a half full flagon of ale from a nearby table that still stood, turned and headed for the door to the street, dragging the comatose dwarf behind him.

Cyrillis followed. The stranger stood and fell in step, obviously curious to see how this was going to play out.

Thrinndor brushed aside the curtain and squinted at the bright morning light from the sun beyond. It had been dim in the tavern. He searched right and left before spotting what he was after—a watering trough for horses and pack animals.

He strode purposely toward it, the feet of the dwarf making ruts in the soft dirt of the street. When the paladin neared the trough, he easily hefted the dwarf and slung him so that he cleared the edges, making a huge splash in the trough as he landed.

There was much spluttering, splashing and cursing from the confines of the trough as the barbarian fought to sit up. He used a massive paw to wipe the water from his eyes, by now open. "What the—!" bellowed the dwarf, glaring at the blurry figures arrayed before him, all well out of arm's reach.

"Here," said the paladin as he thrust the flagon of ale in the angry dwarf's face.

Vorgath eyed the paladin, curses unspoken on his lips. Without looking at it, he reached out and grabbed the flagon, put it to his lips and emptied its contents in one swig. He twisted his face up at the taste of the warm, stale ale and cast the empty container aside. "Thanks," he said. "I needed that!"

"You are welcome," replied Thrinndor pleasantly. He reached out his right hand, which the dwarf grasped. The paladin lifted him clear of the water and set him on boardwalk behind. He was always amazed at how quickly his friend was able to recover from…whatever. "What in the name of Valdaar happened?" the paladin asked, although he was certain he could guess some of it.

"Huh?" asked Vorgath, still blinking at the bright light. "Oh," he said as he scrunched up his face in thought. "I flirted. Boyfriend objected. I kicked his ass. We drank." He looked up sheepishly at his friend towering over him. "I don't remember much else."

"You kicked his ass?" queried the paladin. "You look terrible!" Indeed, Vorgath's right eye was black and swollen almost shut, one lip was split and there were several cuts and abrasions on his hands and face.

"Yeah, well," said the barbarian, puffing out his chest, "you should see the other guy!" He smiled as he added, "He was even bigger than you are!" He was obviously very proud of himself.

"We saw him," said Cyrillis, shaking her head in disgust. "He looks like he got ran over by a freight wagon!"

"Yup," said the dwarf, spotting the cleric for the first time. He held up his ham-like fists. "These two freight wagons!"

"Who is your other friend?" asked Thrinndor, looking around for the man who had spoken in the tavern. Startled, he realized he was nowhere to be seen. He was certain the stranger had accompanied them out to the trough. The paladin scratched idly at his head.

He was still looking around when Vorgath asked, "What other friend?"

Confused and now wary—Thrinndor's senses did not just lose track of people like that—the paladin said, "There was a man in the bar who tried to stop us from waking you." He glanced around again, paying particular interest to any shadows. Nothing. "I could have sworn he followed us out onto the street."

Cyrillis said quickly, "He did." She looked around as well. "He was right behind me…" Confusion muddled her tone.

"Oh," said Vorgath, "that would be Breunne." He glanced around as well. "Remind me to tell him he needs to do a better job at stopping you next time." He grinned up at his friend. "He's a sneaky bastard, all right. I never saw him in the tavern before he walked up to say 'Hi.'" He shook his head. "Never thought it could be done."

"Never thought what could be done?" asked a figure as it detached itself from a shadow.

Startled, Thrinndor reached for the haft of his sword.

"Easy there!" said the voice, "I am indeed a friend."

"That has yet to be determined," said the wary paladin. Cyrillis also held her staff at the ready.

"You another of those damn rogues?" asked Vorgath suddenly.

The man laughed as he approached, his empty hands held before him for all to see. "Hardly," he said as he strode purposefully—and yet somehow not in any way intended to threaten—up to Thrinndor. "Breunne at your service," he said as he extended his right hand.

"Breunne?" said the paladin, his right eyebrow arching higher than the left as he reached out his own right hand and they grasped forearms. "Breunne the ranger?"

"I see my name goes before me," the ranger said, bowing slightly at the waist. "I don't believe I caught yours."

Wary and still more than a little surprised, Thrinndor released the man's grip and said. "I am Thrinndor," as he turned to indicate the cleric, "and this is Cyrillis." The cleric stood unmoving on the boardwalk; her staff remained at the ready.

"Ah, yes." Breunne said. "Thrinndor of the Paladinhood of Valdaar." He turned to face the cleric and reached for her hand, bowing as he did so and placing his lips on the back of it, kissing it lightly. "And the lovely Cyrillis, a Cleric of the Order of Valdaar." He stood and looked deep into her eyes and smiled. "Well met, my lady."

An astonished Cyrillis blushed a deep red. She was not certain what response was required, but civility seemed to be appropriate. Finally she managed to stammer out, "Thank you."

Breunne turned back to face the paladin. He lowered his voice and said, "We must talk." He allowed his eyes to quickly survey the street. "But not here."

With an effort, Thrinndor regained his composure. "How is it you know so much about us?" he asked.

Breunne merely raised an eyebrow, as if the answer should be obvious. "I listen," he said, shrugging his shoulders as he did.

"But—" began Thrinndor.

"Again," interrupted the ranger, "this is not the place." His eyes again darted up and down the almost empty street. "There are ears everywhere."

"So it would seem," said the paladin, his brow deeply furrowed in indecision. He wanted badly to continue this line of questioning—he must know how this man knew of him—but grudgingly agreed that further discussion should not be in the open. "Very well," Thrinndor said as he spun on his heel and started up the street. "Follow me." He said no more as he turned right, taking a narrow passage between two buildings and ending up in the alley behind.

When it became apparent where they were headed, Vorgath announced, "I will meet you there in a few minutes." He turned and started down a side alley. "I need to get my weapons."

Breunne started to protest, but he knew it would have no effect. The dwarf was going nowhere without his weapons.

The livery was only a short distance away. Thrinndor marched in and retrieved his steed that only minutes before had been put to stable. Most of the grain indeed was still in the bin before the huge horse. He rolled his eyes inquisitively at this intrusion into his little bit of peace. "Sorry, boy," said the paladin. "We have a short ride we must make." He winked at the huge horse and rubbed his neck affectionately. "I will have you back here ere noon."

He knew his horse, however, and this steed would be ready to go anywhere, anytime. There was no animosity in the animal's eyes, only curiosity. Once stabled, he was usually left alone for several hours by his master. Hence the only slightly consumed grain.

"Mount up!" snapped the paladin as his hands deftly smoothed the saddle blanket before reaching for his saddle. The others had been standing around, assuming this was a place they could talk.

At his command, they scattered toward separate stalls, saying nothing.

All except the dwarf. Vorgath stood with his arms crossed in the center of the stable, where had he suddenly reappeared. He stood where the sunlight from the door fell upon him. He liked the feeling of it upon his back—there was a definite chill in the air as fall rapidly approached.

Thrinndor eyed his friend from over his mount's back, knowing the dwarf's distaste for riding. "I intend to move fast," was all he said.

Vorgath raised an eyebrow, turned, and spat into the dust at his feet. "I'll keep up," he said.

Thrinndor smiled as he slapped his horse to get him to exhale and then cinched up the straps. "I am sure you will, old one." He winked. "I was just trying to spare you any further pain knowing your present condition."

"What condition?" the dwarf snorted. He puffed out his chest and thumped it with a fist. "Good as new!"

"Whatever!" said the cleric as she rolled her eyes and pulled herself onto her mount's back. It was a fine mare, a beautiful dappled gray that was almost as big as Thrinndor's horse, obtained for her by the paladin from some friends of his while training for his new rank.

Thrinndor grasped the edge of his saddle and hauled himself up. "Damn," he muttered, "I just got out of this thing!" After three days on horseback, he had been looking forward to some rest, figuring he and the cleric would be early to the rendezvous.

"Shall we get a move on?" Thrinndor asked of no one in particular. "I would like to be back by noon."

"No," said Breunne as he rounded the corner on a lean-looking chestnut stallion that looked like it was built for speed. "We'll be a couple of days at least." His eyes roamed the stalls and loft area.

The paladin made to protest, but Breunne raised his hand to cut him off. "At least." His eyes bored into those of the paladin as he passed by. Without saying anything more, the ranger guided his mount out through the double doors into the bright sunlight beyond.

Vorgath looked up at the paladin, his right eyebrow arched as best it could over his new shiner. "What gives?" he asked as he turned to look after the departing ranger.

"I do not know," said the fighter, his eyes also following the ranger. "But I mean to find out." He started his horse with a gentle nudge to the animal's flanks and followed the ranger out through the double doors of the livery.

Cyrillis started her mount and fell in behind them both.

Vorgath shrugged and fell in behind her.

Without hesitation, the ranger led them down an alley to the main street, where he turned east and picked up the pace to a fast trot. Not that there were many other options as to the direction he took. West was the open water and south led to the bay. There were no roads north—at least not until one had traveled a couple miles out of town. Farreach was essentially on a small peninsula.

To forestall any conversation, Breunne kept the pace brisk. A couple of miles past the fork heading north he finally slowed, allowing the others to group up.

Finally, Thrinndor could wait no longer and moved his horse up next to Breunne's. The ranger did not even look over to acknowledge his presence. "Where are we going?" the paladin asked.

Breunne looked over and locked eyes with the paladin's unwavering gaze. "A place I know not far from here where we can talk," he said. As his eyes released those of the fighter, he turned to look ahead, adding, "Trust me."

Thrinndor returned his eyes to the path ahead. "Very well," he said, "until we have reason not to." He allowed his horse to fall back as the ranger nodded.

A short distance farther the road made a slight bend to the north and topped a rise. Again, the ranger slowed his mount.

He kept moving, his eyes combing the trees on both sides of the path. As the others got within range of his voice, he turned to fix the paladin with a stare. "Pick the pace back up after I'm gone. I'm going to circle around behind to see if we've been followed." After a brief pause he added, "I'll catch back up before you get far."

Knowing they were too far down this path to turn back now, Thrinndor nodded as Breunne wheeled his horse and kicked the mount into a full run, heading for the trees to the right of the road where they quickly disappeared.

Within moments they could not tell where he had gone and even the sound of the hoof beats faded to nothing.

Without saying a word, Thrinndor did as asked and resumed their earlier pace. He could tell his friend was laboring bringing up the rear, but he knew that to slow for his sake would result in some harsh words from the dwarf. Still, ever so gradually he managed to slow their pace a tiny bit. They were in no hurry that he knew of.

He took the time to review what he knew about this man Breunne, which was almost nothing. A ranger by trade—and one of no small renown—that he knew. He had been involved with some forays into the Anar Mountains; that much he had heard. Why the ranger went there, Thrinndor did not know.

The big fighter shrugged. They would find out soon enough, he surmised. Or else...

They continued along the road for about an hour when they all turned at the pounding of hooves that came up behind them.

It was Breunne.

He slowed his horse as he drew even with Thrinndor. He said nothing as he turned off the road to their left toward the river, motioning for the others to follow.

Cyrillis, silent to this point, looked to the paladin, but he ignored her and turned to follow the ranger. She started to protest, then shrugged angrily and moved to follow.

Vorgath, working hard to hide his heaving chest, said nothing as he too stepped off of the path onto the grass still damp from the heavy morning dew.

Their pace slowed somewhat as they entered the trees, which followed no path any of them could discern.

Right, left. Left, right. Their way twisted and turned, and they could tell from the sound of the rushing water they were getting closer to the bank of the river.

Emerging from the tree line, the members of the party walked their horses into a small glade surrounded by trees on three sides and the river on the fourth. There was a small, shallow pool where the runoff from a ten-foot waterfall had worried out forty or fifty feet of bank.

Breunne continued until he reached the center of the glade, where he dismounted. He allowed the reins of his horse to drop to the ground, and then he walked to the edge of the water, bent and scooped out a couple of handfuls and drank deeply.

Vorgath needed no urging as he trotted on past everyone and dropped to his knees along the pool's bank and immersed his head to the shoulders in the cold water.

Thrinndor waited, an amused smirk on his face, until the dwarf emerged, his beard and eyebrows dripping water down his neck and under his tunic.

The dwarf rolled over so that he was sitting with his hands behind him, his chest heaving.

"You leave any water for the horses, old man?" Thrinndor's arms were crossed and his tone playful.

Vorgath's bushy brows knitted together into one. He took in a deep breath, held it, and then let it out noisily. He started to chuckle as he said, "You're lucky a lady is present!"

"Whatever!" began the paladin, but he was interrupted by an angry cleric.

She pushed her way past Thrinndor and shoved her face into that of the ranger. "Did you have to push the pace so hard?" Her eyes were blazing. "What is the God-Almighty hurry?"

Breunne took a step back and raised his hands chest high, palms out. "Whoa!" he said defensively. "I don't know and that's what bothered me."

"But why?" she persisted.

Regaining some of his composure, Breunne squared his shoulders and said, "Look, I had to be sure you were not followed—"

"What?" broke in Thrinndor.

"—by making sure we were not followed."

"Why would anyone want to follow us?" asked Cyrillis, her tone somewhat subdued but doubtful.

The ranger turned to face her squarely. "Your destruction of the Temple of Set at Horbalt raised quite a stir along the east coast. Indeed, it was but a few days before the entire region knew of it."

"You what?" said the dwarf, sitting up quickly. He stood and puffed out his chest to protest.

Thrinndor shrugged. "We had a little disagreement."

It was Breunne's turn to arch an eyebrow. "If wiping out an entire compound—burning it to the ground in the process—and killing the Shugaard twins is classified as a 'little disagreement'…" He shook his head in wonder. "…then my friend, we are indeed well met!"

"You did all this without me?" said a dejected Vorgath. He was busy moving a pebble around with the toe of his boot.

Thrinndor took the one step necessary to put him at his friend's side, where he put his hand on the dwarf's shoulder. "Sorry, old friend," he began. "There was not time to call for your assistance." He squeezed his friend's shoulder slightly. "Rest assured you were sorely missed and know that if I had had time, you would have been summoned!"

"Bah!" groused the dwarf, not convincingly. His eyes were still locked in on the pebble at his feet. He looked up suddenly; his eyes filled with a combination of suspicion and belligerence, and said, "Those kills do not count toward the next total!"

Momentarily taken aback by his friend's vehemence, Thrinndor stifled a smile. "Of course not!"

Breunne leaned toward Cyrillis and whispered, "What are they talking about?"

She rolled her eyes. "You will have to ask them!" She turned on her heel and stalked to the water's edge with a stiff back. "I will not be a party to that nonsense!"

The ranger smiled as he watched her bend to splash water on her face. Thrinndor looked at him and raised an inquisitive eyebrow. "What was that about?" he asked, not hearing the prior exchange.

"I'll explain later," replied Breunne without taking his eyes off the cleric.

"Very well," said the paladin, now also watching Cyrillis as she rinsed her water skin and refilled it, "that can wait." He paused for a moment, "However, it is time for you to explain a few things."

The ranger turned his attention to the paladin, smiled and raised his own eyebrow. "What is it you would have me explain first?" he said pleasantly.

"Let us start with just why it was so important to bring us all the way out here?" Thrinndor said as he looked around the clearing and crossed his arms on his chest.

"Easy," began the ranger, "I actually already partially answered that one."

Thrinndor's demeanor did not change one iota. Cyrillis moved closer so she could hear what was being said.

"Your recent endeavors have drawn attention—both good and bad—far and wide," Breunne began. "It was necessary to get this discussion out of town because you now have a bounty on your heads." He looked from Thrinndor to Cyrillis as he said this.

"What?" snapped the paladin. "That is absurd!"

The ranger turned back to the big fighter standing before him. "Is it?" he said. "Really?" When no one said anything, he continued. "You led an assault on their temple—"

"They attacked me!" said the indignant healer.

Breunne shifted his focus to her. "Yet you were at their temple." He said this with a shrug of his shoulders. "Their place of worship was burned." He raised his voice slightly. "Their priests were slain."

"They were going to sacrifice her!" Thrinndor pointed at Cyrillis, his voice almost a shout. "We were only there for information!"

Breunne backed up a step and raised his hands chest high, palms out. "Hey," he said, "It's not me you need to convince." His eyes went from the paladin to the cleric and back. "I say, 'good riddance!' as far as I'm concerned. Their kind is not needed in these parts."

Thrinndor started to speak, but the ranger went on quickly. "And that isn't they story the Minions of Set are telling. It's said that the High Priest of Set is beside himself with fury and has placed a bounty on your head large enough to get even the good citizenry of Farreach looking for you when they hear of it!"

Cyrillis started to speak, but Thrinndor was quicker. "How is it you know all of this?" he asked, suspicion putting an edge to his voice. "It has only been three—"

"Four," corrected the ranger.

"—days?"

"Did you slay all at the compound?" Breunne asked as he crossed his arms on his chest.

The big fighter thought for a moment. "No," he said finally, his shoulders sagging.

"You should have," said the ranger with a sigh. "Their priests can communicate over great distances with just their thoughts." He raised his eyes up to meet those of the paladin. "Your names and descriptions went out to all temples that same day."

"Again," said Thrinndor, "how is it you know all of this?"

"I listen," Breunne said. "I hear things." Thrinndor's suspicious stance did not change, so he added, "Look, when large bounties are put in place, I have a tendency to get involved."

The paladin's eyes went wide and he took a step back, drawing his sword as he did so. Vorgath, who had been listening intently, immediately followed suit. "Spread out!" Thrinndor said intently, his eyes darting from shadow to shadow among the trees surrounding their position. Seeing nothing, he asked, "Is this a trap, then?" His eyes continued to search the trees.

"Heavens no!" said the ranger, whose hand wisely never moved toward a weapon. "While I certainly have sought—and claimed—my share of bounties," he went on trying to calm the paladin, "I have no liking for the Minions and distrust them even more." The big fighter relaxed slightly. "You have no need to fear me. I am indeed acting as a friend."

Thrinndor eyed him, his suspicions not yet allayed. "Why?" he asked simply.

"Good question," replied the ranger. "Yet not one I am able to speak to at this time."

The paladin still did not relax. He repeated, "Why?"

This time Breunne looked into Thrinndor's eyes. "I am not at liberty to say," he said. The big paladin took in a breath to protest, but the ranger held up his hands to forestall him. "You must trust me in this."

The ranger took in a deep breath. "I will say this much," he said, "but please do not press me on this—for now." His eyes searched those of each of his new companions, trying to gauge their compliance. "A mutual friend asked me to seek you out and bring you to this place, and he bade me to ask you to wait for him here until such time as he can join you."

"Sordaak," said the paladin with a snort.

"That wily bastard," agreed the barbarian.

"How long must we wait?" asked Cyrillis.

Breunne shrugged. "That I also don't know," he said. "However, I have reason to believe it will not be that long." He shrugged again. "Certainly no more than a few days."

"A few days!" said the cleric. "We came out here in such a hurry we did not have time to provision!"

Thrinndor continued the thought for her. "We came with only what we had on us and our mounts. We have pack animals back in the livery, and we need to prepare for whatever will be our next quest."

"And I need my pack," said the barbarian, his arms folded across his chest.

Again the ranger threw up his hands and stepped back. "I will obtain all of that for you when I return to town this evening under the cover of darkness." He hesitated before continuing. "However, I will be gone a couple of days." He walked over to his horse and removed two large bags that were tied there. "This should last you until I return," he said as he set the heavy bags onto the ground.

"What?" asked Cyrillis.

"Why?" asked the paladin.

"I have a plan," Breunne said simply.

"What kind of plan?" asked the paladin, suspicion still in his tone.

"Well," said the ranger as he took in a deep breath, "I have to admit it is not much of a plan, but it is a plan." He looked at the paladin. "It's a 'work in progress'…"

When the ranger said nothing more, Thrinndor prodded him. "Go on," he said.

"Well," Breunne began slowly, "I am going tell those in Farreach that you are all dead."

"Dead?" said Cyrillis. "How?"

Thrinndor and Vorgath both crossed their arms and waited for the ranger to explain.

Breunne shifted his feet uncomfortably. "I mentioned I sometimes claim a bounty, didn't I? I will tell them I laid a trap for you." He shrugged, signaling the end of his narration.

"What?" said the cleric. "That is your plan?"

The ranger raised his eyes to meet hers and, his tone belligerent, said, "I said it was a work in progress!"

She took in a breath to continue telling him just what she thought of his plan, but the paladin came to Breunne's rescue.

"No," Thrinndor said quickly. "That just might work." His tone was thoughtful. "If the Minions think we are dead, they will not continue their pursuit of us."

"Right," agreed the ranger.

"They'll require proof," said the dwarf. He also sounded less than enthusiastic about the plan.

"No," replied the ranger, "because I have no intention on cashing in on your demise." He smiled. "I will seek out the local order, let them know I have slain you and that I will travel to their home temple to collect my reward."

"Ice Homme? But that is in the far northern province of Tithgaard," said the cleric. "That is more than a week's hard journey."

"Closer to two," said the ranger.

"But—" she started to protest again.

"You're missing my point," said the ranger. "I'm not actually going to Ice Homme." His smile broadened. "I just want them to think I am!"

"I see," said Thrinndor, "while they are waiting on you to come claim your reward, they will not be looking for us."

"That should buy you a few weeks without their minions breathing down your neck."

"That just might work," said Vorgath, "for a while anyway."

"You?" asked Cyrillis.

"What?" said Breunne as he turned back to face her.

"You said, 'That should buy you a few weeks without their minions.'" She hesitated. "Will you not be coming with us, then?"

Breunne appeared to think about it for a moment. "No," he said simply. "Two reasons: One, I was not asked. And two, I prefer to work alone."

When no one said anything, he added, "Large groups tend to make me nervous. They move slow and are too noisy."

"Noisy?" said Thrinndor, his tone injured.

"Slow?" said Vorgath. His tone wasn't.

"Yes and yes," the ranger said. He was about to explain further but the paladin spoke first.

"Will you not consider it?" Thrinndor asked. "We are not all that large, and we move very fast when necessary." He paused to allow that to sink in. "And we could use another sword. Vorgy here—" he waved an arm in the direction of the dwarf "—is getting a bit long in the tooth."

"Pfft!" said the dwarf.

"Am I being asked?" said the ranger, his forehead furrowing in thought.

"You are," replied the paladin. "Join us and you will get an equal share of any loot. We have done well thus far."

The ranger appeared to consider his options. "Just what is it that you are after?" When no one spoke up, he added, "Because it certainly isn't 'loot'."

Thrinndor hesitated. Vorgath spoke first. "We could tell you, but then we'd have to kill you!" He smiled hugely as he patted the haft of his greataxe.

"What?" the ranger asked quickly, clearly not certain he was being teased.

Thrinndor laughed. "He is jesting, of course. However, our cause must remain secret." He thought about it for a few seconds before continuing. "Ride to take care of the aforementioned business. That should give you adequate time to consider your decision and also allow us to discuss among ourselves the options available to us concerning bringing you up to speed on our quest."

Breunne cocked his head to one side as he considered what was before him. "Very well," he said. "Wait here and I will return with your belongings in two—maybe three—days' time." He sprang effortlessly onto his mount's back. "Depends on how far I have to go to find a temple of Set."

"I believe there is one not far from here," said Thrinndor. "But it is the opposite direction from how you must travel to get back to Farreach."

"Oh?" said the ranger.

"Yes," replied the paladin. "Perhaps a half-day's ride south of here, along the coast. You should have no trouble finding it." He turned and pointed across the river and to the south. "However, I would be happy to accompany you, if you like."

Breunne laughed lightly as he turned his mount toward the river. "I don't think that would be a good idea," he said. "One: You're supposed to be dead, remember?" He laughed again. "And two, we kind of need this group alive so they can pass the word along of your deaths!"

"What are you saying?" demanded the paladin, not smiling.

"Well," began the ranger cautiously, "that you kind of left the last bunch of minions you dealt with kind of dead!"

"They attacked us!" snapped Thrinndor.

"Whatever!" said the dwarf as he turned and headed for the shade of a nearby tree. "Meanwhile, I'm going to get back to that which was so rudely interrupted!" With that, he plopped to the ground and proceeded to get comfortable.

"I'll go it alone," the ranger said, stifling a laugh. "I'll be fine."

As he started his horse toward the river, Thrinndor stopped him. "Can you at least tell us who it was that sent you?"

"Sordaak," said the dwarf. "We decided it was Sordaak."

"Well," said Thrinndor, "We may have decided, but our new friend here did not speak it—and I saw in his eyes at the mention of Sordaak's name that it was not correct."

"You saw that, huh?" said the ranger. "I thought I'd dodged that particular question well." His eyes sparkled. He took in a deep breath and let it out slowly.

"Very well," he said at last. "I guess I can tell you that much." He locked eyes with the paladin. "While I do know of the Sordaak of whom you speak, I have not seen him in more than a year."

"Then who?" came a muffled voice from under the helm that the barbarian had pulled down over his eyes.

"Savinhand," the ranger said as he kicked his horse lightly to start him into the river.

Chapter Six

More Minions

Thrinndor watched the ranger ride around the pool at the edge of the glade and into the water of the river proper. He longed to ask more but decided it could wait.

He turned to find Cyrillis, but she was already working on refreshing herself; clearly she did not desire company. Vorgath was snoring loudly on the edge of the glade. It was doubtful he wanted company, either.

So the paladin walked to the edge of the glade and carefully made his way to back out the way they had come in, taking extreme caution to not be seen—if there was anybody, or anything, to see him.

As he neared the edge of the trees closest to the road that had brought them here, he squatted on his heels and waited.

After more than an hour, he stood slowly and walked to the road and looked at the myriad tracks on it. Slowly he worked with a leafy tree branch he had brought for the purpose and erased any indication that they had left the road.

He also worked his way back toward Farreach about half a mile, trying to remove any sign of their passage.

Satisfied, he looked up at the late-day sun, wiped the sweat from his brow and made his way to the trees, again careful to leave no sign of his passage.

Slowly he made his way back, stopping and listening periodically for anything that was not supposed to be there. When he finally made his way back into the glade, Vorgath was working to set up a lean-to under the tree that had provided cover for his nap. Seeing the paladin, he said loudly, "Where have you been?"

"Keep your voice down!" said the paladin as he approached. "Voices will carry enormous distances when they are not where they are supposed to be!"

"Huh?" groused the dwarf. "I'm sure that made sense to you, but I'm gonna leave it be—for now!" He stopped what he was doing and repeated, much quieter this time, however, "Where have you been?"

"Thank you," said the paladin formally. "I went out to watch the road to see if we were followed."

"And?" the barbarian said as he went back to shaping a sapling he had cut.

"I saw no one," said Thrinndor as if he had not been interrupted. "I took the time to wipe out the tracks of where we had left the road and back toward town, as well." When the dwarf remained silent, the paladin eyed his handiwork. "I see that you also have been busy."

"Yup," replied Vorgath. "I figured if we were going to be stuck here for several days we might as well try to stay dry!"

"Dry?" queried the paladin. "There is not a cloud in the sky!"

"Not now, there ain't!" replied the dwarf. "But on the morrow you'll be thanking me for my foresight!"

"Rain tomorrow?" asked the fighter, knowing better than to argue with the dwarf. He was always right about the weather. Somehow…

"Yup," the barbarian repeated. "And a cold rain at that." He stopped and looked at where the sun was dipping toward the horizon. "The weather is changing. It's going to be cooler—at least for a while, maybe even a few days."

Thrinndor nodded and said, "We will require a fire, then." He looked around at what Vorgath had been working on. "If we make this large enough we can have a small fire inside." He inspected the thatching of the roof. "This should also help to dissipate any smoke so it will not be seen from the road."

"Yup," agreed the dwarf.

Now working together, the two brought rapid shape to the structure. As the sun dipped, they set about building a fire pit inside their new home away from home.

Cyrillis had not been idle, either. Seeing what the men were doing, she went about the task of making utensils for cooking and eating.

As darkness approached, both men scoured the forest for dry wood, both knowing it would smoke less. When they had gathered enough for the night, Vorgath got a small fire going.

Cyrillis started working on a meal while Thrinndor continued to weave more branches into the walls and ceiling of their makeshift hut.

Satisfied, he gathered the animals and loosely tethered them back in the trees where they could get good grass, water and had some shelter from the coming rain. It would have to do.

He headed back for the shelter and his nose told him there was something good cooking inside before he even got there.

As Thrinndor entered, he hung one of the saddle blankets over the opening they had left for getting in and out. That done, he returned to the pack for a second blanket. He hung this one inside the opening. The temperature was dropping. It looked like the predicted weather was getting close, he thought as he sat down on a rock he had drug inside for that purpose. He then accepted a plate offered to him by Cyrillis.

"Thank you," he said as he suddenly realized he had not eaten since break-fast. The healer nodded her reply.

He dug in hungrily and quickly cleaned his plate. He accepted a second, as did the barbarian, when offered.

Hunger satisfied, Thrinndor leaned back and sighed his contentment. "That was good," he said.

"Very good," agreed the dwarf.

"Thank you," the cleric said, not all of the color in her cheeks was from the fire. "And thank both of you for this fine shelter! It is a marvel you were able to build it so quickly."

"Yeah, well," began Thrinndor, "the weather dwarf over there says we are in for some rain, so it seemed appropriate."

"Cold rain," interjected the barbarian with a smile. "But we'll be nice and warm in here.

They were silent for a few minutes, during which they could hear the wind picking up in the trees outside.

"Not long now," Vorgath said as he rummaged around. "Damn! Ran off and left my pipe! A bowl of tobacco would sure be good right now!"

Cyrillis snorted her contempt for that particular pastime, stood and gathered up the dishes from the meal. Once she had them bundled in her arms, she pushed the blankets aside and screamed.

Vorgath and Thrinndor surged to their feet amid the crashing of plates and utensils.

Cyrillis stepped back from the doorway and the fighters were able to see a figure standing there—a hooded figure leaning to one side, holding onto the large branch that was the frame for their door.

As the paladin and barbarian swung into action, the figure's hand slipped from the frame and pitched forward into the room, landing on his face next to the fire.

Cyrillis was the first to recover, and she knelt next to the now unmoving figure.

"Wait!" said Thrinndor as she reached a hand toward him. "Better allow me."

In two steps he was beside her and helped her back to her feet. She started to protest but knew that would only serve to delay her doing what she was certain was going to be needed to be done, and soon. Her senses told her this man was badly hurt.

"Isn't that Breunne's cloak?" said Vorgath as he stepped closer.

Thrinndor saw that it was indeed Breunne's cloak and that it was not only damp from being in the river or rain but also had several dark patches that looked like blood. There were several large gashes in the cloak that revealed where his hardened leather tunic had been pierced.

A lot of blood!

Now with less caution and more worry, the paladin rolled the figure over, revealing the ranger's face.

"No!" breathed Cyrillis as she stepped back in. But the paladin didn't move, nor did he hesitate. He leaned forward and placed both hands on the ranger, closed his eyes and raised his face toward the ceiling of their crude structure.

The paladin's hands glowed momentarily as the healing power poured into the prone body. Wounds stopped bleeding, and skin seemed to knit together before their eyes.

But the cleric could see it was not enough. Breunne's wounds were grievous, indeed. How he had made it here, she had no idea. Regardless, she started chanting and touched the wounds she could see that still required attention.

As she did, each wound mended completely, not even leaving a scar behind. "Get me some water," she said through clenched teeth as she continued to work her healing arts on the unconscious figure.

Without having to be asked a second time, Vorgath bent over and picked up two skins, one empty, the other half full. This one he handed to Cyrillis. He brushed aside the curtain and sprinted through the makeshift door into the night.

With Thrinndor's help Cyrillis sat him up. The paladin said, "He may yet be bleeding internally."

"No," she said with a brief shake of her head. "I have searched out and repaired several places where he was bleeding within, but no longer." She held the skin to the ranger's mouth as he opened his eyes. "And I have repaired several of his bodily functions that were damaged, some badly.

"What he needs right now is water." She was speaking to the ranger now as well as the paladin. "He must replenish the fluids lost by so much bleeding."

Breunne acknowledged by greedily swallowing the water she poured into his mouth. He then surprised her by grabbing the skin from her hand and pouring the remainder into his open mouth.

"Easy," she admonished. "Do not choke yourself." The ranger fought back a spasm of coughing.

He raised an amused eyebrow toward her as the barbarian burst back into the lean-to, a dripping, freshly filled skin held out before him.

Breunne cast aside the empty skin and accepted the one from the dwarf. "Thank you," he said hoarsely as he turned it up, allowing the life-giving fluid to pour into his mouth more slowly this time.

After he had taken several long pulls from the container, he set it aside and tried to stand.

"Whoa!" said Thrinndor.

"Not so fast," chastised the healer. She pushed him gently backward so that his back came in contact with the brush wall behind him. "Just sit right there and let me check you over more thoroughly, please."

Breunne opened his mouth to protest, but Thrinndor said with a smile, "Just do as she says and we will all be spared the tongue lashing!"

Cyrillis threw him a withering glance, but the paladin simply smiled in return.

The ranger did as directed; retrieving the water flask he had dropped when he tried to stand. He now sipped its contents instead of guzzling.

Cyrillis sat back, absently brushing aside a stray lock of blonde hair that had wandered into her vision. "I believe you will yet live," she said with certainty.

"I agree," said Breunne. "Thanks to you, I will," he added quickly. "I'm feeling much better now!"

"What happened?" Vorgath asked.

The ranger looked at the dwarf and then turned to look at Cyrillis. "They wanted your staff."

"What?" she said, taken aback.

Breunne took another sip of water. "When I told the minions I had killed you and wanted my bounty, they only asked about the staff." He took another sip. "And when I told them I had hidden it to ensure I got my reward, they surrounded me and said they would get from me its location one way or another!" After yet another sip he added, "And then they attacked."

"How did you escape?" asked the cleric.

"Escape?" Breunne said. "I didn't escape." He locked eyes with the healer. "I killed them."

"All?" asked Vorgath.

"Yes," replied the ranger. "At least I am fairly certain I got them all. I certainly didn't see any walking around as I left. However, I didn't spend much time looking!"

"That's it!" ranted the barbarian. "You guys have got to stop going to these temples without me!"

"What?" asked a suddenly confused Breunne.

"Do not mind him," said the paladin. "He is only disappointed that there was some killing going on that he was not part of."

"Damn straight," muttered the dwarf. "How many?" He crossed his arms on his chest.

"I'm not sure," said the ranger, still confused by this line of questioning. "They came at me pretty fast. Let's see..." He looked toward the ceiling and began ticking off numbers on his fingers. "Hmmm...I'm not sure about this, but I think there was eight or nine."

"Not sure!" the barbarian fairly bellowed. Then he turned his ire to the paladin. "There ain't no way he can be part of this group! Not keeping track is a grievance of the highest order!" He grabbed the previously emptied skin and the almost empty one right out of Breunne's hands and stomped out through the opening into the night.

"What in the name of the seven hells was that all about?" asked the ranger, his eyes looking at the doorway through which the barbarian had disappeared.

Cyrillis wrinkled her nose in distaste. "Do not worry about these two." She flicked yet another nasty glance in the paladin's direction. "These barbarians have a running contest during the course of a quest or adventure to see who can kill the most." She again wrinkled her nose. "Hence the concern for number of kills."

"Really?" said a suddenly interested ranger.

Abruptly the curtain was thrown aside and a wet dwarf pushed his way through. It was obviously now raining outside—unless Vorgath had fallen into the pond. He threw a freshly filled skin into the lap of the ranger and set the other by the door.

He then spun and poked a stubby finger into the face of the cleric. "Hello!" he said loudly. "I am a barbarian! It's what we do!" He then stomped back over to his rock and plopped down on it, folding his arms in such a manner that precluded further discussion on the matter.

"Well," began the ranger, not sure exactly what to make of all this, "I fear I'm going to have to throw my lot in with yours whether I want to or not."

"What do you mean?" asked Cyrillis. She avoided looking at the dwarf.

Breunne continued. "Now these Minions of Set will be after me." He looked from Cyrillis to Thrinndor. "Whether or not they believe I killed you, they believe I have this staff of yours." He looked back at the healer. "And they most certainly want that!"

Thrinndor said, "The good news is that I do not believe there is another temple of Set in this region."

"No," agreed Breunne. "The nearest is probably the one down in the Workman's Promontory area—and that is several days' hard ride to the south."

"Only one day by sail," said Vorgath. All eyes turned to look at the barbarian.

"My," said the ranger, "aren't we the bearer of glad tidings…"

"He is however correct," said the paladin. "They may even already be on their way."

The ranger sighed deeply. "You're right," he said. "And to make matters worse, that is their regional command center—second only to their university at Ice Homme."

"So?" said the barbarian.

"So?" mocked the ranger. "That means they will have more Minions there than we have yet dealt with. And," he added, allowing a taint of worry to creep into his voice, "there will be at least one High Lord among them." He shifted his gaze to the paladin. "Possibly two."

"My," mimicked the barbarian, "aren't we the bearer of glad tidings!" When no one said anything, he stood slowly. "I say 'good'!" He grabbed his greataxe, brandishing it before him with one meaty hand. "Bring 'em on!"

He glared at first the ranger and then the paladin. When neither spoke, the barbarian spat a "Bah!" and sat back down, again folding his arms on his chest.

Breunne climbed unsteadily to his feet. "That settles it."

"Settles what?" asked the paladin, steadying the ranger with a rock solid hand.

"I must leave immediately," the ranger answered with a shrug.

"What?" asked the paladin.

"Why?" asked the cleric. "You must rest!"

"No," said Breunne. "I've got to get to Farreach before the Minions do." He turned to face the paladin. "It is now even more important that those at Ice Homme believe I am on my way to them."

"But you are in no shape to travel!" the healer insisted.

"Young lady," the ranger said with an easy smile, "Thanks to your ministrations, I am in far better shape than when I usually travel."

"Yet your body requires sustenance and rest," she said, though less forceful this time.

Breunne took in a deep breath. "Well," he said, "I suppose tarrying a few minutes for a bite to eat would not affect the outcome of the known world!" He smiled. "That is assuming these barbarians left anything to eat of whatever it is that smells so good."

"Of course!" Cyrillis exclaimed as she reached for the pot sitting next to the fire. She waved a hand at Thrinndor and Vorgath. "Although they did not leave much!" She threw each of them a withering glance.

"What?" said the barbarian.

"How could we possibly know we would have company this evening," responded Thrinndor, sounding hurt.

"Hmph!" muttered the cleric as she dumped the remaining contents from the pot she had been using onto a clean plate. Well, she reasoned, at least it looked clean! "I am indeed sorry, but this is all that remains."

Actually, there was really a nice pile of the thickened stew-like mixture they had all had earlier for dinner. It was still warm and steamed nicely in the warm, comfortable air of the lean-to.

"Thank you," he said as he accepted the plate. "This will do just fine."

Cyrillis quickly untied the sack hanging along one wall that contained some bread that had been in the bags left to them by the ranger several hours before. "Here is some bread to go with that," she said as she broke off a large chunk.

"Thank you again," Breunne said around a mouthful of the stew. "Excuse my manners, but I just realized I haven't eaten since breakfast and I am suddenly very hungry!"

"By all means, eat!" she replied.

As he neared the end of what was on the plate, Breunne settled back and slowed his chewing. Thrinndor, who had been waiting semi-patiently for this move, said, "Perhaps we can take a few minutes before you leave to ask and answer some questions?"

The ranger looked over the top of the heaping spoonful he was about to insert into his mouth, raised an eyebrow and said, "Very well." He put the spoon and its contents into his mouth and continued while chewing. "But we must keep it brief."

"Agreed," said the paladin.

"Me first," said Breunne, still munching on a mouthful of the stew.

Thrinndor nodded his acquiescence, and indicated the ranger should proceed. "What is so important about that damn staff?" he asked without preamble.

Thrinndor and Cyrillis exchanged looks, and she nodded her permission for the paladin to talk. He sighed deeply. "That, Breunne, is a long story—one that I will attempt to shorten for you. However, you must first answer a question for me."

Breunne stopped with another spoonful poised at his lips. His right eyebrow shot up questioningly. "If I can," he said.

The paladin took in a deep breath. "Why did Savinhand send you to warn us?"

Breunne put the still full spoon back down on his plate. "That, Thrinndor, is a long story." He grinned. "One that I will attempt to shorten for you." He again picked up the spoon and put it in his mouth.

After he finished chewing, he washed down the stew with yet another pull from the skin at his side.

At last he looked up to meet the paladin's eyes. "Short version: It's politics."

"What?" Vorgath asked before Thrinndor could say anything.

"I assume you would like more?" Breunne asked. Thrinndor merely nodded.

"Slightly longer version: Their leader—the leader of Guild Shardmoor, that is—has gone missing." The ranger now had their undivided attention. Even the dripping of the rain seemed to go silent. "And is presumed dead. Savinhand has been asked to remain until a new leader is selected."

If the shelter was quiet before, now the silence was positively deafening.

"It also seems that a number of the guild's prized assassins have also gone missing," the ranger added.

Vorgath coughed and said, "We might know something about that last part."

"I thought you might," replied the ranger.

Thrinndor's eyes never left those of Breunne. "Phinskyr is dead?"

"Presumed dead," corrected the ranger.

"How is a successor selected?" asked the paladin.

Vorgath answered for him. "A panel is convened," he said. "The panel will select four candidates." He paused as he tried to remember what was next. "A candidate may refuse the process, if he wishes—but the consequences are dire." His eyes met those of the paladin. "Those that remain will contest for the right to lead."

A silence fell over the group.

"Contest how?" asked Cyrillis.

"Last man standing," answered the dwarf, quietly.

"And what has this to do with Savinhand?" asked the paladin, knowing the answer already.

"He was selected by the panel," replied the ranger.

"He what?" said a startled cleric. "Savinhand?" She stood abruptly. "Our Savinhand?" Her tone was both incredulous and worried.

"That bumbling excuse for a thief?" intoned the dwarf.

The shelter was silent for a moment save for the whistling wind and the falling rain.

"Rogue," corrected the ranger. "While he has yet to achieve master status as a rogue—"

"You got that right!" snorted the barbarian.

Breunne ignored him. "—do not discount his abilities." The ranger's tone implied a warning. "His time as a monk left him as heir apparent to lead their order when Borromiir stepped down."

"What happened?" asked Cyrillis.

"He was not ready for leadership, so he went out in search of something more," replied the ranger quietly. "It is said he dabbled in the mystic arts as a youth as well."

"But," interrupted the dwarf, "lead a band of thieves?"

"Rogues," corrected Breunne again. "And he did not search them out. Rather Shardmoor took him in, recognizing his skills as potentially valuable to them."

"So it would seem," mused the paladin.

"OK," said Vorgath in the lull that followed, "we are talking about the same Savinhand, right?" He looked from the paladin to the ranger and back again. "Tall ugly guy? Dark hair? Rather skinny?"

"Sounds like the same guy," replied the ranger with a shrug.

"He most certainly is not ugly!" said Cyrillis. When everyone turned their attention on her, she blushed slightly. "Just saying…"

Thrinndor raised an eyebrow in query. "What was his response?" He turned his attention back to the ranger.

"He said he needed time to consider his options," replied Breunne.

"And?" pressed the paladin.

"And they refused." The statement lay flat on the pressed-down grass on which they were standing. "None are allowed to decline the contest," Breunne said quietly. "His options—as outlined by the panel—were to contest, leave the guild, or die."

Chapter Seven

Their Number Grows by One

The silence in the lean-to was enough to hear the occasional sizzle as a drop of rainwater found its way through the thatched roof to land with a hiss when it hit the fire.

Thrinndor cleared his throat. "How long ago was this?"

Breunne cocked his head in consideration. "Let me see." He stared at a drop of water as it formed and then fell noisily into the fire. "Two days observing Vorgath—"

"What?" spluttered the dwarf. "You were only in Farreach one day!"

"I assure you it was two," said the ranger. "One day waiting for your arrival and..." He ticked off a couple more fingers. "...two days travel to get to Farreach." He looked back at the paladin. "Five, maybe six days. No more."

Thrinndor looked first at Cyrillis, then turned to Vorgath. "We must ride," he said.

"What?" asked the ranger, sitting up quickly. "No, it is I who must ride." He looked at the cleric for support. "You must remain here for when Savinhand arrives."

"He may require our assistance," said Cyrillis, worry in her voice.

"I assure you he does not," said Breunne. "The first round of the contest was to be two days ago. I'm certain our friend would prevail easily over this first opponent."

"And the second?" queried the paladin.

The ranger took in a quick breath and held it for an instant. "That is another matter," he said at last. "The second—and final—round was to be today."

It was Cyrillis' turn for the sharp intake of breath.

Before she could say anything however, Breunne continued. "His second opponent was of course to also be determined by another first round contest—but I have little doubt of that outcome as well."

"Why is that?" asked Vorgath, wanting to be a part of the conversation.

"Because one of those is Shivluur," replied the ranger.

"Shivluur?" said Thrinndor. "The assassin?"

"I see you know him," said Breunne.

"Know of him," corrected the paladin. "And what I know is not good." His tone also grew worried. "He is said to be very skilled at his craft."

"Indeed," said the ranger. "Very skilled…"

"But why would the panel pit an assassin against Savinhand to determine the leadership of their guild?" asked the cleric. "It makes no sense!"

"On the surface it does not," agreed Breunne. "But if a little digging is done—and I have done so, I assure you—I believe some reason to their apparent madness surfaces."

"Please explain," said the paladin.

"Well," began the ranger, "Shivluur and his small band of assassins have grown troublesome to the guild and many want them out."

"Then why—" blurted the healer.

"Allow me to finish," the ranger said tersely, "and I believe your questions will be answered." He threw a stern glance her way. Her eyes flared but she said no more.

"On the other hand, Savinhand has brought much good accord to the guild of late—especially tales of this most recent escapade." Breunne paused for a moment. "So it was not hard for his name to gather the required support when brought forward by the council." Again he paused. "There were two assassins on the panel—guaranteeing Shivluur's nomination, as well."

The ranger hesitated as he searched for words to voice his thoughts. "The way I see it, the rest of the panel allowed Shivluur's name to be brought forward hoping he would be slain. Another of his band of assassins was pitted against Savin in the first round, which would further weaken their stance in the guild should our mutual friend prevail.

"Even if Shivluur were to win the contest, his ranks would be weaker still, and I believe the guild would either have him killed outright, or possibly perform a vote of no-confidence, thereby ousting him and what remains of his nasty band.

"If Savinhand were to win the day, then he and the guild would either chase off or kill the remaining assassins—and he would have accomplished their main goal for them.

"Now," he continued after pausing to think, "Savin made it known to the panel that he had prior obligations—I assume that is where you guys come in—and would step down in favor of another, selected by him and approved by the panel.

"So the panel is in a win-win situation if Savinhand is victorious. Either he steps down until his obligations are complete or he accepts the position and rules until such a time as his rule becomes untenable."

"What happens then?" asked Cyrillis when he did not immediately continue.

"He is…disposed of and another panel is convened, of course!" replied the ranger.

"So," said the paladin, "why were you sent to ask us to wait here?"

"In part to warn you that you were being actively sought by the Minions of Set," Breunne replied. "And also to let you know he was going to be delayed."

"Delayed?" asked the cleric, wryly. "How is he going to notify us if he is dead?"

Breunne shrugged. "Good question. One must assume he will have made other arrangements were that to be the case."

She stared at him for a few moments, and then her eyes flashed as she lowered her voice. "If you are—as claimed—a friend of his," she said, "then why did you not stay and help him?"

The ranger met her gaze, his eyes unwavering. "One, because he asked me to," he said. "And two, because to help him would have gotten us both killed." He lowered his voice to match hers. "No intervention is permitted; under penalty of death."

Silence again weighed heavily in the shelter. Feet shifted uncomfortably in the grass and droplets continued to sizzle as they landed with a splat on a blazing fire.

Finally Breunne broke the quiet. "I have answered your questions to the best of my ability. Now if you please, answer mine, which has grown by one. Why do the Minions seek her staff?" His eyes bored into those of the paladin. "And why do you care so much about what happens to a thief?"

"Rogue," corrected the paladin. Breunne bowed his head slightly in acknowledgement. Thrinndor sighed heavily and allowed his shoulders to slump. "It is complicated," he said quietly.

"I expected nothing less," said the ranger.

Again the paladin looked to the cleric to see if she still agreed with his decision to speak of their quests to this stranger. Her eyes widened in uncertainty and she shook her head slightly. But then she lowered her eyes as her shoulders also sagged. She again nodded her assent.

Thrinndor straightened his shoulders and seemed to pull confidence from the air around him. "Very well," he began, "these words are not meant for ears that do not believe. You must never speak of what you are about to hear."

Breunne's eyes searched those of the paladin for a moment, and then abruptly he slid a small, thin dagger from its sheath at his belt with his left hand. His eyes never left those of Thrinndor's as he raised his right hand and held it against the dagger.

Without flinching, he drew it slowly across the palm of his right hand, leaving behind a growing trail of blood. Cyrillis gasped. "Give me your hand," he said in an even tone.

Without hesitation, Thrinndor stretched his right hand out, palm up. Breunne grasped it and drew it toward him. He held the blade so that it hovered, still gleaming with his own blood, above the hand of the paladin. Still he said nothing.

Slowly he drew the dagger across Thrinndor's hand as he had his own, again leaving behind a small trail of blood.

The paladin's expression did not change. This was a ceremony of which he had heard, but never witnessed.

Abruptly Breunne flipped the dagger so that it spun and buried itself into the soft loam of the earth at their feet.

Still the eyes of the ranger bored into those of the paladin as he reversed his right hand and grasped that of the paladin such that the incisions on their hands were aligned perfectly.

"As our blood on the blade mixed and became one and then together enriched the earth, so let our purpose become one to the enrichment of the other.

"I give you my word on this our bond that I will not speak of that which you implore me not to.

"Furthermore, I pledge my sword, my bow and my very life if the need arises to this cause of yours."

Breunne started to release his grip, but Thrinndor grasped the ranger's hand tighter and poured forth his healing. The power surged through the clasped hands until the paladin released his grip. The ranger looked down at his hand and saw that it was completely healed, leaving behind no indication of what had transpired save the blood on his palm.

Thrinndor spoke first. "Why?" he asked.

Breunne did not hesitate. "Savinhand," he said as if that would be enough.

It was.

Thrinndor nodded.

"Very well," he said. "Be seated." He smiled for the first time in several minutes. "Even in brevity these tales will take some time."

Breunne did as directed. As he made himself comfortable he said, "I do not intend to be rude or belittle that of which you are about to speak. But please be as brief as you can, as I have tarried here longer than I should. I must get to Farreach ere the morning sun rises."

Thrinndor nodded his assent as he also lowered his tall frame to the ground and made himself comfortable. Vorgath and Cyrillis did likewise.

"I will only cover the highlights required to answer your question," said the paladin. "The details can wait until we have sufficient time."

The ranger nodded his agreement.

Thrinndor cleared his throat and said, "I will begin with Cyrillis' staff. It is known as Kurril and is very old. It is an artifact of great power, once wielded by Angra-Khan—a member of Lord Valdaar's High Council.

"It is also one of the three artifacts required to perform the ceremony that will return Valdaar to the material plane." He paused for a moment. "It is our quest to find the other two.

"I do not believe the Minions of Set strive to obtain Kurril for their own use—for I am sure they know they would be unable to do so—but they mean to ensure it is not used for the purpose as foretold in the teachings of old."

Thrinndor paused again as he noted the ranger nodding his head in apparent agreement. "You know of this?"

"No," replied the ranger. "However, what you have said fits with what little I know of The Prophesy, and with what I have learned since." He turned as his eyes sought out the staff. "So that is Kurril then?"

"It is," replied the paladin.

"Why would the Minions care about this dead god?"

"He is not dead," said the paladin, his voice resonating with certainty. "His life force has been banished from this the material plane of existence. The ritual will return him to us.

"As to why the Minions seek to stop his return, that is a simple concept." He paused to see if the ranger could guess what was coming next, but it was obviously not so. "Their god—Set—is not a true god. But in Valdaar's absence his stature has grown as he has had little or no contention for the creatures of the land that tend toward what has been called the darker teachings.

"No, Set and his Minions will certainly do everything in their power to stop us from returning my lord to this plane." He paused and looked over to where Cyrillis was sitting, her staff cradled in her lap. "It appears their current plan to do so is to take the staff from us."

There was silence in the shelter as Breunne considered what he had been told. He again nodded. He stood suddenly, saying, "Then it is even more vital that I get to Farreach before the Minions from the southern region do." His gaze once again fell upon the staff. "When they arrive, they must believe that I am on my way to Ice Homme with the staff."

"Why?" Vorgath asked.

The ranger turned to address the barbarian. "Because if I don't, they'll likely head to the temple I just laid waste to," he said. "And that would bring them right by here and they will have skillful huntsmen with them. They would probably discover this place."

"Good!" said the dwarf with vehemence, surprising the ranger. "Bring them on! This waiting shit is growing old." He glowered at the ranger, daring him to defy his reasoning. "A little skirmish would most certainly bring a much needed distraction!"

"Skirmish?" Breunne scoffed. "Distraction? There is a veritable army of them at their outpost in the south."

Thrinndor came to the aid of his long-time friend. "Yes, however it is doubtful they could mobilize that army to get them here by morning."

"Yeah!" said the hopeful dwarf.

"Agreed," replied the ranger. "But the advance party—assuming they are coming—will include one, if not two, High Lords and their immediate entourage." He paused to let that sink in.

"And I'm sure," he continued, "that I don't need to tell you we are not currently properly equipped to deal with them!"

"Bah!" snorted the barbarian. He again crossed his arms across his chest and glowered at the ranger but said nothing more.

"I thought not," said Breunne. He turned back to face the paladin before the dwarf could react to that.

"I presume you have a spellcaster as part of this austere group?"

"Yes," replied the paladin. "The aforementioned Sordaak is our caster." He paused for a moment. "And leader."

"Leader?" said the ranger. Clearly this was not what he expected. Paladins were almost always the leader of any party they were part of. This was truly an interesting development. "He must be quite the caster, then." He looked thoughtfully at Thrinndor. "I can't wait to meet him." When no one said anything, he added, "Where then, pray tell, is this leader of your party?"

"He is studying with Rheagamon," the paladin replied.

The ranger who had looked away to again place his eyes on the staff—or perhaps Cyrillis—whipped his head back around. "Rheagamon?" he said quickly. "The Rheagamon?"

Thrinndor merely nodded.

"I'd heard he had retired," said the ranger. "And was taking no more understudies."

"Well," snorted the barbarian, "it appears you heard wrong!" He was clearly still smarting from the High Lord thing.

"It appears Sordaak was able to convince him otherwise," said the paladin, throwing a warning glance at his friend in the process. Vorgath shut up and went back to glowering.

"Well," said the ranger. "I guess maybe this Sordaak of yours is worthy after all."

"I wouldn't go that far," said the barbarian, unable to contain himself.

Thrinndor threw his friend another nasty glare, who stared back in defiance. After a bit, the dwarf let a breath out noisily and said, "Just sayin'!"

"If that is all you have to say," reprimanded the paladin, "then I will thank you to not say anything!"

Vorgath took in a sharp breath but decided to let it go. He again let out the breath noisily, letting all know that he was giving in, for now.

His attention once again focused on Breunne, Thrinndor continued. "He is also very important to our cause, for he is the only known direct descendent of Dragma."

"Really?" said an incredulous Breunne. "Very interesting!" His gaze took on a faraway look as he appeared to be studying the place where water was getting through the roof to drip into the fire.

"You seem to know a lot of The Prophesy," said Cyrillis, joining the conversation at last. Her tone held an almost hidden undercurrent of distrust. Almost...

"Some," the ranger replied. "Not near enough." He again surged to his feet. "However, that will have to wait for another day."

Breunne looked around at the others who also stood—except for Vorgath. The dwarf remained seated with his arms crossed on his chest. He stared intently at some apparently very interesting ember in the fire.

"I must be on my way," Breunne said. "As much as I have enjoyed the warm fire, the company and the food," he nodded at Cyrillis, "I want to gather your belongings in town, plant the seed of my conquest of this group—"

Vorgath snorted, but said nothing.

"—and declare my intentions to get what is mine from Ice Homme. All before any boat from Desert Homme makes it to Farreach."

"Here," began the healer, "at least take some fresh clothes to ward against the rain and wind." The wind had indeed picked up, as had the rain. An occasional flash of lightning could now be seen through the blanket that served as a door, with the accompanying crash of thunder. Some strikes sounded very close.

"No," said the ranger. "You wouldn't have me show up in Farreach in pristine condition, would you? I must appear as if I had just fought a hard battle, barely escaping with my life." He grinned to remove any hint of reproach from his voice.

She hesitated before answering. "Your raiment certainly looks the part."

He grimaced when he looked down at his tattered garments. "Yes. I guess it does at that!"

"The townspeople will not yet have heard about the local temple you eliminated," began Thrinndor.

"Good point," said the ranger. He thought briefly. "I think I can use that to my advantage."

"How so?" asked the paladin.

"I will say I came upon your group after you wiped them out," he said, grinning. "And that made my job all that much easier." Vorgath again snorted. Breunne looked his way. "After your decimation of the Temple at Brasheer, they will want to believe you sought out this temple and killed them all as well." He smiled. "Your legend will certainly grow!"

"Gee, thanks!" said the paladin, sarcasm dripping from his voice.

"Yeah, well," said Breunne, "better yours than mine!" He grinned at the paladin. "Maybe I can keep my reputation clear!"

"Yeah, right!" moaned the dwarf.

Everyone ignored him as the ranger paused with his hand poised to push aside the curtain. "I will probably be a couple of days," he said. "I must take care not to lead the Minions back here."

"Wait!" said Cyrillis. All eyes turned to her. "What about Sordaak?" She went on more calmly. "I mean, we were supposed to meet him in Farreach by the end of this week." Her eyes went from the ranger to the paladin. "How will he know we are here? And, if he shows up in town and starts asking about us any Minions in the area will probably detain him for questioning." She bit her lip. "Or worse…" She carried her own thought forward when no one immediately answered.

"Good point," replied the ranger. After a moment's consideration he added, "Change of plan." Thrinndor's right eyebrow arched. "Rheagamon's Keep is a couple of days' travel north from Farreach." The ranger was obviously changing plans as ideas occurred to him. "That's the direction I must travel anyway." He turned back to face the cleric. "So I'll swing by there to warn him to stay out of Farreach." He turned his attention to Thrinndor. "Here's what we'll do. You all wait here for Savinhand, as planned. But only for three days."

Thrinndor's eyebrow inched incrementally higher.

Breunne answered the unasked question. "The final contest would have been today. If he yet lives, Savin will be here within that time frame."

"But, if he lives," said Cyrillis, "will he not then be leader of Shardmoor? Will he not be required to stay?"

"No," said the ranger. He held up a hand as the healer drew in a breath to protest. "I'll let him explain that to you. Rest assured, however, that if he yet lives, he will be here within those three days."

Cyrillis again started to protest but Breunne said, "He will be here." His tone implied certainty.

The healer reluctantly nodded.

"There is a small unused cavern a half-days travel north of Rheagamon's Keep," the ranger said. "Maybe a mile west of the river's ford—"

"I know that cavern," said Vorgath, surprising everyone as he re-entered the conversation.

Breunne swung around to face him. "Very well," he said, "I'll go to Farreach as previously discussed and claim your belongings as bounty for myself. Then I'll pick up Sordaak and we'll meet you there in, say, five days' time?"

Thrinndor nodded. "Sounds like a plan," was all he said.

"All right then," began the ranger as he once again reached for the blanket keeping the rain and wind out—well, most of it anyway. Abruptly he spun on the ball of his foot and took the one step required to stand before the healer.

He grasped her hand, bowed and put it to his lips. "Until we meet again, my lady." Standing, he looked deep into her eyes. He then spun again, pushed through the doorway and disappeared into the darkness beyond without another word.

"This is getting complicated," groused the dwarf, who was staring at the now empty doorway.

"Yes it is," replied the paladin. His eyes were on the cleric, who was also staring at the same empty doorway. Her expression was somewhat different, however.

Chapter Eight

Sordaak

Sordaak's initial conversation with Rheagamon had not gone exactly as he'd planned. In fact, it had not gone anything like he had planned.

He had expected that he would have to persuade the old drow to take him on as a student. To that end he had asked Vorgath to wait for him outside the keep while he went in to request an audience with its master.

The keep was small by current standards—really not much more than a walled compound hosting several small buildings. The walls, however, were impressive in height and girth.

Sordaak estimated them to be about thirty feet in height, and they were close to fifteen feet thick. He guessed correctly that there was probably a hidden corridor that ran between the exterior and interior walls. There was only the one entrance, and that was protected by two massive iron and stone gates that were obviously opened and closed by the use of counterbalances. No amount of brute strength would raise either of them.

There was no palace. No main house. No elaborate temple. The one feature that stood out was a tall tower. Perhaps a hundred feet in height, it looked down on the entire valley floor for miles in every direction. It was windowless, save at the top. There at the top there was a balcony that encircled what Sordaak assumed to be the living quarters of the drow sorcerer. At the base of the tower sat a beautiful garden with trees and flowers in abundance.

Sordaak strode through the gates and followed a path that led him to the garden. He was not challenged. In fact he saw no one until he got to the entrance to the garden.

There he spotted a stooped old man clipping flowers from a large rose bush.

The mage strode purposefully up to the old man, whose back was to him as he approached. He stopped several feet short, and when the man did not immediately turn around Sordaak cleared his throat noisily.

The old man continued cutting flowers and gave no outward sign that he had heard the caster. Sordaak cleared his throat again, this time even louder.

When the man still did not turn, an exasperated Sordaak said, "Excuse me, would you please inform Lord Rheagamon I would like an audience?"

The old man snipped one more flower and placed it in the basket perched on a stool put there for that purpose before slowly turning to eye the intruder.

Sordaak fought down the urge to gasp in shock as the old man's face was revealed to him by the light of the sun.

His hair was long, white and wound in small braids that hung down onto his chest. The skin was weathered and old.

But it was the eyes that caught and held his attention. The eyes were intense and ablaze with the hue of the red hot coals of a fire!

Sordaak could not see the ears due to the hair, but he suspected they were pointed. This was Rheagamon? "I–I," he stammered.

The eyes grew even more intense as the man's brows knitted together in a frown. "I know who you are, young man," the old drow said in a voice that was somehow both soft and commanding. "And I know why you are here."

It was Rheagamon!

"Yes, sir," blurted Sordaak, struggling to regain his composure. "I—"

"Silence!" snapped the old man. "We don't have time for that!" he said as his eyes bore into those of the caster standing before him.

"Tell me," Rheagamon said abruptly, "why is it you seek to eschew the teachings of Chaos..." He spat the last word as if it were distasteful to utter. "...only then to embrace the way of Law?"

Sordaak was taken completely by surprise that Rheagamon already knew that much about him. Knowing his answer would probably determine whether his fate was to be tied to this old drow made him break out in a cold sweat. So he hesitated. The mage closed his eyes and took a deep breath. When he opened them, he pulled his robe straight and stood to his full height—which by human standards was not tall, yet he was several inches taller than the old man before him.

He swallowed hard to rid himself of the bile that was creeping up the back of his throat. When Sordaak spoke, it was with a clear, unwavering voice.

"I was taught the ways of Chaos as a young apprentice," he began. As he spoke, he gained confidence and his voice became stronger. "I embraced that philosophy in part because my master taught it, but more because it was how I wanted to believe." He looked straight into the burning eyes of the master sorcerer before him. "I didn't want to believe that my destiny was predetermined.

"I wanted to believe that only I controlled my fate—no one else! And certainly not that of any rumored legends or fairy tales taught to children!"

When he found that he was raising his voice, he forced himself to be calm and lowered his tone back to a conversational one. His shoulders slumped, and his eyes fell to the ground at the old wizard's feet. "Yet deep inside I knew that to be false." Now the young mage's voice was barely above a whisper. He raised his head back up and his eyes again found those of the master. "The cosmos do not exist for me. While I certainly have a place in them, I do not control them. There is a plan and I am part of that plan. Even time has laws," he continued, his voice rising again, "and those laws must be respected." He brought his volume back down. "Revered, even." He was silent for a moment. "I am who I am. I must learn who that is all over again and how to fit into my place within the boundaries of the Law."

The old man's eyes searched those of the young man before him for any sign of deceit. He found none.

"Very well," Rheagamon said as he also stood to his full height—which was taller than he had looked at first glance—and then he waved a hand in the direction of the gates. There was a thunderous crash as both slammed to the ground, sealing the keep.

"Follow me," the old mage said as he turned and headed for a previously unseen entrance to the tower. "We have a lot of work to do."

Sordaak stood his ground and said, "I came here with a friend."

"The barbarian has been dismissed," the old drow said as he disappeared into the tower. His voice echoed back to Sordaak as he did not turn to speak. "You must have no distractions if you are to complete your required studies in the allotted five weeks." This last came as he rounded a corner and disappeared into the shadows inside the doorway.

Sordaak hurried so as not to get left behind, and therefore lost.

Dismissed? Sordaak wondered silently to just what that meant. However, he became determined to do as his new master said and put all distractions out of his mind.

Vorgath could take care of himself.

*

And so the next five weeks became a blur to him. When he passed through the door to the tower, he left everything—everyone—outside that door.

He threw himself into the studies with an abandon that surprised not only Rheagamon but also himself. Sordaak was relentless. He lost track of days and nights, only eating and/or resting when his body or mind could do no more without doing so.

His new master warned him against this, informing him that the mind functioned better when it was not distracted by hunger or lack of sleep. Sordaak did his best to apply that teaching, yet often found he was unable to pull himself away from a particular tome or manuscript.

Rheagamon taught him that he was not like the clerics. "They derive their power from their gods," he said. "We sorcerers get it from the rocks under our feet. From the clouds in the sky. From the animals in the field. We get our power from whence it lies, waiting for us to release it.

"Our mind directs that power and sends it forth in whatever form we ask of it. However, each incantation takes a little piece of us with it. The more powerful the spell, the larger part of you that is required.

"As you grow in power and stature, you will learn how to better control your mind and limit what each spell takes from you. After years of study, even the most powerful of spells will seem to consume a more seemingly insignificant part of your mind.

"So you must rest. You must eat. You must take care of yourself. Always remember that a weak, lazy body is because of a weak, lazy mind. Keep yourself fit in mind and body."

Rheagamon paused then and his voice grew unexpectedly serious. "A wise sorcerer must never exhaust himself completely. For when that happens, you leave yourself vulnerable to whatever comes your way. You are ill equipped for hand-to-hand combat, and you must avoid that at all cost." He paused for a few moments before continuing. "There is another reason," he said quietly. "Every time you exhaust your mind to the point where it is no longer able to defend itself, you take a chance that you will damage it." He had looked up suddenly, his eyes boring into those of his pupil. "As a sorcerer," he said, "your mind is all you have! You must not take that chance!"

A reply seemed indicated, so Sordaak said, "Yes, master. I understand."

"See that you do," Rheagamon said. "For in you I see the potential for a strength of mind like this land has not seen for many a century! My own power is limited not only by what is in here..." he tapped the side of his head lightly "... but also by what spells my master was able to pass along to me and what spells I was able to pick up on my own." His flaming red eyes bored into those of Sordaak. "You have no such limitations!" His voice rose to almost a shout. "Your mind has the capacity that until now I did not believe was even possible!" He lowered his voice until it was barely above a whisper. "And you have Dragma's Spellbook!"

Sordaak felt certain he should have wondered just how the old man knew that, but he was way beyond any wonder at what the old man already knew.

"You understand little of what it contains, I know that," Rheagamon continued. "But you will! With it you have no limitations!" The old man looked around suddenly as he whispered, "Let no one know you have it! There are many who would kill you just to get a chance to look inside!"

Sordaak was taken aback by the old sorcerer's vehemence. He quickly decided the book was too important to carry around in his pack. "I cannot risk losing it then," he said as the old man turned to head for the door. "Can I leave it here for safe—"

Rheagamon spun around and jabbed a finger at his pupil. "No!" he shouted. "Do not tempt me so!" He was suddenly breathing hard. "The book can have only one master!" The old man paused to regain control of his emotions. "Rather," he continued more calmly, "one master that lives."

The old sorcerer looked into the eyes of his student. "A few hundred years ago I would have slain you myself for that tome." That caused Sordaak to start. "I even searched for it myself briefly." Rheagamon's eyes took on a faraway look as his mind traveled back through the centuries.

With a shake of his head the old master returned to the present. "No," he said, his voice weak from expended emotion. "You must keep it with you, for now." He smiled, "At least until you have built a keep of your own."

He then turned his back and headed for the door to the library in which they had been studying. "That is all I can teach you at this time," he said. "You must return to me following your next adventure.

"You have a visitor at the main gate."

Stunned, Sordaak watch the old drow disappear through the doorway into the inner passage beyond. As the muffled sound of the old man's shuffling footsteps diminished, he shook his head trying to clear it.

He needed some time to reconcile what he had just heard. It was several minutes before he remembered he had been told he had a visitor.

Quickly, he took the steps of the tower two at a time until he reached the bottom. He hustled toward the main gates and was startled to see them open. He was not aware when that had happened. Or how…

As he passed through the outer gate he looked around, expecting to see Vorgath. But the dwarf was nowhere to be seen.

Instead, there was a tall, slender human clad in leather armor with a long, flowing cloak over it.

"Sordaak?" the man said.

"That depends on who is asking," replied the caster cautiously. He kept a wary distance from the man.

"I am Breunne," the man said as he took a slow, non-threatening step towards the mage, his right hand extended for greeting.

Still unsure of this man's intentions, Sordaak reluctantly grasped the forearm and returned the gesture. "Am I supposed to know you?" he said, ready to leap back should the need arise.

"I doubt that you would," the man said. "However, Thrinndor sent me to warn you."

Still not convinced—while they had worked to keep their alliance secret, surely there were some out there who knew of it—he released the man's grip and stepped back.

Sordaak decided to get more information before he committed. "Who?" he said. "And warn me about what?"

Breunne's face took on a wry smile. He had anticipated this. "Thrinndor. Big, tall guy. Wears black armor? Travels with a good-looking healer named Cyrillis and a grouchy dwarf named Vorgath?"

"Oh," replied the caster, also now with a wry smile on his face. "That Thrinndor!" The smile disappeared. "What warning?" He knew he was supposed to meet the rest of them in Farreach soon. He was going to have to ask Rheagamon how long he had been here, because he had no idea.

The ranger looked around quickly. "Is it safe to talk here?" he asked, concern apparent in his expression.

"If not," said a grinning Sordaak, "we're screwed." He knew there was no one around and what was about to be said his mentor probably knew already! "So, talk."

"Very well," said Breunne. "Your friends have been...busy. They managed to piss off every Minion of Set in this region—probably in all the land."

"How?" the mage asked, looking around for his friends.

"Long story short," the ranger said, "Thrinndor and Cyrillis went to their Temple at Brasheer to ask them about her heritage. They tried to take her staff." He paused as Sordaak took in a sharp breath. "Thrinndor prevented them."

Sordaak let the breath out slowly. "I'll bet he did!" He raised an eyebrow. "That it?"

"Well," said the ranger who was suddenly obsessed with a pebble down at his feet. "There might have been another minor altercation with the temple south of Farreach that involved decimation and destruction."

The mage's eyebrow climbed higher. "Might have?" he asked.

"Well," Breunne repeated, "they kinda got themselves wiped out and the blame again lies at your friends' feet." He looked up sheepishly. "Kinda."

"And?" Sordaak had a feeling there was more—far more.

"Look," said the ranger as he again looked around furtively, "can we talk about this as we travel?" His eyes were almost pleading.

"Why?" asked the caster. "I'm going to need more information than that!" But now he knew something was amiss—he could feel it.

"We have reason to believe the High Lord from Desert Homme is on my trail!" Now the ranger was starting to fidget.

"At the risk of getting repetitious: Why?" Sordaak was getting good at these one-word questions.

"Because the Minions might believe I have slain your friends—"

"What?"

"—and am in possession of the staff." He finished with a rush. "Look," he said again, "I believe the High Lord to be not far behind me—or rather where I led them to before I came here. I have hidden my trail here well."

Knowing what he did about the Minions, Sordaak said, "No one can hide their trail from them that well." His tone implied he did not believe it was possible.

"I am a Ranger," replied Breunne as if that settled the matter.

The mage was not sure whether it did, but there was at least some comfort knowing that it was at least possible now.

"Let's get back to my 'dead' friends," said the caster as he folded his arms across his chest. He was prepared to wait this man out.

"Not here," replied the ranger tersely. "We must be on the move!" Once again he looked about nervously. "You don't want to take the chance they would follow me here, do you?"

Sordaak stood there with his arms crossed, trying to decide what to do. Rheagamon had said he was through with him for now, after all. He only had a few belongings.

He made up his mind. "Very well," he said. "Wait here. I will return in a few minutes with my mount and gear."

"Hurry!"

Breunne's insistence was beginning to be felt in Sordaak. He turned and ran back through the gates.

Sordaak packed quickly. He did not have that much to begin with.

He donned his old robe, noting that it had been cleaned and the holes/tears repaired. He idly wondered how. He had not seen anyone except the old drow his entire time he had been here.

No one! Yet, meals were always ready when it was time to eat. He always had clean garments to wear. His room was always clean with fresh linens when he returned—no matter what time of day that was.

Odd…. And it was odd that he hadn't thought to notice it before.

He couldn't remember seeing anyone! He had been too busy to notice…maybe. But, surely he would have remembered had he seen servants or other staff members.

Packed, he briefly looked for Rheagamon, but the old sorcerer was nowhere to be found.

Sordaak got the strange feeling he had been dismissed. He shook that thought off and decided he didn't have time to consider it further. Breunne had been more than a little convincing in his desire to get on the road quickly.

He went to the livery and found his horse fattened and ready to travel. He was even saddled, his reins tied to a post.

His curiosity piqued, he looked around for who could have gotten his horse ready so quickly. That's when he discovered his mount was not alone. Tied along-side was a pack animal, fully loaded with provisions and equipment. Sordaak even thought his nose detected the aroma of fresh bread!

He dropped the reins he had picked up and was about to investigate when he heard Breunne shout his name.

"Shit!" he muttered under his breath. He bent to retrieve the reins and swung none too easily into the saddle. It had been after all more than a month, he reasoned, and he had not been all that great a rider in the first place!

He grabbed the leads of the pack animal and swung his mount toward the door. He made a mental note to talk to Rheagamon about who took care of things for him when he returned.

Chapter Nine

The Wait

Breunne had switched directions many times, and at several other points they had ridden where there was no trail at all. They did not arrive at their destination until evening of the second day.

Sordaak, whose outdoor skills were not very far off of the bottom of his priority list, was hopelessly lost. He had no idea where they were in relation to where they had started.

And he was not all that happy about it.

However, Breunne had done as promised and filled him in on what had transpired with his friends, why they were in such a hurry and why he was being so careful about being followed.

They had ridden well into the night that first day, making a dry camp with no fire when they did stop. They had ridden in streams and rivers for miles at a time—emerging only on hard rock surfaces. Even then they tied cloth bags over the hooves of the horses and pack animals to preclude them from leaving a mark on the solid rock underfoot.

At first, the mage had complained, but it was not long before the ranger's caution infected him to the point he was constantly looking over his shoulder trying to see any movement that wasn't supposed to be there.

Apparently satisfied, Breunne had at last led them up a long, grass-covered slope toward a cliff face. A small stream bubbled gently along where their animals' feet fell silently on the grass.

The ranger dismounted as they approached a large boulder that blocked further progress. There was still enough light to see that there was not much to see.

"This is it?" said the mage. His ass was sore from two days in the saddle, and he intended to let someone know about it. He dismounted and looked around but could find no sign of the promised cave.

Breunne ignored him as he stripped the saddle from his horse and picketed him over by the stream.

Sordaak considered pursuing the conversation further but ultimately figured it would be a lost cause. He, too, stripped and picketed his mount. By the time he was done, the ranger had started removing the supplies from the pack mule. Together, they accomplished the task in only a few minutes and had the animal picketed next to their horses. Next the ranger picked up his saddle and slung it over his shoulder, stepped around the boulder and disappeared.

Not wanting to chance fighting with the saddle and any narrow opening he might encounter, Sordaak left his behind as he quickly followed in Breunne's footsteps.

Behind the boulder, the darkness was complete. The mage fumbled around some, but when he bumped his shin for the second time on an unseen rock, he cursed and muttered the words to a spell.

A bright light lit up the surrounding area as he held up a dagger he had cast the spell on.

"Put out that light!" snapped the ranger from somewhere ahead.

"But—"

"Now!"

An annoyed Sordaak did as requested and hid the brightly illuminated dagger under the folds of his cloak, extinguishing the light.

"Thank you," said the ranger. "That light can be seen for miles in any direction from up here," he said by way of explanation.

Sordaak cursed as he stubbed his toe on an unseen rock. Unseen because any adjustment his eyes had made to the darkness—which was not all that much in the first place—had been undone by his spell.

Breunne smiled and said, "Once we are far enough back in here, a light will certainly be welcome." There was a pause as he moved further ahead. "As will a fire—a small fire."

"If I live long enough to see that fire," groused the mage as he stubbed the toe of his other foot, stifling yet another curse.

He put his hands out and waved them back and forth in front of him blindman style, and that seemed to help. It was not long before the passage opened up somewhat, and he could no longer find a wall on either side.

"Is some light OK now?" Sordaak asked, sarcasm dripping from his voice.

"Yes," said the disembodied voice of the ranger, somewhere off to the caster's right.

The mage reached down and removed the dagger from its hiding place, allowing the light from it to wash over the chamber. It was larger than Sordaak had expected, perhaps an irregular twenty or twenty-five feet in diameter.

There was a fire ring built off to one side, but try as he might, he was unable to see where exactly the smoke would exit. Someone, he decided, must have verified that it did—this place had been used many, many times by the look of it.

"Now what?" asked the caster.

Breunne looked at the sorcerer and raised an eyebrow. "Now we wait," he said simply.

Sordaak started to question further but decided it was not worth the effort. There was probably nothing more to learn.

He propped the dagger up on a shelf he located near the fire ring and used a small amount of energy to light a torch he found in a holder nearby.

With the torch in hand, he circled the chamber and lit two more. There were others, but he left them alone—it was rapidly getting dark outside, and he wanted to keep the adjustment time for his eyes to a minimum.

Meanwhile, the ranger set about the task of starting a fire in the pit provided with wood from a stack conveniently nearby. He too kept it small.

Sordaak summoned Fahlred, and that quickly drew the attention of the ranger. "What is that?" he asked, concern deep in his voice and his hand on the pommel of his sword.

"What?" replied the mage absent-mindedly. "Oh, him. This is Fahlred, my familiar."

Still the ranger did not take his eyes from the creature. He said nothing.

"He is a Quasit," the sorcerer explained. His tone conveyed pride.

"He is a devil!" the ranger exclaimed.

"Actually," said the caster as if he were attempting to reason with a child, "he is a demon."

"Whatever!" snapped the ranger. "You have a demon as a familiar?" He was obviously having trouble wrapping his mind around that fact.

"Yes," replied the caster. He then turned away from the ranger and focused his attention on Fahlred. He suddenly realized he had spent so much of his time with his new master that he had completely ignored his friend.

He closed his eyes and focused. No words were necessary, they communicated by a form of telepathy. Briefly he apologized—knowing it was not necessary, but he felt better for doing so—and then he explained what it was that he wanted.

He asked Fahlred to search every nook and cranny of the cavern and check for other ways in or out. After that, he told his familiar to stand watch over the entrance so he could rest.

After the Quasit had winked back out of existence, Sordaak went about the task of preparing their first hot meal in two days.

The ranger still had not moved. However, his demeanor was no longer defensive but more thoughtful. "Pardon my ignorance," he said.

"Of course," replied the caster with a dismissive wave of his hand. He had grown accustomed to such reactions to his familiar.

"But it has been many a year since a demon has answered the call of a sorcerer."

"Many a hundred years," corrected the caster as he hung the pot on the hook provided for the purpose.

"Yes, well," Breunne continued, "be that as it may, it is certainly an indicator of your skill." This drew an interested glance from the mage. "And it would certainly lend credence to what Thrinndor was trying to explain to me concerning the times that are upon the land." The ranger was no longer talking to Sordaak, but more to himself. He rubbed his chin in thought.

"So it would seem," agreed the caster, who was also deep in thought. He spun and waved a wooden spoon at the tall man across the chamber. "Just what is your place in all of this?" he asked suddenly.

Now it was the ranger's turn to be cryptic. "I do not know," he replied with a sigh.

"Huh?" said Sordaak. "That's it?"

Breunne took a defensive stance. "I am a longtime friend of Savinhand," he explained. "And I took the blood oath with Thrinndor, pledging to him my sword and my life all for a cause I do not yet understand." He shook his head silently.

A silence fell over the chamber, interrupted only by the occasional sap popping in the mostly dry wood in the fire.

"Perhaps you can explain it to me further," said the ranger morosely as he stared into the coals of the fire.

"No," replied the caster, drawing a quick glance from the ranger. "That will have to wait for the paladin. I too have been a part of this quest for only a brief period."

Again both fell silent as Sordaak ladled some of the meat and tuber mixture he had prepared into wooden bowls. He handed one to the ranger.

"Thanks," Breunne said. Sordaak merely nodded.

They ate in silence.

Finished, the mage cleaned up and set about the task of making his bed. "We must rest now," he said. "I have a feeling we will not have the leisure of such opportunity in the future."

Breunne nodded and stood. "I'll take first watch."

"No," the sorcerer said. "Fahlred will watch over the approach." His eyes met those of the ranger. "He does not require sleep."

Breunne nodded, deciding he was in too far to question the mage on this. He rolled into his blanket, put his hands up behind his head and began to ponder the last few days.

Everything seems to have happened within a whirlwind.

He searched his mind to see if he could recall just how it was he happened to be in this cavern, with this mage, at this time. He had begun life as the only child to a drifting father who was a sometimes rancher, sometimes farmer, all the time drunkard who had no goal in life save for that next drink. His mother had died while giving him life—a fact his father had never let him forget. Perhaps that was why he drank so much—to aid him in forgetting. Whatever, Breunne had decided. He was not going to follow in the footsteps of his father.

So it was that one night, when this man who was old before his time due to the drink had passed out from a particularly long night at the local tavern, Breunne he took what little coin he had been able to hide away and made a run for it. He stole off into the night with nothing more than those paltry few coins, the clothes on his back and a bow he had made himself.

It was the third such bow, each fashioned by own hands and each progressively better than its predecessor. He became quite good in the manufacture of his own arrows, as well. And he had become quite good with their use. He practiced countless hours with them until he could hit a large rat (of which there always seemed to be a never-ending supply) while he was at a dead run—and the rat moving, as well.

He learned the hard way to be careful with his arrows. For while he could make them himself, the materials to do so—at least for the good ones—were much harder to find.

Initially he made his own way, preferring to avoid any human contact and their peculiarities, regardless of what those peculiarities were.

But soon he began to crave companionship, at least on occasion. So he started to visit towns whenever he happened upon them. He never stayed long—finding he still preferred to make his own way. Rely on no one.

Then one day during such a visit that he ran into Markwonne.

While he stayed away from the strong drink, Breunne hung around in the taverns in whatever town he happened to visit, knowing them to be a clearinghouse for all sorts of information. If there was something to be found out about a town or a region, it would be talked about in the local tavern.

That day Markwonne had asked to see the bow Breunne had slung over his shoulder and his cache of arrows.

Reluctantly, Breunne had handed them over. For some reason he selected two of his best efforts for the arrows.

The man had inspected them closely. "You make these?" he had asked.

Unsure why the man wanted to know, Breunne merely nodded.

"Very good," the man had said. "Crude, but good."

"Crude?" Breunne had asked. He was very proud of those two particular arrows.

"Yes," replied Markwonne. A quick glance at the boy told the old ranger he needed to say more. "But good." He unslung a bow from somewhere under his cloak and handed it to the boy. Next he pulled two arrows, seemingly at random, from a quiver Breunne had not seen and handed them over.

Breunne marveled at their workmanship. Indeed, he had never seen the like of the arrows. Straight and true, with perfectly matched feathers at one end and a metal head that was very sharp on the other.

And the bow… If the arrows were masterfully made, then the bow was perfection incarnate. It was long—as long as he was tall! It was gently curved and made of a wood that he as a boy had never seen. It was worn smooth by years of use, yet it showed no signs of wear. There were small, intricate runes covering the dark wood from one end to the other.

It was beautiful!

It felt so right in his hands, too. He looked up in wonder at the man who stood before him. Markwonne was in his early middle years, no more than thirty-five or forty Breunne was sure. He had an easy confidence about him that was effusive. Breunne was still only seventeen, but he had been on his own for more than four years and considered himself a skilled huntsman. However, without knowing why he suddenly felt inadequate.

He reluctantly handed the bow back to the man, who reached out and tousled his hair. "Come with me, lad," the man said as he turned and strode through the door, apparently confident Breunne would follow. Without knowing why, he had.

They had gone outside and the man led him to the livery, where he had picked up two crude bags and filled them with hay from the loft. He packed the hay in as tightly as he could and then handed one to a curious Breunne.

He then set foot on a path that led out of town without saying a word. He never even turned to see if he was followed.

They stopped not far out of town in a meadow where Markwonne tied the bags such that they hung from the limb of a tree. He pulled a piece of coal from a pouch at his belt and drew rings on both bags, each ring larger than the other.

Now Breunne got the idea. He smiled; confident he was in his own element. Still, the fancy bow and the ultra-straight arrows bothered him.

They exchanged shots, Breunne holding his own, making each of his arrows count. Then Markwonne smiled and started the bags to spinning and swinging on their ropes.

Still Breunne continued to shred the material at the center of the circles.

"Not bad, kid," Markwonne had said as he approached the boy with a rag hanging from his right hand. As he got close he reached toward Breunne's head, but the boy jerked away.

"Relax," the older man said holding up both hands, palms out. "I want to see what you can do when you can't see."

"What?" asked Breunne, confused.

Markwonne held up the strip of cloth. "I want to blindfold you with this to see if you can hit what you can't see."

"What?" said an incredulous Breunne. "That makes no sense!" Still, the man covered his eyes. "I can't hit anything with this on!"

"You sure?" asked Markwonne.

"What do you mean?" replied Breunne, now blind and completely confused.

"You must learn to use your other senses," said the older man. "Your eyes may not always be there to guide you. Or what you see may not always be what is there." He walked to where he had hung the targets.

"What?"

Markwonne again started both targets swinging. "Take your best shot," he said, ducking behind a tree in the event he had misjudged the lad.

Breunne's head jerked about, exasperated. "You have got to be joking!" he said, his bow still held at his side.

"I said," Markwonne said more sternly, "take your best shot!"

"I don't understand!" replied Breunne.

"Just do it!" snapped the older man.

Breunne let out a noisy sigh. "Whatever!" He reached into his quiver and snatched out an arrow. He quickly notched it, drew back the string and raised the bow, pointing it in the general direction of the swinging bags. He hesitated only briefly and loosed his arrow. It sailed harmlessly into the woods behind the swinging sacks.

Breunne reached up to snatch the blindfold off. "See?" he said, frustrated.

"Stop!" shouted Markwonne.

Breunne's hand stopped as the thumb hooked under the strip of rag covering his eyes.

"Try again," said the older man, his voice once again lowered.

Breunne's hand fell again to his side. "What?"

"I said try again," repeated Markwonne. "This time, use your senses!"

Frustrated, Breunne bowed his head. "This is stupid! I can't see!"

"Exactly!" said the older man calmly. "However, you are not looking!"

"Huh?" said Breunne. "Of course I'm not looking! You have my eyes blindfolded!"

"You are not listening, either," Markwonne said, his voice still calm. "Reach out with your other senses."

Breunne, still exasperated, snatched another arrow from his quiver. He quickly notched it and drew back the string. He took a deep breath and waited.

There! He could hear the bags swinging! He hesitated, trying to gauge location and then released the arrow.

This time there was a satisfying thud as the arrow struck the bag on the left!

Breunne quickly stripped of the blindfold and yelled, "Yes!" He held his bow high above his head in victory.

Markwonne looked at the arrow, barely snagged in the top of the bag, well clear of the circles.

"Again," he said, looking back at the boy. "This time try to hit the mark!"

"What?" cried the teen. "I hit the damn bag!"

"Yes," replied Markwonne, still calm. "But you missed the mark."

Breunne stared at the older man, aghast.

"Put the blindfold back on," said Markwonne, an edge to his voice this time, "and hit the mark!"

Breunne did not move, instead staring at the man as if he'd lost his senses.

"If you want to become my student," said Markwonne, "you will put the blindfold on and hit the mark!"

"Student?"

"Put the mask on," repeated Markwonne, his patience wearing thin.

Breunne continued staring at the man, not sure what to do. What if he missed? What if he hit the mark? Did he even want a master?

Slowly, deliberately he lifted his hands and replaced the blindfold.

Markwonne walked over and gave the bags another shove, starting them in motion once again.

He then turned and faced the teen. "Now," he said as Breunne reached for yet another arrow, "take a deep breath and reach out with every fiber of your being."

Breunne hesitated briefly, and then reached back into his quiver, dropping the first arrow his fingers grasped. They groped silently until he found what they sought—his most prized arrow. He never missed with this one. Now was not the time to start, he thought absently. He slowly withdrew the arrow, raising it and the bow at the same time. He took his time, slowly notching the arrow and bringing it back to his ear. Once there he paused and took in a deep breath and held it. And waited. Slowly he began to feel something. He felt the breeze soft on his left cheek. He smelled the burlap of the bag and the sharp tang of the stale hay. He heard the creak of the twine as it strained against the limb.

"Feel it!" insisted the older man, his voice barely audible over the noises of the forest.

Breunne released his breath as he loosed the arrow. Again there was a thud as the arrow hit home—but this time there was something else.

Slowly he reached up and slipped the rag off of his head.

Markwonne was grinning at him, his back now to the bags—both held in place by the one arrow! The feathers of the arrow pressed against the center of the circle of the outer bag, and stuck into one of the outer circles on the other.

"In time," said Markwonne, still grinning, "you will learn to hit the mark on both bags!"

Breunne drew in a breath to protest, but the older man began to laugh. After a brief delay the teen joined him.

Breunne had spent two years learning the craft of a ranger from Markwonne, and he returned to him from time to time for a refresher or to learn even more.

That had been almost ten years ago—a lifetime for some, a blink of an eye for others.

Savinhand. He had first met the rogue when Savinhand was still learning from the monks. And it could possibly be said that he himself had been somewhat responsible for his leaving the monastery in the first place. For it was he that had planted the seed that there was a vast world beyond the walls of that compound into the mind of the young lad.

Savinhand had been all too eager to hear tales from beyond those walls.

Between adventures, Breunne had taken to stopping by to relate tales to this young monk so eager to learn. And early on he could tell that the lad was destined for more than the monks could provide. Thus it came as no surprise when he swung by following one of those adventures that he was informed that Savinhand had chosen to leave the monastery. When Breunne had asked where the boy had gone, the old monk simply pointed west, shrugged and turned to go back inside the walls of his compound.

Breunne lost track of Savin for a time, only to run into him almost two years later in a tavern in the small farming community of Hargstead.

There he learned Savin had been inducted into Guild Shardmoor and had rapidly risen through their ranks as a rogue and locksmith.

Over the next few years, they adventured together and separately. Their friendship grew, and on occasion they called upon one another for assistance. It was on one such occasion that seemed just like those that had come before that Breunne had been summoned to Grandmere.

This time, however, had been different. Savinhand needed Breunne to deliver a message—to Thrinndor, Cyrillis, Vorgath and, of course, Sordaak.

He—Savinhand—was going to be late.

*

Late on the second day Sordaak and Breunne again gathered at the fire for the evening meal.

This time it was Breunne who was stirring a mixture of freshly killed venison in the pot with herbs and some roots he had dug.

Sordaak lounged on the far side of the cavern, absently reading through some scrolls when he said, "It's been two days…" He left the thought out there, hoping for a response.

"Yes," Breunne said, not looking up from the pot as he sprinkled more seasonings in from a small pouch he had pulled from his pack. He said nothing else.

The sorcerer rolled his eyes and said, "You said they should be no more than two days."

"It appears I may have been wrong," replied the ranger, still not looking up from his creation.

Sordaak looked up as he re-rolled the scroll he had been working on. He briefly considered pressing the issue further but instead shrugged and leaned back on his pack. "Smells good; like maybe something Savinhand would make."

"Thanks," replied Breunne. He continued stirring, and it was a few moments more before he looked up. "I taught him everything he knows." He smiled. "About cooking, anyway!"

"Heh," said the caster as he shifted his weight to the other elbow.

Breunne hesitated and then lifted an eyebrow. He detected more than a hint of worry in the caster's demeanor and that surprised him. "They'll be here soon enough."

"Sure," said the mage without looking up.

Breunne was not convinced.

Suddenly Sordaak sat bolt upright and appeared to stare at a point on the wall opposite him.

"What is it?" asked Breunne, suddenly concerned.

The caster held up a hand to preclude further questions. Instead he closed his eyes and appeared to concentrate. Without opening them, he said, "Someone approaches."

Breunne dropped his spoon and strode to the cavern wall where his gear was. He quickly grasped his quiver, bow and had his hand on the hilt of his sword when Sordaak opened his eyes and said, "It appears you were correct."

Breunne's eyes opened wide in surprise.

"They're here!" the mage said as he surged to his feet.

Just then Vorgath stepped around the bend in the entrance to the cave and said, "Miss us?" He stepped into the cavern, Cyrillis was right behind him.

"Where's Thrinndor?" asked Breunne. He removed his hand from the sword.

"Outside tending to the horses," replied Cyrillis. Her eyes went from Breunne to Sordaak. There they lingered.

The mage stood quickly when he saw her, his eyes on hers. "Good to see you again," he said, his cheeks tinged with red as he bowed at the waist slightly.

"Good to see you as well," she replied formally, a smile playing on her lips. She then quickly took the three or four steps necessary and threw her arms around him and hugged him tightly.

The mage's face colored even more, and he lifted his arms to awkwardly returned her embrace.

"Ahem," he said as he pulled back, his face now a bright crimson.

Thrinndor made his appearance as the two separated, his right eyebrow lifted slightly as he noted the exchange.

Breunne smiled as he watched the two separate. His expression turned to one of concern as his eyes fell upon the paladin.

"Where's Savinhand?" he asked, his eyes trying to penetrate the darkness behind the big man.

Thrinndor's expression immediately turned to concern, as well. "He did not show." His eyes locked with those of the ranger. "We even waited an extra day, figuring he might have been detained…"

"Damn!" exclaimed the ranger.

"We almost elected to send word to you two," said the paladin, "and head straight to Grandmere. But we figured we would probably require a full party should he require assistance."

"Damn!" repeated the ranger.

"We should leave immediately!" said Sordaak. He turned to pick up his pack.

"No," Breunne said, stopping him short. "Assuming he yet lives and requires our assistance, a night will not make that big a difference."

"That is what we ultimately decided, as well," agreed the paladin.

"But—" began the mage.

Breunne again stopped him, "It is a day-and-a-half hard ride to Grandmere from here," he said. "If we get an early start and ride until we run out of light tomorrow, we can make it by mid-morning the day after." He looked to the paladin for agreement

Sordaak hesitated and then allowed his shoulders to drop. "Very well," he said as he turned his attention back to the cleric. "You must be very tired." He turned to the paladin. "Get some rest. We will be in the saddle at first light."

Everyone was quiet for a while as the newcomers settled in for the night and got themselves something to eat.

Cyrillis came to sit by the caster, who was sitting next to the fire and staring into the coals.

She respected his mood for a time and was silent, content to stare at the coals as well. After a bit she decided to see if he would talk.

"How was it with Rheagamon?" she asked quietly.

The sorcerer turned to look at her, seemingly unaware until then that she was sitting next to him.

"What?" he asked, his reverie broken. "Oh…Rheagamon. Well, that is one smart old man!" He smiled as he continued. "I learned more from him in that five weeks than in two years with Quozak!" He spat the name of his former mentor.

"Really?" Cyrillis asked, her voice genuine.

"Yes," replied the caster. "I feared I would have to start over and thus be way behind in my studies, but the old man worked me so hard that I am more than three full ranks further along than I was previous!"

"Wow!" she exclaimed. "Three?" He nodded. "Did you learn any new spells?"

"Hell yes! I can't wait until I get to try them out in battle!" He grinned hugely now. "How about you?" He was enjoying her company more than he would like to admit.

"I picked up several new ones, as well," she said. "At least two that should come in handy: Neutralize Poison and Raise Dead!"

"Nice," agreed the caster. "That should come handy for our bumbling rogue!" Realizing immediately he had stepped over a line, he said "Dammit!" He looked over at Cyrillis to check her reaction. She was suddenly looking down at her hands, and Sordaak could see a tear trying to work its way free of an eye.

"I'm sorry," he said, wanting to reach out and put an arm around her shoulder but not daring to do so.

"No, it is all right." She turned her misty eyes up to meet those of the mage. "I know you did not mean harm and that you two are friends."

'Yes, yes," Sordaak stammered. "Friends."

After a few seconds of silence, Cyrillis stood. "I must go now and get some rest."

Sordaak stood quickly. "Me too." He spun on the ball of his foot and quickly strode to where his bedroll lay.

The healer stared after his receding figure, smiled and shook her head as she also went to where she had set up her things.

The group milled about briefly, but soon all were settled and knowing the day that was ahead of them, they slept.

Chapter Ten

Grandmere

The trip to Grandmere was relatively uneventful, and they made good time. Thus it was well before noon on the second day when they approached the town.

It had been decided the night before that only Sordaak would go into town, as he was presumably the only one not actively being sought by the Minions of Set. The encampment where Guild Shardmoor made their headquarters was less than five miles to the other side of the settlement known as Grandmere.

As Sordaak rode on alone, the others melded into the trees and set about the task of skirting a ridge, working hard to ensure none from town knew of their presence.

Sordaak now had two pack animals (one of them belonging to Thrinndor) trailing him—both with only empty sacks tied to their backs—a situation the mage planned to remedy at Grandmere's somewhat better than adequate shops.

As he made the rounds, ticking items off of the substantial list he had been given, he listened for any news concerning either the situation out at Shardmoor or any activity associated with the Minions.

As the last of the supplies were being loaded for him, he was sorely disappointed by the lack of any aforementioned news. None. Even his subtle questions and occasional rumor dropping resulted in nothing.

His last hope was the apothecary. He had several items on a personal list that he needed filled, and the spell component shops were generally a clearinghouse for information.

His past dealings here in Grandmere had always been beneficial in this regard, provided one was willing to barter for said information.

Although it had been two or three years since last he visited, he had no reason to believe now would be otherwise.

However, he was to be disappointed yet again.

No amount of poking, prodding or offers of coin gave him any more information than he had ridden into town with! In fact, by just his asking questions, several of the townspeople were considerably more knowledgeable from his having been there!

Shaking his head, he emerged from the apothecary and quickly gauged the time of day by checking the position of the sun. It was now well past noon and sneaking up on mid-afternoon. He was supposed to meet up with the others by late afternoon.

Quickly storing his precious components onto one of the animals, he made his way to the nearest tavern, conveniently located right next to the apothecary.

He entered the darkened inn, guessing correctly that its proximity to the apothecary would make it a hangout for those more inclined to his line of work: sorcery and possibly other forms of magiks as well.

As it was still relatively early, there were few patrons currently within. All but one looked up when the additional light from the brushed aside curtain spilled into the modest establishment

Sordaak was purposely not wearing his new robes (those given to him by Rheagamon) or his new hat (ditto). Instead, he was in somewhat of a disguise, wearing a light leather upper tunic that chaffed badly and leather leggings to match. He hoped he would not be recognized, but even if he were he had a story prepared: He was cross-training as a rogue.

That would explain any perceived interest in Guild Shardmoor, should any think to ask. As of yet none had.

He approached the bar and ordered a flagon of wine and then, deciding he didn't have time to work the five or six other patrons one at a time, he ordered a round for the house.

He circled the room, approaching first the group of three seated at a table and then moving on to the two others seated at the bar in short order. He avoided the direct approach, instead spinning his tale and listening for any news of interest.

After about an hour, he was a few silvers shorter in the pocket and knew nothing more than when he walked in. The replies to his subtle inquiries were almost always identical—the headquarters for the Guild had been very quiet of late. Too quiet, some said. But none knew anything as to why.

He dared not ask directly about any activities of the Minions, instead discussing gods and their disciples in a general fashion. Nothing there, either.

He looked around for the sixth person he had seen when he entered but quickly realized the man was no longer in the tavern. This alarmed him slightly because he had seen no one leave.

Curious, he thought. He was fairly certain there was one other here when he came in.

He made his exit, thanking those that remained inside for their attention, and was thanked in return for his generosity.

As his feet padded lightly on the boardwalk outside the inn he glanced about quickly, seeing if he could see anyone, or anything, that might not want to be seen.

Seeing no one, he stepped out of sight between buildings and summoned Fahlred.

Quickly he explained that he sought a man who may or may not have preceded him out of the inn, and for the familiar to remain out of sight as he searched for him. Look for anyone suspicious, he said.

His quasit nodded, indicating his understanding and winked back out of existence. Sordaak knew he was nearby, though. He could feel his presence.

The sorcerer again checked the position of the sun and decided he had time for one more such visit, but it needed to be shorter.

He quickly surveyed what was the main street of this sleepy little town and selected an establishment he figured might be somehow connected to the Guild.

After all, it was called Rogue's Roost.

Subtle, he thought as he again tied the reins of his animals to the rail out front and pushed his way into an interior only slightly more lit up than the previous one.

Slightly.

This establishment, however, was deserted save for the barkeep, who was polishing his glassware as Sordaak allowed the curtain to fall in place behind him.

Wait! There was another curtain behind the bar and to the left, and that curtain was settling back into place! Someone had just gone through that opening!

The mage silently sent his familiar to investigate, getting a silent acknowledgment from his Quasit.

Sordaak plastered a big smile on his face, approached the bar and ordered still another wine.

The barkeep looked up and smiled through crooked and broken teeth. "We're closed," he said simply and went back to polishing the glass he had been working on.

Suddenly nettled—and feeling the effects of the previous three flagons of wine he had already consumed—the mage replied, "Well then, now you're open!" He reached into a pocket on his vest and withdrew a single silver piece and slapped it loudly onto the top of the bar.

The barkeep started slightly at the sound exaggerated by the emptiness of the room. He eyed the coin briefly, obviously weighing something in his mind.

The barkeep shrugged and put the glass he had been polishing in front of Sordaak. He reached for a corked flask at his side, put the cork to his mouth and pulled it out with his teeth.

He sloshed some of the contents from the flask into the glass, spilling a considerable amount in the process. The bartender was about to put the cork back in—again with his teeth—when Sordaak said, "Since you are 'closed,'" he reached into the pocket and removed another silver and tossed it onto the bar, "pour yourself one, as well."

The barkeep hesitated as he watched the second coin roll to a stop near the first. He looked up and his eyes met those of the mage. He spat out the cork and said, "Don't mind if I do!" He again smiled his broken smile and added, "Since I'm closed." He then placed another glass on the bar and sloshed wine into it.

They both worked on their drinks in silence for a bit. Finally, the barkeep grunted and said, "You're not from around here are you?"

Sordaak looked up and into the eyes of this unkempt man, trying to decide just how much he should reveal. He shrugged and said, "No."

The barkeep took a swig of his drink and waited, certain there would be more. He was not disappointed.

Sordaak also put his wine to his lips, but he only sipped his. "As you can probably tell from my attire," he said, "I have been in training as a trap-smith and lock-pick," he lied. "I was told I could find Guild Shardmoor here in Grandmere," he went on, "and this seemed a likely establishment for information as to where I might find some information on them."

The smile left the barkeeps face and he looked about nervously. "You'll have to come back later," he said.

"Why?" asked Sordaak, knowing there was more to be had.

The man hesitated. "I ain't at liberty to say," he said stubbornly.

Sordaak lifted an eyebrow and again delved into his pocket. This time his fingers emerged with a gold coin. He flipped it onto the bar where it joined the other two.

"There'll be another if you tell me why," said the caster, measuring his words carefully.

The barkeep eyed the coin greedily, but still he hesitated.

"Look," said the mage, "I'm looking for a friend. A man who earlier this season started me down the path as a rogue. He promised a place in the Guild if I pass the entrance requirements." He took a deep breath. "He told me I was to meet him here in Grandmere before the weather turned cold." He waited. "And here I am."

The barkeep still said nothing, but Sordaak could tell his resolve was wavering. He decided it was all or nothing at this point. "I've been searching all over, but so far have seen no sign of Savinhand."

"Savinhand?" the man blurted out. "He's your contact?"

"Ummm....yes," replied the mage, certain now he was getting somewhere. He kept his manner benign. "Is that a problem?"

The man shook his head slowly. "Not for me it ain't," he said. "But fer you?" Again he hesitated. "That you'll have to find out on yer own!"

"What?" replied the caster. "What do you mean? Has something happened to my friend?"

The man crossed his arms on his chest and shook his head resolutely, indicating that was all he was going to say on the matter.

Sordaak rolled his eyes and his hand again moved to his pocket. This time however his fingers emerged with yet another silver-looking coin, but this one was smaller than the two previous versions.

The barkeeps eyes widened when they saw the coin. Although he had seen very few of them, he recognized a platinum piece when he saw one.

"Look," the bartenders said as he licked his lips in anticipation of getting his hands on the coin the caster was flippantly rolling around on his fingers, "you are not a member of Shardmoor—"

"Yet," interrupted the caster.

"Yet," agreed the barkeep. "There can't be no harm to givin' information to a soon-to-be member, can there?"

"Of course not," coerced the mage.

"Of course not," repeated the man, his eyes never leaving the coin in Sordaak's hand.

"Still," the barkeep said as he tore his eyes away from the coin to bore into those of the man across the bar from him, "If'n you are asked, you didn't hear any of this from me!"

"Of course not," repeated the sorcerer as he abruptly slapped the coin onto the bar and pushed it toward the barkeep.

The barkeep slowly reached for the coin, but his hand stopped just short. "They'll kill me if'n they find out," he said, his eyes still locked on those of the mage.

"I doubt that," said the caster in his best soothing tone. "You're too valuable to them."

"Yeah, well," the barkeep said, again licking his lips nervously. "You don't know them. I do!"

Sordaak decided he'd better say nothing more, instead crossing his arms on his chest, obviously waiting for more.

The barkeep looked around nervously, verifying again they were alone. "A little over a week ago," said the barkeep, "all guild members were recalled to Shardmoor." He lowered his voice until it was barely above a whisper. "I was told there was to be a contest of sorts. And that all guild members not actively adventurin' must be present."

"A contest for what?" asked the caster.

The barkeep merely shrugged his shoulders. "Dunno," he said. "But I figger it had somethin' to do with that Savinhand fella you mentioned."

"Why?"

"Dunno that, either," the man said. "'Cept his name kept coming up in various conversations." He winked. "If'n you know what I mean."

Sordaak didn't, but surmised this was not the time or place to admit as such. He nodded knowingly and returned the wink.

Instead, he again put his fingers in the coin pocket and moved them around so that the faint clinks could be heard through the material. "Anything else that might provide useful?" he asked, his eyes hopeful.

The barkeep again licked his lips; both eyes now fixated on the casters fingers deep within the pocket. "Not that I can think of," he said, regret plain in his voice.

"Where are they now?" Sordaak asked suddenly.

"Huh?" the man said, his eyes finally moving from the pocket to fix on those of the mage.

"Your place," Sordaak said, waving an arm around at the empty tables and chairs in the room. "Although it's only early afternoon, I would assume that this place is usually starting to fill up by this time of day…"

"Hmmm…?" the barkeep said, his eyes straying back to the pocket as the sound of coins again made itself heard. "Oh, yes, of course!" He then looked at the caster and lowered his voice. "Everyone was called back out to Shardmoor again today."

"Why?" asked the caster—even he was tired of saying that, but it was all he had.

"That I can't answer," said the barkeep. "Not because I don't want to, either. "I never heard no reason for this summons." His eyes went back to the pocket, then to those of the caster. "Ya gotta believe me!"

"Do I?" asked the caster, his head turned sideways, obviously trying to decide whether he should or not.

"Well," the man said as the coins yet again jingled in the pocket, "Less'n it had somethin' to do with them assassins…" His voice trailed off hopefully.

With considerable effort Sordaak reined in his emotions and asked blandly, "What about 'them assassins'?" His heart was suddenly pounding in his chest.

"Well," the man said as he leaned both elbows onto the bar so he could get closer, and therefore speak softer, which he did. "Them assassins have always had their own separate guild, and yet them and Shardmoor always worked together—kinda like a pact."

He again checked his surroundings. "But, late last week something happened." Sordaak had to lean closer to hear what the man was saying. "Several known to be assassins for Shardmoor were seen in town together," he said. "And when they left, they rode out together. They was headed away from Shardmoor!"

He allowed that to sink in before he went on. "That in and of itself ain't all that unusual," he said. "But rumor has it the assassins have been kicked out! Permanently!"

"What?" For some reason, the mage found he was whispering as well.

"Hey," said the barkeep as he stepped back. "You didn't hear it from me!"

Sordaak allowed that to digest for a few moments, then his eyes searched those of the man before him. "I still don't see what all this has to do with my friend Savin…" he said, his voice laden with hope.

"You don't get it, do you?" asked the barkeep.

"No," admitted the mage. "Get what?"

The barkeep raised his eyebrow and again crossed his arms on his chest, indicating he was through.

However, Sordaak knew what was required to get the lips moving again. Rolling his eyes, his hand went to the pocket and appeared to search around in there for the proper coin.

The barkeep pretended not to notice, but his eyes were not-to-surreptitiously watching every move of the mage's fingers.

After a show of searching, finally another platinum coin emerged. The barkeep was unable to contain himself and his hand shot out and snatched the coin from the caster. As an afterthought, he also raked the coins sitting on the counter off into a waiting hand. They quickly disappeared somewhere into the man's tunic.

The barkeep then leaned forward again resting his arms on the bar. He made a show of making sure they were still alone and said, "Rumor has it your friend Savinhand is now the leader of Shardmoor!"

"What?" cried an obviously incredulous mage. "Impossible! Savinhand? Are you sure?"

"Hell no I ain't sure!" snapped the barkeep. "But that's how the rumors go!"

"Really," Sordaak's tone was thoughtful. "But certainly his life is forfeit?"

"Well," agreed the barkeep, "it's said he bested the leader of the Assassin's guild to become the guild leader and that he has survived more than one attempt to send him to the afterlife, since!"

The barkeep paused for effect. "That's why he kicked the assassins out of the guild," he said. "Or so I hear."

Realizing what he had been saying, the man looked around quickly, suddenly terrified. "Now, get out!" He was almost shouting. "You didn't get any of this from me!" He pointed at the door. "I will deny I ever saw you, if asked!"

"See that you do," Sordaak said as he again reached into his pocket, withdrew another platinum coin and flipped it at the man.

"Huh?" said a confused barkeep, his eyes not leaving the coin as it spun toward him. He deftly snatched it out of the air and watched as the caster crossed the room toward the door.

"Forget you ever saw me," replied the sorcerer as he pushed the curtain aside and stepped onto the boardwalk.

He had to squint as he went from the dimly lit room to the bright afternoon sunlight. He blinked several times as he looked up and down what should have been the main street of this town.

No one. He saw no one! That was starting to bother him.

Quickly he snatched up the reins of his animals, leapt into the saddle and applied his heels none too gently to its flanks as he turned the animals head down the road and out of town.

Toward Shardmoor. He briefly thought about heading the other direction, but Sordaak figured—at a minimum—that the barkeep would keep tabs on him, and probably others as well. He had asked questions about the guild. Certainly it was expected he would go there.

So he did.

Though every window and every doorway he checked appeared empty, he could feel the eyes boring into his back. It might have been his overactive imagination, but he doubted it.

He recalled Fahlred as soon as he was clear of town, and his familiar informed him that the unseen man had preceded him down this path shortly after he had snuck out of that first tavern.

Interesting, Sordaak thought. Now Shardmoor was going to be alerted to his presence, as well.

*

Sordaak met up with the others of his party at the appointed place—well off of the main road and only a mile or so from Shardmoor.

"I'm probably being followed," announced the caster as he rode up to the group who were lounging in a dry camp. Some were lying in the shade out of the light of the sun. Still others were purposely lying in the light.

Sordaak was sure there were reasons for this, but he didn't have time to figure it out as both the ranger and the barbarian jumped up and melded into the brush, disappearing instantly.

"Was it something I said?" asked a semi-amused caster.

"Yes," replied Thrinndor. He was not amused.

"What did you find out?" blurted out Cyrillis.

"It appears our rogue friend yet lives," Sordaak said with a shrug.

"Interesting," said the paladin. "It would seem that our friend was—is—more than he led us to believe."

"So it would seem," agreed the mage as he dismounted amid a cloud of dust.

"What do you mean?" asked the cleric. It was obvious she was just happy he still lived. Yet these two acted as if they needed to know why.

"If Savinhand yet lives," began Thrinndor, "then he does so only after besting Shivluur in The Contest." His eyes went from Cyrillis to Sordaak. "And that would have been no easy feat!"

"Agreed," said the caster, meeting the eyes of the paladin.

"Why does that matter so?" asked Cyrillis.

"Because," replied Thrinndor, "the rogue that accompanied us and fought side by side each of us did not appear so skilled."

Sordaak nodded.

"However," admitted the big fighter, "I confess that I was too busy most of the time during the fighting to observe his skill set appropriately."

"Did anyone think to ask Savinhand how many he killed during our most recent adventure?" Sordaak asked thoughtfully.

Thrinndor's face twisted in a big grin. "No," he said. "Come to think of it, I do not think that came up!"

Unable to restrain himself, Vorgath came crashing back into the small glade where they had been resting. "We could probably work the math backwards from the critters we killed, minus those we knew to be in the opposing parties," said the dwarf, doubt clouding his voice.

"Or you could just ask him," said a voice that materialized at the caster's right elbow.

Sordaak almost leapt clear of his skin.

"I told you NOT to do that!" he said through clenched teeth, his heart pounding in his throat.

Savinhand just grinned and stuck out his right arm.

Sordaak glared at him for a few moments as his heart slowed a bit. Then he grinned hugely and grasped the proffered forearm in greeting.

Cyrillis moved closer, waiting for the two to release their clenched grip. When they did, she flung her arms around the rogue's neck and said "Where have you been?" It was meant to be a reproachful question, but in her exuberance she could not quite pull it off.

Savinhand's face briefly turned red and he was momentarily at a loss for words.

"Ummm..." he managed to stammer out. "They've been keeping me pretty busy."

Cyrillis stepped back and her eyes searched those of the rogue. "They?" she asked.

"Shardmoor," Savin replied. "My guild."

There was a silence among the group.

Finally, Thrinndor asked, "So it is true?"

Savinhand briefly considered dragging out the conversation, but he knew what the paladin meant and decided not to push his luck. "Yes," he said, his attention on the paladin. He knew what bothered Thrinndor.

"You can recall Vorgy and the ranger," he added. "Those are my men that were following Sordaak." He looked over at the caster. "I'll have to speak to them about being detected."

Thrinndor obediently called for the two to return.

Sordaak smiled. "Don't be too hard on them," he said. "I would have never known had not Fahlred warned me. Nothing can escape his attention when he is looking." His smile broadened. "And I had him looking."

"Ah, yes," replied the rogue. "I had forgotten about him. Duly noted."

Vorgath and Breunne stepped into the clearing. The ranger immediately stepped up to clasp arms with his friend.

"Vorgy?" the barbarian said.

Savinhand stepped around Breunne to confront the dwarf. "No slight intended, I assure you," he said.

Vorgath grinned. "None taken."

Savinhand returned the grin. "It's good to see you again, old friend," he said as he stuck out his right hand and clasped the forearm of the dwarf.

"It's good to be seen," replied the barbarian.

"So you were able to defeat Shivluur, then?" asked the ranger.

"Yes," answered Savinhand. "This surprises you?" He was teasing his long-time friend, and Breunne knew it.

"Hell yeah," the ranger said. "He was one bad-ass assassin." He was smiling from ear to ear. "And to hear these guys tell it, you are but a bumbling excuse for a thief."

"Rogue," corrected Sordaak. He also had a big smile on his face.

"How were you able to defeat him?" asked the ranger, his tone eager.

Savinhand hesitated and then shrugged his shoulders. "Shivluur relied too much on his poison skills," he said. "I was...prepared for him." He grinned. "His hand-to-hand skills were not as good as they should have been."

"Really?" said the ranger. "I'd like to hear all about it."

"Some other time, I'm afraid," said the rogue, his demeanor turning serious. "Right now we have other fish to fry."

"What about the Library?" asked the mage. "As Head Thief in Charge, you can get us in there, right?"

"Rogue," Savinhand corrected. He paused, searching for the right words. "And, no not exactly." He shifted his weight to his left foot uncomfortably.

"What do you mean?" asked the paladin.

"Yes," said Sordaak, "please explain." His arms were crossed and his brows knitted together as he waited for what he was sure was going to be unacceptable reasoning.

"Well," Savin began, "It's complicated." His eyes showed uncertainty. "And it's why I'm here."

"Make sense, please," said the caster.

"I'm trying!" snapped the rogue leader. "If you'll shut up, I'll explain it to you!"

Sordaak raised his eyebrows in astonishment. This was clearly a different Savinhand before him. Much more assertive.

Savinhand took in a deep breath. "Sorry," he said. "This leadership thing has taken me by surprise, and it is a big change for me."

The sorcerer merely nodded.

"The Library of Antiquity is indeed mine by right of ascension," Savin began. He took in another deep breath. "However, the previous master is supposed to guide his or her successor to it and show them how to get in." He again shifted his weight.

"You don't know where it is, do you?" asked the barbarian, a taint of humor in his voice.

"Oh," replied the rogue, "I know where it is."

"Then what's the problem?" asked the caster.

"The path to the Library will be heavily trapped," Savinhand began.

"Oh, no!" interrupted the dwarf. "Not again!"

Savinhand looked at him crossly. "However," he said, "that will not be the biggest problem. I have worked hard on my trap detection and disarming skills and I feel comfortable I'll be able to handle that part."

When Savinhand paused for what seemed an inordinate length of time, Sordaak prompted him again. "What then is the problem?"

"There are those within the guild—and some from without—that will try to prevent me from gaining access to the Library."

"But you are the Guild Leader, are you not?" said Cyrillis.

Savinhand looked at her. "Yes," he said, "but there are those on the council that only agreed to allow me to participate in the Contest because they were certain I would fail."

"What?" said the cleric.

"Shivluur was seen as the obvious choice by many to succeed Phinskyr," Savin said. "Either they were not aware of my background as a monk, or had dismissed it as irrelevant because they were merely amused when my name was put forward to challenge for the Rite of Ascension."

He again paused, trying to decide how much of this he needed to tell now and what could wait for when they had more time. "My first official duty as Leader was to disband the Assassin's sub-guild and ask them to leave."

"You what?" said an incredulous barbarian.

Breunne had known Savin was going to do this, and Sordaak had already heard the rumor. To Thrinndor it made sense. However, saying and accomplishing the task were certainly two different things.

"Some left willingly when asked," replied the rogue. "Others had to be convinced."

"I'll bet," said the dwarf.

"But even among the remaining council members," Savinhand continued, "there were those that supported Shivluur—and they have followers in the Guild."

"So you lead a guild divided," summarized the paladin.

"Yes," agreed the rogue. "However, in the last few days I have been able to win a few of those over with promises to return Shardmoor to prosperity."

"Nice," groused Vorgath.

"Yes," said the rogue, "well, the guild has been essentially without a leader for some time now."

"Huh?" said the dwarf.

Savin rubbed his chin in thought, unsure if he should reveal his next big surprise. Ultimately he shrugged and shifted his eyes to meet those of the cleric.

"It seems Phinskyr had been leading a second life," he said slowly. "One that kept him away from his duties at Shardmoor for extended periods of time." His eyes searched those of Cyrillis to see if she knew where he was going with this. It was apparent she did not.

"From one such trip he failed to return," he continued slowly. "It was only when I heard the name he went by before his joining Shardmoor and his ascension to power that I was able to make the connection."

He paused, uncertainty gripping him.

"What name would that be?" asked the cleric, her eyes not leaving those of the rogue.

"Ytharra."

Chapter Eleven

Savinhand

"Who?" replied Vorgath.

"Ytharra—the man who helped raise and train Cyrillis?" Sordaak asked.

Savinhand ignored them. Instead, his attention remained on the cleric. And thus he was in position to catch her as she took a step back and stumbled.

Thrinndor, who had figured out where this had been going moments before the rogue made his revelation, had also moved to help her if needed.

He was. Savinhand and the paladin each caught an arm and kept her from falling. Her staff slipped to the ground with a thud.

"Easy," Thrinndor said as she regained her balance and gently shook off the hands supporting her.

"You are certain of this?" she asked, her eyes searching those of the rogue.

"Yes," Savin said, nodding. "I did some research into the matter once I learned his name. I found out he was old—very old. He had taken control of the guild more than a hundred years ago, a fact few seem to have noticed."

"But," Sordaak broke into the conversation, "why would one of the Guardians of Valdaar want to lead a bunch of thieves and assassins?"

The rogue turned to look at his friend. "That question I have been trying to answer since I discovered this. While I don't have an answer, I do have a couple of theories." He turned his attention back to Cyrillis. "First of all, as leader of the predominant rogue's guild in the land he would have access to a vast information-gathering network, also one of the best in the land. I think he used this network to track those of the lineages required to return his god to power." Savinhand's eyes searched those of the healer. "I think that is how he found you."

"But," she said, "we—Jacinth and I—found him."

"Did you?" asked the rogue. "Jacinth, who I also believe to be a Guardian, was probably summoned by Ytharra upon the death of your parents."

"But," Cyrillis said, "If he was a Guardian, why did he not just tell me of my heritage? Certainly he knew."

"I'm certain he did," agreed the rogue. "However, he must have felt he needed to protect you."

"Protect me from what? From who?" asked the cleric. "I can see that while I was but a child…" Tears came to her eyes as she recalled the end. "…but before he died, surely he should have told me!"

"He did," said the paladin as he put his hand on her shoulder to reassure her.

"He most certainly did not!" she replied forcefully.

"Remember what he told you at the last," Thrinndor said. Cyrillis looked confused. "He told you to 'find from whence it came.'"

"What?" she said. Then realization came, and her eyes opened wide. "Find from whence it came!" she repeated. "The staff. Dragma's Keep." Her eyes searched the paladin's. "Find you." She turned to the caster. "Find Sordaak." Her voice was laden with wonder.

"Right," said the rogue.

"Second," asked the caster. His eyes had never left Savinhand.

"What?" asked the rogue.

"You said you had a couple of theories," replied the caster. "That was the first. What is the second?"

"Ah yes," said the rogue. "Second, I believe that Phinskyr wanted access to the Library of Antiquity."

"Damn," said the caster. "It does all seem to make sense."

"Back to the Library," said the dwarf. All eyes turned to him, but no one said anything. He rolled his eyes. "What, other than a few dissident thieves and some easy traps—"

"I never said easy," interrupted Savinhand.

"—is keeping us from this pile of dusty books?"

Savinhand took in a deep breath and let it out slowly. Now all attention was back on him. He was beginning to get used to this. "A couple of things—three actually. First, I don't know the Libraries exact location," Savinhand said.

"But you said—" interrupted the dwarf.

"I know what I said," cut in the rogue. "I do know where the entrance is." He paused, trying to formulate the words so they'd understand. "But the Library is not necessarily there."

"What?" asked the barbarian. "Make some sense man!"

"If you would shut up," Savinhand said, "I will explain!" He stared down the dwarf, who shrugged and folded his arms.

"Go on," Vorgath said, glowering at the rogue from under his bushy eyebrows.

"Very well," said the rogue. "As I said, I know where the entrance is, but once inside there are multiple options. Selecting the wrong course may seal the Library forever."

"A puzzle," said the caster. "Great!" His demeanor indicated that he remembered all too well his last encounter with a puzzle. That one didn't go so well.

"Yes," answered Savinhand. "But with a twist." Sordaak lifted an eyebrow. "Get this one wrong and the Library could be lost forever." The rogue's eyes bored into those of the caster. "No second chances."

"Great," said the sorcerer. "I presume you have some information to help select the correct path?"

"Yes," replied the thief. "However, it too is a riddle."

"Sweet!" Sordaak said, rolling his eyes. "We'll have to study that when the time comes."

"Yes," repeated Savinhand. "I will certainly welcome other eyes and minds." The leader of the rogues took a deep breath. "Second, the chamber is warded."

When he did not immediately continue, Sordaak said, "How so?"

Savinhand had been looking at the toes of his leather boots. He looked up and into the eyes of the caster. "The entrance is password-protected."

"Password?" Thrinndor asked.

"Yes," replied the rogue. "The problem is Phinskyr took the password with him to the afterlife." He paused for effect. "The outgoing guild leader is supposed to pass along the password, or at least where it can be found, but Phinskyr died before he had the chance."

"Perhaps," said the paladin thoughtfully.

"Huh?" asked the rogue.

"Ytharra would not have taken that password to the afterlife if something in the Library is needed by us," said the paladin.

"So," began the rogue, "you're saying we don't need to get into the Library?" He sounded almost relieved.

"No," Thrinndor said. "I am saying that he would have given the password to someone." He turned to look at Cyrillis.

"What? No." She shook her head. "There was never any mention of a password. Or even the Library, for that matter." However, all those books he had brought her—she had to admit that Ytharra indeed must have had access to this Library. Yet...a password? Not that she could remember.

"Perhaps he may have been subtle," the paladin said. He knew better than to press the issue, however. "That is something we can revisit at a later time as well, I think."

Thrinndor turned his attention back to Savinhand. "It is too late for us to get started this evening," he said as he checked the position of the sun on the horizon. No more than a couple of hours of light left.

"Third?"

All eyes turned to see Sordaak standing with his arms folded on his chest. His eyes remained on the rogue who was again studying something at his feet.

"Third," answered the rogue, not looking up from his feet, "the library is guarded."

"Of course," the barbarian said, also turning his attention to the rogue. "But surely the guards will allow the new guild leader inside?"

"It's not guarded by guild members," said the rogue, his voice ominous.

"Who then?" asked Breunne, joining the conversation at last.

"Not necessarily a 'who,'" said the rogue, his voice barely audible. "It is not known exactly what—or who—will be guarding the library."

Savinhand smiled for the first time in several minutes. "The keys to the Library of Antiquity are not simply handed over to any that survive the Rite of Ascension. Rather, the survivor must defeat the traps, solve the riddle of the entrance, give the password and defeat this final guard.

"Then each new curator of the Library must capture, raise and train a new guardian to replace the one they slew when they gained access for the first time."

"So," intoned Sordaak, "we don't have any idea what this final test will be?"

"No," said Savinhand with a shake of his head.

"A dragon," said Cyrillis, her voice barely above a whisper.

"What?" came several voices at once.

"A dragon," she repeated, louder this time, more sure of herself.

Again everyone spoke at once. After a bit of that, Savinhand, who was staring curiously at the cleric, held up his hands until one by one the voices died out. "What makes you think Phinskyr trained a dragon?"

Cyrillis took in a deep breath and returned his stare. "He was fascinated with them." When Sordaak took in a deep breath to protest, she held up her hands. "Not only that," she added, her gaze still on the rogue, "he mentioned on a number of occasions that dragons could be trained—"

"Bullshit!" snorted the dwarf.

Cyrillis' penetrating stare pinned the barbarian to the tree he was standing beside.

"I mean no disrespect to you or your dead mentor," Vorgath said by way of apology, "but dragons are mean, nasty creatures that only concern themselves with loot and plunder!"

"Have you met one?" replied the cleric coolly.

"No," the dwarf muttered, suddenly finding something at his feet that drew is interest. He quickly looked back up. "But that don't mean I haven't studied them!"

"I am sure it does not," the healer said, her voice frigid. "However, dragons are intelligent creatures that are deeply misunderstood."

"Bah!" snorted the dwarf. "Have you met one?"

Clearly Cyrillis had been anticipating the question. "Yes," she said. "As a matter-of-fact I have!"

"What?" came several replies, again at once.

"Ytharra—Phinskyr—once brought one to our place in the hills and introduced me to her."

"Her?" asked the barbarian.

"Yes," she replied haughtily. "You have a problem with that?"

"Hell no," answered the barbarian. "As long as you don't have a problem with me killing her!"

Cyrillis took in a sharp breath for a nasty comeback, but Savinhand spoke first. "I'm afraid we will have no choice in the matter," he said.

The healer's expression went from anger to worry to fear in the span of a couple of heartbeats. Her face took on a pained expression. "No!" she moaned.

The rogue nodded his head, not wanting to say what was next. "With the death of her master, the only way to release the dragon from her geas will be by her death." His tone showed the sorrow she felt. "That's the way the guardianship works. And this is not the first time the guardian has been a dragon."

"Lucky us," muttered Breunne.

"Damn straight!" said the barbarian forcefully, his greataxe Flinthgoor clutched in one ham-like fist. "I finally get to bag my dragon!"

"You might want to rethink that before this is through," replied a thoughtful Savinhand.

"What?" said the barbarian. "Why?"

"Phinskyr had more than a hundred years to train this particular dragon," Savinhand answered.

"Whatever," said the dwarf. "You'd better figure out what you are going to train as her replacement, because this one is as good as dead!" He raised his greataxe above his head and shook it for emphasis.

"What a blowhard!" said the paladin, trying to relieve the tension that had suddenly taken hold on the gathering. "If you were only half as good as you talk, you would be well on your way to being a god!"

"Who says I'm not?" snapped the barbarian. He also was grinning hugely—however, his was for a different reason. For the past hundred years he had been searching for a dragon. They had become so scarce in the land that they were seldom seen.

Thrinndor turned back to the healer and his tone softened. "What kind of dragon?" he asked.

"What?" she asked. Her mind was not in the conversation.

"Color," the paladin plied gently. "What color are the dragon's scales?"

"Green, I think," she answered hesitantly. "It was a very long time ago. I was but a young girl then."

"Green," said the ranger. "Acid, right?" he asked no one in particular.

"Breath weapon would be a poison gas," corrected the paladin.

"Great!" said the ranger sarcastically.

Thrinndor turned back to the healer. "You are sure of this?" he asked, his tone gentle.

"Green?" she asked. "Well—"

"No," interrupted the paladin, "that the guardian will be a dragon."

Cyrillis shook her head slowly. "Not sure at all. It just fits with what has been said here and with Ytharra's fascination with dragons." She looked at the paladin with something akin to hope in her eyes. "It was so long ago. I could be mistaken…"

"Perhaps so," said the paladin. "But we must be prepared as such in the event you are not." His voice trailed off.

"Yes…yes, of course," Cyrillis replied.

"Look," said the rogue in his best soothing voice, "if it is this dragon you met, she may not remember you." The healer gave him a hurt look. "That was not really what I wanted to say," he said quickly. "She has been enchanted to stop whoever tries to enter the Library other than her master. Even if she remembers you, her geas will require her to….stop you."

"Are we certain we must enter the Library?" the cleric asked suddenly.

Everyone was taken aback by the question.

Savinhand finally recovered enough to speak. "Well," he said, "it is certain that I must." He looked to the paladin for support. "I am now the curator."

"And he is a member of our party," said the paladin gently but firmly. "He requires our aid to see this through."

Cyrillis' shoulders slumped. "Very well," she said quietly. "I must hope that I am wrong and there is no dragon."

"Well," said the dwarf loudly, "I for one hope there is one!" He again brandished his axe in a menacing manner.

Thrinndor threw the dwarf a withering stare. Vorgath glared back but said nothing more.

"But," said the cleric softly, "she let me ride her."

"What?" said the others in the party.

Cyrillis looked up defiantly. "You heard me! She let me ride her!" Her eyes took on a faraway look. "It was glorious!"

A stunned silence fell over the group.

Finally Breunne found his voice. "It has been many a year since a dragon has permitted man to ride." His tone held reverence.

"Be that as it may," said a resolute Cyrillis. "She took me high above the mountains—above the clouds, even." She paused as her mind struggled with returning to the party. "The perspective from up there was amazing!" she said, her eyes misting over.

Silence again fell over the glade.

Vorgath cleared his throat and moved over to stand next to Thrinndor. "Ummm," he said as quietly as he could and yet still be heard by the paladin, "do we have a problem here?"

Before Thrinndor could reply, Cyrillis spun and fixed him with her eyes ablaze. "No! We do not have a problem here! My first allegiance is to Valdaar.

My second is to this party!" Her chest was heaving with the effort of controlling herself. "If we are required to fight and kill this dragon," she went on, her voice lower, but the implied threat behind it no less, "you can count on me to do my utmost to keep your body and soul as one, barbarian." She backed up a step and stood to her full height. "That is assuming you have a soul!"

She spat the word barbarian as if it were bile in her mouth. Cyrillis spun on her heel and left the clearing in a rush, her back ramrod straight.

"Was it something I said?" asked the dwarf, his tone indicating he was not really concerned one way or the other.

"One day," replied the paladin, staring where the cleric had disappeared into the trees, "your lack of tact will get you into trouble."

"Barbarians need no tact," Vorgath snorted.

"With allies," Thrinndor said as he turned his attention to his old friend, "tact can be a useful tool."

"Bah," said the dwarf. However, he sounded less convinced, even to himself.

In the uncomfortable silence that followed the group began preparing the evening meal. Sordaak had purchased in town many supplies, and Breunne had killed a small deer earlier that would provide fresh meat for a couple of days at least.

As they milled about, Thrinndor caught the rogue's attention. "Tell us about the Rite of Ascension," he said.

"And how you found out about Ytharra," added the caster.

Savinhand looked from one to the other. "Very well. I suppose I can take the time for that." He looked at the sun which had just about disappeared behind the rise. It would be dark soon. "My people were expecting me to return this evening." He tried to figure out how important that was.

"Your people," said the barbarian. "How easily you slip into that role."

"However," continued the rogue, ignoring the jibe, "I doubt they'll send in a rescue party should I not show up for evening meal." He grinned at the paladin.

Savinhand walked over to a small cask set on a rock well away from the fire and poured himself a cup of wine. The others similarly got themselves something to drink—Vorgath and Thrinndor an ale, Breunne and Sordaak a wine.

As they settled in, Cyrillis walked back into the clearing, her back still ramrod straight. She walked to her pack and withdrew her cup.

Knowing all eyes were on her, she made a show of ignoring the dwarf, filled her cup to the brim with wine and marched over to sit across from Savinhand and next to Sordaak.

She took a sip of her wine and then raised her eyes to meet those of the rogue leader. "Please continue."

"Very well," replied the thief. "If all are ready?"

When he had obtained a nod from each, Savinhand cleared his throat and his eyes took on a faraway look as the memories came flooding back to him.

Had it really only been a month? So much had happened. It seemed a lifetime ago when he had ridden from the camp following the looting of Dragma's Keep.

"I made the trip to Grandmere without incident," he began, "and in good time." He smiled at the barbarian. "I was anxious to begin work on certain skills.

"Upon arrival at Shardmoor HQ, I was informed that a movement was afoot to choose a successor to Phinskyr." His tone took on a sing-song tenor. "He had been absent this time for going on two years—by far the longest he had ever stayed away." His eyes strayed to Cyrillis. "He had taken to long absences for the past ten, fifteen years—we now know where he had been going." He smiled. "He had explained he had been taking extended pilgrimages in preparation to name his successor, so he was left to his own accord.

Then the rogue leader scowled. "It was during these recent absences that a group of assassins led by Shivluur weaseled their way into Shardmoor and worked their way into ever increasing positions of power.

"It was commonly known—but never said out loud—that Phinskyr would have never allowed such an alliance. It was also widely believed that Shivluur had had something to do with the guild leader's demise—assuming, of course, he was no longer among the living.

"This is how it's done, of course. Kill, or otherwise arrange for the death of, the guild leader so that a Contest will then be called." He paused while he considered. "But I'm getting ahead of myself." He looked at the paladin. "Like I said, I noticed a lot of talk about convening a council to call for a Contest, but to date it had only been talk.

"That all changed one day while I was working with the guild trapsmith trainer. The old-timer said his father told him of the day when Ytharra had come to the guild—and he had not been young, even then.

"I stopped him and asked him if he was certain of the name. The old-timer had replied, 'Absolutely'. The old man wanted to know how I knew the name." Savinhand paused for a moment. "So I told him I had heard Ytharra had died.

"The old man did not ask how or even when. Rather, he immediately took me to the acting leader—Phinskyr's second—and bade me to tell the story." Savinhand looked purposefully at the paladin at this point. "Ever mindful of your request, and my geas, I told him only what I knew, and I was sketchy about that. I merely told them that I knew of an old man who had gone by that name that had recently passed into the afterlife while serving as a mentor to a young girl." He smiled. "They merely assumed he had been working to train his replacement and had asked nothing further of me."

Savinhand's eyes drifted to the cleric. "Apparently they were more than content just to have some sort of verification of his death so they could push forward with their plans to call for a Contest."

His eyes went back to the paladin. "Which they immediately did. Then they sent word for all available guild members to return to Shardmoor to select their champions.

"As you may have heard, the Rite of Ascension—also known as The Contest—is how the Guild Leader of Shardmoor is selected.

"The four factions, one controlled by the sub-guild of assassins until recently, each submit a name to represent them in The Contest." He paused to smile. "Dice are used to determine who fights who in the first round—but those die are rigged, of course. Would you expect anything less from a group of thieves, rogues and assassins?"

He didn't wait for a reply. "Of course not!" he said, his smile broadening. "But again I get ahead of myself." He cleared his throat before progressing. "Shivluur's name was submitted by the assassins, as was another assassin's name who Shivluur wanted out of the way—Scrailogg. The third name submitted was Uriahlt, a legitimate, so to speak, candidate from Phinskyr's own faction who had been trained by the master himself.

He took a sip from his wine. "This is where things get a bit crazy. As it turns out, the old trapsmith I had been working with, and have known since I became guilded, is the leader of the fourth faction." He put his cup to his lips and took a long pull at the wine this time. "He—much to my surprise—submitted my name."

Another pull at the cup. "He refused my questions as to why, instead working to focus my efforts on surviving."

His next drink emptied his cup. Savinhand paused as he stood, walked over to the cask and refilled his cup. He made his way back to the rock he had been using as a seat and looked down at it. He rubbed his butt with his free hand and instead chose to remain standing. "Afterward he explained it like this: Shivluur was certain to meet Scrailogg on the first round and just as assured to best him. As I was an unknown, he wanted me pitted against Uriahlt—a match he intended to have scouted to determine a weakness he could exploit. Regardless, the old trapsmith had said, Shivluur had quietly arranged for some assistance with whoever he was to face in the final battle. The old man had smiled at me and continued. 'However,' he said, 'when one knows what is coming, one can prepare for how to deal with it.'

"Still I pressed him with 'why me?' The old man's face turned serious and he said, 'I've seen you in action, son, and I know from whence you came.' By that I assume he knew of my training with the monks. 'You can best them,' he said, 'any of them—with some proper preparation.' He had smiled again, and refused to say more."

Savin took a small sip from his cup, deciding that a headache in the morning wasn't worth it. "Contestants selected, the Rite was scheduled for a week later. So I asked Breunne to find you and let you know I would be late." He smiled. "But first he worked with me in hand-to-hand and informed me what weaknesses he knew about concerning my coming opponents.

"Ever true to our guild creed, 'If you're not cheating, you're not trying,' there was a lot of background stuff going on. Side bets. Offers to throw the match. Offers to buy me out and leave the guild forever." He took another sip from his cup. "And at least two attempts on my life—but we had been ready for those.

"When finally the day arrived, Shardmoor home ground was packed with guild members. Our small arena was filled to capacity, and then some.

"First up were Shivluur and Scrailogg. That was not a match. Shivluur arranged for a distraction and pierced the heart of the other assassin in less time than it takes to blink.

"My match with Uriahlt went considerably longer. But, obviously, I prevailed." He smiled. "Uriahlt was certainly adept with a variety of weapons, yet he was not prepared for my ability to wield short sword and kukri simultaneously. Although we were both bloodied during the match, he never harmed me seriously.

"When my eyes met those of Shivluur, his were wide in surprise. Clearly he hadn't expected me to advance." Again Savin smiled and took a sip of his wine. "Shivluur called for an immediate commencement of the final battle, knowing I was weakened by loss of blood. He was denied." He raised the cup to his lips, but changed his mind. "The final Contest was scheduled for the next day.

"The old man washed and dressed my wounds and he gave me some potions to return my strength."

He now had their undivided attention. "When the final battle approached, the old man took me aside and placed a pendant around my neck." He reached down under his leather tunic are pulled out a small, gem-encrusted gold medallion held in place with a metal chain. "He said that it would protect me from most blade-borne diseases.

"And then he had me drink a potion, saying it would protect me from most known poisons." Savinhand paused as he reflected. "Finally, he bade me to trust my senses and my skills.

"The last thing he told me was to ignore the darts—they were merely a nuisance and there to distract me. He told me to hurry, as the potion had a limited time span that it would protect me. When I asked him how limited, he had just shrugged and smiled.

"So I stepped into the arena and made ready to do battle." This time he took a drink of the wine before continuing. "Shivluur charged immediately, clearly a change in tactics from his last bout designed to confuse me.

"I fended off that flurry easily and felt the sting of at least two darts in the process. Silently I hoped the potion would work against whatever was on the tips, but had no time to worry as Shivluur again charged. He sensed my hesitation as assurance the poison was working.

"Again I fended off his attack, but one of his blades drew a line of blood across my forearm. Shivluur grinned a knowing, evil grin then, assuming I would be dead in seconds.

"I stepped back, shook my head and dropped to one knee. With a yell claiming victory, Shivluur charged in with his guard dropped, intent on the kill.

"At the last second I surged to my feet and swung my shortsword in an arc that connected with the neck of a very surprised assassin."

Savinhand again took a pull from his wine—what the hell, he thought, and made it a long one. He wiped the back of his hand across his mouth. "The wide-eyed surprised look was still on his face when his headless body fell in the dirt!"

He grinned at the stunned looks he got from the faces across the fire and withdrew his shortsword from his belt. "Thank Valdaar for providing me this vorpal sword!" He held the blade high above his head, pressed his cup to his lips and emptied it.

Chapter Twelve

Shardmoor

Thrinndor stood, crossed his right arm on his chest and bowed, his arms extended in salute.

Vorgath hesitated, and then he too stood and thumped his chest in salute.

Breunne also stood, but instead of saluting, he stepped to his friend and stuck out his right hand. Savinhand grasped his forearm, and the ranger yanked hard, pulling the rogue toward him as he flung his arms around his friend in a tight embrace. "I feared for you," the ranger admitted as he pushed away. "Oh, I always believed you could hold your own against any of those three, yet their treachery knows no bounds!"

"I'm glad you didn't give me that shot of 'confidence' before you left!" Savinhand grinned so as not to offend.

A hand reached up and tapped the ranger on his shoulder. He turned and then stepped aside. Cyrillis stepped in and threw her arms around the rogue's neck. She clung tightly to him for a moment and then stepped back. She looked deep into Savinhand's eyes. "I am certainly glad you yet live," she said, her face stern. "However, you are an idiot!" She spun on her toes and marched off into the trees, her back again ramrod straight.

"What?" the rogue leader said, his voice plaintive. He turned to the paladin and said, "Did I do something wrong?"

Thrinndor shrugged in response. "I think she does not approve of your fight for leadership."

"I agree with her." All eyes shifted to Sordaak as he stood and faced the rogue. "That most certainly did not show your brighter side." The mage went on, smiling. "However, if our quest is ultimately successful, history will quite possibly smile favorably on the results!"

"Hear, hear!" toasted the paladin as he raised his cup.

Sordaak, Breunne and Vorgath all followed suit.

"Whatever!" said the barbarian after he had quaffed his remaining drink. "I agree with the young lady. You're still an idiot!" He then stomped over and refilled his cup from the cask.

They all got a good laugh out of that.

When the laughing stopped, Savinhand wiped the mirth from his eyes. "So tell me. Other than aggravating the entire Set nation, what have all of you been up to?"

*

They had talked deep into the night, Cyrillis returning to the campfire sometime later with wet hair and carrying her armor. As the sun was just barely making its presence known over the distant mountains, Savinhand stood by the fire, slicing bacon into the pan. "Coffee on?" Startled, he turned to see the cleric approaching the fire to his right.

"Yes," he replied. "Of course." He carefully picked up the pot, trying not to disturb the grounds, then poured the steaming black fluid into the cup in her outstretched hands.

As she put the cup to her lips, Savin warned her, "Careful, that's hot!"

She eyed him over the rim as she gently blew into the cup to cool it. The look said, Are you kidding me? The lips said nothing.

"Sorry," he said. "Reflex."

"I know," she said. Then she smiled.

He had not realized he had tensed up until he felt his shoulders relax. He sighed in relief.

There was silence while he turned the meat.

"I am sorry for my actions last eve," she said finally.

"Think nothing—"

"Allow me to finish, please," she said gently.

Savinhand closed his mouth and nodded.

"Thank you," Cyrillis said. "Allow me to explain." She took a deep breath. "All my life I have watched those I care about most die," she said as she stared at the coals. She waved an arm in the direction of where the others slept. "You guys are my only family—all I have left." She was silent for a moment. "I do not want to lose any more."

Savinhand opened his mouth to speak but thought better of it.

"Please know that I am eternally grateful for what you have done for our cause," she continued. "However, had you been killed in your efforts to gain control of the Library..." She turned to look into the eyes of the rogue, a tear trailing down her cheek. "I do not believe I could have suffered that."

Savinhand put down the fork he had been using and reached up with his hand and brushed away the tear. He then wrapped both arms around her shoulders as she began to sob. He held her that way until her shoulders stopped shaking, and then he pushed her away and held her at arm's length while he looked into her eyes. "I had no choice," he began. When she made to protest, he put his finger on her lips. "To refuse the Rite would have meant my certain death." His eyes held hers. "However, even if allowed to walk away, I couldn't have. The Library of Antiquity is too important to your mission. Our mission!" He took in a deep breath. "It was you—and Thrinndor—that saw me through the Rite." His eyes beseeched her to understand. "I knew I must not fail you!"

"But," she said, "we are not certain of the Library will aid our cause!" She shook her head to emphasize her point.

"I considered that," he said. "But, if not the Library, then what's next? There is no other option at this point!"

She hesitated for a moment, and then her shoulders slumped as she nodded. "You are right, of course" she said.

He lifted her chin with a finger and smiled at her.

His smile turned to a frown and his tone got serious when he saw the scar on her lovely neck. "You were closer to the afterlife than I," he admonished. "And that would have ended your mission before it really began." He paused while he searched her eyes. "And broken my heart."

"Ahem," Thrinndor cleared his throat as he approached the fire. "Any of that coffee left?"

Savinhand dropped his hand to his side curious as to the paladin's timing. "Plenty," he replied, his voice tinged with regret as he reluctantly shifted his attention away from the cleric's powder blue eyes to those of the big fighter.

He noticed for the first time that their color was identical.

One-by-one the others meandered up to the fire, most with their hands extended to warm them. There was a definite chill to the air this morning. Winter was not far off.

Savinhand served up plates of eggs, pans of bacon, and more than a dozen of his pan-fried biscuits. Not to mention three pots of coffee—a sure sign that the night before had indeed gone long.

By the time everyone had eaten, cleaned up and readied the mounts and pack animals, the sun had been up for two hours and the chill from the previous night but a memory.

Silently they started their animals on the trail that lead to Shardmoor.

As they topped the rise that overlooked a deep, green valley that held the sprawling complex known as Shardmoor—in reality a small town—Thrinndor reined in his mount and waited for the others to catch up and gather around. "What is our plan?" he said, speaking to the rogue, who also stopped his mount.

"Well," Savinhand replied as he pushed back his hat to let the sun shine into his eyes, "I don't have much of a plan." He grinned at the paladin. "I'm supposed to present the group I'll be taking with me to complete my assault on the Library to the council."

"Present?" asked the barbarian. "Aren't you the leader of this group of scum?"

"Hey!" Savinhand feigned hurt feelings. "Those are my scum you're talking about!" When the barbarian grinned back he continued, "Yes, however I am not permitted to pull resources from the guild itself for the assault." His eyes drifted down to the compound below. "Rather it is my 'final test' to prove that I have sufficient support from outside the guild to lead it properly. Or some such nonsense!"

"Whatever!" groused the dwarf.

"So I will go on into the compound," the rogue leader said, "and announce I have formed my alliance." He shifted his eyes so that he was able encompass each of them with his gaze. "I will then send for you when they are ready to... meet you." He looked at the paladin. "It won't take long."

Savinhand paused for a moment. "I want to thank each of you for your support in this matter," he began.

"Support?" Vorgath laughed. "I'm here for the loot! And maybe to send some worthy opponents to meet whatever god they serve in the afterlife!" His grin grew broader. "So tell me now, if'n there ain't no loot, then I have someplace else to be!"

"Dragon?" reminded the paladin.

"Oh, yeah!" said the barbarian. "I forgot about that!" He slapped the handle of his greataxe. "Sign me up for whatever support you require!"

"Whatever!" returned the rogue leader with a grin.

"Does your guild have a Crier?" Sordaak asked suddenly as Savinhand turned his horse to go.

"What?" asked the confused thief. "Crier?"

"Yes," replied the mage patiently. "I have an idea."

"What sort of idea?" Savin asked suspiciously. "And no, we don't have a crier."

"How about a bard?"

"That we have. More than one, even."

"Could you send one up here while we wait, please?"

Savinhand eyed the sorcerer with one brow raised in question. He didn't move his horse.

Sordaak exaggerated rolling his eyes. "If we are going to be presented before this council, we might as well be formally announced." His face split into a big smile.

"I'm not sure I like the sound of that," replied the rogue. "However, I'll play along. You'll have your bard."

"Send your best," said the caster, smugly. When Savinhand just sat there, he added, "You can run along, now." He waved his arm in the direction of the compound.

Thrinndor, also wary of what the mage had in mind, dismounted as the rogue leader rode away shaking his head.

The group was silent as its members went about preparing a noon meal.

The paladin wanted to ask Sordaak what he had going on inside that head of his but decided he would find out soon enough.

The bard had shown up right after lunch. He announced that they would be summoned shortly before the evening meal and that they would all be invited to stay—assuming they were found to be acceptable.

Sordaak and the bard walked off a short distance, deep in conversation. The bard was nodding, smiling and making an occasional notation on a parchment he was preparing.

Thrinndor was not sure this was going to be good.

*

They were standing in what must have been considered an antechamber but in reality was not much more than an ill-kempt side room lined with shelves that were scattered with various books, scrolls and other various documents in no detectable form of organization.

They had indeed been summoned as expected in the late afternoon. After arriving, Sordaak told them to listen for their name to be called and to enter the adjacent chamber in a combat mode, swinging their favorite weapon as if their lives depended on defeating whatever imaginary quarry they could dream up.

Because their lives just might…

The main chamber was much larger than expected, with a long table on one end at which five large, matching chairs lined up. The centermost of the chairs was empty. In the others were seated, presumably, the four members of the council.

Along the other three sides of the chamber was bleacher-like seating, filled to capacity. Sordaak estimated close to a thousand rogues, scoundrels and other low-life waited in the room. He hadn't realized there were that many rogues in all the land!

Savinhand went first before the council to inform them he had gathered his champions to assist him in gaining access to the Library of Antiquity. After doing so, he returned to the antechamber to join his friends, as prearranged.

Sordaak signaled the bard, who dressed in his best attire—somewhat embellished by several trinkets supplied by the caster—and stepped into the center of the chamber. A troupe of trumpets filled the air with the sounds respectful of a coronation.

Thrinndor looked at the caster and raised an inquisitive eyebrow, but the mage ignored him, instead concentrating on what the bard was doing. Curious, the paladin also turned his attention to the chamber.

Once the trumpets had quieted, the bard unrolled a scrolled parchment and cleared his throat.

"Here ye! Here ye!" he declared in his most formal voice. "I come before this august body to present for your consideration a most excellent group of individuals destined to breach the Library of Antiquity with our most esteemed Leader, the Great and most Adept of all, Savinhand and his blades of whirling steel!"

The leader of the rogue guild turned an amused eye upon the mage, who grinned sheepishly and pointed into the chamber.

The rogue leader returned the smile, shrugged, and leapt into motion.

There was a blur of movement as his hands drew his shortsword in his right hand and a wicked looking dagger in his left. He sprinted down the short, narrow hall that separated the antechamber and the main room. As he entered the main hall, he began a tumbling run, flicking his blades right and left as he tumbled, spun and jumped high into the air.

At the apex of one such leap, his blades flashed and—while spinning through the air high off of the ground—he cut into a large gourd hung there for the purpose.

As the rogue leader deftly landed on his feet and skidded to a halt, he looked up as the slightly swinging gourd.

All eyes in the chamber followed his, revealing a smiling face neatly carved into the otherwise smooth surface of the pumpkin.

The crowd, which had been holding its breath in anticipation of they knew not what, erupted in applause and cheers.

The bard waited for the raucous crowd to subside, his raised eyebrow the only emotion he allowed himself to display.

He went on. "Next I present to you the leader of this experienced and well balanced party, the uber-powerful sorcerer Sordaak!" The bard drew out the name, getting louder with each syllable.

Thrinndor turned to stare at the caster, but he quickly realized he was not standing next to Sordaak anymore. Confused, he looked out into the main hall just as a bright flash next to Savinhand almost blinded him.

As his eyes readjusted following the flash, he saw that it was replaced by a cloud of smoke.

As the smoke dissipated, everyone in the hall could see first the tall pointed hat of the caster, and then the rest of him materialized.

Again the hall erupted in appreciation.

Savinhand waved his arms and coughed lightly as the smoke got into his face and eyes.

"Sorry," muttered the mage under his breath.

Savinhand just grinned at him.

At a nod from Sordaak, the bard again raised the scroll and resumed his recital.

"Up next we have the giant-strong dwarven barbarian, Vorgath Shieldsunder of Clan Dragaar, pride of the Silver Hills!"

Vorgath rolled his eyes and let out one of his blood-curdling yells that caused even Thrinndor's heart to leap. Then the barbarian raised his greataxe over his head with both hands and sprinted into motion, the axe whirling all about him as he ran. When he skidded to a halt, he continued to swing the blade in an extended display of strength and skill that silenced the crowd, awestruck. His last move was to swing the blade in a broad circle and snap it to a stop, his chest heaving.

Again the crowd erupted, now even louder than before.

Vorgath bowed, his weapon held off to one side in a single meaty fist.

Sordaak nodded again to the bard as the crowd noise diminished and they sat back down. The bard turned crier read from his script, looked up and said loudly, "Next is Breunne! A Lord Ranger of the highest order, and adept in all things related to the forest!"

The ranger lifted an eyebrow before striding into the room, bow in hand. As he moved quickly toward the three already standing before the council table, his hand reached back and drew an arrow from the quiver slung across his back.

He spun and pointed his bow into the crowd, drew back the string, and released the arrow at a fat man seated halfway up the grandstand. The man, and those seated around him, ducked and dodged. But the arrow curved at the last moment and shot straight up toward the high ceiling. There it burst with a loud bang, and two each red, yellow and orange sparklers drifted slowly toward the floor, hissing as they fell.

Breunne's hands flashed, and he notched and released a series of arrows in blurred succession, each arrow slamming into the sparklers in yet another explosion as they drifted slowly down.

Six arrows, six targets, six explosions.

The ranger—who had not stopped moving the entire time—stopped next to the barbarian and bowed.

The gathering again surged to its feet, the response louder still.

This time the bard did not wait for the sorcerer to signal. "Next in this most intimidating lineup of sorcery, strength and dexterity we have the heart and soul of the troupe, the Magnanimous, ultra-strong Paladin, Thrinndor!"

Thrinndor smiled to himself, pulled his helm down and strode into the chamber. In his left hand he held the new shield he had obtained in Dragma's Keep, and in his right he held his Flaming bastard sword, deeming it to be the more impressive looking of his arsenal.

He was correct. Rather than an improvised series of thrusts and parries, he elected to perform the recently learned battle preparation for the Paladinhood. None here would know it was meant for a group of paladins, not just the one before them.

Again, he was correct.

Again the room was silenced as he went through a series of steps, thrusts, parries and chants designed to transform a group of ten paladins into a single entity capable of doing battle at a much higher level than each could individually.

The crowd sat mesmerized as the figure clad in black armor, with a black helm, a black oversized shield and a huge flaming sword performed some sort of choreographed dance before them that left them breathless and wanting more.

When Thrinndor completed the regimen, as an afterthought he tilted his shield and loosed the single bolt from the crossbow mounted behind it at the gourd on which Savinhand had carved the smiling face. The bolt pierced the pumpkin between its eyes and emerged out the back of the "head" in a spray of orange as the gourd burst into small pieces.

The crowded room sat initially stunned in silence, then again exploded to life, surging to their feet, shouting and whistling at a level even greater than before.

When the gathering finally quieted and returned to their seats, the bard again without a signal shouted for all to hear, "Last, but certainly not least, we have the most wise and most beautiful high priestess in all the land, Cyrillis of Myanmoor!"

Cyrillis blushed slightly as she set her jaw to enter the arena. How she was going to follow what the paladin just did, she knew not. Knowing this bunch of rabble would not understand her healing arts—and she could figure no way to showcase those in a setting such as this—she elected to sling the staff all about as if she were a disgusting battle cleric.

As she marched in, she called up a Blade Barrier just for show. The waste of spell energy abhorred her, but she deemed it necessary this one time.

Apparently some part of her marching in with her staff whirling about her head had the desired effect, because the rabble rose to its feet and cheered her on.

About halfway to the group, she noticed that Sordaak also had his fingers to his lips and was whistling loudly, stomping his feet and waving his arms in the process.

Uh oh, she thought as she approached him, he had that far-away look in his eyes. He was not really present in the room! He was having one of his mind exchange episodes!

And he was staring straight through her!

She was not certain what was going on that puny brain of his, but it most certainly involved her.

He was definitely enjoying himself.

Mad, but not exactly sure why, she approached the group as she finished her planned maneuvers with her staff. In her ire, she slammed the heel of Kurril to the stone floor.

As the metal heel contacted the smooth stone in a brief shower of sparks, flames erupted from the gem suspended in the head of the staff and quickly launched themselves in the general direction of the caster and rogue, both of whom stood to her left.

Even in whatever reverie he was in, Sordaak saw the flames coming and had time to dodge to his left.

Savinhand, however, had been watching the council closely for their reactions, and only the sound of the flames warned him that something was amiss. He turned toward the sound, and so took the blast full in the face. His hands instantly came up to shield himself as best he could. While that helped, only the additional distance from the cleric and her ire kept him from serious injury.

Savinhand lowered his hands, blinked twice, and said "Ow."

Utterly surprised by what she had just done, Cyrillis found she was fighting her anger, her need to go to Savinhand's aid, and maintaining the charade for the council. In the end, she could tell the rogue was not badly hurt, so allowed a mildly satisfied grin to settle on her lips. At the look of astonishment on Thrinndor's face, she muttered out of the side of her mouth, "It has never done that before!"

The paladin recovered quickly and replied—also out of the side of his mouth—"Not for at least a thousand years, anyway!"

Sordaak, who was close enough to hear the entire exchange said, "Well, you'd better get control of that staff, sister!"

This added fuel to the flames of her outrage. Cyrillis took the one step necessary to put herself in the sorcerer's face. "What did you see?" she demanded, hissing the words through clenched teeth to keep from shouting.

Sordaak took a step back. "I…ummm."

Cyrillis refused to let him escape, and stepped after him and again put her face only inches from his. "What did you see!" she repeated.

Seeing she was not to be denied, the caster swallowed hard. "We were in a much larger arena," he began meekly. He dearly wanted to be somewhere else, right now. "The crowd was cheering. You were marching in front of a large group of people playing musical instruments wearing…" He stopped and again gulped hard.

"Yes," she said, her eyes narrowing to mere slits.

"You were wearing a…much shorter tunic," his voice trailed off to the point where it was barely audible.

Cyrillis' eyes widened in astonishment, and she searched the mage's for any sign of deceit. They stood that way for a moment, and then her right hand shot out and she slapped the caster across his face. Hard. She then spun on her heel and moved off to stand next to an extremely confused paladin. He had heard nothing of the exchange between the caster and the cleric. His eyes went back and forth from one to the other.

"Ask not," the healer hissed.

Thrinndor who had been about to do so, merely nodded, his attention distracted by Savinhand moving to stand next to the caster.

Savinhand had a curious look on his face reddened by the flames. "Was it worth it?" he whispered so only Sordaak could hear.

"Oh, yeah!" Sordaak returned the whisper. He dared not rub his stinging cheek.

Unable to stand it, Cyrillis exhaled loudly and again marched over and put her face mere inches from the mage. This time, Sordaak stood his ground, and even allowed a small amount of defiance to cross his visage.

"How short?" she asked through clenched teeth.

"Very short," he replied.

Her eyes again searched his for a moment. Her hand again shot out, and she gave him another ringing slap.

Sordaak did not budge.

The healer spun on her heel and walked stiffly to stand next to the paladin.

The crowd still cheered, although some were confused about the healer slapping the leader of the party before them.

Savinhand leaned over. "Nice legs?" he whispered.

"Damn nice," replied the caster, finally allowing himself the luxury of rubbing his stinging cheek. "I probably deserved that," he added with a smile.

"Next time you go wandering through dimensions," said the rogue, his eyes on the healer, "take me with you!" He returned the smile.

Sordaak merely nodded as the council stood to their feet, still clapping loudly.

The ranking official—the woman of the group, as it turned out—motioned for quiet, and after a few moments received it. She was of moderate years but had taken good care of herself, Sordaak decided. In fact, she was quite beautiful. Raven black hair falling almost to her waist. Average in height, well-proportioned for that height and she was wearing leather armor that accentuated those proportions.

Her piercing green eyes locked onto those of the caster. "Do you have a name for your..." She searched for the correct word. "Group?"

Sordaak stepped forward, his face still red from his recent encounter with the healer, and the left side of his face even redder from that same encounter.

A name? He briefly looked right and left. He had not even considered a name. His eyes caught Savinhand sheathing his short sword out of the corner of his eye. "Vorpal," he answered quickly. "We are called Vorpal!" He then bowed, not sure whether that was required in this setting but knew that a little subservience to a council such as this would seldom be wasted effort.

The female council member bobbed her head in acknowledgement of his bow. "Thank you. That...performance was most...interesting."

"Thank you!" replied the sorcerer with a broad smile.

"I hope you can fight as well as you can act," she said. Her demeanor indicated she found that unlikely.

Sordaak returned her smile and said, "I believe you will find us up to the task!"

The smile disappeared in a flash from the woman's face. She was trying to decide whether she was being mocked. Ultimately she decided it did not matter. "Very well," she said with a smile that was only half of what it had been previous. "It seems that Savinhand has indeed chosen well." She shifted her attention to the rogue and bowed slightly.

Chapter Thirteen

Reorg

Sordaak opened his eyes slowly and tried to figure out where he was and just exactly why he was awake. Unable to do either, he allowed himself to ease slowly back to the pillow beneath his head. Damn! His head hurt!

Pillow? So soft, he thought vaguely as he eased back into slumber.

Bam…Bam…BAM!

There it was again. An incessant knocking on a door. His door!

He sat up quickly—too quickly, as it turned out. The tiny men with war-hammers inside his head renewed their effort to get out.

"Son-of-a…" he spat the curse through the growing pain behind his eyes. "Go away!" he shouted.

The latch rattled and the door slowly swung inward, letting a blinding light from the hallway into the darkened bedchamber. A figure stood in the doorway, partially blocking this light. A huge figure.

"I am afraid I cannot do that," said the man as he strode into the room and threw open the curtains that had done an efficient job of blocking out the light of a mid-morning sun. Until now.

"Ugh!" said the caster as he again allowed his head to slump back to the pillow. He drew the blanket up over his head. "Go away!" he repeated through clenched teeth.

Thrinndor anticipated such a maneuver. He strode the short distance to where the caster lay and jerked the blankets from the bed. "Get up," the paladin said none-too-gently. "The day is old and we must be on our way."

"Must?" said the caster, his eyes screwed tightly shut. "Whatever it is can wait until tomorrow."

"No," Thrinndor said. "Our destiny awaits and we must journey forth to meet it."

Still without opening his eyes Sordaak muttered, "Surely this destiny would be better served—" He yelped slightly as a ham-like fist grabbed the front of his tunic, abruptly jerked him out of the bed and set the mage unsteadily on his feet.

Now his eyes were open. They stared malevolently at the man who dared to stand before him after such mistreatment.

"Surely it would," said the paladin. "However we are stuck with you!" He grinned insolently at the sorcerer. "Now clean yourself up and get something to eat. We depart within the hour."

With that, the paladin spun on a booted heel and strode toward the door. There he stopped and turned to observe the mage as he headed back toward the bed.

"Do not!" Thrinndor commanded severely. "Either prepare yourself or I will carry you to your mount and tie you to your saddle as you are!"

Sordaak bit off an angry reply as he glared at the man blocking the door. The very thought of food made him nauseous—well, more nauseous.

Finally the mage nodded and muttered, "All right."

"What was that?" demanded the paladin.

Again the caster bit of a sharp reply as he straightened his tunic. "I said all right!" His tone told what he thought of this exercise.

Thrinndor nodded and walked out into the hallway. "One hour," he said, not looking back.

Sordaak briefly eyed the bed and then turned to look after the rapidly receding paladin. Damn, he muttered. That had been one hell of a party! Well, what he could remember of it, he thought as he scratched the mop of black hair on his head with one hand and the center of his chest with the other.

He looked back at the bed longingly, cursed, and shuffled his feet over to the convenient in-room facilities and began the process of making himself presentable.

Fortunately, a bath was already drawn for him, as it was going to be a long process.

*

Just over an hour later, a freshly bathed and shaven Sordaak was led by a chambermaid—a rather cute one, he noted with a sigh—down to the group gathered outside the main stables.

His mount was freshly groomed and saddled for him. His pack animals were also loaded and ready to go.

He became acutely aware his friends had been waiting for him.

"About damn time!" announced Savinhand, a disarming grin displayed on his face.

"Do all men take so long to get ready in the morning?" There was no smile on Cyrillis' face, but her eyes belied their mirth.

"Whatever!" snorted the caster.

His eyes settled on the rogue. "I hope you can finally tell us where we are going?"

"Nope," replied the rogue, maintaining the agreed-upon charade that only he knew of the Library. "But I can show you. That is if you are finally ready to go?"

"I was born ready!" snapped the mage good-naturedly.

"Ha!" snorted the cleric as she leapt onto her mare's back and pointed her toward the path out of the compound. But Cyrillis didn't start her mount yet.

Sordaak smiled when his eyes came across the barbarian, who was also obviously feeling the effects of the previous evening's festivities as well.

"Damn, if this bunch of thieves don't know how to throw a party!" the caster said with a wink.

Vorgath, who had been slouching against a fence rail, pulled himself up to his full height—which brought his eyes about level with the center of the mage's chest—and returned the wink. "Damn straight!" His eyes twinkled.

Sordaak smiled as he turned to face the cleric, whose back was now to him. "Hey sister," he said. "How about one of those restoration spells to set me straight?"

The healer spun angrily in her saddle. "I told you to not—" She bit off the rest of the reply when she caught sight of the huge grin on the caster's face. "I would not waste the spell energy on such an endeavor!" she said with a huff. "Your misery is just rewards for your deeds!" She turned away stiffly, mostly to hide the smile on her face as she did so.

Sordaak's face took on a pained expression as he again looked at the dwarf. "What deeds?" the caster asked plaintively. "A little wine, perhaps. But certainly no deeds!"

"A little wine?" said the paladin, amusement plain in his tone. "You two—" He waved his hand to include the dwarf. "—put the winemaker's guild into shift work!"

Sordaak smiled and raised his hand, which the dwarf promptly slapped in agreement. "Damn straight!" he echoed the words of his new drinking partner.

"That," said the cleric, again spinning so she could look down her nose at the caster far below, "and you flirted and hit on anything in a skirt." Her eyes flashed. "And several in pants!"

Sordaak's grin grew even bigger. "My, my," he said. "Jealousy certainly does become you!"

"Jealousy!" Cyrillis was almost shouting. "Well I never!" Her eyes flared. Seeing she was being mocked, however, she again turned away from the caster and folder her arms resolutely across her chest and said no more.

A grin plastered on his face and suddenly feeling better than he had a right to, Sordaak edged up to his horse and was about to climb into the saddle when he spotted the woman from the council table subtly motioning him over.

He vaguely remembered talking with her the previous night but couldn't remember what about. Or if anything else had occurred…

He looked around quickly and saw that Cyrillis was trying too hard not to notice. She was obviously more than a little concerned with what this woman might want.

The mage shrugged and walked the short distance to where the woman stood silently. As he did, he wracked his brain but could not remember her name—assuming he ever knew it. Damn! She looked good!

Cyrillis watched out of the corner of her eye, all the while pretending not to do so. The two had a low, short conversation, the caster nodding occasionally and shaking his head once.

As the conversation wrapped up, the woman—Bealtrive, he suddenly remembered—peered over his shoulder at the cleric who was sitting stiffly in the saddle intently studying some imagined speck of dust on her robe.

Bealtrive suddenly reached out and snaked an arm behind Sordaak's head and pulled him in for a long, passionate kiss. When they separated, the woman winked at the caster and said loud enough for all to hear, "Thank you for last night, sugar!" She winked at a the mage's obvious confusion and whispered, "That was for the benefit of your little girlfriend over there." She again winked and spun to leave.

Sordaak turned to see the cleric turn suddenly away, kicking her horse into motion the opposite direction, her back stiff as she stared straight ahead.

"Huh?" said Sordaak, turning red. He faced Bealtrive, but she was already walking away, her backside swaying back and forth in a most interesting fashion. The mage was suddenly certain that the hip action was also not meant entirely for him. However he was also not certain it was noticed by the other intended party, as she was leaving the area in a big hurry.

It was.

A befuddled caster stumbled his way back to the group and noticed three of the four staring at him slack-jawed, Vorgath being the lone exception. A devilish grin was plastered on the dwarf's face. "You dog!" he said. "Well done!"

The mage returned the grin and climbed aboard his horse. He looked around. The others had yet to mount.

"I presume when you requested my presence in such a hurried manner," Sordaak said, his tone laden with sarcasm, "that you wanted to get on the road?"

Hurriedly, Breunne, Thrinndor and Savinhand grabbed the reins of their mounts and also climbed aboard. Vorgath shouldered his pack and prepared to follow.

Once settled in the saddle the paladin looked at the caster, lifted an eyebrow and said, "What, if I may ask, did she want?" His eyes went to the doorway through which Bealtrive had disappeared.

"My body," Sordaak said as he applied his heels to the flanks of his mount and started after the rapidly receding cleric.

Thrinndor shook his head as he started his mount to follow at a more leisurely pace.

Savinhand walked his mount up even with the paladin's. "I'm sure there's more to the story than that!"

"Fascinating reaction," replied the big fighter as his eyes followed the caster. "Sordaak?" replied the rogue leader. "Nah, Bealtrive always gets her man!"

"Not his," corrected Thrinndor. "Cyrillis'."

That startled Savinhand a bit. "Oh, now that you mention it, you're right!" He turned to see the caster just as he disappeared into the trees to the north. "Interesting."

"Should you not be leading the way?" asked the paladin, pulling his eyes away with some effort from the edge of the trees.

Again startled at the abrupt change in the conversation, Savin looked at the paladin to see if he could tell where this was going. "Nah," he said after careful consideration, "we'll stay on this road for the remainder of the day." His eyes went back to the approaching tree line. "We'll catch up with them long before it's time to make camp." His eyes strayed back to the paladin beside him. "Tomorrow morning we'll make the final approach."

"We had better pick up the pace a little," Thrinndor said, "if we want to catch them before their mounts tire out!"

"Right," replied the thief as he urged his horse forward to match the canter the paladin had set.

"You all right back there, old one?" Thrinndor asked as he turned to see the dwarf running easily alongside the ranger.

"Don't worry about me, your high-and-mightiness!" replied Vorgath, no sign in his voice that he was laboring in the slightest. "I'll be running long after that nag you're on passes out from carrying your fat ass!" The barbarian smiled, showing his uneven teeth.

Thrinndor opened his mouth to defend his steed but thought better of it and smiled in return. "That you might, old one," he said. "That you might!" He turned back to the road ahead as the party entered the trees.

*

Catch them they did, but not before the shadows grew long and a chill returned to the air as the day drew to a close.

Obviously nothing between the caster and the cleric had been resolved as she rode twenty or thirty feet ahead of the dissolute mage, her back still ramrod straight in the saddle.

Thrinndor chuckled to himself—nowhere near loud enough to be heard by the pair, of course. He was not sure why, but the scene was comical to him in some way.

Savinhand, who knew the area relatively well, led them off of the main road shortly after they had regrouped. He stopped them at a small glade surrounded by small hills and large trees.

"This is as good a spot as any to make camp," he said with a shrug. Indeed, there was a small stream not far off to provide water for the usual operations, as well as several large trees and some brush to provide privacy.

"How much farther to the Library?" asked Thrinndor as he helped Vorgath gather wood for a fire.

The rogue leader took in a breath to answer, paused and then let it out with a sigh. "Good question."

"What?" asked the paladin.

"Huh?" said the dwarf. "I thought you knew where we are going?"

"Well," said the thief as he began to fidget, "I never actually said I knew where it was." He held up his hands to forestall the coming protests. "I said I know where the entrance is." Suddenly his hands got very busy unloading pans and bags of food.

"Speak some sense, man!" groused the dwarf. "That's nothing but pure gibberish!"

Savinhand spun and stabbed a finger at the dwarf. "Look," he said sternly, "I don't know a lot more about this than you do! Phinskyr—or Ytharra, as you knew him—never had a chance to pass along to me in the normal fashion the particulars of getting into The Library!"

Vorgath was momentarily taken aback by the vehemence in the rogue's tone.

Savinhand took in a deep breath as he took a step back. "Sorry," he said as his shoulders slumped. "This is going to be an adventure for all of us, I'm afraid." He looked around the group, meeting the eyes of each of his friends.

"He gave you nothing?" said the barbarian, his tone slightly more sympathetic than before, but not so much than most could tell.

The eyes of the rogue leader flared briefly, but he calmed himself. "I didn't say that, either." This time all were silent as Savinhand prepared what he wanted to say. "Phinskyr feared that during his long absences his quarters would be ransacked looking for information about the Library—and they were. More than once and by more than one individual or group of individuals." He smiled suddenly. "But Phinskyr was smart. He left several false clues, and several traps." His smile broadened. "I found several large blood stains and the remains of more than one would be perpetrator." He now paused for effect. "All the while he seemed to know he would not return, and left a journal with the only person in the land he trusted." He turned slightly to confront the ranger. "Breunne."

All eyes followed those of the Leader of Shardmoor. Breunne gave a half smile followed by a half bow. "Guilty as charged, master," the ranger said.

"You do seem to get around, do you not?" queried the paladin.

Breunne simply smiled in response.

Savinhand reached into his tunic and removed a small package covered in a leather wrap and bound with leather thongs. He deftly undid the ties, pulled back a flap and removed a small, old-looking leather-bound book.

"Nice," said the caster. "So we do at least have a guide of sorts."

"Not exactly," replied the rogue, sheepishly. Sordaak raised an eyebrow. "Everything in this journal is encrypted," Savin said.

"Oh goody!" said the magicuser sarcastically. "More puzzles!"

"You should be good at them by now," observed the cleric, joining the conversation at last, her tone frosty enough to throw a skin of ice on the nearby stream.

Sordaak opened his mouth for a biting reply but quickly thought better of it. The look on Cyrillis' face indicated that had been a good move. Instead, he folded his arms across his chest, knitted his brow, sunk his chin to his chest and said nothing as he stared longingly at the journal.

"Yeah, well," said the paladin, suddenly uncomfortable. "May I see that?" He coughed politely and reached toward the book.

"Actually," Savinhand began apologetically, "I would prefer this not left my hands—"

"You don't trust us?" asked Sordaak.

The rogue leader's eyes flashed. "Trust is not the issue," he snapped. "Rather, this manual is very old—older than even Phinskyr. It has been handed down for many centuries and it is very fragile." His ire dissipated. "Please understand." His eyes pleaded with all in the group. "It's not in very good shape and I am told 'order' is crucial as it pertains to our journey." He took in a deep breath. "It's obvious several pages are loose and they must not be jumbled. I'm sorry."

Silence pervaded the encampment.

"Besides," interjected the ranger, "it's enchanted such that only the Leader of Shardmoor may handle the book." His tone was lecturing. "Any other contact will turn it to ashes."

Savinhand looked surprised. "You never told me that."

"You never asked," replied the ranger with a shrug. "It would have come up if it became necessary. It has."

The mage's face went from curious to disbelief to distrust then back to curious in a matter of seconds. "That will make studying it closely difficult at best."

Savinhand smiled for the first time since pulling the book out. "I'll make sure I put it on a table for all to see once we are inside." His eyes pleaded with the mage to understand. "Tomorrow, and not before. It wouldn't make any sense to try to figure out any of this, now." He shifted his eyes to those of the paladin. "Trust me on this—I've been there!"

Thrinndor's right eyebrow shot up, but he said nothing.

Sordaak eschewed silence. "What? You've been there? When?"

"Let's see," answered the rogue, his hand going to his chin as he rubbed it in thought. He was obviously retracing his last few days. "Four, maybe five days ago." He looked again at the caster. "I'm not really sure, and I don't believe it really matters, does it?"

"No," agreed the mage. "I don't suppose so." His face then took on a note of belligerence. "You could've told us!"

"What did you see?" asked the paladin.

Savinhand turned his eyes upon the big fighter. "Well," he began slowly, "I didn't exactly go inside."

Vorgath beat several of the others to the obvious question. "Why not?"

"Well," the thief repeated and then he hesitated. "Look…It's time for choices."

"What choices, exactly?" said the barbarian.

"If you would shut up and let me finish," replied the rogue, "I'll tell you." He stared at the dwarf until Vorgath nodded. "That goes for all of you," Savin added, looking at each in turn and getting the same response.

"See," said the mage, looking at the paladin, "you guys are rubbing off on him, too!"

Savinhand glared at the caster for a moment before his face split in a grin. "I believe you are correct," he said, mimicking the paladin in tone and inflection.

"Ha, ha!" Thrinndor said in mock indignation. "It is all for the good, that is certain!"

"Whatever!" said the magicuser as he rolled his eyes.

The seriousness of the moment evaporated as the group all chuckled. Savin was more than willing to delay what he needed to say, but he knew it needed to be said, nonetheless.

After a few moments the group's attention was again on him, the rogue cleared his throat and said, "This is kind of where I need to make certain each of you knows I don't know exactly what we are facing here." He looked down at his hands as silence once again fell upon the group, the levity of the previous moment evaporating just as quickly as the seriousness had before.

"I cannot tell you how much I appreciate that each of you are willing to put your lives on the line in this quest to gain what is mine," he went on still looking at his hands. He looked up and turned to face the paladin. "I know that you hope that knowledge of your god and his sword will be contained within."

Thrinndor nodded but said nothing.

"And you," he turned to face the cleric, "search for verification of your ancestry." She, too, nodded.

"You," he looked next at the caster, "your fate is tied with them, bound by your common goal. That and you yearn for everything that is knowledge."

Sordaak followed suit and also nodded.

"And you, old friend," he said as he turned to face the ranger, "you and I would assist one another in taming the flames of the Seven Hells with a small bucket of water if the other but asked." A small tear formed in the corner of his right eye. "So I know why you are here."

Breunne, feeling the solemnity of the moment, nodded as well.

"But you," the rogue leader said as he turned to face the barbarian, whose meaty arms were crossed on his chest, "you I have to give the option to depart." He went on quickly before there could be a protest. "I don't know what we will find where we are going or even whether we will return…"

In the silence that followed, the dwarf dropped his arms to his side and leaned closer to the thief. "Dragon?" he said gruffly. "You mentioned a dragon." He said it as if that answered all. Next, he slung his greataxe off his back and waved it menacingly at the group. "If any of you try to get between me and that dragon…" He whipped the axe and split a log cleanly in two with one well-placed cut. Then he grinned into the stunned silence that followed. "Just see that you don't!" He again folded his arms across his chest, leaving the axe buried in the stump the piece of wood had been sitting on. "Besides," continued the barbarian, "Super-pally over there and I have a similar working relationship as you and the tall, skinny—"

"Wiry," corrected the ranger.

Vorgath blinked at the interruption, and then grinned hugely. "Wiry guy over there. Except," he added as he turned to face the paladin, "recent events have put a strain on said relationship."

"Huh?" said Savinhand.

Thrinndor grinned. "Do not mind him," he said. "He is merely a bit grumpy—"

"More grumpy," corrected the ranger.

The paladin looked at the ranger, lifted an eyebrow and said, "More grumpy," he admitted, "since I did not call for his aid before going to the Temple of Set at Brasheer."

"That was you?" said an intrigued thief.

The big fighter nodded. "And Cyrillis."

"I had little to do with that outcome," intoned the cleric solemnly.

"You single-handedly took on and wiped out a major outpost of Set," replied the rogue, obviously still trying to wrap his head around that tidbit.

"They were," Thrinndor said as he searched for the proper word, "unprepared." He shrugged as if to shift attention elsewhere. "And I would hardly call it a major outpost."

"They would," replied the rogue. He stared as his relatively new friend with a newfound respect. "What happened?"

Thrinndor told him.

It was also the first time Sordaak had heard the story in full. He fidgeted uncomfortably on the rock on which he had been sitting and stared at his hands, which were also fidgeting. Finally, unable to stand it any longer, he surged to his feet and moved deliberately over to stand in front of the cleric.

She ignored him, continuing to stare at her own hands.

The gathering was silent as the magicuser struggled within, obviously irritated. "They were going to sacrifice you?" he said suddenly, a mixture of anger and deep concern apparent in his voice.

She nodded slowly but did not look up.

"Bastards!" the mage spat. "Why?"

"They wanted my staff," she said as she finally looked up and acknowledged his presence.

Suddenly, the caster was trembling, whether in fear, rage or a combination of both was not clear. He reached down and pulled at the loose scarf she had been wearing about her neck of late. The not quite healed scar of her close brush with death was now plain for all to see.

Sordaak took in a sharp breath as his hands knotted into a fist at his side. His face turned a mottled red as he continued to tremble. "You should not have gone there without me!" he said stiffly, his voice a rush of emotions.

Cyrillis' eyes searched those of the caster for signs of anything—emotion, rage, affection. She knew not what. When finally she spoke, her voice was low and thick with emotion. "Why do you care?"

Sordaak was taken aback by the intensity in her voice. And by the question. Why did he care? That was not a question he had even asked himself.

Why did he care? It was obvious he did.

Sordaak said the first thing that came to mind. "Because without you, Valdaar could be doomed to remain locked in that crystal for a thousand more years!" he said in a rush.

Again the cleric's eyes searched those of the caster. "You do not know that!" she said softly. "We are not even certain I am of the lineage of Angra-Khan!"

"I am," began the mage.

"No. You are not!" snapped the healer, her voice rising. "None of us are!" Her eyes flashed briefly. "I am not even certain who my parents are, let alone my entire lineage!"

"And now," she lowered her voice, her emotion spent, "I will never know!" She buried her face in her hands, which muffled her voice. "The records that might have proven one way or the other have been destroyed!"

Sordaak wanted to reach out to comfort her, but he dared not. He didn't know what to say.

"I'm sorry," he said. It was all that would come out.

She looked up, her red-rimmed eyes and tear-stained cheeks hopeful. "What? Why?"

"For not being there," he said quickly. Too quickly! Damn! That's not what he wanted to say!

Cyrillis' face twisted in sudden anger. "You are an idiot!"

Sordaak fought back one reply, then another. In the end he threw his hands up in despair. "Whatever!" he said as he spun and marched back to his seat. As he started to sit, he suddenly stopped and turned to face the paladin, who was watching the whole scene play out before him with a quizzical look. "I've had it!" snapped the caster.

Thrinndor's right eyebrow marched incrementally higher.

"I put this damn group together!" The caster's eyes roamed the group, daring anyone to contradict him. "However it has become obvious to even me I am not the right person to lead it." His eyes sought those of the paladin. "You're a damn paladin! You're born to lead!" He sat down unceremoniously on his rock and folded his arms across his chest. "I hereby relinquish all right to lead and/or command this party." He dropped his chin to his chest and glowered at the fire as it slowly came to life.

"Ummm," said the paladin, clearly caught off-guard. "Very well." It was the best he could come up with. Even to him it sounded inadequate.

Sordaak looked up suddenly, and his eyes narrowed to mere slits. "However," he said, "I reserve the right to have my suggestions heard as I deem necessary."

"Of course," the big fighter replied. He was still not sure what had just happened.

"And," said the caster wryly, "I reserve the right to inform you when you're being stupid."

Thrinndor said nothing, his expression impassive.

The caster's eyes went back to the fire and he returned to glowering. "All right then, you're the boss." He spoke as if that were the end of it.

And it was.

An uneasy silence settled on the group. Savinhand looked from one to the other, wondering what else he had missed.

He cleared his throat noisily and when the others—except for the mage, who continued staring intently into the fire—turned to look at him, he said, "So I suppose it was you who also destroyed the Temple of Set at Farreach as well?" This was directed at the paladin.

"Ummm," Breunne raised his hand rather meekly. "That would have been me."

"What?" replied the rogue. "How?"

Breunne told him.

When he finished, Savinhand crossed his arms on his chest, his eyes roving over the group. "My, my. You have all been busy." His eyes settled on the mage, who was still staring intently at nothing in the fire. "Is there anything else I might have missed that could be deemed important?"

Sordaak continued to ignore the rogue. Cyrillis' attention was also now locked in on something in the fire. Vorgath was obviously still miffed at the two fighters for leaving him out of their respective frays as he poked morosely at the embers. Breunne and Thrinndor shrugged.

"OK, then," said the rogue. "I guess I have my answers."

Savinhand put his hand out, palm down, toward no one in particular. Instead he leaned in toward the fire. "We are Vorpal," he said formally, using the name tossed out in haste. "And we go in as one."

Thrinndor and Breunne stepped forward and put their hands over that of the rogue leader.

Vorgath heaved himself to his feet and did likewise.

Cyrillis looked up from the fire, stood and moved to put her hand over that of the dwarf, her expression blank.

All eyes turned to the mage, who had not moved. With obvious effort he tore his eyes from the fire and locked with those of Savinhand. Finally he nodded, placed his hands on his knees and pushed himself upright. He then wedged his way into the opening left for him and placed his hand over that of the cleric.

"We are Vorpal," the rogue leader repeated, solemnly.

"We are Vorpal," all six said as one.

Chapter Fourteen

No Honor Among Thieves

Sordaak felt a tug at his senses. He had been deep in slumber, and it took a few seconds for him to realize it was Fahlred doing the tugging. And then he was instantly alert.

Someone—something—was approaching their camp. More than one. They had left the Quasit to stand guard. He did not require sleep.

The mage fumbled around with his right hand until his fingers closed on a pebble. This he flung in the direction of the lump of bedding he knew to be the paladin. From the way the blankets stiffened, Sordaak knew his friend was instantly awake.

The fire had burned down to where just the coals remained, but in the complete darkness that engulfed the gathering, it was enough for the mage to see the big fighter roll silently out of his blankets and move to the nearest bundle, which proved to be that of the dwarf.

The paladin put his right hand on the barbarian's shoulder and the index finger of his left to his lips. Vorgath was instantly awake and nodded his understanding of the situation.

Next Thrinndor moved to wake the ranger, who also silently acknowledged the need for stealth with a nod of the head.

Vorgath went to where he knew Savinhand made his bed, but his bedroll was empty. A quick touch revealed the blankets were still warm. The dwarf looked around and saw a shadow detach itself from a tree and wave silently in his direction. Vorgath returned the gesture.

Meanwhile, Sordaak padded silently over to where he knew the cleric was sleeping. Unsure how to wake her without either a struggle or her screaming in surprise, he hesitated. Finally, he tapped her on what he hoped was a shoulder.

He saw her tense under her blankets, but the cleric said nothing. When she rolled over to see who disturbed her, the mage held his finger to his lips and

waved his other hand at the surrounding trees. She grabbed her staff and nodded her understanding as she silently rolled out of her blankets.

Sordaak motioned for them to all gather away from the steady glow of the fire.

Once they were all together, the mage whispered, "Fahlred woke me. There
are several creatures approaching."

"Do we know what they are or how many?"

"No," hissed the caster. "Six to ten. Humanoid and they dispersed as they
approached our camp."

"Not friendlies then," said the paladin.

Sordaak shook his head in agreement. "I have a plan," he said, which he explained.

Now they each waited in a hiding spot that allowed them to see their bedrolls,
which had been made up to look like each of them were still nestled warmly inside.

A trap.

Savinhand waited, more curious than concerned. He was fairly certain those
approaching were from his guild. He wondered idly which faction dared to
attempt to obtain the journal in this fashion.

Although he had been careful never to mention its existence before showing
it to his friends the day before, he figured the others in his guild surmised there
must be such a book. That and he was also certain they had been followed.

Possibly by more than one of his guild members.

Possibly by more than one faction.

He could neither hear nor see any movement, yet Savin knew they were out
there. He heard an occasional owl that wasn't an owl. An occasional insect that
wasn't an insect.

He waited, his senses on high alert.

Thwap! Thwap! Thwap!!!

The sound of arrows and/or bolts smacking solidly into the rolled-up blankets was followed immediately by the whispering sound of rushing feet as the
attack commenced.

Savinhand made it to the preordained count of five and then separated himself silently from the tree with which he had been one for the past half hour or
so and shielded his eyes.

The fire in the center of their camp, which had died down to the coals, suddenly burst to life in an explosion of both sound and flames. The sound was by
way of one of Cyrillis' Sound Bursts, and the fire by way of a Wall of Fire spell
courtesy of their caster.

There were several startled yelps and one or two screams of those who
found themselves too close to the fire, but most of the attackers—now clearly
visible to the companions—were simply too stunned to move.

Yet one or two had been able to roll or dodge their way from the worst of
the spells and were hastily trying to make their retreat.

"Stop!" Thrinndor shouted. "Drop your weapons, stand where you are and we may yet allow you to live!"

Two of the cowardly assailants released the dagger and/or short sword that they had buried into the bedroll before them and quickly raised their hands above their heads, their eyes watering from the effects of the suddenly brightly lit clearing.

The rest either stood and attempted to flee or had already tumbled their way as far from their previous objective as was possible in the two or three short heartbeats since the attack had begun.

Breunne loosed the arrow he had notched and drawn back for the purpose and immediately followed that with another. One of the dark clad assailants groaned as the arrows hit him in the back and he pitched forward onto his blackened face and lay still.

Another got too close to where Vorgath had been hiding and the barbarian cut loose with one of his barbaric yells and cut the slender young man before him nearly in two with one swing of his greataxe.

Thrinndor drew his flaming bastard sword from its sheath—he had kept it there to preclude the flames from it alerting their adversaries—and swung it in one motion, hitting his target in the neck just above the shoulder as the fleeting figure tried to dart by. The Halfling screamed in pain and collapsed to the ground, unconscious and possibly dead.

Savinhand parted yet another from his miserable life as his Vorpal weapon flashed in the firelight and neatly lopped the head off of one of the assailants who had tried to escape past him.

As quickly as it began, the skirmish was over. The two remaining intruders kept their hands where they could be seen, not wanting any undue attention from anyone.

Thrinndor reached down and grasped the unconscious assailant at his feet by the tunic and easily drug him into the firelight and deposited the man none too gently next to the ring of rocks. He scowled at the nearest attacker and said evenly, a grim expression on his face, "Are there any more?"

The man tried to shy away from the attention, shrugging without commitment.

The big paladin took two rapid steps and was suddenly in front of the cowering rogue. He reached down with his left hand—his right held his flaming sword—and grasped the tunic of the now terrified man and lifted him clear of his feet. Thrinndor twisted his torso so that the man dangled over the rejuvenated fire, his booted feet among the flames. The thief's eyes widened in terror, but still he said nothing. The big fighter leaned forward so that his face was only a few inches from that of the sweating rogue and said menacingly, "I asked you, are there any more?"

As his pant leg caught fire the man shook his head and said, "No!"

The paladin, much to the man's dismay, lowered him a couple more inches so that his feet brushed the top logs of the fire. "Are you sure? Because if I find out otherwise, I will roast you slowly over these very flames and feed you to the wolves!"

With the attention of the group diverted to the scene at the fire, the other assailant tried to meld with his environment and slip out unnoticed. Breunne had expected such a maneuver. He quickly notched and loosed an arrow that caught the man in the back of the leg, just above the knee joint. The rogue howled in pain, pitched forward onto his hands and knees and then rolled over, both hands going to the wound. Still, the man looked about wildly to see if he was near enough to the edge of the trees to make a run for it.

"That was not a miss," said the ranger, his tone impassive. "Try to escape again and my next arrow will penetrate your back between the shoulder blades, just to the right of your non-existent spine."

The man stopped fidgeting and sat very still. He even stopped moaning from the pain of the arrow buried deep in his leg.

Thrinndor's eyes never left those of the one he held before him. He noticed that the man's leggings were now smoldering in several places from the proximity to the flames. "Well?" he asked.

The man's eyes darted nervously to where his companion sat on the ground with the arrow sticking out of the back of his leg and back to those of the big man that held him precariously over the fire.

"Yes!" he blurted. "There's one more!" Sweat ran freely down his face, whether from his feet inches from a now very hot fire or from fear was not certain.

In the end it really didn't matter.

Thrinndor pulled the man from the fire and dumped him unceremoniously on the ground. There the man used his partially gloved hands to pat out first the flames that had started on his right ankle, and then set to work on several spots that were merely smoldering.

The paladin ignored him. "Show yourself and we may yet allow you and your companions to live!" he said, his voice loud enough to carry quite some distance into the night, but not quite a shout.

They waited in silence, the healer in Cyrillis wanting to aid those in pain, the assailed in her not wanting to aid the enemy.

After a few moments, they all clearly heard the rapidly retreating hooves of a horse ridden hard.

Breunne leapt into motion and was into the ring of trees before Thrinndor could stop him. Not that he would have, but the big fighter was fairly certain that nothing could be done. Instead, he turned his attention to those that remained in the clearing. "All right," he said, "let us see what we have here." His eyes surveyed the scene. "Bring those that yet live into the light of the fire so that Cyrillis may attend to their wounds."

Vorgath glanced over at his victim. "Don't bother with this one," he said as he applied a none too gentle toe to the man's side, rolling him over. His lifeless eyes stared accusingly up at the stars.

"Ditto," said the rogue, looking over to where the head of the man he had encountered landed, which was several feet from where the body lay contorted. "He's a goner." Savinhand then walked over to where the man lay that Breunne had shot at the outset of the action. "This one is still alive," he said, noting the slight rise of the man's back from labored breathing. While he watched, however, the man took in a deeper breath, exhaled noisily and then lay still. All signs of breathing stopped. "Wait," he said as he bent down for a better look. "Never mind. This one is currently introducing himself to whichever god he ignored during his miserable life."

"Well," said the paladin with a glance toward where he had been hiding and encountered the Halfling, "I believe that one yet lives." He pointed with the sword still in his right fist.

"Figures!" said the barbarian with a roll of his eyes. "Never could finish a job right!" He shook his head and clucked his tongue in clear disappointment.

"Silence, peon!" commanded the paladin, a wry smile playing at his lips. "At least I do not swing first and ask questions later!" His smile grew. "I believe that may qualify as an unfair advantage!"

"Why talk when it is already known the scum need to die?" the dwarf queried. "Maybe we should finish the job." He brought his axe to the ready position and stepped toward the still smoldering thief, whose eyes immediately grew wide in fright.

"These 'scum,'" broke in a suddenly reflective Savinhand, "are members of my guild!" He looked at the dead one at his feet. "Or were, as the case may be."

"What?" said the dwarf as he stopped in his tracks. "We dined and partied with these guys the night before last?"

"Yes," answered the rogue leader. He looked down at the faces he could see and identify. "Well, some of them anyway."

"Really," said the barbarian thoughtfully as he turned to see if he could recognize the man lying at his feet. He didn't.

"I suppose the old adage 'no honor among thieves' has a ring of truth," said Thrinndor.

"Indeed," agreed the dwarf.

"This surprises you?" Savinhand asked with a circumspect tenor to his voice.

"No," said the paladin as he turned his eyes upon the rogue leader. "However, I will have to admit that how quickly they turn on their new leader, does."

"That can be explained easily enough," said a female voice from beyond the light of the fire.

The bushes parted and Bealtrive stepped into the clearing, Breunne was right behind her with his longsword poised at her back.

All eyes were on them as they came to a halt near the fire.

Thrinndor's eye's widened slightly in surprise. "Please continue."

Savinhand surveyed the group. Vorgath stood impassive to one side, leaning on the haft of his greataxe. Sordaak was busy trying to do a disappearing act by crawling under the nearest rock. Cyrillis was alternately applying her disapproving gaze on the caster and the new arrival—a move not missed by the paladin.

Nor Bealtrive either, apparently. "Well, hello there Lover Boy," she said as she blew the mage a kiss and gave him an exaggerated wink.

If Sordaak was uncomfortable before, he was positively miserable now. Sweat was beading together and running freely down his temples. His mouth worked, yet no sound emerged.

"I see you're happy to see me too," she said, winking again. She turned to the ranger. "I think you can put that weapon away now. You certainly made sure I was carrying none of my own!"

Thrinndor's eyebrow marched incrementally higher as his eyes turned to the ranger. "What?" Breunne asked defensively. "Of course I had to search her."

"Whatever!" said Bealtrive, making a show of adjusting the tight leather garment covering her ample breasts. "Just pray that I don't tell my new boyfriend how thorough your search was!"

Now it was Breunne's turn to shift uncomfortably.

The councilwoman was obviously enjoying this. She was about to say more when the paladin cut her off.

"You said you could explain. Please do."

"Oh that," she said with a frown. She waved dismissively at Savinhand. "Our new leader was not supposed to win that contest." She scowled at him. "I had an arrangement with Shivluur. By nominating him he would share the rule—and more importantly, the library—with me."

"So, you figured you would come take what your deemed rightfully yours," the paladin continued for her when her pause grew overly long.

She looked at the paladin with wide, innocent-looking eyes. "Something like that."

"So," said the rogue leader, his mind churning over the possibilities, "you are after the journal?"

"What journal?" she asked, her attention suddenly piqued. "There's a journal?"

Savin was momentarily taken aback by her seemingly genuine ignorance.

"Of course," she continued, the wheels in her mind also churning, "I knew there had—has—to be something of the sort. Phinskyr was gone too long, too often to ensure he was able to pass along the required information." Her eyes turned to Savin. "There's a journal, then?"

"Something like that," the rogue leader mocked her.

Her eyes widened and then she nodded slowly as they narrowed. "Perhaps we underestimated you," she said.

"Perhaps," Savinhand said. "Certainly Shivluur did!"

Bealtrive nodded and laughed. "He did, at that." It was not a nice laugh. Abruptly, she spun and used an open hand to slap the now drooping sword of the ranger aside as she sprinted quick as a cat for the edge of the trees.

"Stop her!" shouted the paladin. He was too far away to be of any use—she had planned her escape so as to take her the opposite direction.

But she had underestimated the quickness of the barbarian. Vorgath leapt into action, whirling his greataxe in a blur of motion and flinging it at the rapidly exiting rogue. She saw the flash out of a corner of her eye and dove hard to her right to avoid the blade. The blade missed, smacking with a thud into a tree. The blade bit deep there and stuck, its haft blocking her path. She was committed now, however, and tried to leap over it, but failed as her left foot caught. She spilled head over heels onto the ground just beyond.

Ever quick, she rolled and tried to surge back to her feet when her breath left her lungs in a whoosh! Vorgath, unbelievably quick for one of his size, had followed his throw and jumped onto the back of the rogue as she tried to regain her feet.

The barbarian pinned her there as she struggled mightily. It was like riding a hellcat, he thought briefly as he fought to hang on. She cursed, spit, raked her nails, bit and whatever else she could think of to get the dwarf off of her back.

"Whoa, lassie," Vorgath said as he grabbed a fistful of hair when she twisted yet again. Finally he had had enough and he clubbed her with his right fist on the side of her head. Her eyes rolled back into her head as her body went limp under him.

The barbarian looked like he had been in a fight with a hellcat! He bled from several scratches, his beard was in complete disarray and he breathed heavily.

As he started to rise, there was a shriek off to his right that completely took him unawares.

"Get off of her!" snarled a high-pitched voice.

Startled, Vorgath turned to confront this new adversary just as a figure launched itself at him. He had time to put up an arm to ward of the attack, but no more.

The figure crashed into him, knocking him off of Bealtrive's back. He tumbled hard to his left and was almost clear when he hit his head on a rock. Immediately, stars blurred his sight. The stars were still swimming in front of his eyes as he tried to rise, but the figure pressed its attack relentlessly and he was kicked hard in the head.

That was it. Out went the lights.

The remaining company had been taken completely off guard by this new attacker. They had been content, amused even, to let the barbarian deal with the councilwoman, but the ferocity of this new attack left them dumbfounded.

Startled into action by the barbarian going down, Breunne dropped his sword and snatched his bow off of its resting place on his shoulder. Quickly, he reached for an arrow.

Thrinndor was only a split second slower. He leapt in the direction of the downed dwarf, his bastard sword poised high above his head for a strike.

Savinhand started that direction as well but changed his mind when he saw one of the prisoners start to edge his way to the trees.

"Move again," snarled the rogue leader, "and it will be your last!" The man stiffened and then eased himself back to where he had been and remained still.

"Stop!" shrieked Cyrillis.

Breunne was about to release the arrow he had notched, and Thrinndor was almost within striking distance when he slid to a stop as the figure leapt off of the down barbarian and spun to face his new attackers, a shortsword in hand.

He held it low and menacingly, indicating to all he knew what he was about with the blade.

"He is just a boy!" the cleric said.

The paladin did a double-take. Sure enough! The lad could be no more than eleven or twelve years of age! Knowing he now had something to hold over his barbarian friend, he lowered his sword and relaxed as he stood upright.

"There now, son," he said soothingly with a chuckle. "Put down that sword before someone gets hurt!"

Instead of complying, the boy jumped at the relaxed and unprepared paladin. He was unbelievably quick. Thrinndor only had time to raise his left arm to meet the attack.

The shortsword flashed in the light of the fire and sliced a deep furrow in the meaty forearm of the big fighter. Thrinndor clenched his teeth to keep from howling in pain as he whipped his arm up and knocked the slight figure of the boy back a couple of steps. His blow should have been enough to knock him out, but the boy had rolled with the punch and took most of the blow on his shoulder. Still, the youth was clearly stunned as he turned to face the big fighter.

Breunne, unsure what to do, kept the arrow notched and at the ready should it be needed.

Fighting through the pain in his arm, Thrinndor again faced the boy, this time more wary. Blood ran freely from the gash as he held it before him to ward off another attack should one come. "I will give you one last chance," snarled the paladin. "Drop your weapon and face the consequences of your actions, or die."

The boy, dazed slightly from the blow he had taken, eased his stance and appeared about to comply. But again he leapt at the paladin, the shortsword in his hand again flashing in the firelight.

This time, however, Thrinndor was ready for him and easily side-stepped the thrust. Not wanting to kill the boy—not yet, anyway—he brought the haft of the huge sword in his right hand down hard on the back of the boy's skull as he rushed past.

There was a satisfying thonk as the hard metal met skull and the boy dropped hard to all fours, where he shook his head side to side in obvious pain.

"You do not listen all that well," said the paladin as he kicked the sword out of the boy's hand, sending it far out of his reach. He then reached down with his left hand and grasped a handful of tunic at the back of the boy's neck and easily lifted him clear of the ground.

The boy kicked and clawed at the air. "Stop struggling," said the paladin loudly, "or my next blow will certainly knock some sense into that thick head!"

The boy kicked twice more until Thrinndor pulled back his right arm with the flaming bastard sword in plain sight.

"Put me down!" said the boy, a belligerent look on his face. His eyes, however, never left the flaming sword.

"Very well," replied the big fighter as he took two steps to back into the clearing and flung the boy down next to the ring of rocks surrounding the fire. "Bind him," he snarled as looked around at what remained of their assailants. "Bind them all."

Cyrillis rushed forward and knelt by the boy. "Did you have to hit him so hard?" she shouted, inspecting the growing knot on the side of the boy's head.

Thrinndor was momentarily taken aback by her concern for the boy, and her ignoring the blood pouring from his own wound. "Yes," he said finally. "It could have been harder, I assure you. And maybe I should have!"

The cleric turned and started to snap off a heated reply, but the look in the paladin's eyes caused her to change her mind and the cleric returned her attention to the boy.

Sordaak, his expression grim, stepped to the fire, knelt behind the boy and none too gently lashed his hands together behind his back.

Cyrillis glared at him but said nothing more as she administered to her new charge.

Thrinndor shook his head silently, closed his eyes and said a brief prayer as he poured some healing magic into the gash in his arm. Almost as quickly it had opened the wound stopped bleeding and closed. As he stepped over to check on the barbarian, he noted the councilwoman beginning to stir. A quick glance showed Vorgath to be in no danger, so he turned his attention instead to the female rogue. In two steps he was at her side and planted a knee in the small of her back. She started to struggle, but a command from the paladin stopped her. "Be still," he hissed quietly, "or I will not be so easy on you as the dwarf."

She stiffened and then relaxed.

"Good," he said. "Give me your hands slowly." He set his sword aside and removed a couple of leather thongs tied at his belt.

She complied without further struggle.

When he finished trussing her up tightly he helped her unsteadily to her feet. He noted that the barbarian was beginning to show signs of life.

He guided Bealtrive toward the fire and shoved her roughly to the ground beside where the cleric was still working on the boy.

"Hey!" both women said at once.

"Be silent," replied the paladin as he turned quickly and strode back to where his friend had risen to a sitting position and was shaking his head slowly in an attempt to clear the cobwebs.

"Easy there, old one," chided the paladin. Vorgath looked up to stare at his friend indolently.

Thrinndor offered a hand, which the dwarf took. The paladin easily lifted the dwarf to his feet, where he stood unsteadily for a moment.

"What in the name of the Seven Hells hit me?" the barbarian said as the cobwebs cleared slightly.

"Here," said the paladin lightly, a smirk in his voice. "Let me show you." He put his hand on the dwarf's shoulder and guided him slowly to edge of the fire, where Cyrillis was standing not far from the boy.

Thrinndor stopped in front of the boy who looked up to stare at the paladin with a mixture of fear and hatred in his eyes.

"There," said the big fighter, amusement ringing in his voice, "meet your assailant!"

Vorgath stared down at the boy, his mouth agape. "What's this?" he demanded. "A joke?"

"No joke," replied the paladin, neither able nor wanting to hide the humor he was feeling. "This boy was the one who knocked you senseless. Well, more senseless!"

"Har-har," mocked the barbarian. "I ought to…" He drew back a fist and stepped toward the boy.

"If you do," Cyrillis said, her voice low, "you will have me to deal with, as well!"

Thrinndor raised an eyebrow. "You know," he said slowly, "this motherly shit can be carried only so far." Vorgath nodded. She turned to look at him, her eyes flashing. "This boy," he spat the word, "tried to kill us!" He waited for a reply. Getting none, he continued. "He is lucky to still be alive." He turned and strode off in the direction of the other prisoners.

"Are they bound tight?" he asked the caster as he approached. "These are, after all, thieves and would certainly be adept at bindings and freeing oneself from them."

Sordaak nodded. "Yes. They won't be escaping those bindings unless I release them!" He smiled smugly and crossed his arms on his chest.

"Thank you," replied the paladin. "We have one at least who places the well-being of the party before that of our enemy!"

Cyrillis bristled at the barb. "We were in no danger!" she snapped. "Unless you fighter-types are unable to handle a small boy!"

"I'm not small," said the boy. He puffed up his chest, but with his slight frame that did little to support his argument.

Thrinndor glared at her but wisely chose to carry the conversation no further.

"So," started Sordaak, "what are we going to do with them?" He waved his arm at the four who were now seated near the fire but not close enough to aid one another. The unfortunate thief to have fallen upon Thrinndor at the outset of the battle had also succumbed to his wounds and passed to the afterlife, so these four were all who remained.

The man who had briefly tried to escape and had gotten an arrow in his leg for his troubles had not yet been tended to and was markedly less happy than the others.

"Good question," said the paladin. "We cannot leave them here. And we certainly cannot take them with us." His eyebrows knitted together in thought as he pondered a solution.

Vorgath shrugged. "We finish what they started," he stated flatly. "We kill them."

The grouping was silent for a moment. Bealtrive and the boy both stuck their jaws out in open defiance but said nothing. The eyes of the other two took on a haunted look.

"I don't think that will be necessary," Savinhand said as he stepped forward and positioned himself between the two adult male thieves.

"Rats," muttered the barbarian as he lowered his weapon, turned away from the fire and stepped to the edge of the light.

The rogue leader smiled as he watched Vorgath walk away. "I would suggest there be no more attempts at escape or our barbarian friend will get his way." His eyes followed the barbarian as he took up position.

Thrinndor crossed sheathed his sword and crossed his arms, clearly content for the moment to see what Savin had up his sleeve.

Savinhand turned his attention back to the two men before him. His smile vanished even quicker than it had appeared. "Swear fealty to me," he said suddenly, his tone grave, "and I will allow you to return to Shardmoor."

He waited for the obvious response. He got it. "If we don't?" snarled the one who had his leg wrapped from his recent encounter with one of the ranger's arrows.

The rogue leader hooked a thumb behind him in the direction of where Vorgath stood. "Then I'll allow you to take your chances with my dwarf friend over there." He grinned wickedly. "I might even give you a chance and let you both go at him at once."

"Please," chimed in the barbarian. "I would prefer a little action to start my day!"

"How do we know you will do as you say?" said the other thief.

"You don't," replied Savin, his eyes piercing. "However, if fealty is sworn, you have my word as Leader of Shardmoor that you will be allowed to return there and bring them news of your failure."

"How do we know they will do as told?" inquired the paladin, not sure he liked where this was headed.

The rogue leader turned his gaze upon the group leader. "A good question from those uninformed as to how our guild—any rogue guild—operates," he said evenly. He again turned to the two before him. "Once fealty is sworn," Savinhand intoned slowly, "those swearing are bound legally to me personally and are as such protected." He paused briefly. "However, should they chose to break the vow, they will be hunted down like the dogs they have become and killed." Again a pause. "Slowly."

Both thieves looked at one another as Thrinndor spoke. "So," he said, "let me see if I have this correctly." His eyes never left those of the wounded thief. "The way I see it either a fast death at the hands of our barbarian..." He twisted his gaze to look in Vorgath's direction. "...and, just so you know, these will not count toward the kill total at the conclusion of our objective."

The barbarian started to object, but he stopped and nodded, not quite suppressing the smile on his face.

"Or," continued the paladin, returning his attention to the two seated in front of him who were shifting uncomfortably on the cold ground, "you swear fealty to your new leader—which I do not understand why that has not happened to date—dying a slow death should that vow be broken." He looked at Savinhand. "Do I have it correct?"

"Very good," said the rogue leader. "I see you do understand after all!" He looked at the two, his smile again gone. "What's it to be?"

The two men looked at one another. The one with the bandaged leg said, "What about them two?" He jerked his head in the direction where Bealtrive and the boy were seated.

"I suggest you concern yourselves with your own hide," Savin said evenly. "I have other plans for them. Plans that do not concern you." Again, the two exchanged glances. "Yet you hesitate," said the rogue leader, shaking his head slowly. He turned and made eye contact with the barbarian standing at the edge of the firelight who was leaning on the haft of his greataxe. "Vorgath?"

"Wait!" said the one with the bandage. He was obviously the senior of the two. "Please understand, our only hesitation is that we previously pledged our blades to the service of her." He turned to look at where the councilwoman sat.

Savinhand also turned to look at her, his eyebrow rising inquisitively. "Is this true?" he asked.

"Yes," Bealtrive said smugly.

Savin thought about it for a moment. "Well," he said slowly as he again turned his attention on the two men before him, "we have a few options here as I see it.

"One—she can release you from said service, or two—I can vacate that service as Leader of Shardmoor, at which point she would have no further claim to you." The rogue leader smiled, however it was not a smile that instilled joy into the hearts of the two prisoners. "Or three," he again jerked a thumb in the direction of Vorgath.

There was an uneasy silence over the group. Savinhand noted idly that the sky was starting to lighten to the east.

He looked over at where the rogue councilwoman sat. "Will you release them?" he said evenly.

Bealtrive knew her position of power was diminishing rapidly. She licked her lips nervously. "What's in it for me?"

"You might yet get to live!" snapped the barbarian.

Without turning in his direction, Savinhand raised a hand to forestall further interruptions. "I have plans for you," he said. "Plans I do not believe you would object to."

Bealtrive's eyes narrowed as several nasty rejoinders came to mind. Her shoulders drooped and she looked down at the ground, defeated. "Very well," she said quietly without looking up. "I release you from your service to me."

The fire popped just then, causing those seated next to it to jump slightly.

Again, an uneasy silence settled over the group.

"What's it to be?" repeated the guild leader, impatience edging its way into his voice.

Once again the two bound thieves looked at one another. Both nodded at the same time.

"All right!" said the one with the bandage, testily. "I swear fealty to you unto death! And as required by the bylaws of our guild, I demand protection from those who would stand against you until such a time as you are able to assume full leadership of our guild."

Savinhand nodded. "And you?" he said to the other.

"I also swear fealty to you unto death. And all that other stuff, as well." His eyes narrowed. "I don't know how you're going to protect us from all those who want to kill you, though."

The thief with the bandage nodded his agreement.

"I assure you," said the rogue leader, "you will be protected until I return to assume full responsibilities of leadership."

"If you return," said a sneering Bealtrive.

Savinhand turned to look at her and smiled. "I'll return." His tone brimmed with newfound confidence. "That I vow to you!"

Her eyes widened in astonishment at the vow. This changed things. A lot. "See that you do!" she said, not sure what was happening.

Savinhand smiled and nodded in her direction. "Release them." He waved his hand dismissively in the direction of his two newest subjects.

"Damn!" muttered the dwarf, loud enough for all to hear.

Thrinndor laughed and stepped forward as he was the nearest. He drew a thin stiletto from a sheath at his waist and cut the thongs that bound the two men hand and foot.

Both rubbed at their wrists and ankles vigorously to get the blood circulating again. Sordaak had indeed tied them well.

At Savin's direction, Cyrillis applied some of her healing powers to the bandaged leg, and soon both were standing without assistance.

Savinhand walked out of the clearing with them as the sun broke over the hills to the east, telling the others he would be back shortly.

He was.

"Release them," he again commanded. This time, Thrinndor looked at him doubtfully.

"You are sure?" he asked.

"Yes," replied the rogue leader, confidence again welling to the surface. "They will not try to escape. Nor will they attempt any further harm." He looked long and hard at both Bealtrive and the boy, silently imploring them to obey.

Thrinndor shrugged and again stepped forward, dagger in hand.

Their bindings released, they too rubbed blood flow back into their extremities.

"Let's go," Savinhand said as he started for the clearing.

"What are you doing?" queried the paladin.

"My business with them is private," said the rogue over his shoulder as he disappeared into the trees.

"You sure about this?" Sordaak's tone left little doubt that he was not.

"Yes," replied Savinhand without turning his head.

Bealtrive looked at the boy, who returned her look. She then shrugged and moved to follow the rapidly receding Savinhand.

"What's that all about?" asked the barbarian.

"I know not," replied the paladin, who was staring at the point where the three had departed. "But I mean to find out!"

Chapter Fifteen

Reins of Power

By the time Savinhand returned to the clearing, the sun was high over the hills and the remainder of the party had prepared a nice breakfast. They had even begun packing for what they had been told was a short journey to the entrance.

Sordaak breathed a sigh of relief when the rogue walked back out of the brush and into the clearing. The mage had started to get worried, and he was not the only one.

"We have a choice to make," Savin said cheerily. He directed this comment at the paladin, their new leader.

"What would that be?" the big fighter said, somewhat startled by the thief's sudden appearance. He was one of those who thought Savin had been gone too long.

The rogue leader looked up at the sun, shielding his eyes. "Our destination is but a couple of hours that way." He pointed off to the northeast, essentially following the nearby stream out of what appeared to be a shallow cul-de-sac into the hills. "Our caster-types have burned some of their precious spell energy," he continued with a smile and a dip of his head in difference to both the healer and the mage. "Although that amount might be slight, it might be wise to step inside at as close to full strength as is possible…" He took in a deep breath. "…under the circumstances."

"Oh?" said the paladin. "And what circumstances would those be?"

"Well," the rogue leader shifted his weight nervously from foot to foot, "for one, I don't know exactly what to expect once we are inside."

"Great!" muttered the caster.

"You expected different?" Savin said, his eyes boring into those of the caster. "I told you this at least once before."

Sordaak merely shrugged and went back to sorting stuff in his pack. "Whatever."

"And the second reason?" asked the paladin.

"Second?" replied the thief. "Oh yes, I did say 'for one,' didn't I?"

Thrinndor nodded.

"Well," continued the rogue, "the second is a guess, but a pretty good one. I have reason to believe there will be few—if any—places to rest to restore spell energy once we are inside."

The mage's head whipped around. "Come again?"

"In Dragma's Keep, we managed to take time out to rest, recover from various injuries and restore spell energy on several occasions," Savinhand answered him patiently. "I have reason to believe we will not have that luxury once inside." He took a deep breath. "Well, possibly one such place just prior to entering the Library itself."

"How do you know this?" Now it was the caster's turn to attempt the stare down.

Savin rolled his eyes, not fazed by the query. "I don't exactly know. It's just something mentioned in the journal about conserving spell energy for the end fight." He again shrugged and smiled.

The mage shook his head in mock disgust and turned his attention to the paladin. "Very well, I will cast crowd control spells—web, dancing ball, prismatic spray, that sort of stuff. I can give you a complete list if so desired. And I'll only cast when you ask for them."

Thrinndor nodded his agreement.

"I'll hold back on any offensive spells unless you deem them necessary."

Again the paladin nodded.

"And I shall keep my energy reserved for only healing purposes as well," Cyrillis said.

"Sounds like a sound plan," stated the big fighter. "With three fighter types and one sneaky bastard…" At this, he grinned at the rogue, who grinned back. "…we should be able to make do with whatever we encounter with the standard 'sword and board.'" Thrinndor looked at both Vorgath and Breunne, getting confirmation from each. "Very well. From the looks of the path forward, we should probably continue on foot?" This he directed at the rogue.

"That would probably be wise," Savin said. "I have made arrangements for those of my guild to take our animals back to Shardmoor—"

"What?" snapped the caster. "Why?"

"Well," said the rogue leader, "when we emerge from the Library, it will almost certainly not be back to this place."

"Come again?" repeated the caster.

"Again," Savinhand said, "I don't know this; it's just another cryptic entry in the journal that mentions 'spatial shift' and something about selecting a new location for said Library."

"You know," groused the barbarian, "this is starting to sound better all the time."

"No one is forcing anyone to enter," replied the rogue.

"Dragon?" replied the dwarf. "Helloooooo!" His attempt at humor was not lost on the party, and several of them chuckled in response.

"Very well, then," said the paladin. "Any ideas as to how many days' rations we should carry with us?"

"Hmmm," replied the rogue with a shrug of the shoulders. "I should think no more than two or three days should be sufficient."

"A week it is!" said the barbarian. When everyone turned to stare at him he added, "Hey, I got hungry in that last little escapade we wandered so slowly through!" He grinned at the rogue. "No offense intended, but I don't intend to go hungry this time!"

Savinhand laughed. "None taken. And the extra should not slow or hinder us significantly." He turned his attention back to the paladin, who had waited through the conversation.

"A week it is," Thrinndor said. "A scant week, if you please! I do not want you carrying a cask of both ale and wine after all!"

"Dammit!" groused the dwarf. "There went that plan!" He smiled at the paladin in return. "I'll limit myself to two skins of each. Someone else can carry the damn water!"

Thrinndor laughed. "Very well, I think that can be arranged."

He turned his attention back to Savinhand. "You said your guild members would attend to our mounts. Who exactly, if you do not mind my asking?"

Savin took in a deep breath before replying. "Bealtrive and Scumdog."

"Scumdog?" Cyrillis' head snapped around, away from the pack she had been working on. "Surely you cannot mean that little boy?"

"Actually," replied the rogue sheepishly, "I do." He held up both hands to ward off the coming protest. "Relax. I intend to rectify that upon my return."

The healer let the breath she had about to unleash upon the rogue leader out with a sigh.

"He showed up at Shardmoor a couple of years ago," Savin continued, relief apparent on his face. "A self-described street rat that got caught once too often stealing from those in the guild." He shook his head in wonder. "It is a wonder he yet lives."

A twinkle of mirth came to his eyes. "Bealtrive spared him, took him under her wing and has been teaching him the trade."

"She gave him that awful name?" Cyrillis was again inflamed. "That bitch!"

"No," laughed the rogue. "The court gave him that name when he was unable to produce one of his own when he was at his sentencing. They needed a name for the records. One faction pushed for 'Scum' and other for 'Dog.' They could not decide. Ultimately it was decided it was not worth arguing about and recorded it as 'Scumdog.'"

"Sentencing?" asked the dwarf.

"He was to have his right hand cut off."

The healer's hand went to her mouth in protest. "Dear Valdaar!" she exclaimed. "How barbaric!"

"Hey!" broke in the dwarf. "I resemble that remark!" He smiled at the cleric's confusion.

"Actually," agreed the rogue leader, "it is a common practice used to prevent thievery."

"But—" she stammered.

"Does anyone besides me see the contradiction here?" asked the dwarf in the brief opening left him by the healer.

At the blank stares he got, he added, "Thieves cutting off the hands of thieves?"

All eyes shifted back to Savinhand.

"Actually," he said, "stealing from a thief is most heavily frowned upon, hence the rather drastic punishment." He waved a hand in dismissal. "Regardless, Bealtrive had pity on him and took him in. He was released to her on probation." He grimaced at the thought. "If he ever gets caught stealing from the guild—or anyone in the guild—again, they will remove both hands!"

"Really?" Cyrillis asked.

Savinhand shrugged. "It was a condition of him being released to her. The punishment doubles should he be caught again." He paused to let that sink in. "A condition to which they both readily agreed."

The party was silent for a bit.

"We will have to leave this matter to your guild, I am afraid," said Thrinndor with a shake of his head.

"Sort of," said the thief. He was suddenly interested in a pebble that he was pushing around with the toe of his leather boot.

"Is there something you are trying hard not to tell us?"

"Such as?" Savin did not look up.

"Such as what it was that you had to leave the clearing for to deal with Bealtrive and Scum…" The quick look shot to the fighter by the cleric caused him to change what he had been about to say. "…the boy?"

Cyrillis folded her arms across her chest.

Savin's eyes flared briefly. "That is a guild matter," he said sharply.

Thrinndor crossed his arms resolutely, his eyes still locked onto those of the rogue. "If you insist."

Savinhand returned the glare. "I—" he began, but apparently something changed his mind. "Aw, hell, it's not like it's a state secret!" He continued glaring at the paladin, who did not budge. "Since I am a member of this party and I have sworn service to you and this quest of yours, I guess it won't hurt to tell you."

The rogue leader shrugged. "I have informed Bealtrive that I have other matters to attend to that will require me to be absent for long periods of time—"

"They should be accustomed to that," interrupted the dwarf.

"You are, of course, correct," replied the rogue as he allowed his shoulders to droop. "However, it's not how I wanted to begin my tenure as leader."

He looked around the group, trying to gauge their reaction to what he was about to say. "I've asked Bealtrive to act in my stead until such a time as my service is no longer required here."

"What?" Thrinndor said

"Really?" Sordaak asked.

"The bitch?" said the cleric, incredulous.

"Yes," replied Savinhand. He had guessed about right. "I needed her cooperation for several reasons, which will remain known only to me." His tone left no room for argument.

The big fighter reluctantly nodded.

"And the boy?" It had been awhile since Breunne had spoken, and the sound of his voice startled Savin.

"He is to remain in Bealtrive's tutorage until such a time as I can take over that role." He grinned at their sudden wide-eyed stares. "What?" he asked defensively. "As guild leader I may take as my understudy whomever I wish!"

"But they boy?" asked the mage. "He tried to kill us! Well actually, he tried to kill our esteemed barbarian."

"And nearly succeeded!" said the paladin. His grin was even larger than that of the caster.

"Bah," spat the dwarf. "A couple of lucky shots!" He glared at the paladin. "I was in no danger!"

"Whatever!" Sordaak rolled his eyes.

"Did you see him move?" said the rogue leader, admiration plain in his tone. "He's quick, strong and fearless!"

"He comes at me again," said the barbarian, "and I'll show him the meaning of fear! That I assure you!"

"He's only twelve," Savinhand said.

"Better he learn early," said the dwarf, "or he may not live long enough to test these skills you so easily praise."

"The boy now has the protection of Shardmoor," said the rogue leader, his voice teeming with the newfound strength of leadership. "He is a full guild member, and you may rest assured he will behave as such!"

"That means you don't have to worry about him attacking you again," said the caster with a wink to the rogue.

"Just see that he don't," groused the dwarf. "Are we going to stand here jawing all day? I'd kinda like to at least see this place before the sun goes down!"

Thrinndor chuckled. "The late breakfast played well into our hand." He looked up at the sun, now high overhead and slightly to the north, as was proper for this late time of the year. In another month the snows would come to these high places, he thought. "We will finish our packing, turn over our animals to Shardmoor and begin our march."

He looked at Savinhand. "Two hours, correct?"

"Thereabouts," replied the rogue. "We'll be more heavily laden than I was when I came this way a couple of weeks ago. So add maybe an hour to that."

Thrinndor nodded. "Very well. Finish getting your things ready." He again checked the position of the sun. "We depart in one hour. We will make a leisurely pace and set up camp within sight of this entrance." He looked at the rogue. "I presume we will have a place to set up camp nearby?"

"Yes," replied the thief. "There is a nice knoll overlooking our destination. It is easily defensible—although I expect no further trouble."

Thrinndor stopped in his tracks. "Why is that?"

"Because part of the reason I have made Bealtrive temporary leader is that I asked her to call off any other missions sent to deter us."

"There are more?" asked the paladin.

"At least one," said the rogue leader. "Could be two."

"Will she be able to stop them?" asked Breunne.

Savinhand hesitated. "I believe so. It's a matter of her remaining scouts finding these expeditions and getting them word that she's in charge." He smiled. "She can be pretty persuasive when she wants to be."

"Damn right," muttered the caster, busy poking around at the stuff he had dumped out so he could decide what to take. He didn't look up to see the nasty look Cyrillis shot him from where she was doing the same thing.

One by one they went back to where their packs had been left. Each had a different way to determine what he or she needed to take.

Sordaak pulled a funny-looking pie-shaped object out of a small leather sack tied at his waist. He carefully unfolded it until it resembled a round black disc, perhaps eighteen inches in diameter.

Next he put his hand against its surface and it passed right through, disappearing from sight!

Breunne, who having finished sorting his supplies and arranging them in easily carried sacks that did not hinder either his sword hand or his ability to quickly bring his bow into play, happened to look over and see what the mage was doing. "Is that a Portable Hole?" he asked, his tone more than just curious.

"Yes," replied the caster, looking up from the device in his hand as he pulled his hand back out with a rather large, lumpy sack in hand.

"I've heard of them," the ranger replied, as he moved closer to get a better look, "but I've never actually seen one. How does it work?"

Sordaak was more than happy to explain. "Well, think of this circle as a permanent, movable entrance to another plane of existence. On the other side is really a finite area—sort of like a bag, or maybe a chest. "You put things in…" He demonstrated by putting back the bag he had just removed. "…and they stay there." He pulled his empty hand back out. "When you need something from inside, you merely reach in and fumble around for what you are looking for." He again put his hand back into the black circle and it disappeared completely up to his elbow. "And pull it back out." He removed the large bag again.

"Remarkable!" the ranger said.

By now, attracted by what Sordaak was saying, Thrinndor, Vorgath and Savinhand also walked over just as the caster was again removing the sack from the hole.

"Where did you get this wonderful device?" asked the paladin.

"It was given to me by Rheagamon," the mage replied proudly. "It's a safe location for my spellbook—among other things."

"Very nice," said the dwarf. "How much will it hold?"

"Well," said the spellcaster, "that is not exactly known." He looked down at the disc. "He told me that I must be careful not to 'overfill' or 'overload' it. There are apparently three different sizes of these, although this is the only one I know of. Small, medium and large." He looked at the dwarf standing close by. "He told me this is a medium one."

"What happens if you overfill it?" asked the paladin.

"Not exactly sure about that, either," Sordaak said. "I did some research and, from what I understand, overloading can cause the entrance to tear, and you will no longer have access to what is inside."

"That would suck," said the barbarian.

"You got that right!" replied the caster. "I cannot afford to lose this spellbook now that I finally found it." He looked at the group standing before him. "Therefore I just use it for additional potion and scroll storage, besides my book."

"Sweet," said the ranger.

The others agreed and went back to what they had been doing.

Vaguely, Sordaak wondered where Cyrillis had been. He dearly wanted to show off his new toy. Ah, well...Maybe another day. He went back to checking his potions and scrolls, making sure he had some of each in appropriate locations in and around his tunic for immediate use. Those in the Portable Hole were for backup use, to replace any consumed during the course of action.

As each of them readied his or her pack, they moved to be near the fire. Or, more correctly, where the fire had been. Vorgath had been working to ensure it was extinguished before they moved on.

Savinhand had moved outside the clearing and summoned those of his guild. To his surprise, only the boy showed up.

Scumdog quickly explained that Bealtrive had left earlier to get back so she could recall any other groups who were trying to get whatever it was that the rogue leader had.

Savin nodded his approval and helped the boy gather the animals together. When at last that task was accomplished, he took the boy out of earshot of the others and bade him to sit.

"I want you to be my eyes and ears back at Shardmoor," the rogue leader said quietly. "There will be those who want to defy my rule, and there will be those who will not recognize Bealtrive as their leader." He paused. "Or both."

The boy nodded his agreement.

Savin handed him a piece of parchment rolled and tied with a leather string. It was sealed with wax and imprinted by the ring the rogue leader had on the index finger of his left hand. "Keep this hidden, and only use it if things start to get out of hand."

"What is it?" the boy asked.

"It's a decree by my hand that I prepared giving her leadership of the guild until such a time as I am able to return," Savin said.

"Why don't I just give it to her now?" Scumdog asked.

"Because I don't want to give her that much power right away," the rogue leader said. "I should be back in only a few days, and I hope she can keep those dogs at bay for that long." He smiled at the boy. "And because when I return, I will make the announcement myself—it's better that way. Too many will believe the document is forged."

"Ah," said the boy.

"Look," the rogue leader went on, his tone serious, "I see in you some of what I myself went through when I was but a lad your age." He shook his head remembering those days. "I had nothing. A chance encounter changed my life forever." He smiled down at the boy. "So it will be with you.

"Can you read and write?" Savin asked suddenly.

The boy fidgeted on the fallen tree on which he was sitting. "Some," he said quietly, looking at his hands. "Not much." He looked up into the eyes of his new master.

"Learn," Savinhand said as he reached out and ruffled the boy's hair. "Tell Bealtrive I told her to get you a tutor and to get you in school."

"Why?" asked the boy, suddenly belligerent. "Why does reading and writing matter?"

"Because," replied the rogue leader softly, "without that, you can't write—or read—this," he held up the parchment scroll he had written out for Bealtrive. "Nor can you learn your trade properly. Some books will be required reading if you want to advance through the ranks as a rogue!"

"All right," Scumdog said, "I'll learn! I'll learn faster than you even know!" He smiled. "I'm smart!"

"I know you are," Savin said with a wink. "But books and reading will make you smarter!"

The boy beamed.

"Scumdog is not a proper name for an apprentice rogue," said the thief thoughtfully. "From henceforth you shall be called Nichron."

"Why?" the boy scowled. "What's Nichron?"

"Nichron is a name I knew as a lad," Savin said. "It's a name I remember as being tied to a powerful man who governed our whole region."

"What happened to him?"

"Oh," said the rogue, "he died long ago, defending his keep and thousands of others from an orc attack." He fought back emotion as he continued. "I'm told he may have been my father."

There was a pause while Savinhand regained his composure. "It is a name I want you to have."

The boy looked up at this man who so recently he had been intent on killing and said solemnly, "I will bear this name proudly. Nichron. Yes, I like the sound of that."

"Good!" Savinhand again ruffled the boy's hair. "Now get going, and keep an eye on my guild!" As the boy leapt to his feet Savin said, "And keep an eye on Bealtrive—don't let them kill her…yet!" He smiled as the boy nodded.

"Yessir!" Nichron said as he grabbed a handful of mane hair and pulled himself up onto what was to be the lead horse.

Savinhand slapped the flank of the horse, starting the animals moving. He then reached up and brushed away some errant moisture that seemed to have gathered in his left eye. Only to discover it was also in his right eye.

Damn, he chastised himself! He was getting emotional in his old age. After all, he thought, twenty-eight is old—as a boy, he had never expected to see twenty.

He strolled slowly back toward the group, whistling a tune he had picked up recently while hanging around in all those taverns.

Chapter Sixteen

Smoke Wars, Part Deux

Vorpal encountered no problems on the slow march to the entrance. However, they took no chances and marched in formation. It had been decided that Breunne with his woodsman skills should now scout ahead. He therefore was well ahead of the group, off the path and unseen.

Vorgath marched point, Flinthgoor held at the ready. He was followed immediately by Thrinndor, Sordaak at his side, both ready for whatever might come their way.

Cyrillis was last in the formation, her job to heal as necessary or throw down an area of effect spell if called for.

Savinhand was now in the more classic role of the rogue in a group—sneaking around behind the last person. This was to ensure they were not followed and to stay hidden in the event of attack. He would then use his sneak-attack skills to work in behind any enemies encountered and attack from that position, stealth being his greatest ally.

The stream they had been following skirted a gentle knoll on top of which stood the ranger in plain sight.

The rest of the group climbed the slight slope and joined him there. On the other side was a small, windowless dwelling.

Vorgath spoke what each was thinking. "That's it?" He looked around for the rogue. Not seeing him, he went on anyway. "That shack is this Library of Antiquity?" He left no doubt he did not think much of that possibility.

"No." Savinhand's voice startled the dwarf as the rogue materialized out of seeming thin air. "That is merely the way in."

The dwarf stared at the rogue and tried in vain to figure out where he had come from. He knew that rogues worked on hiding in shadows and such, but there were no shadows! Sure, the sun was getting low on the horizon, but on the top of this knoll there were as of yet no shadows.

"Whatever!" groused the dwarf. "One of these days you are going to surprise me at the wrong time and I am going to take your head off!" He waved Flinthgoor menacingly.

Sordaak snickered quietly under his breath. He had fallen prey to Savin's sneaky ways many times in the past and was now less startled when he appeared as such.

"Whatever!" taunted the rogue leader. "I'll be sure to take appropriate precautions."

The two glared at one another until the barbarian grinned. "Just the same," he said as he turned to look at the small shack down the other side of the knoll where it sat beside the stream. "That's the entrance?"

"Pretty good disguise, huh?" replied the rogue.

"Pardon me?" intoned the paladin.

"If you are looking for this massive, mystical library," replied the rogue, "you would not suspect it behind that door, would you?"

As one, they turned and again looked at what from all outward appearances looked like a rundown shack.

"Nope," said the barbarian as he dumped his pack unceremoniously to the ground and began scouting around for rocks with which to ring a fire. He found them aplenty down by the wash of the stream.

The remainder of the party followed suit, each doing his or her part to get the fire going, preparing the evening meal, or setting up some other part of the camp.

Savinhand prepared the evening meal, as usual. He had a gift for making even the toughest of game palatable, and the others were more than happy to allow him to do so.

The group ate in silence, most content to slay their own demons without the hindrance of conversation.

Once the cleanup was complete, they again gathered around the fire, which the barbarian built high to ward against the chill of the descending darkness.

After a particularly loud pop as some embedded sap in one of the logs startled several in the party, Thrinndor cleared his throat. "This night we will turn in early," he said as the sun completed its disappearing act behind the hills to their west. "I want to be ready to enter at first light."

Sordaak looked over at the big fighter he had come to rely on over the past few months and nodded. He then pulled his pack over and began to rummage through it. He removed his pipe and a small leather pouch and set about building a smoke.

Vorgath lifted a bushy brow inquisitively and then patted his chest lightly until he discovered where he had put his pipe. Sensing an opportunity to work on his smoke figures, he spent what would seem to others an inordinate amount of time packing his bowl, carefully tamping down each layer as he did. He felt a growing excitement for the competition when he glanced up from his work to see the caster doing the same. The barbarian smiled in anticipation.

The others in the group also felt the tension begin to grow. All except for the ranger—he of course had not been present for the previous competition. Breunne looked around curiously as the others shifted their seats, or moved outright, so they could both get a better view and give the two ample space to work their craft.

Satisfied with his pipe, Sordaak held up an index finger, nodded his head and a flame appeared on its end with an almost inaudible pop.

Breunne raised an eyebrow as the caster put the end of the pipe in his mouth and held his lit finger to the bowl.

He puffed lightly, sucking the fire into the contents. Soon he had good head of smoke going. He sighed contentedly and held up his lit finger in the direction of the dwarf and bobbed his head deferentially.

Vorgath, who was strategically near the ring of fire, shook his head slightly, reached over a meaty paw and selected a thin brand that was lit only on the one end and drew it out. He put it against the tobacco in his bowl and began puffing lightly.

The mage shrugged indifferently and the fire on his finger went out. He held the finger up briefly, inspecting it to assure himself that no damage had occurred. It hadn't.

"New pipe?" the dwarf asked between puffs.

The caster nodded and smiled. "Also a gift from my new master."

"I hope you had time to work with it," Vorgath said with a smile.

The mage returned the smile and again shrugged. "Some."

After a brief stare down, the barbarian said, "Good." He took the onus, drew deeply on the pipe, pursed his lips and blew out a grouping of three rings in succession, each successive one smaller than the first.

Finally figuring out what was going down, the ranger found an open spot in the circle surrounding the two contenders and sat down.

The smaller ring silently floated through the ring next size up and appeared to lock itself in position within that ring, sides not touching. And then the two together sailed silently toward the largest ring and in like manner settled into position, again the sides not touching.

In position, the rings began to spin. The innermost ring began to rotate on its left and right edge. The middle ring spun on its top and bottom. This spinning started slowly at first and then sped up until the rings became a blur.

Cyrillis clapped her hands together appreciatively, and the others followed suit.

Sordaak rolled his eyes and likewise took in a short, quick draw. He raised his head, pursed his lips and released a long, thin tendril of smoke.

Quickly the smoke coalesced into the shape of an arrow. It hung poised there, not moving until Sordaak puffed his cheeks and appeared to blow gently in the direction of the arrow. However, instead of moving slowly, the arrow launched as if shot from a powerful bow and sped directly at the blur of concentric circles, leaving a thin trailer of smoke as it sped on its way.

Unconsciously, the grouping held their breath as the arrow approached the rings, not knowing what to expect.

As the arrow got to the rings, something unusual happened. The rotation of the rings appeared to slow as the arrow, also slower, made penetration.

The arrow completed its passage without making contact. However the rings appeared to catch on the trailer as if it were a solid mass instead of the smoke it obviously was.

Instead of continuing straight past the rings, the arrow turned hard and reversed course. The arrow then made two or three more passes through the center of the now completely stopped circles.

Sordaak smiled and then reached up and grabbed the tendril of smoke left by the arrow and jerked hard. Immediately the rings tumbled to the ground as if pulled there.

On impact with the ground, the rings and the tendril holding them immediately dissipated with an audible poof.

Again the applause erupted within the party, with the cleric leading the charge.

Vorgath's eyes widened in what passed as mild surprise, and he nodded at the caster, acknowledging defeat in round one. He nodded again, signifying it was Sordaak's turn to lead.

Sordaak bowed his head slightly, put his pipe back to his mouth and revived the bowl with several quick, intense puffs. He then took in a slow, deep draw and paused as he considered. With a wicked smile, he again pursed his lips and began blowing out a tremendous cloud of smoke. He was curious to see what the barbarian would do with this one.

The smoke, slowly at first, began to take shape before all their eyes. Still the mage drew on his pipe, puffing out more of the noxious stuff.

A mountain! Cyrillis was certain a mountain was forming before their eyes! It was...huge!

Still Sordaak pulled on his pipe, pouring even more smoke into the mountain that was now blocking from view what little was left of the light from the setting sun.

Vorgath was indeed having trouble figuring out just what to do with this apparition. Finally, tired of waiting—and almost sure his pipe was either out or going out—he began a series of rapid puffs of his own.

His pipe was not out.

Soon he was pouring out smoke like a chimney, as well.

Ignoring the dwarf, the caster continued to work on his mountain. Now there was a snow-capped peak on it and it towered high over their heads. Sordaak allowed it to drift northward with the gentle breeze so that all could properly appreciate the scale of what they were seeing.

Vorgath began working on the form for his figure and soon a humanoid began to take shape before them. A dwarf! This one was different from his last, however. While this dwarf indeed had a large great-axe, it was strapped to his back. In his hands instead he held a pick and a length of rope.

This dwarf meant to climb the mountain rising up before their eyes! And climb he did. Slowly at first, but gaining confidence he climbed ever higher.

Still the barbarian and the caster poured smoke into their creations. The mountain continued to grow almost as fast as the figure climbing it crawled steadily up its flanks.

Sordaak paused and, catching the attention of the dwarf, winked. Suddenly there was a tremendous explosion that caused everyone on the knoll to duck in either fright or surprise—or both! The top of the mountain blew away! It was a volcano!

When the air cleared, the companions could see that the top quarter of the mountain was missing and that lava was beginning to pour forth from the jagged remains of the peak.

The dwarf figure had been knocked to the ground by the force of the blast. However, he quickly regained his feet and saw the blood red magma begin its slow but sure descent toward him, picking up speed as it went.

The figure on the mountain reversed course and quickly began to retrace his steps, albeit at a much faster pace.

It was apparent to all that he was not going to make it. The lava worried not about ravines, boulders or trees that blocked its path, a luxury the dwarf didn't have.

Realizing his plight, the figure abruptly changed tactics and climbed as high as he could onto a small ridge below which the magma already ran freely. All watching knew it was but a brief respite as more and more lava poured from the depths and was soon to override everything on that side of the mountain.

Including the dwarf…

The figure looked around briefly and seemed unaware, or not concerned, with his plight. Instead of running, he stopped and shook out a loop with the rope he held in his hands. He began to swing it in broad circles over his head. Greater and greater the loop got as he swung it wider and wider. Finally, when the loop seemed impossible to control further, the dwarf sent it sailing toward the summit.

Impossible! The loop seemed to open wider as it flew ever higher until as it reached the summit, it settled neatly over the mouth of the volcano.

The companions unconsciously held their breath as the scene unfolded before them. The lava was so close. Even Sordaak was wondering what would come next…

They had not long to wait. As the rope settled over the mouth of the volcano, the dwarf figure jerked hard and the rope tightened slightly. The lava was too close!

Just as it seemed there was no hope—the lava was mere inches from where the dwarf stood—the dwarf leapt off of ridge on which he stood. Directly into a valley that was already flowing with the blood of the mountain!

He sailed down and away from the summit. However, there was no place that was not already flowing with lava! As he was about to meet his fiery death, the dwarf again jerked mightily on the rope held tightly in both hands and that, combined with his momentum, caused him to swing wide of the ravine at the last possible moment.

Jerking on the rope also appeared to serve another purpose. Impossible! The noose was tightening on the mouth of the mountain, choking it ever so slowly shut!

Higher and wider the dwarven figure swung, using his momentum and his powerful arms to pull himself from the lava just as it seemed certain he was about to be consumed by it.

And with each loop and each jerk, the noose tightened a bit more, pinching the mouth of the volcano more closed as it did. Until finally, with one more tremendous heave, the mouth was snuffed completely closed!

The volcano seemed to surge against its new bindings and then puffed a small cloud of smoke and went silent.

The figure swung high and hard in one more loop and released his grip on the rope as it flung him clear. He landed hard on his feet, tumbled three or four times and skidded to a halt, again on his feet. He then doffed his helm and swept it in a wide gesture as he bowed to the group who were now on their feet, applauding wildly and cheering.

As the smoke apparitions, now released by their masters, lost focus and began to dissipate, Sordaak also arose slowly to his feet and clapped his hands together—although his applause was notably less enthusiastic. "Nicely done," he said as he bent slightly at the waist, bowing to the barbarian. Nor was his smile all that genuine.

Vorgath beamed his pleasure and returned the bow. "Thank you, thank you," he said as he also turned and bowed to the others, obviously pleased with the adulation.

"However," said the caster slowly, "I am not finished."

The smile disappeared from Vorgath's face as he again turned to face the magicuser. "Yes, you are," he said as he looked at the pipe in the caster's hand. "Your pipe is out."

Annoyed, Sordaak waved the pipe dismissively. "Easily remedied," he said and snapped his fingers and the flame again appeared on the end of his index finger.

"I think that is enough for this evening," said the paladin as he looked at the now almost completely dark sky. Only the light from the fire and the glow from the lava had allowed them to see what had transpired. "I want to enter by first light."

Sordaak stared at the big fighter without moving a muscle. Finally the flame on his finger went out and he said, "Very well."

Thrinndor breathed an inward sigh of relief.

The caster turned and again bowed, this time more formally, to the dwarf. "Another time, perhaps."

"I look forward to it," the barbarian said formally. "Know that I have been dueling with smoke for more than a hundred years. And it has also been longer than that same hundred years since I have lost such a duel." He paused as the mage continued to stare at him impassively and then he started to turn away. "And that was the furthest I have been pushed in at least half that time." Sordaak stopped and again faced the barbarian. "That was magnificent!" Vorgath said.

The magicuser stood still long enough that a nervous tic twitched unnoticed at the edge of his mouth. "Thank you. I think." He turned to walk away, but stopped. "You're not bad, either," he added without turning. He again started toward his bedroll and then abruptly spun around. "However, next time you'd better bring your 'A' game, because I have a new, super bad-ass smoke and I am going to kick...your...ass!" He once again spun and marched out of reach of the firelight.

"Well," said the cleric with a disapproving note to her voice, "are we not a bit competitive!"

"Damn straight!" came the disembodied voice of the caster from the darkness. Cyrillis turned up her nose and marched off in the opposite direction.

"What's with those two?" asked the ranger.

"That is a good question," mused the paladin, his eyes looking first after the cleric, then the caster. "I am not sure I want to know the answer, however." He too headed for his bedroll.

Breunne was left staring after the paladin. Shaking his head, he also headed to where he had set up his bed. He passed by where Sordaak was preparing his blankets. "What have you planned?" he asked from a polite distance away.

"Not a clue," replied the mage without turning his head.

"Gotcha," said the ranger with a smile.

Chapter Seventeen

Going In (Finally!)

Breakfast was a quick but sustaining affair. Savinhand had said he was unsure when their next hot meal would be, so he rose early and prepared what amounted to a lavish meal: bacon, sausages, eggs, biscuits, various cheeses and even some fruit he had picked up from a vendor back in Shardmoor.

Vorgath complained about being spoiled but ate nonetheless. Two plates' worth. He mumbled something about being a growing boy and requiring stored energy for the coming battles.

Thrinndor reminded him that he had plenty stored energy already while pointing to the dwarf's ample midsection.

The dwarf rolled his eyes, quickly finished the plate he had been working on, sighed and stood for the standard morning stretching ritual of whooping the shit out of the paladin.

A grinning Thrinndor also stood and moved off so as to not destroy the camp with their antics.

However, Cyrillis stopped them before they could get started with a fierce command. She told them she had learned—just for their benefit—some stretching exercises that did not involve knocking one another's teeth out.

The two fighter-types reluctantly agreed and followed her lead as she showed them how to loosen their muscles after a rest period.

Once finished, Thrinndor felt invigorated and let her know as much. Vorgath muttered something about the paladin's manhood, his needing a dress and some dainty shoes for his morning routine. They very nearly went back to the old way of exercise when Cyrillis again stopped them with a sharp command.

She stepped in front of the dwarf with her staff at the ready and her face red. She asked him something to the effect of whether he was ready to defend such remarks.

Vorgath backed up, his hands held before him, obviously not wanting to cross paths with the cleric. He also said that he had just been funnin', and that he also felt better—ready for battle. He even thanked her.

Thrinndor was on the verge of teasing the barbarian back but thought better of it when the healer had turned her stare on him and said, "Well? Do you have anything to add?"

The paladin also backed up with raised hands. "No, my lady!"

And so they now stood before the door to the shack, each of them having had searched the perimeter at least twice.

"Hmmm…" said the paladin. "No windows and only this one door." He looked over at the rogue. "Odd."

Savinhand shrugged and said, "It will look different from the inside. Trust me."

"Do we knock?" asked the barbarian. "Or just kick the door down?"

Savin rolled his eyes. "Neither. We simply lift the latch and go in." He demonstrated by doing so and pushing the door inward. The hinges protested lightly by squealing as the door traveled inward.

The paladin's eyes went from the rogue to the open door. "You said it will be different inside. Perhaps we should stake the door so it cannot close behind us?"

Savinhand shook his head. "Won't work. We must all be inside and the door closed before we can access the next portal."

"Portal?" queried the caster. "You didn't mention a 'portal' before?"

The rogue let out a deep sigh. "Portal may be the wrong term." He thought hard to come up with the correct one. "The room will change, and we will have options."

"Huh?" said the dwarf. "Make some sense, man!"

"I would if I could," replied Savinhand tersely. "Look, this 'shack' is not the entrance. It is but a portal to the entrance." He looked at the ranger for help. "Once we are inside and trigger the mechanism by closing the door, we will be in another place."

"A teleporter!" announced Sordaak.

"Sort of," replied the rogue, "but not exactly." The barbarian made to speak again, but the thief went on before the dwarf could get started. "Could we just go in and get this rolling?"

Vorgath changed what he had been about to say. "Works for me!" Abruptly he shouldered his axe and stepped through the door.

Thrinndor stepped to the opening but did not go through. Instead he watched his friend from that vantage point.

Vorgath moved to about the center of the room and turned to look back at his friend.

"What do you see?" the paladin asked.

"You, dumbass!" retorted the barbarian with a smile. "Now can we just get on with it?"

Savinhand pushed his way past the paladin and moved to stand next to the dwarf. "Come on in," he said.

"I think I'll leave Fahlred out here," the mage said, uncertain which way to go with this.

"That might not be a good plan," replied Savinhand, his voice muffled by the doorway.

"Why?" asked the caster stubbornly.

The rogue leader shifted his feet uncomfortably. "Because once inside and the mechanism is tripped, I don't know where we will end up." He paused for a moment. "Or when."

"What?" Vorgath's smile disappeared and his head whipped around.

"Fact is," said the rogue, gathering confidence as he spoke, "this 'teleporter,' as you called it, could send us across the valley." He turned his gaze to the walls off to his left. "Or it could send us to a different plane." His eyes went back to those of the paladin. "Or we could be sent anywhere—anytime! We won't know until we get there!"

"Shit!" said the caster.

"And when we are through?" asked the paladin, his tone low and concerned.

"As I said before," the rogue said, matching the concern of the big fighter blocking the doorway, "I don't know where we will end up. That's why I had our horses taken care of. It comes down to this: If we complete this quest, I get to choose where the entrance is located –"

"Then choose here!" replied Sordaak.

"Not an option," Savin said. "Think about it. The location of the entrance must remain a secret. So by necessity it will relocate every time a new administrator is chosen. It will also change in appearance. I have not yet decided where to put it or what it will look like, but that is a decision I must confront before I leave the Library."

There was silence among the group as they considered this.

Finally, the mage could not hold back any longer. "You could have told this to us before now."

The rogue turned to face his friend. "Would it really have made any difference?" he said.

Sordaak started to reply angrily, but then he exhaled slowly. "No," he said. "I don't suppose that it would."

Again there was a pause as each considered what this meant.

Thrinndor was the first to speak. "You said 'if we complete this quest.' What if we do not?"

Savin turned slowly to face the paladin. "You're good at catching that stuff," he said evenly. "But that answer is much simpler than the last. Think about it."

The big fighter looked at him blankly.

The rogue rolled his eyes. "If we don't complete the quest, the entrance will end up right back here. And it won't matter because we'll be dead!" He waved his arms wildly to help make his point. "The guild will have to select a new administrator and the process will begin all over again!"

Realization came to the paladin in a rush. "Shit!" he said, causing a number of raised eyebrows. He ignored them. "Got it." He stepped quickly into the room and joined the barbarian and the rogue in its center. As he turned to face the door, he commanded, "Let's go."

Breunne was the first to comply. Cyrillis followed him in, with Sordaak close on her heels.

They all looked at each other when nothing obvious happened.

"What's next?" said the barbarian.

"We close the door," replied the rogue. He stepped forward to handle that task.

"Wait!" said the caster. Everyone turned to stare at him.

"What now?" said an exasperated dwarf.

Sordaak ignored him, turning to face the paladin instead. "You said 'let's.'"

"What?" said the paladin, confused.

"Not 'let us', but 'let's'!"

"And 'shit'," said the dwarf, suddenly interested.

Thrinndor looked from one to the other, blinked twice and said, "You are rubbing off on me," he said with a straight face.

Sordaak forced back a smile. "Well," he said, "just see that you keep that to a minimum, OK? Someone in this group must maintain some modicum of decorum." Now he smiled.

Cyrillis made a sound indicating she agreed with that particular insight and rolled her eyes.

The mage spun on her and was about to try to get to the bottom of whatever was eating at her but instead clamped his mouth shut. Now was not the time, he decided.

That was probably a good decision because he heard a clunk behind him as the door closed and the latch slide into place. He was not sure what he felt next, but it was certainly not normal and was instead kind of dizzying.

"Ready or not," announced the rogue, "here we come!"

The caster spun and was about to lambaste the impudent thief, but he stopped suddenly as he looked around the cabin they were in. Quickly his ire dissipated as he realized their surroundings had changed.

There were now four doors, all identical to the one they had come through. Otherwise, the room was the same.

"Would it have hurt you to wait until we were all ready?" the mage said, irritated at being caught unprepared.

Savinhand and Vorgath both said "yes," at the same time. They grinned at one another.

"If we waited for you to be ready all the time," said the dwarf wryly, "we would still be somewhere deep underground in Dragma's hell-hole!"

"Whatever!" groused the caster as he turned his attention first to the doors and then to his senses.

"I believe we have traveled," said the paladin. "Somewhere."

"Duh!" snapped the caster as he reached out for his familiar. He wanted to be sure Fahlred had made the journey to wherever they were. He had. He asked the Quasit to see if he could shed some light on where they were. No help there.

"Duh?" Thrinndor said.

"It's a term used to indicate that one had just stated something obvious to all," replied the caster, his mind elsewhere.

The paladin tugged absently at an earlobe. He briefly considered pressing the point, but even he could not figure out how it would be relevant.

"Anyone have any ideas, feelings or other insight as to just where that some-where might be?" the paladin asked instead.

"Or when?" said the ranger.

"About that," began the rogue, "in the effort to be clear, there has only been one—maybe two—recorded instances of the chamber transporting its occu-pants through time."

"That's certainly good to hear," groused the barbarian. "Out of how many of these recorded instances?"

"Dozens, I believe," Savinhand replied.

"Wait!" said the caster, spinning to fix his stare on the rogue. "You mean you have 'dozens' of these 'instances' recorded in that book?"

"No," Savin said. "This journal is but a small portion of the documented his-tory associated with the Library of Antiquity. It's maybe a couple of hundred years of observations and musings of the then current administrators of the Library."

"And most of those by one man," Breunne stated flatly.

"Phinskyr," agreed the thief.

"Where would be the rest of this documented history?" asked the caster, already knowing the answer.

"The Library of Antiquity, of course," replied the rogue.

"Of course," mimicked the mage.

"A lot of good that does us!" groused the barbarian.

"You must understand," Savin said defensively, "this documented history is not to help outsiders in." He looked from the dwarf to the caster. "It's to aid the new administrator in setting up his defenses for the Library itself."

"Defenses?" asked the cleric. "What defenses are required for a building? Especially a Library?"

Savin turned to face the healer. "You must understand. The term "library" is actually inadequate in its description."

"Oh?" asked the caster, distracted from his communicating with Fahlred.

"Yes," replied the rogue leader without turning. "Because stored, itemized and categorized within the austere walls of this particular library are not only the standard books, tomes, charts and recordings, but…" He paused, not sure just how much he was allowed to reveal at this early stage. "…artifacts, jewels, armor and…" He turned to face the paladin. "…ancient weapons are sequestered there, as well."

"What?" said the big fighter, his eyes narrowing in suspicion. "Weapons?" His tone went from suspicion to one of hope in the blink of an eye.

"Yes," Savinhand replied.

"Could it be?" Thrinndor's voice held hope, but it was the hope of one who had had such hope crushed on more than one occasion.

"Yes it could," replied the rogue. "However—"

The paladin interrupted. "How is it you have not mentioned this before?" Somehow he managed to sound both hurt and suspicious at the same time.

"Easy," Savin said. "Three reasons: One: I was trying to prevent just this reaction. Because, two: The likelihood that the blade you seek is hidden in the Library is about the same as our dwarven friend over there becoming an equestrian expert."

"Not gonna happen," Vorgath said, his mighty arms crossed semi-patiently on his chest.

"Exactly," replied the thief. "And Three:" the rogue leader continued hastily before he was again interrupted, "when exactly would I have had time to discuss this with you? I only learned of the Library a week ago. And that there are items within its lofty walls other than just books within the past couple of days!"

Thrinndor let the breath out that he had not realized he had been holding. He also allowed his broad shoulders to sag at the same time. "Very well." His demeanor brightened slightly. "We will just have to go see."

"Correct," said the rogue leader. He shifted his weight from one foot to the other. "One more thing: On the very slight chance that Valdaar's Fist is indeed stored in the Library of Antiquity, there it must remain."

"What?"

"It is sooth," said the caster solemnly. "This much I know: What is kept in the Library must remain there."

"Or?" replied the paladin, his voice menacing.

"No 'or,'" said the rogue. "Nothing may be removed from the Library of Antiquity." His tone was level and solid. "Ever!"

"If Valdaar's Fist is there," said the big fighter, "I will claim it and it will leave with me."

"It will not be permitted," Savinhand said.

"Who—or what—will stop me?"

Savin looked up at the paladin and their eyes locked. The rogue had been afraid of this. He did not back down. "I, as caretaker and administrator of the Library, will."

"You?" sneered the paladin.

Sensing the hostility, Cyrillis stepped between the two. "Boys, boys! This is something we can resolve should the need arise."

Their eyes did not waver.

"No," said a resolute thief. "It is better we resolve it now." He finally tore his eyes from those of the paladin and put them on the cleric. "I want no misconceptions when we reach our goal."

"Agreed," responded the paladin.

Savinhand turned back to face the paladin. "While I do not believe the sword you seek is in The Library, do not discount my ability to do what I have said I will." Now his tone was also laden with the confidence to back up his statements. "Recently there were two who did, to their detriment."

Thrinndor's jaw dropped in open surprise. "You threaten me?"

"No," the rogue replied evenly, "I am telling you that nothing retained within the walls of The Library may ever be removed. By anyone!"

The paladin's eyes narrowed. "You swore an oath! An oath to support this quest to the end."

"I did," agreed the thief. "However, you don't understand!"

"Help me to understand," replied the paladin.

"I will, if you'll give me the chance!" Savin's eyes flared briefly.

Thrinndor crossed his massive arms on his just as massive chest. "Go on," he said, his voice rumbling from deep down inside.

Savinhand took a deep breath and a step back. "Thank you," he said. The rogue leader looked around the room, but he needn't have bothered. He had everyone's full attention.

"From what I understand," he said, "The Library is more like a museum, if you will." His eyes strayed back to the paladin. He had not budged. "It has been as such for more than two thousand years. It's really a collection of curiosities and various works of art—as seen by whatever curator put them there to begin with.

"Long ago a deal was struck, with whom—or what—is not recorded, and no one remembers." He took in a deep breath. "Ancient enchantments were induced and pacts formed. The Library was created." His eyes again wandered the room, but quickly came back to those of the paladin. "And it was given life." This drew gasps from several in the room. He nodded. "The Library is said to be a living entity." He paused as he allowed that to sink in. "Do not doubt it. Over the centuries many books, manuscripts, tomes, trinkets, weapons, gems and some just plain curiosities were enshrined within. They were categorized, lovingly cared for and stored.

"The Library of Antiquity lives to maintain these treasures." His eyes held those of the paladin. "The pact entered upon requires that items may only be brought in, none removed."

The paladin searched the eyes of the rogue, not sure where to go next. "Then we must pray that Valdaar's Fist is not among these treasures."

"Exactly my point," replied the rogue. "It is for the simple reason that your quest requires the sword that I must believe it is not among the collection maintained therein."

Again Thrinndor searched for what he should do next. "Agreed."

He spun and fixed the mage with his stare. "Any luck on finding out where— or when—we are?"

"No," replied the caster with a shrug of his narrow shoulders. "These walls seem to be enchanted such that neither I nor my familiar can sense anything beyond them."

The paladin turned to the dwarf. "How about a direction?"

"Sorry," Vorgath said with a shake of his head. "My sense of direction is infallible when I have a reference point." He looked at one of the doors and pointed. "That door is the one we entered through. When we came in, that was the West door." He looked back at his friend. "Whether it is now or not, I can't tell."

The paladin turned back to the rogue. "Now what?" he asked simply.

"Now it gets complicated," responded the thief.

"Duh!" said the barbarian.

Everyone turned to look at him. "I kinda like that word," he said with a smile. "Simple, quick and to the point."

Savinhand chuckled as he reached under his tunic and removed the leather wrapped parcel he kept there. As he unwrapped the tome he said, "According to this journal, only one of these doors will take us to where we want to go."

"And the others?" asked the mage.

"The others will be wrong, and we'll have to pass a test just to get back to this room and try again," Savin said.

"What kind of test?" asked the dwarf.

"The book doesn't say," replied the rogue. "It's my understanding, however, that monsters, puzzles and other hindrances are among the possibilities."

"Great!" announced the caster. "Are there any clues in that book that might be of assistance?" He glanced around the room. "These damn doors all look identical to me!"

"You're not looking hard enough," said the ranger. He pointed at an insignia on one of the doors. It was a small depiction of the sun. He then pointed to the door opposite the one with the sun; it also had an insignia in the same place, but this one was of the moon.

Sordaak looked again. "Damn," he whispered. "I didn't see that." He quickly looked at the other two doors, noting insignias in the same place on both—one the universal symbol for land, the other water. "Anything else I might have missed?" he asked dryly.

When no one said anything, the mage looked accusingly at the rogue. "Any mention of these symbols in that book of yours?"

"Yes," he said. "And no."

"Here we go again!" griped the dwarf. "Which is it?"

"Well," started the rogue. "It only mentions them as being the first test." He looked at the caster, clearly hoping he understood. "Possibly a puzzle of sorts."

"Great!" the mage repeated. "Did I mention that I flunked out of that part of my training? Puzzles make my head hurt."

Thrinndor stepped to the doors, each in turn and studied the insignias closer. The others in the room watched him.

"Could it be," he said as he studied the symbol for the moon on the door in front of him, "that it has to do with their order in the formation?"

"Huh?" said the barbarian.

"The Formation," explained the paladin. "Legend has it that the sun was formed first. Then the ground on which we stand. Next was the moon, or moons—I am not certain why only one is depicted here. And finally water was introduced."

"The Order of Formation!" Sordaak said excitedly. "Of course!"

"Then we should go through the door with the sun on it first," said the cleric. She walked over to also study each emblem.

"And if we're wrong?" queried the ranger.

"We'll try again," replied the mage, shrugging as he did. It seemed a simple matter to him at this point.

"Ummm…" said the rogue as he cleared his throat. All eyes returned to him as he turned the page in his journal.

"What now?" asked the caster.

"It says here," the thief said softly, "that we will only have one chance at each puzzle."

"What?" Cyrillis said.

"How so?" asked the paladin.

"Well," Savin said, "that it doesn't exactly say. But the implication is that if we get it wrong, we will have to work our way back to this room and the doors will have reset—possibly with a different set of emblems."

Sordaak took in a breath to again express his thoughts on this process, but evidently changed his mind. He let the breath out with a sigh. "That changes nothing," he said wearily.

"Agreed," acknowledged the paladin. "We proceed through this door." He walked up to the one with the sun on it. From there he turned back to face the others. "Unless there are any objections or further insights?"

The silence he got, along with a couple shakes of the head, was all he needed. The paladin turned his attention back to the door.

"If I may," Savin said as he stepped up to stand at the paladin's left elbow while rewrapping and storing the journal.

Thrinndor turned his head to peer at the man next to him. "Surely you do not suspect these doors are trapped?"

"I 'suspect' nothing of the sort," the rogue said lightly. "This chamber was designed by a thief to keep other thieves—among others—out." He looked up at the big fighter and grinned. "I expect it to be trapped!"

"Well put," said the ranger, taking a couple of steps away from the indicated door.

"Very well," agreed the paladin with a sigh as he stood aside to give the locksmith ample room with which to work his trade.

Savinhand stepped up and immediately began examining the door, the latch, the jamb and everything else in the immediate vicinity. After a few minutes he stepped back and placed his hands on his hips. "That's odd," he said.

"What?" more than one voice asked.

Savin ignored them as he removed a small bag tied at his belt, reached inside and removed a small cloth-covered item. He re-tied the bag to his belt and then carefully removed the cloth, revealing a piece of glass about the size of his palm. Then he stepped back to the door and again began his search, this time looking through the odd-looking piece of glass.

"What's that?" asked the cleric.

"Shhhh…" chastised the ranger. He looked at her and whispered, "It's a magnifier glass." He looked back to where the rogue was inspecting the door frame slowly. "It allows him to see what is in front of him in far more detail."

"Oh," whispered the healer. "Thanks."

The cabin was silent enough that each could hear the breathing of the others. All attention was on the thief as he carefully inspected the door.

Finally Savin stepped back and again put his hands on his hips. "Damn!" he exclaimed into the silence.

"While we're still young!" griped the barbarian. Thrinndor turned to say something, but Vorgath cut him off. "Don't say it!"

The big fighter grinned at his friend.

Savinhand turned to look at the gathering. "I don't get it!" He waved his hand in the general direction of the door.

"What?" Cyrillis asked for them all.

"There are no traps!" replied the rogue.

"You mean you can't find any traps!" corrected the dwarf.

Savinhand turned slowly and fixed his stare on the dwarf. He did not back down. "No," he said succinctly, "I mean there are no traps!" He bit off each word and even took a short half step toward the dwarf.

In response the barbarian drew himself up to his full height—still almost a foot shy of the rogue—and said, "You've been working on that." It wasn't a question.

"Damn right I have!" replied the thief. "Before I could contest for the right to lead," his eyes continued to bore into those of the dwarf, "I had to achieve the status of Master Trapsmith and Locksmith!"

"No," Vorgath said before Savin could continue. "You've been working on that look!" He grinned his toothy grin.

A startled thief stood upright and then grinned in return. "Yes, that, too," he said as he brushed a wayward lock of black hair back in place. "It comes in handy when dealing with those rogues!"

"Ha!" snorted the ranger.

"Could we please get on with this?" begged the caster. "As our not-so-eloquent barbarian said—"

"Hey!"

"—we're not getting any younger!"

"That's not what I said!" said the dwarf.

"Whatever!" Sordaak waved his arm dismissively. "Can we please get on with it?"

"Yes," replied the rogue leader. He strode back to the door and lifted the mechanism. "It's not even locked. Just the same, I would stand back in the unlikely event someone got cute on the other side of the door."

"Cute?" Breunne asked.

"Traps," Savinhand said as he pushed the door open and stepped through the frame.

"But you said—" began the healer. "Oh, never mind!"

The group waited patiently for the thief to say something. After a few moments Savin poked his head back through the door. "You guys coming?" He smiled and disappeared back into wherever—whatever—was on the other side.

"Standard maneuvering formation," said the paladin as he drew his sword and readied his shield.

"Standard what?" Vorgath asked, his eyes narrowed to mere slits.

"Maneuvering formation," Thrinndor said patiently. "That means we assume our usual marching protocol in our movement."

"This leader shit has made you daft!" said the dwarf, shaking his head as he readied Flinthgoor.

"Just get in position, old one!" snapped the paladin.

The barbarian did as requested, shaking his head.

The others followed suit.

Breunne stepped silently through first followed by the barbarian. Thrinndor motioned for Sordaak to go through next, which the mage did without comment, the paladin right behind him. Cyrillis immediately followed.

On the other side she found the others in standard battle formation, waiting expectantly for…what?

The walls and ceiling were indistinct—bathed in some mixture of light and fog. Even the size of the room was indefinite.

"Where are we?" she said as she stepped through the door.

Once clear, the door closed behind her of its own accord. There was an ominous thud as it seated in the frame and the mechanism slipped into place.

The mage and the paladin exchanged looks when a voice suddenly broke the silence. "You have chosen poorly." The voice echoed off of the walls as the door shimmered and then disappeared.

Chapter Eighteen

Heads or Heads

Silence held the group for a few moments as the mist faded and the chamber began to take shape.

"Defensive posture!" Thrinndor snapped.

In a matter of seconds Breunne moved ahead and to the barbarian's right with Cyrillis and Sordaak close behind. Thrinndor stood a few paces behind them. Savinhand was nowhere to be seen as usual.

The room was not really a chamber so much as a large, elongated cavern they were standing in one end of. The other end was not quite visible through the lingering mists.

The path on which they stood ran alongside a meandering stream. The water bubbled lightly over the rocks as it stumbled slowly in the direction they were obviously meant to go.

The chamber was lit by light that filtered through the mists over their head. It was eerily similar to the large cavern they had encountered while searching for the entrance to Dragma's Keep.

After a few moments in which nothing happened, the paladin relaxed his guard slightly. "Looks like our current destiny lies further down this path."

Sordaak rolled his eyes. "I gave up the leadership position for that?" He looked at the big fighter. "Shall we?" He waved an arm sarcastically in the indicated direction.

"Just say the word and leadership will be returned to you," replied the paladin.

Breunne shook his head in mock concern and turned to begin striding down the path before more could be said.

And so the group fell back into their regular traveling formation, with one noted exception: Weapons were drawn and at the ready. The warning from Savinhand that they would have to pass a test had everyone on full alert.

The path meandered farther back into the cavern while following the stream.

Soon, however, they could see that the stream slowed and broadened out into what appeared to be a shallow pool. The walls of the cavern followed suit and also spread out until they were no longer visible on either side. The ceiling also lifted higher until the mists were far above their heads.

The path veered right, following the shoreline in that direction. There, Breunne waited for the others to catch up to him. "Curious," he said. "I can't tell whether we are inside a cavern or outside in the open air."

"Inside," the barbarian stated flatly. "There's no sky up there." He craned his neck as he tried to penetrate the mists with his unusually sharp vision. "But I don't sense the rock, either. As you said: curious."

"Perhaps that can explain," said the mage. He pointed out into the water.

Everyone turned to see a large shape rising silently out of the pool. Initially only the heads were visible—multiple heads! It soon became apparent the heads were a part of one creature.

The monster was rising out of the water because it was moving slowly toward them!

Sordaak counted five different heads, each a different color. There was one each red, blue, green, black and white.

"Hydra!" shouted the paladin. "Spread out!

"Each head is able to produce a breath weapon similar to that of a dragon—just on a smaller scale—each according to the color of the head," said the ranger as he took a few steps toward the water and moved to his right.

"Correct," said the paladin. "Cyrillis, try to apply to the fighter the appropriate resistance to according to whatever head he is facing, please."

"Got it," the cleric said. She began murmuring prayers.

"I'll take fire," said the barbarian as he stepped to his left, moving to confront the red head of the hydra.

"Cold here," Breunne said. He stepped so that the white head was directly in front of him. As the monster continued to move toward them and thus out of the water the ranger added. "Damn, this is a big one!"

"I will focus on whichever head stays around here in the middle," said the paladin. "Probably the acid and poison cloud ones." He turned slightly to ensure the mage could hear what he said next. "Sordaak, can you slow it down some with a fog or cloud?"

"I can try," the caster replied as he pulled a small pouch from the thong that held it in place at his belt. "However, each head will have its own resistance check to being hindered by anything I throw at it." He eyed the beast doubtfully.

"Anything to distract the heads we are not immediately attacking will help," replied the paladin.

"Got it," replied the spellslinger.

"Go for the heads first," said the ranger. "Cutting them off will temporarily stop the breath weapon." He stood at the ready, an arrow notched in his bow. "But to kill it, we must attack the body."

"Temporarily?" Sordaak asked.

"Yes," Breunne said raising his bow. "The heads regenerate rather rapidly."

"Wonderful!" replied the mage as he waved his arms over his head, chanting as he did.

The healer was busy doing as she was directed when Thrinndor asked, "I wonder why it has not attacked—"

Before he could complete the sentence, the blue head reared back, spread its jaws and released a flash of light at the paladin. Lightning bolt! He had forgotten about that one!

He didn't have time to think about it as he brought his shield up to deflect the bolt. While it appeared he had been successful—the shield seemed to absorb most of the energy—it was metal and some of the energy was passed through it to the paladin's left hand and arm.

In an instant severe pain flashed through his arm and it went numb, completely numb. And also completely useless.

"Shit!" he shouted as his left arm and the shield dropped to his side.

"The hydra needs to get close enough for its breath weapons to be effective," the ranger answered his own question belatedly. He loosed three arrows in rapid succession into the body of the creature, all striking home. None seemed to have any effect on the monster save to divert some attention his way.

As the white head turned its attention on the impudent creature just out of its reach, the ranger ducked and ran a few steps farther away. He withdrew arrows from the quiver slung on his shoulder as he did.

"Thanks!" muttered the paladin as he shook his arm in an attempt to get feeling back.

Somewhere about then, Vorgath yelled at the top of his lungs and charged into the water, obviously unwilling to wait for the monster to come to him. His blade flashed and though he was unable to reach high enough to strike at the head or neck area, it bit deep into the muscular shoulder area that supported one of the necks.

The hydra screamed, bent the neck with the red head on it toward the dwarf, opened its maw and breathed fire onto the barbarian down below.

The dwarf jerked his axe free from where it had lodged and immediately dove into the thigh-deep water, hoping to put out the flames in his beard.

Cyrillis continued to work her spells. Lightning resist for Thrinndor. Fire resist for the barbarian. Cold resist for Breunne. That should do it for now. Where was Savinhand, the cleric wondered briefly? She hadn't seen him since the hydra appeared.

Wait! There he is! She thought as he suddenly materialized next to the water's edge, sprinting toward the monster with a long stick—staff?—in his hands. As she watched, he planted the shaft of wood on the shoreline and used his momentum to launch his body through the dense cloud created by the magicuser, over the blue head, which was still intent on the paladin, to land neatly on the back of the hydra.

Releasing the stick as he flew, Savin's hands flashed to his belt and each came back with a weapon: his now trusty Vorpal shortsword in his right and a long, thin dagger in his left. He had assessed the situation on the way in and decided the green head, which was focused on the splashing in the water that was the dwarf, would be his target.

Just then the blue head spat out another lightning bolt, this time catching the paladin square in the chest as he waded into the water, his left arm still hanging uselessly at his side.

The sword in the rogue's hand flashed, catching the neck of the green head right at its base, completely severing it at that point!

Now he had the beast's attention! It surged upright, nearly throwing the thief into the water. But Savin quickly stabbed hard with his left hand and his dagger bit deep, giving him a hand-hold to allow him to remain on the creature's back as it bucked and rose up.

The remaining heads screamed in unison and turned their attention to the pest now hanging on for dear life on its back.

"Ugh-oh!" muttered Savinhand as four sets of malevolent eyes focused on him simultaneously. His Vorpal again slashed hard at the nearest neck—blue, as it happened—but the crazed thrashing of the beast beneath him caused him to miss badly. His momentum was too much for the meager hand-hold his left hand had on the dagger and he tumbled toward the water where he landed with a splash.

Thrinndor, who had been knocked back a step by the lightning bolt to the chest, had recovered somewhat and was finally within range with his sword. He ignored the easy target of the neck before him, instead his flaming blade flashed in the gloom and bit deep into the body of the creature.

"Body!" he shouted. "Attack the body!" He could see through the mist that the green head was already growing back.

Just then a spluttering Vorgath surged from beneath the surface with a roar. Now he was really mad! At least half his beard had been burned away, and he had worked more than a hundred years on that beard!

Breunne loosed three more arrows, all again hitting their mark in the main trunk of the beast. Although he was sure he was hurting the creature, the arrows seemed to have no effect.

This creature was going to require more 'attention' than his arrows could provide. Quickly, he made the change from bow to sword and waded in.

Spotting the ranger through the mists, the white head turned on him and breathed a blast of cold frost that caught him unprepared. The icy cone knocked him from his feet and sent him tumbling backward into the waiting water.

Momentarily stunned, he fought his way back to the surface only to find that the continued blast of cold from the hydra's mouth had formed a thick layer of ice on top of the water!

He fought down panic, knowing the ice could not extend far in any direction. Still, it was several heartbeats before his struggles found a spot where there was no ice. He lunged out of the water, his oxygen-starved lungs gasping for air. Briefly he noted that he couldn't remember the air tasting so sweet. He cast about wildly in the now ice cold water, but could see nothing through the fog. The caster had certainly been thorough!

Listening, however, he was able to tell his recent encounter had carried him past the creature. Trying not to make a splash and thus alert the beast, he attempted to make his way back to the fray. Fortunately he had his sword at the ready, for when the mists parted the white head was only an arm's length away. They simultaneously spotted one another and the beast opened its maw, again releasing its breath weapon.

Breunne held his ground as the icy blast hit him square in the face. "Not this time," he said through clenched teeth as his blade made a wicked arc through the air, connecting with the monster at the base of the skull.

The remaining three heads screamed in pain as the neck that had held the white head jerked back. Breunne then had the creature's full attention, as those three remaining heads turned on him and released their breath weapons.

Fire, lightning and acid washed over the ranger, knocking him unconscious as he slipped below the surface of the water.

"Cyrillis!" shouted the paladin. "Breunne's down!" He cursed his inability to immediately go to his comrade's aid, but the monster was between him and the submerged ranger, and now the beast was turning its attention back to him.

"On it," the healer replied as she splashed into the water toward where the ranger had fallen.

Thrinndor didn't have time to see if she was successful as the mists thinned. Sordaak's spell was dissipating. The big fighter swung his sword in a mighty arc, but the creature was nimble for its size and dodged.

As he righted himself from the missed blow, the paladin took a moment to assess the situation. He did not like what he saw. The green head was almost fully regenerated and would soon be able to deal its breath weapon. The white head was not far behind.

His left arm started to tingle fiercely, and he quietly wished it had stayed numb. The hydra was bleeding from several wounds to its body, but none appeared to be mortal. Certainly it had slowed not at all.

He made a snap decision as he again brought his sword to bear. "Sordaak!" he shouted, not taking his eyes off of the blue head squaring off for another bolt in his direction. "Go on the offensive! Now!" Fortunately, the beast could not deal its weapon continuously. It had to build energy back up between each one.

"Been waiting for that!" muttered the caster as he pointed his right index finger and launched is quickest spell, Force Darts. They did not do much damage, but they never missed and his increased rank gave him more of them. They were also now more potent than before.

Indeed, the missiles darted unerringly into the massive chest of the creature, doing little noticeable harm. Yet the creature screamed and the black head focused its malevolent stare on the caster. The body of the creature began to move again, toward the shore and this new threat that it deemed most significant.

Sordaak ignored the beast as he waved his arms over his head in preparation for a second, more powerful spell. He had been prepared, already having selected the spell components for his first two or three spells and had them in his fingers.

He knew from his studies that using like energy on a particular head of a hydra—say fireball on the red head—actually aided that head rather than harming it. Thus, an area of effect spell that harmed one head could actually help another.

So fire, cold and electric based spells were out. Unfortunately, those were his primary focus. He had no use for acid or poison gas spells. He knew the missiles he had used were force-based and thus were effective—just not effective enough. He again pointed his finger and said the release word to the spell he had decided on. It was a spell he had just learned. The mage had not tried it in battle yet and was mildly intrigued to see how well it worked.

Several small balls, five in all, leapt from the end of his finger and raced toward their target. The mage had aimed for the body of the hydra, knowing the heads had too much mobility and this spell did not hit its intended target unerringly as the missiles did.

With some additional effort, the caster could maintain a small amount of control over where the projectiles went even after he released them. Sordaak kept his finger locked on to the chest of the beast, so that when it dodged to his right to avoid the first ball, now much larger in size, the mage followed him with his finger and the remaining four followed the ill-fated monster and struck it square in the chest, one after the other.

The first ball, now more than a foot in diameter and buzzing loudly as it approached, knocked the hydra back a step. It screamed in either rage or pain as the second orb hit it in roughly the same spot. This time the beast was knocked from the huge pedestals it used as legs. It fell back with a tremendous splash and writhed in the water, more angry than hurt.

Still, Sordaak followed the creature with his finger and the remaining two orbs plunged into the water where the creature struggled to regain its footing.

Both struck with sufficient force to again knock the creature deeper into the pool. Still, it struggled to rise. However, some of the virulence was missing from its motions and the monster appeared sluggish.

"I believe it to only be stunned," said the mage, surveying the scene with a critical eye. "Now would be a good time to finish it, I think."

Needing no further enticement, Vorgath and Thrinndor leapt at the creature, their weapons held high. Savinhand materialized out of nowhere and again jumped onto the creature's back.

Cyrillis had found the ranger and was slowly dragging his unconscious body toward the shore. She had already determined he was going to live, as long as she got him out of the water quickly. She did.

Sordaak folded his arms and watched the melee with satisfaction.

The blows from the paladin, ranger and rogue were raining down hard and fast on the hydra, and the monster couldn't recover fast enough to use its breath weapons. Still, it had five heads full of razor-sharp teeth and claws at the ends of each of its feet. It remained a formidable opponent.

As such, it did manage to inflict occasional harm to the three fighters but was soon destined to fall. Sordaak launched another volleys of missiles for good measure.

The water roiled red with the blood of the creature, and more than a little of that of the three trying to kill it. Minus three of its heads, it fell back into the water and lay still. Vorgath removed the two remaining heads with one mighty swing of his axe and kicked the beast just to be sure.

After verifying it was indeed dead, the three turned toward shore and made their way to the beach where the mage still stood with his arms crossed. He had one eyebrow arched high above the other but said nothing.

Thrinndor stopped before the caster. "What was that spell?" he said between gasps, unable to hide his curiosity.

"Meteor Swarm," replied the mage with a toothy smile.

The paladin nodded. "Nice," he said as he spat blood onto the light brown sand at his feet. "You have indeed gained in strength and stature since last we fought."

Sordaak nodded. "Yup." He then uncrossed his arms and raised his right index finger to his lips and blew on it.

"What was that?" asked the paladin.

"What?" replied the magicuser.

"You just blew on your forefinger," replied the big fighter.

"Oh," said the caster. "That's just something I saw during one of my visits to the other reality." He then turned to see the cleric had the ranger sitting up. Breunne was still a bit woozy from his recent encounter.

"I thought you assured us hydra breath was on a smaller scale than that of a dragon," said the barbarian as he surveyed the damage to his beard. More than half of it was burned off, and what remained was charred and brittle. It bore little semblance to that which he had worked on for more than a hundred years.

Thrinndor laughed. "That was smaller scale." He shook his head. "If that had been a true red dragon, old one, you would have lost far more than just your eyebrows and half your beard!"

Vorgath got a surprised look on his face as he reached up and touched where his eyebrows had been. He cursed vehemently.

"Ahem," interrupted the rogue.

"What?" shouted the barbarian.

Savinhand pointed meekly at the red-faced cleric helping Breunne to his feet.

"Oh," replied the dwarf. "Sorry." Savinhand couldn't tell, but he was pretty sure Vorgath's face was red from more than just his recent confrontation with the hydra.

"Yeah, well," Cyrillis grunted as the ranger sagged unsteadily, leaning on her to keep from falling, "I have heard worse." She tried to grin. "Not much worse, mind you, but worse."

"Sounds like a challenge!" replied the barbarian, returning her grin.

"No, no," Cyrillis said. "That was quite adequate!"

Vorgath started to protest the classification, but changed his mind as he turned his attention to the rogue. "Well, what's next?"

"Good question," Savin replied. He backed up a step and raised both hands to forestall the protest he knew to be on the way. "However, I think we will find the door that will take us back into the cabin where we left it."

The barbarian exhaled noisily the breath he had taken in to lambaste the thief, satisfied instead with a nasty glare.

His eyes releasing the rogue at last, the dwarf turned to look back the way they had come. However, the cavern wall where they had come in was too far off to see anything clearly.

"I think we should rest briefly and get ourselves back to full strength before we continue," said the cleric.

"Healing up is certainly a good idea," began the thief. "However, as I said before, I think we'll find that resting will not provide the usual restorative effects."

"Just the same," Thrinndor said, "I believe our healer's advice is sound." He looked to the rogue. "Unless you know of some reason we should not?"

"No," replied the rogue stubbornly. "However, I'm certain that we won't be attacked while in the cabin. I can't say the same out here—wherever here is."

"Point taken," said the paladin. "As soon as Breunne is ready to travel—"

"You're not waiting on me," the ranger said through clenched teeth. He stood to his full height and released his grip on the healer. She stood by ready to catch him, nonetheless.

"Very well," the paladin said. "Let us move out." He kept a dubious eye on Breunne as he moved ahead of the party. "We will travel together for this short trip back."

"I'm fine!" said the ranger. However, his clenched teeth belied that statement.

"I do not want the group spread out at this juncture," Thrinndor said in his best diplomatic voice as he stepped forward and placed a reassuring hand on the ranger's shoulder. "The healer needs to be near all of us right now." He squeezed Breunne's shoulder and stepped forward with an exaggerated limp.

Even Savinhand remained close to the party, tagging along just behind. His limp was not exaggerated.

Getting back took longer than Thrinndor remembered; he was starting to worry they had come the wrong direction. However, soon the wall could be seen. And in that wall a door.

He looked at the thief. "Should we check for traps?"

"Nah," replied the rogue as he pushed his way past the paladin to stand in front of the door. He lifted the latch and pulled. The door opened easily, revealing the familiar four-walled interior within. "That damn hydra was trap enough from this side."

"Amen," said the caster as he followed the thief inside.

Thrinndor was the last through and he pulled the door to behind him. They party looked at one another.

"Now what?" the barbarian asked.

Thrinndor cleared his throat. "We heal up and try to make better sense of these symbols before we continue."

"Sounds like a plan," agreed the ranger.

"I have a complication we should consider," said the mage. He studied the walls between the doors.

"What would that be?" asked the party leader.

The spellcaster turned his attention to the paladin. "We shouldn't tarry here, either. Something here, or nearby, is draining my spell energy."

Chapter Nineteen

No Rest for the Weary

A silence fell over the group. Sordaak certainly knew how to get their attention.
"What?" asked several in the party in unison.

"I'm not sure if this phenomenon extends to our healer or not," he looked her way, but she did not immediately answer. "But I have noted a small, but not insignificant, decrease in my available spell energy since returning to this chamber."

All eyes turned to the cleric as she closed her eyes and appeared to search within. After a moment she opened her eyes and shook her head. "No," she said, "not such that I would notice, anyway."

"Good," replied the caster. He looked first at Thrinndor and then at Breunne. "Either of you notice anything?" He knew that both had limited spells available to them.

Thrinndor shook his head after he also closed his eyes and checked his energy. "Not I," he said.

The ranger closed his eyes and furrowed his brow. Suddenly his eyes popped back open. "Yes," he said. "I'm most definitely down some energy." He shook his head. "Damn! I wouldn't even have noticed had you not said anything, though. It's very slight."

"Right," agreed the mage. "It seems that whoever designed and or built this place did not want questers to rest here."

"That holds true with what little I was able to glean from the journal," chimed in Savinhand. "This quest is as much a test of stamina and strategy as it is strength of party."

"Very well," replied the paladin, thinking quickly. "Cyrillis, tend to the various injuries as quickly as possible while the rest of us work on the riddle of the doors."

"Shit!" said the magicuser suddenly.

"What now?" queried the big fighter.

"The doors," Sordaak said, pointing to the one in front of him.

"What about them?" asked the barbarian as he turned to investigate the one nearest him.

The sorcerer rolled his eyes. "You're looking but not seeing! The emblems." He again pointed to the one on the door in front of him. "They've changed!"

"What?" repeated the paladin. When his eyes followed the finger of the caster, he saw what Sordaak was trying to say. "Shit!"

Breunne was the first to read off what was now on the doors. "Snake, bird, scorpion and cat," he shook his head. "Now what?"

Vorgath swore.

"That is not going to help," muttered the cleric as she made her rounds.

The barbarian bit off a quick reply. He said instead, "Depends on what it is you're trying to help!"

Cyrillis shook her head as she applied some salve from a pot she held in her left hand to the frost burns on the ranger's face and neck.

"Snake eats the scorpion," said the paladin. "Bird eats the snake, and cat eats the bird!"

"It was that sort of logic that got us through the wrong door the first time," said the caster as he folded his arms across his chest. He was studying each emblem with care.

"Besides," said the dwarf as the healer applied some of the cream to his face, "a big bird can easily carry off a small cat."

"And a large snake can consume a bird," said the ranger. "If it were to catch one."

"We can argue the size of the creatures and their respective place in the food chain for hours!" moaned the rogue leader.

"Or we can look for some other relationship," replied the caster as he studied the emblem depicting the cat.

"Such as?" Vorgath had had just about enough of these puzzles.

"Such as possibly the shape of the emblem itself," replied the caster as he leaned forward to get a better look at the emblem with the bird on it.

"What?" Thrinndor's head spun, looking briefly at each of the markings.

"See here," said the caster pointing to the bird. "This one is round in shape." He took a few steps and stood before the door with the snake on it. "This one is a square. Over there—" he pointed to the emblem of the cat "—a triangle." Finally he pointed to the scorpion. "And that one has the top and bottom slightly longer than the sides. A rectangle."

"I now see what you mean," said the paladin. "But how does that help us?"

"I say it's the animals," said the barbarian as he crossed his arms on his chest, hoping someone would argue with him.

"You could be right," said the mage with a sigh. "However the walls and doors in this chamber are identical except for these emblems." He scratched his head idly as he thought. "I find it hard to believe that whoever made these markings just chose the shape they were on at random. There has got to be a pattern!"

He stomped to stand before each while the others watched.

"A pattern we must find before I run out of energy!"

There was silence as each spent time looking closely at the markings on the door.

"Anyone else require my assistance?" Cyrillis asked as she put the jar of cream back in her bag. Her eyes stopped on the barbarian, noting several claw marks on his left arm.

Vorgath saw what she was looking at. "Not worth bothering with, young lady," he said gruffly. "A couple of scratches, that's all."

"I will be the judge of that," she said. After a moment's inspection she added, "As I feared. These will hinder your battle skills because they will easily break open and start bleeding once again." She closed her eyes and whispered a prayer as she waved her hand over the damaged skin. Immediately, the scabs healed over, leaving a light pink scar in their place.

The barbarian took in a breath to protest but changed his mind. His only reaction was to roll his eyes. "Whatever!" he muttered.

"What was that?" responded the cleric.

"Nothing," muttered the dwarf.

"Nothing?" she asked. "Because I clearly heard something!" Her eyes bored into those of Vorgath. "We have had this discussion. I get to say who needs healing and who does not!

"You do your job and I will do mine," she went on. "When, during the course of your job you are injured, I will do my best to keep your body and soul together." She lowered her voice. "Unless you require of me not to. At which point we will see how long the mighty Vorgath survives!"

Silence filled the room. Sordaak was pretty sure he could hear that spider breathing as it spun its web in one corner of the room opposite him. Even Fahlred cowered silently on the mage's shoulder.

"And with your penchant for wading into a fray with your axe held high, screaming in a fit of rage," she continued, "that will not take long!"

"Yes, ma'am." The dwarf's tone was contrite. His eyes met hers and sparkled. "You keep me alive and I will do my absolute best to ensure no harm comes to you."

Cyrillis searched the eyes of the barbarian in an attempt to discern whether she was being made fun of.

"Do we have a deal?" Vorgath said. He was not smiling.

"I get to decide when healing is required?" she replied guardedly.

"Of course."

"No more of this silly banter about 'mere scratches' and 'wounds of honor'?"

Vorgath hesitated. "No more," he said with a sigh. "I am yours to heal." Now he smiled.

The cleric returned the smile and the two grasped forearms to seal the deal.

"Aw," said the magicuser, "Get a room!" He too was smiling.

"Jealous?" inquired the barbarian lightly.

"Absolutely not!" exclaimed Sordaak, a bit too quickly. "I didn't need her attention!"

"This time!" the healer finished his sentence for him.

"If you'd done something to get the hydra's attention," added the dwarf, "you might've needed some healing!"

"I did do something!" responded the caster. "I, however, am smart enough to do my damage from a distance!" He smiled smugly. "Besides, with all the attention you were getting, if you were any taller, you'd probably have had your whole face burned off. Not just a singed beard!"

"Ha!" snorted the dwarf.

"Can we please get back to solving the riddle of the doors?" interrupted the paladin. "Before Sordaak runs out of juice?"

"Juice?" said the ranger.

"You know what I mean!" snapped the paladin. He looked at the caster. "Sordaak, what is your status?"

"Still losing energy," replied the mage. "However, the loss is slight. I have yet to lose enough to prevent use of even my lowest of spells." He turned to stare at the emblem of the cat. "Be that as it may, I wouldn't want to remain here much longer."

"My point exactly," replied the big fighter. "Any thoughts on this puzzle?"

"No,. Not really." He looked over at Thrinndor. "It might have been prudent to mark the doors—or maybe the floor in front of them—with the symbols that were there before."

The paladin thought about this piece of information briefly. "We did not anticipate the symbols changing."

"Nor did we even anticipate returning to this chamber," agreed Breunne.

"Just the same," said the caster, "I'm going to mark them now." He dug around in the bag at his waist and pulled out a piece of charcoal and stepped up to the door before him. As best he could, he copied the symbol of the cat onto the face of the door.

He then stepped back to admire his handiwork. He started to turn away, then dropped to his knees and drew the same thing on the floor a couple of feet inside the door.

"Any particular reason as to why?" responded the paladin as the mage moved over to the door with the scorpion.

"Not really," said the caster with a sigh. "But it's possible there is a relationship between a particular emblem we have now and what might have been on that same door before."

Sordaak repeated the process with each of the remaining doors. As he stepped to the last door, the one with the snake on it, he called over his shoulder.

"Thrinn, make a list of reasons why we should select any particular symbol as I finish this."

"On it," replied the paladin.

The others gathered around Thrinndor. "Give me any ideas you may have," he said. "And why."

"Snake," said the barbarian simply. "The hydra was behind that last door. And that beast is classified as a reptile. Same as the snake."

The paladin looked at him inquisitively.

Vorgath shrugged. "Best I could come up with on short notice."

"Right," replied the paladin, dubious. He looked over at the ranger. "Breunne?"

"Not really," he said with a shrug. "That is the door we emerged from." He turned and pointed at the door with the snake on it. "If it's also the door we entered through, then it previously had the emblem of the sun on it."

"Of course!" Sordaak said as he looked up from his rendition of the snake he had been drawing on the floor. "Why didn't I think of that?"

Finished with the snake, he drew a sun next to it, doing his best to mimic what he remembered the emblem to look like when they went in.

The remaining party looked on with curiosity.

When he finished with the sun, Sordaak stepped back to the center of the room and closed his eyes. He then spun and went to his drawing of the cat, dropped to the floor and drew the symbol for the moon next to it. He repeated the process next to the cat he had drawn on the door.

Finished, he again returned to the center of the room. "Now, if I remember correctly," he said, again turning to face the door with the snake/sun on it and then pointing to his right, "that door had the symbol for land on it." He then pointed to his left. "And that one had the symbol for water."

Scorpion was with land and bird with water. He first went to the door with the bird emblem currently on it and added his rendition of the symbol for water. Next was the land added to the door with the scorpion.

He stepped back to admire his handiwork.

"What about the shapes?" asked the cleric.

"Huh?" said the caster, his reverie broken.

"The shapes," she replied. "The circle with the bird and so on."

"Right!" Sordaak said. "I had forgotten all about that." He stepped back to each, drawing the circle with the water and the bird, square with the snake and sun, triangle with the cat and the moon and finally the rectangle with the scorpion and land.

When he stepped back to the center of the room, Vorgath said, "Now what?"

Sordaak turned to look at the dwarf a sharp reply on his lips. "Never mind," he muttered. "Now we search for patterns," he announced to the others, ignoring the barbarian for the time being.

"Very well," said the paladin. "Cyrillis, you and Breunne take the door with the bird and see if you can figure out any patterns."

Cyrillis nodded and stepped up to inspect the indicated door and the ranger stood next to her.

"Savinhand," the big fighter continued, "you and Vorgath take the scorpion." Both men nodded and moved to the appropriate door.

"I will work on this one," he said pointing to the door with the cat.

"I've got the snake, then," said the caster as he stepped over to peer at that door.

After a moment the paladin said, "We will all move to the door to our right after one minute of investigation. We will then meet back in the middle to compare notes when we each have inspected each door."

Nothing more was said as they all gave their full attention to the doors and emblems before them.

After about a minute they all rotated to the doors to their right.

As each finished his or her last inspection, they stepped to the middle of the room as requested.

Sordaak was the last to approach the group.

"Well?" asked the barbarian as the mage stepped in, idly scratching his head with his left hand.

"Deep subject, shallow mind," replied the mage without thinking.

"What?" asked the dwarf, confused.

"Point made," said the magicuser, his mind obviously elsewhere.

Thrinndor stifled a chuckle. "Anyone have any brilliant insights that the rest of us might have missed?"

Some serious toe studying ensued. Nothing was said.

The paladin noted that the caster looked agitated. "Sordaak?" He was clearly distracted as he spun rapidly, looking at first one door and then another in quick succession.

"Damn!" hissed the spellcaster. "There must be something I'm missing!" He stopped turning, his attention on the door with the bird.

"I will take that as a 'no,'" said the paladin with a shake of his head. He looked at each of the remaining party members one at a time. "Nothing?"

Again there was some serious toe searching.

"Very well," said the paladin. "Sordaak, give us your best guess."

"Why me?" snapped the caster. "I picked last time! See where that got us?"

"Well," acknowledged the paladin, shrugging, "you seem to at least have a clue that there may be some sort of a connection. That far surpasses the rest of us."

"Great!" said the mage.

"Maybe we are overthinking this," said the cleric.

"What?" asked the mage, his eyes boring into those of the healer.

In response Cyrillis took in a deep breath. "We are assuming that there is some relationship between the current symbols and shapes, and those previous."

All eyes were on her as she continued. "What if all that mess is there only to distract us from the real puzzle?"

There was silence in the room for a few moments.

"What real puzzle?" asked Sordaak.

Again there was silence.

"I have no idea," answered the cleric.

"You're kidding?" replied the mage.

"No," said the healer, straightening her back as she stood to her full height. "These symbols and shapes have only served to keep us in this chamber while we search for answers." Her voice rang with authority. "Meanwhile, you lose energy!"

When no one said anything, she went on, "What if the correct door selection is merely random?"

"That would suck," said the barbarian.

This time the paladin chuckled. "I believe this theory has merit."

"But—" began the mage. He, however, had nothing to finish the thought with.

"Exactly," Thrinndor said. "If you do not yet have insight into which door is next, we will select one at random."

Sordaak looked up, his face torn with indecision. She could be right! In desperation he pointed at the door with the cat on it and then abruptly dropped his arm with a sigh.

"Damn!" the caster said. "Her proposal has at least as much—if not more—merit than anything I can toss out there!" He looked at the cleric. "Pick one!"

"Why me?" she replied.

"Sorry," said the caster. "But it is your idea, after all."

Her eyes went to the paladin. Clearly this was not what she had in mind. "I cannot be responsible for the possible harm, or even death, of any in this party!"

The paladin's eyes softened. "Random, huh? Very well." He looked over at the magicuser and lifted his right arm and pointed to the door with the bird without looking at it. "We will go through that one."

Sordaak looked up at his friend, thought to argue and changed his mind. He smiled. "Bird it is!"

Without taking his eyes off of the caster, Thrinndor said, "Savinhand, check the door, please."

"On it," the rogue was falling into a routine.

"Everyone else get something to eat." The paladin looked at his old friend the dwarf. "Snack only," he said with a grin. "Make it quick."

"I'll take that as this is no time for the strong drink?" Vorgath returned the grin.

"Correct, o venerable one." The paladin winked at the barbarian. "We will save that for our victory celebration!"

"Makes sense," said the dwarf grudgingly as he dug through his bag looking for something to eat. Actually, it was more of a search for something he wanted to eat. Food was plenty at this early juncture.

Finally he drew out a portion of dried pork and a biscuit. He eyed the wine skin with no small amount of regret but settled on the skin of water instead.

He chomped mindlessly on the biscuit as he watched the rogue go through his paces.

Savinhand stepped back from the door and scratched his head. "Damn," he said. "There aren't any traps here, either!" He turned to look at the paladin. "It too isn't even locked!"

"Perhaps," Thrinndor started, "these traps you are expecting do not apply to this entrance chamber?"

"Perhaps," replied the thief. His tone said he did not know what to believe.

"All right," said the paladin, "defensive posture." He looked over at the ranger. "Breunne, you are in first."

The ranger washed down the biscuit he had been munching on with a quick swig of water and nodded as he climbed to his feet.

While the others also got to their feet and settled their packs, Savin pulled out a biscuit and began munching on it. He shook his head silently, wondering just where all these traps were supposed to be. He washed down the dry bread with a mouthful of water and stored the skin as Breunne approached the door.

The ranger reached out and grasped the latching mechanism with his left hand, lifted it and pushed the door open fully. The door opened silently on well-oiled hinges.

Breunne stepped through the opening and immediately disappeared. Vorgath followed only a step behind, the paladin on his heels. Sordaak and Cyrillis stepped through side-by-side. The mage turned to find the rogue, but Savinhand had already melted into his surroundings.

Sordaak returned his attention to what was before him, shaking his head as he did. Once again he and the others in the party were enshrouded by a fine mist. "Maybe," he said to no one in particular, "we should try to prop the door open?"

"Somehow," the disembodied voice of the paladin wafted through the fog, "I do not believe that will work."

Sordaak sighed. "Nor do I." He kicked the door shut. It latched with a forlorn click. Belatedly, he hoped the rogue had made it through.

At the click of the door mechanism, the mists began to dissipate.

Walls took shape to either side of the door—or rather, where the door had been! When Sordaak checked again, there was no door!

As the mage turned to assess their situation, a deep voice resonated off of the rock walls. "You have chosen poorly."

"Again," added the mage. "Shit!"

The passage was about twelve to fifteen feet wide, with a ceiling that appeared to be twenty feet or so above their heads. The way before them was already lit, this time by some sort of indirect lighting up near the ceiling.

The passage continued away from the blank wall where the door had once been for forty or fifty feet, appearing to branch both to the right and left.

"Everyone in?" asked the paladin. He knew the answer but felt he had to be sure.

"Check," replied the ranger from his point position twenty feet ahead of the group.

"Present," said the barbarian.

"Here," Cyrillis and Sordaak said together.

There was a brief pause, and then the rogue appeared next to the paladin. "We're going to have to find a better way of verifying everyone made it through a door! Kind of negates my sneakiness."

"Noted," replied the paladin as he turned to address the rogue. But he had already vanished. "We will have to work that out."

He looked around briefly. "All right, move out."

The party formed quickly into marching formation and started down the passage. When they got to the end, Breunne stood waiting for them.

Sordaak looked first right, then left. "Shit!" he repeated. The passages were identical, each going fifty or sixty feet before branching in a "T." "It's a maze."

Chapter Twenty

A Disturbing Discovery

"I hate mazes," muttered the caster.

"All right," said the paladin as he studied the intersection. "Sordaak, you are going to have to map as we go." He got a nod from the mage. "Are you still feeling the drain on your energy?"

Sordaak paused to check as his hands fumbled for a piece of rolled up parchment he had brought along for this purpose. "No," he said.

"Good," replied the paladin. "How much did the delay cost you?"

"Well," said the caster, "I lost enough energy to cost me one of my lesser spells. Not insignificant, but not devastating, either."

"We will have to be more expeditious next time in there," Thrinndor said.

Sordaak nodded.

The paladin turned to address the group. "Very well. It seems our casters are no longer experiencing energy loss, and that is a good thing." He paused while considering their options. He couldn't think of any. "So we will therefore proceed with the usual caution in standard formation."

Thrinndor looked over at the mage. "Sordaak is going to map for us. We must make certain he is up to date before making any turns. Mazes, I am sure I do not have to remind you, can be very tricky to navigate."

Vorgath rolled his eyes.

"We must also use caution," the paladin continued, ignoring his barbarian friend, "as this may be where the promised traps lie across our path.

"To that end," he continued as he looked around for the rogue. Not seeing him, he raised his voice. "To that end, I want Savinhand up ahead of the group—he and Breunne will exchange places.

The ranger nodded.

"I'm hard to see," complained the rogue as he suddenly appeared next to the paladin. "Not deaf!"

Thrinndor turned to face the thief. "I am beginning to see why our esteemed caster has a problem with that particular habit of yours."

Sordaak snickered lightly while Savinhand feigned being wounded.

"Can we just get on with it?" moaned the barbarian.

Again the paladin ignored the dwarf. Instead he turned to the rogue and waved toward the end of the passage. "Savinhand, if you would, please."

"But of course," the thief said, bowing formally. He took several steps, which put him past where the ranger had been. "I am going to require heightened awareness, which will allow me to sense traps as we walk."

"I have a spell that will increase you skill level in that regard," said the cleric.

"How long does the spell last?" asked the rogue.

"Several minutes," she replied. "It does not require the use of much energy, and I can renew it as required.

"Very well," Savinhand said. "That would be most useful, I believe."

"Anything to increase your skill level would be most useful," muttered the dwarf while pretending to adjust his belt.

Savin glared at the dwarf. "You know, I find your lack of faith disconcerting." When Vorgath did not reply, he continued. "Back in trap search class, when we were unsure whether we had missed a particular trap, we simply rolled a dwarf ahead of us to check!" His eyes twinkled, matching the smile he bore.

"Just try rolling this dwarf!" rejoined the barbarian. He, too, smiled.

The two locked eyes. After a moment of this, Vorgath shifted the grip on Flinthgoor to his left hand and stuck his right out toward the rogue.

Savinhand also reached out, and the two clasped forearms.

"OK," said the dwarf, "I'll ease up." He grinned broadly. "At least until you miss one! After that, my efforts will redouble!"

The rogue returned the wink. "Fair enough!" He turned to the cleric. "If you please."

Cyrillis obediently waved a hand in the thief's directions and said an unintelligible word.

Savinhand could indeed feel his senses heighten immediately. "Thank you," he said as he turned and led the party down the passage.

Savin walked slightly slower than normal, but not perceptibly so. His senses reached out on all sides, looking for anything out of the ordinary. It's said that a good trapmaster could sense a trap with his eyes closed. He chose not to test that theory, however, as he felt the burden of performing this task for everyone behind, not just himself.

As such, when he approached the intersection in that first passage he felt the alarms going off. He immediately held up a hand for the others to stop.

"What?" asked the dwarf only a few feet behind.

Savinhand waved him to silence, not daring to take his eyes from his task.

"I would back up were I you," he said as he stepped forward to confront what he had yet to see.

Obediently, the barbarian took a few steps back until he stood next to the paladin.

Thrinndor didn't have to be told what was going on. He waited until the others got even with him and held his finger to his lips, commanding silence. It didn't matter that no one was going to say anything. Everyone stood with their eyes glued to their trapsmith.

"There you are," the rogue whispered under his breath. Yet such was the silence in the passage that all heard him.

Again without taking his eyes from the mechanism he had spotted, his hands moved to his belt and removed his tool pouch. Deftly he undid the tie and unwrapped it by feel alone. His expert hands removed his magnifier glass.

He used it to trace the hair-thin wire from where he had spotted it to where it disappeared into the wall. This was a tricky one. He knew from experience that there must be a mechanism nearby that would allow him to disarm the trap, so he began to search for it.

The wall was made of individual bricks, each twice as long as they were high. Again experience told him there would be a fake one somewhere nearby.

There! The mortar used for that brick was of a slightly different color, indicating that it was newer than that of the surrounding wall. His hands felt for a release mechanism. Finding none, he put the magnifier into a pocket and slid a dagger from its sheath at his belt.

With that, he carefully worked the mortar until had removed most of it from around the brick. Next he inserted the blade into the revealed gap and gently pried until he felt the brick move slightly. He repeated the process on each side of the brick until he was able to remove it from the wall. It was indeed a false brick, much thinner than those around it.

He set the brick carefully on the floor and again removed his tool pouch from its place behind his belt. He knelt to get a better look into the opening created by removing the cover brick.

The mechanism looked simple enough: The trip wire was connected to a spool that when disturbed would release yet another spool with more wire wound on it, presumably unleashing something nasty.

He preferred not to find out—not the hard way, anyway. He selected a small spike and gently tapped it into a crack in the mortar. Then he pulled a piece of wire from his pouch and ever so gently wrapped it several times around the trip wire, securing it in place by doubling back over the joint multiple times. Next he wound the other end of his wire around the spike, making sure it was tight.

He selected his cutter from the pouch and placed it over the trip wire where it exited the box. He took a deep breath and cut the wire, ready to dodge any direction should his tie-off not hold.

It did.

He let out the breath in a noisy sigh of relief as he sagged back away from the box. Funny, he thought, to himself briefly, he was not perspiring. Confidence, he thought briefly. Quickly he raised his right hand to his head and knocked three times. Knock on wood. He smiled.

He pulled the now slack trip wire through the wall and followed it to where it had been secured to the opposite wall and cut it there. He then coiled up the wire and put it in his pouch for later use. Placing the magnifier and tools back into the pouch, he rolled it up, retied the thong and slipped it back into its place behind his belt.

"What was it?" inquired the cleric.

"Not sure," replied the thief, his eyes searching the wall for what might have happened had he not disabled the trap. Absently his hands slid silently over the brick until he found what he was looking for: a slot in the wall hidden by a spell.

Once his hands discovered the slot, the illusion spell dissipated, revealing the slot on both sides of the passage.

Cyrillis gasped as he peered into the crevice. He could make out the sharp edge of what was probably an axe.

"Axes," he said, his eyes following the grooves in the wall. "Triggered by that trip wire. They would probably have swung out from this point." He pointed to a larger gap at one end. "Slashing into whatever or whoever was in their path."

"Nice," said the barbarian, noting that the slot height was just high enough to hit the average victim mid-back. For him it would have been mid-neck.

"That was an unexpected place for a trap," said the rogue as he again pointed his attention down the hall toward the intersection, now only a few feet away. "This must be the source of what the journal speaks to. I will have to use extreme caution."

"Please do," agreed Thrinndor. "Take all the time you require. We are in no hurry."

Savin nodded as he turned his attention back to the path in front of him. He took in a deep breath as he again moved ahead.

The rest of the party needed no urging to remain even further back. Cyrillis was poised to heal at the first sign of danger.

"Right or left?" asked the rogue as he approached the intersection.

"Right," replied the paladin. "In a maze, we will always turn right if a choice is required."

Savinhand again nodded and moved to the right side of the passage, his senses reaching out as far as he dared, while still paying the most attention to his immediate vicinity.

"Why?" asked the cleric, voicing the question that more than one in the party had on their minds.

"Convention," replied the paladin. Seeing this did not fully explain by the look on his healer's face, he explained further. "If we always turn the same direction in a maze, there is no question from which way we came should we have to make a hasty retreat." He smiled at her. "That and now I do not have to answer that question every time we come to an intersection." His smile grew broader.

"Makes sense," Cyrillis said.

Meanwhile the rogue had again stopped, this time at the entrance to the passage that branched to the right.

There was in inconsistency in the brick in the right wall. The mortar also appeared...different. However, try as he might, he could neither sense nor detect anything amiss.

The others in the party again stopped a respectful distance away, this time saying nothing. They recognized a pattern the trapmaster was following and did not want to disturb him.

"Interesting," Savin muttered more to himself than to be heard. But again the others had no trouble hearing him.

Still no one spoke.

Savinhand reached out his right hand and said a word unintelligible to those behind him. The energy of a spell was obviously released, and the floor at the center of the intersection began to glow a faint blue.

"Damn," muttered the thief. "The old son of a bitch is using magic traps, too!"

"What sort of magic?" queried Sordaak as he took a couple of tentative steps forward.

"I don't know," replied the rogue, his eyes searching for the trip mechanism.

"Allow me to investigate," said the caster as he approached the intersection.

"Sure," agreed the rogue. "Just don't get too close to that area highlighted in blue."

Sordaak threw Savin a nasty you-don't-have-to-tell-me-that look, but the rogue's attention was already elsewhere. Deciding it would be a waste of time to carry forward with that thought, the mage instead turned his attention to the blue area on the floor.

Not finding anything to help him figure it out, he reached into his pouch and removed a pinch of dust flecked with sparkles. He made a sweeping motion with his hand, releasing the dust as he did so. He spoke a word from the ancient elfish tongue to finish the spell.

Something he did showed him what he was looking for because after a moment he said, "Damn! That's a teleportation spot!" He looked up at his friend the rogue. "Was this Phinskyr a sorcerer?"

Savinhand hesitated before speaking. "Not that I'm aware of. He was, however, known to dabble in the mystic arts, but to what depth is unknown."

"Well," said the spellcaster matter-of-factly, "Teleportation is no 'dabbling' spell!" His face mirrored the concern spoken by his voice. "I have yet to master that particular spell!"

The thief looked dubious. Sordaak continued. "I suppose it's certainly possible he used a scroll or other magic item to set this trap—"

"Either that," the ranger continued for him, "or he spent more of that extralong life of his 'dabbling' in magic!"

"Agreed," said the rogue. He didn't like this, not one little bit! Magic traps threw an unwanted complication into this mix. He had not studied them near enough at this point in his career.

"Teleport to where?" asked the cleric.

Taken aback by the question, everyone looked at her. "What?" asked the rogue.

"Not what," she replied, "where. Where would have this spell sent whoever triggered the trap?"

"There's no way of knowing," answered the mage, "short of activating it and finding out the hard way."

There was silence for a bit as each digested that tidbit of information.

"Do you not think it important?" she pressed.

"Not really," replied the mage. "Generally these 'traps' are used within a maze to confuse and/or split up a party." His eyes held hers as he continued. "If you are thinking that maybe this is a device to bypass the maze completely, two things come to mind to refute that concept." He took in a deep breath. "One: It would not be placed in a location where it could be accidently triggered by an unknowing group of adventurers." He could tell his guess had hit the mark—she had thought this might be a quick way through the maze. "And Two: The voice told us we had chosen poorly. Therefore, it would not be the normal way whoever knows the way would use."

Deflated, Cyrillis merely nodded.

"Sorry," said the caster said as he turned back to look at the trap.

"Can you remove it?" asked the paladin.

Sordaak waved a hand negligently in the direction of the intersection. "Done."

Indeed the faint blue of the magic indicator was gone.

"Guys," began the rogue as he shook his head slowly. "This adds an element I wasn't prepared for." He shifted his gaze to the paladin. "I'm fairly confident I can find and remove just about any conventional trap." His eyes went back to the intersection. "But magic traps? That's a different animal altogether."

"Understood," Thrinndor said. He turned to the caster. "Is there anything that can be done to detect these traps?"

Savinhand spoke first. "I general, if it is indeed a trap I still have a good probability to find them—even the magic ones."

"Is it a matter of then being able to remove them?" asked the paladin.

Savin hesitated. "Sort of." Thrinndor started to protest. "Allow me to explain," the thief said hurriedly. The paladin nodded.

"Thank you," said the rogue. "First of all, my trap sense will usually detect even a magic trap." His eyes wandered back to the brick in the wall that led to his investigating the intersection further. "It's disabling the trap that gets tricky."

Again he hesitated before continuing. "My trap sense tells me one is nearby, but it doesn't tell me what is nearby." He looked back at the paladin. "That makes it difficult—at best—to disable said trap."

"But you found this one," said the ranger.

"Yes," replied the rogue. He held up his right arm to reveal a leather bracer on his forearm. "With the aid of this device. This bracer is enchanted such that when activated it will reveal any magic in the area."

"Nice," Sordaak said. "I was going to ask you how you discovered the spell."

"So," interrupted the ranger, "what's the problem?"

"Two things," said the rogue. "First, the use of this device is limited to three times per day—or rest periods." He looked back over at the intersection. "Second, it only tells me that there's magic in the vicinity, not what it is."

"Got it," said the paladin. He turned to the mage. "Can you help out with these?"

"If he can find them," replied the caster, "I can dismiss the magic."

"Good," the big fighter said. "Problem solved!"

"Not exactly," Sordaak said.

Thrinndor waited for the mage to continue saying nothing. He was starting to get used to this sort of banter.

"All of these spells use energy," explained the caster. "Once our esteemed trapmaster here uses up the available energy from that device, every time he senses a trap but is unable to find it, I will be required to first use the Detect Magic spell. Then once I know what I'm dealing with, I'll have to Dispel Magic— again a spell."

Thrinndor nodded. "I see a pattern developing here. I believe Phinskyr is possibly trying to remove—or at least limit—our ability to use a caster further down the road."

Sordaak nodded his agreement.

"Can't we just rest should the need arise?" queried the ranger.

"Hmmm," began the paladin. "We know we cannot back in the entrance chamber." His eyes narrowed as he thought. "However we might be able to do so out here—"

"Wherever 'here' is," muttered the dwarf.

"—if the need were to arise." Thrinndor turned to face the party. "We shall have a rest period to test this."

"No need," said the mage, his tone bitter.

The paladin faced the magicuser.

"Since we stopped and began this conversation," Sordaak continued, "I have noticed more energy drainage."

"Really?" said the rogue leader.

"Not really surprising," answered the spellcaster. "Seeing all the effort this Phinskyr guy has put into making sure I—we—don't dawdle, I would find it surprising if I were allowed to rest!"

The party stood in stunned silence for a moment while digesting this information.

"I do have an ability which will restore some lost spell energy to one in the party," the healer said quietly. She was looking at the mage.

Sordaak's eyes searched those of the cleric. "I've heard of such abilities, but I've never seen them in action. How much?"

"Very little, I am afraid," she said, not letting her eyes leave his. "This ability has multiple uses—ten at my current rank." Her voice trailed off. "After that I must rest to be able to use the ability again."

All were silent, letting that sink in.

"Can you use it on yourself?" queried the caster.

"No," she said. "Only on another."

All eyes shifted to the paladin. It was obvious he needed to make a choice.

"I do not see an option," he said. "Cyrillis, do what you can to restore some spell energy to our caster."

The cleric nodded and raised her hands above the head of the magicuser. She again whispered an unintelligible word.

Sordaak felt an energy surge and smiled.

Cyrillis repeated the word an additional nine times, moving her hands only slightly between each.

Finished, she looked hesitantly at the caster, not knowing how much she had been able to help.

Sordaak's smile grew. "Excellent! That'll help tremendously!"

"Really?"

"Absolutely," responded the caster. "That additional energy will provide several more spells—at a minimum!"

"Nice," said the paladin. The room fell quiet.

"In an emergency," Cyrillis said into the silence, "I have a very limited supply of energy potions, as well."

The mage's head whipped around. "Pneumonic Enhancers?"

The cleric nodded. "Very limited."

"Bless you," the caster said, a huge smile on his face. "Those are very expensive. We will have to prudent with their use."

The healer nodded.

"Very well," said the paladin. "We must still limit your energy usage to strictly what is necessary."

The mage again nodded.

"However," Thrinndor said as he turned back to the rogue, "I see no way around its use while we yet endure this maze."

"Agreed," said the mage.

"Me, too," Savinhand chimed in. "I'll proceed as before, except I will ask for assistance when I find something, but unable to find said something." He smiled.

"Are we done talking?" griped the barbarian with a roll of his eyes. "Because if we're not, I'm going to need something to drink!" He unslung the wine skin from his shoulder to make his point. "I know I heard something about a rest period!"

"Easy there, old one!" replied the paladin with a wink. "We are moving out now." He nodded to the rogue, who obediently started down the right passage.

Vorgath slung the skin back to its spot on his back, muttering.

Abruptly Savin stopped and turned to face the party. "Another boost spell if you please," he said to Cyrillis. "That last one seems to have expired."

The healer nodded and did as asked.

Satisfied, the rogue again turned his attention to the passage before him and moved out slowly.

Thrinndor got the mage's attention and again lifted his eyebrow.

Sordaak knew what he wanted. "As soon as we started moving again, the energy drain stopped."

The paladin nodded as he turned to watch the progress of the thief.

The mage did the same. "You know," he said as he watched Savin stop to look over something he considered suspicious, "I'm not the only one who's going to go without rest."

The paladin did a double-take. "Excuse me?"

"Unless I am mistaken—and that is doubtful at this juncture—we as a group must continue to make progress else the energy drain will begin again." Sordaak started to move slowly down the passage, not wanting to get separated too far from the thief.

Chapter Twenty-One

Trap!

The paladin fell in step with the mage, who cocked an inquisitive eyebrow at the big fighter. "You understand what I'm saying?"

"Yes," replied the paladin. "What I want to know is…" The pair stopped while the rogue again paused to investigate something that caught his attention. "…how this guy is able to accomplish all of this from the afterlife?"

"I've wondered about that myself," said the caster as he again started moving slowly, mimicking the steps of the rogue ahead. "There's a lot about this place I don't like."

"Like this," the mage said wryly as Savinhand motioned for him to come to where he was intently checking over a place in the wall. "This could get annoying real fast!" He moved toward the rogue slowly. "We're not a hundred steps into this maze—which we have not a clue how big it is—and we have already found two traps!"

"Three," said the thief as the caster approached.

"Damn," said the caster. "See what I mean?" He flung a disgusted glance over his shoulder at the paladin, who shook his head.

Thrinndor turned to face the others as they approached. Vorgath's demeanor was the same as that of the caster's. Less than pleased.

"This could take a while," the paladin began, his voice lowered.

"Ya think?" said the barbarian as he clunked the head of his axe on the stone floor and leaned on it. "If'n I don't get some ass to whoop here soon, I'm-a gonna have to take it back up with you, leader boy!"

"Whatever!" said the paladin, still whispering.

The ranger approached the group silently from his new position at the flanks. "What gives?"

"Nothing," replied the paladin. "Stumpy over there is getting restless."

Vorgath growled deep in his chest but smiled as he leaned on the haft of his greataxe. "I think it's time for some liquid refreshment." He looked insolently at his leader. "Past time, truth be known. Unless you disapprove, of course?"

Thrinndor hesitated. His first thought was indeed to disapprove, but common sense won out. "No," he said. "I believe a short break to be in order." No sense upsetting the apple cart fifteen minutes into the maze.

Vorgath grunted his acknowledgment as he unslung his wine skin, pulled the cork and took a long swig.

The dwarf then offered the skin to the paladin, who shook his head as he watched the magicuser and the rogue go about the business of defeating yet another trap.

The barbarian shrugged and turned to offer the skin to Breunne.

The ranger started to decline but changed his mind and took the proffered vessel. He needed some fortification after his recent encounter that had gone none too well. He lifted the skin to his lips and took several short sips—he was still slightly weakened from his ordeal and didn't want to overdo it.

Satisfied, he turned to offer to the cleric, but she had passed him and was intently watching the two journeymen up ahead.

Feeling better, the ranger shrugged and handed the skin back to the barbarian. "Thanks."

Vorgath nodded and took the skin. He then put the cork back in and slung it back in place over his shoulder. He, too, felt better. He grasped the haft of his huge greataxe, swung it up and rested it on his shoulder. "Are we there yet?"

Startled at the abrupt intrusion into what had been almost perfect silence, Thrinndor jumped slightly and pressed a finger to his lips. "Shhh!" He was more than a little irritated at the dwarf.

The barbarian's smiled broadened, but he remained silent.

Finally, the mage signaled for the rest of the companions to move up to their position, which they did.

As they approached, Savinhand again moved out ahead of the group toward the intersection that was now not far ahead.

Sordaak waited for them, his eyes following the footsteps of the rogue. Without looking at his friends as they approached he said, "That was yet another enchanted trap." He turned to peer at the paladin, his face stern. "A particularly nasty one."

Thrinndor briefly considered inquiring into the particulars, but Sordaak was already moving to follow the thief.

"If this maze is very big," said the sorcerer as he shook his head, "I will run out of energy long before we get through it!"

He muttered a curse as he again took note of Savin stooping to study a section of the wall just above the stone floor.

"What now?" cried the caster.

In response, the rogue held up a hand asking Sordaak to stop where he was without looking up from what held his attention.

The magicuser did as he was asked, crossing his arms on his chest in disgust.

The barbarian silently walked up to stand next to the caster, immediately followed by the paladin. "Surely there is not another trap so close to this one?" Thrinndor said.

Sordaak just shrugged.

"Damn," cursed the dwarf as he watched Savinhand get down on his knees to get a closer look at whatever commanded his attention.

The rogue shook his head and got back to his feet. "There aren't any traps here, but you need to see this."

Obediently they moved forward as a group.

When they got to where the thief was standing, they could see it was not an intersection at all. Instead, there was an alcove to the right and another long hall to the left.

In the alcove, a metal shaft protruded out of a hole drilled through the stone floor. Attached to the shaft was a round wheel with spokes radiating from where it was attached to the shaft.

"Hello there," said the barbarian as he moved in for a better look. "What do we have here?"

"A valve," replied the caster.

Vorgath threw him a dirty look. "I know that, idiot!" he said.

Sordaak ignored the jibe. "The more useful question would be: What does it do?"

"There's one way to find out!" replied the barbarian as he put his hands on the wheel.

"Wait!" Savinhand quickly brought both hands up in an effort to forestall the barbarian.

Vorgath looked up at the rogue, his arms poised to turn the wheel. "Yes?"

"Notice the markings on the floor," the thief said hurriedly.

Obediently, the dwarf took his hands off of the wheel and looked down at the stone under his feet. "Three," stated the dwarf. There were indeed three identical lines carved into the floor not far from the base of the valve.

"Or one and two," said the thief. He stepped forward and pointed to a gap between two of the lines.

"Could be," acknowledged the barbarian. He was far from convinced, however.

"So," Cyrillis said, "either way, what are they for?"

"I don't know for sure," replied the rogue. He stepped across the hallway to where the other hall branched to the left. "Take a look at this."

Again the others followed to where he stood pointing at a marking on the floor. It was a single carving identical to the first of the markings near the valve.

Vorgath started to say something, but Savin held up a hand to stop him. "Wait, there's more."

He walked over to where the hall down which they had been walking ended and again pointed at the floor. Here there were two of the markings, again identical to the second and third of the carvings near the valve.

"OK," said the ranger. "Now what?"

There was silence for a moment. "Not my job," said the rogue. "I find and point out the obvious." He folded his arms across his chest. "Up to you guys to figure out what they do."

"Do we even want to find out?" asked the cleric as she studied the carvings in the floor. "I mean, we have a passage we have yet to explore." She turned to look at Thrinndor. "Do we want to chance not exploring it?"

"Your point is well taken," said the paladin. "However, it is likely we will encounter more of these 'valves' deeper in the maze, and I believe it would be in our best interest to know what they do."

"Agreed," said the caster as he eyes went from first one set of markings to another and finally to the last.

"Vorgath," continued the paladin, "if you will operate the valve." He waved behind them. "Everyone else back past the entrance to the alcove, please."

The barbarian nodded as he stepped to the mechanism. The rest of the party moved obediently back the way they had come until they were clear of the alcove.

Vorgath again put his meaty hands on the perimeter of the wheel, set his feet and lifted an eyebrow at the paladin.

Thrinndor nodded. "Battle ready," he said as he withdrew his flaming sword from its sheath at his belt and readied his shield.

The others did likewise. Vorgath looked longingly at his Flinthgoor leaning against the wall not far to his left. He sighed and shifted position slightly to be nearer his greataxe.

Gritting his teeth, he set his feet and tried to turn the wheel.

The muscles on his arm bulged and his face reddened, but the mechanism did not budge. He released his grip with a gasp and stepped back, staring at the big wheel.

"Try the other direction," said the caster.

The barbarian threw a nasty look over his shoulder but stepped back up to the valve, put his hands on it and strained to turn it the other direction.

There was a loud squeal as the metal protested the movement at first, but this time the wheel slowly moved.

As the barbarian continued to turn it another sound could be heard: Water. There was definitely water being released by the turning of the hand-wheel.

And then another sound shook the hall in which they all stood. It started as a low rumble but quickly grew in intensity. The wall at the end of the passage they had come down was moving!

Slowly at first the wall swung on unseen hinges. It gathered speed until it met the entrance of the passage that had been to their left with a loud thud and stopped.

"Interesting," said the dwarf, not the least winded from operating the valve. "Hydraulics."

"What?" asked the healer.

That was as far as she got however as a group of humanoid creatures rounded a bend in the passage that had been revealed when the wall shifted.

Sordaak recognized them instantly. "Drow!" he shouted.

The male dark elf in front stopped and drew his sword. "We are the Keepers of the Maze. For your intrusion you must die." His voice was emotionless as he spoke.

Vorgath snatched Flinthgoor from where it rested and roared as he launched himself into a rage.

The roar caught the drow completely off guard, and the leader barely got his sword up in time to deflect the sweeping blow from the barbarian's greataxe.

However, the deflection was slight as the axe merely glanced off of the sword and bit deep into the upper arm of the elf. Still, it kept the blow from being mortal, at least for the time being.

As Breunne stepped forward to confront the remaining drow, he felt a sharp pain in his back. He spun to look behind him. Another group of the drow was running toward them from the direction the party had come from!

"Trap!" he shouted, making sure he got Thrinndor's attention.

"No way!" snapped Savinhand. "There are no—" He cut off what he had been about to say when he turned and saw the dark elves coming up behind them.

"Shit!" shouted the paladin as he spun to face the new adversaries. "Vorgath," he said over his shoulder, "you and Savin on that first group." He did a quick count: five in each group! "The ranger and I will take the others."

Breunne nodded as he stepped to the side to give the paladin room to swing his flaming bastard sword.

"Sordaak," continued the paladin as he spotted one of the drow in front of him winding up to cast a spell, "take care of any spell-slingers! Cyrillis," he lunged at the first of the drow to get within range of his sword, "do that heal-thing as required!"

As the paladin parried a blow from the lead drow, his peripheral vision spotted the arrow protruding from the ranger's back. "How bad?" he asked fending of yet another blow.

"I'll live," replied the ranger as he brought his sword crashing down on the shield of the first drow to get in range. "You worry about yourself!" He grunted as he lunged at the elf on his right, a backswing from the glancing blow he had dealt the shield of the one on his right.

That blow connected, but the damage was minimal. Still, it served to cause that drow to back off a step. Spotting yet another drow trying to circle behind him he spun to his left and put his shoulders on the wall and withdrew a nasty-looking dagger from its sheath at his belt.

As he swung his longsword at the drow on his left, he saw the wound on the other drow close as if by magic. The elf smiled as he stepped in.

"Healer!" Breunne shouted. "They have cleric in the party, somewhere!"

"Damn," swore the paladin. He was getting better at this cursing thing. Damn that dwarf! "Cyrillis! See if you can neutralize that healer!"

"On it!" she replied as she searched both groupings looking for their cleric. There! That female drow with the staff—she must be their healer!

As Cyrillis watched, the female elf pointed her finger and sent healing energy to a drow that had gotten the worst end of an encounter with the barbarian.

"No you do not, bitch!" she muttered as she raced down the passage whirling her staff.

The opposing cleric's eyes widened when she caught sight of the oncoming Cyrillis. She raised her staff too late to ward off Kurril as it flashed toward her head.

The heel of Kurril impacted the drow cleric's head with enough force to knock her from her senses, perhaps even kill her. However, a bright flash exploded from the point of impact and a sizzling pop was heard.

The drow's head snapped over at an impossible angle and she dropped to the ground like a sack of potatoes.

She was dead. Cyrillis could sense that she had gone to afterlife, but was unsure exactly how. She stared briefly at the prone body of the opposing cleric but was jolted back to where she was by the howl of the barbarian as he buried his greataxe into the slender back of a drow warrior who had been trying to flee.

As quick as the battle began, it ended.

Cyrillis looked around using her god-granted percipience to check the status of the others in her party.

What she found astounded her.

Vorgath, breathing hard while still under the influence of his bloodlust, had several nicks and cuts but nothing serious. Savinhand, also nearby, appeared unscathed. As she watched, he knelt to wipe the blood from his blades onto the tunic of an obviously dead drow warrior. Sordaak, too, was unscathed. He stood over the body of what she presumed to be the enemy caster. His lifeless corpse was still smoldering from whatever spell Sordaak had used on him. As she watched, the caster knelt and removed a wand, two pouches and several scroll tubes from the body of the enemy.

Thrinndor had several cuts to his forearms and one nasty-looking gash in his left shoulder where an enemy blade had hit uncomfortably close to home. He would yet live, she determined. The paladin was helping the ranger to sit.

Breunne! She chastised herself for not checking him sooner. He had taken an arrow in the back next to his left shoulder blade. She could see that it had broken off sometime during the battle. Presumably the arrowhead was still lodged deep inside. He also had several cuts to his arms and chest where he had been unable to fend off the ferocious attacks of more than one drow. Some of them were deep. She could tell he had lost a lot of blood.

She rushed to where he now sat and roughly shoved the paladin aside.

"Excuse me?" Thrinndor said as he allowed himself to be moved.

Cyrillis said nothing as she poured her healing magic into the ranger. Instantly she could see wounds close and bleeding stop. But she could tell he was not in great shape.

"Wine!" she cried as she pushed him gently around so she could get a better look at his back. She took the skin Sordaak handed her and gave it to the ranger. "Drink," she said. "You are going to need this!"

Breunne nodded as he lifted the skin to his lips with his right hand. His left remained uselessly at his side. There was too much internal damage to the structure of his left shoulder.

His skin was pale due to loss of blood and his lips were a slightly blue color the healer did not like. Poison? No, she did not think so. Probably the effort of holding himself in a sitting position, she decided.

"I am going to have to remove this," she said, her voice laden with concern.

Again, the ranger nodded as he lifted the wineskin to his lips.

Cyrillis looked around quickly. Spying the other half of the broken arrow shaft, she retrieved it and handed it to the ranger. "Put this between your teeth," she said. She knew she did not have to explain why.

He did as told.

Meanwhile, Thrinndor was directing the remainder of the party. He had Savinhand check out the area revealed when the wall shifted. Sordaak was ordered to see if he could tell where the second group of drow had come from—more to assess if more attacks were eminent than anything else. He had decided to remain with the cleric and the ranger in the event more did show.

Cyrillis had removed the leather the ranger used as armor and cut away his tunic by the time the paladin had returned to oversee the operation. He could also see she was struggling with the pain she was about to inflict on the ranger.

"Would you like me to remove it?" he asked gently.

The cleric threw him a look that caused him to back up a step.

"I can handle this," she said. "I have had to remove worse on multiple occasions." Her eyes softened when she saw the concern on the paladin's face. "Sorry. I can handle this," she repeated, softer this time.

She removed a pouch from her belt, undid the thong that bound it and unrolled it on the hard stone floor. Selecting a pair of tongs, she knelt to get a better look. She poured some water on to a piece of cloth pulled from the same pouch and gently wiped away the blood from around where the broken shaft poked through the skin. What she saw did not please her. The skin had four small incisions around where the wooden shaft pierced the skin. Damn drow!

"It appears the arrow has multiple blades on the head," she said, concern again clouding her voice. "I am going to have to make additional cuts to see if I can get a look at it." She bit her lip. "I cannot take the chance of pulling it without knowing what type of head they used."

Again, Breunne nodded. He lifted the skin to his lips and took a long pull this time.

Cyrillis removed a small sack from her belt and selected a tiny vial from inside. "This will help with the pain on the surface," she said as she tore open the seal and removed the stopper. "However, there is little I can do for the pain removing this head is going to cause."

Once again the ranger nodded, but this time he put the shaft of the arrow between his teeth rather than the container of wine.

Carefully, Cyrillis applied the ointment from the vial to the area immediately around the shaft of the arrow. Knowing that the effects did not last long, she quickly pulled a specially sharpened dagger from the unrolled pouch and went to work around the shaft. Periodically she rubbed more ointment onto his skin and even put some on the edge of the dagger. It seemed to help.

There was so much blood! She had to rinse far more often than she liked. The warrior that fired this arrow must certainly have been strong! The head was far deeper than she had hoped.

Finally she spotted the head. It was as she feared. The metal blades were on springs and designed such that they opened up upon entry into the soft tissue of a body. Damn drow she thought again.

"Hold still," she said unnecessarily, as the ranger had not moved since she began her work. "I am going to have to push this slightly further in to get the blades to retract. Then I will hold them in place and jerk it out of there in one quick movement." Her eyes told the story. "This is going to hurt."

Breunne closed his eyes and nodded. The muscles of his jaws bulged as he bit hard on the arrow shaft.

Cyrillis put the last of the ointment on her blade and made several quick incisions to give her fingers room to work. She took in a deep breath and then pushed on the shaft of the arrow. There! Three of the blade heads snapped back into place, but the fourth was stuck on something. She could hear the ranger gasp in pain as she reached in the dagger and worked the area around the forth blade.

Finally, it too was free. She wrapped the fingers of her left hand around the four blades, gripped the shaft with her right and put her knee against the ranger's back and jerked with all her might.

The shaft was slick with blood and she almost lost her grip. But she clenched just before her hand completely slipped off. With a sickening ripping sound the shaft came free.

Breunne groaned in pain, somewhat muffled by the wood between his teeth. There was a snap as the force of his jaws bit through the arrow shaft between his teeth. His eyes rolled back in his head and he toppled over onto the floor, where he lay unmoving.

Cyrillis inspected briefly the head of the arrow in her blood-soaked hands and then cast it aside with a curse. Next she poured her most potent healing spell into the prone fighter. The bleeding stopped immediately, the skin appeared to knit together, and the ranger's breathing was less laborious. Still, Breunne's eyes remained closed.

Cyrillis used her senses to look under the skin and could see the damage still hiding there. Again she poured her most potent healing into the still fighter, saying a prayer as she did so.

She opened her eyes and this time when she checked the damaged area she could see her spells had done their work.

Cyrillis breathed a sigh of relief and sat back to ease the cramping of her legs that had been too long in the crouched position. She leaned back against the cool wall and absently brushed a lock of wayward blonde hair out of her eyes. "He must rest," she pronounced to no one in particular.

"We can't," protested the caster as he approached the group.

"He must rest!" repeated the cleric as she fixed her best do-not-argue-with-me-stare on the mage.

"We can't!" shot back the caster. "Even though I have used wands as much as possible, I am now below half of full strength!" His eyes grew softer as he pleaded with her to understand. "We don't know how big this maze is! I will soon be of no use to this party if we don't keep moving!"

The cleric's eyes searched his as she fought back a nasty rejoinder.

"I'm fine," said the ranger, the weakness in his voice belying his statement. Then, between clenched teeth as he struggled to rise, he added, "Let's get a move on."

"You must rest," responded the healer as she leapt to her feet and assisted the ranger to his. She sounded less sure now, even to herself.

"I'll have plenty of time to rest when I am dead," Breunne said with a wink at the caster. He was obviously feeling better. "Which, thanks to you, I'm not." He smiled and his eyes twinkled.

Cyrillis did her best to respond, but her percipience told her that he was still in pain. However, there was not much else she could do for him at the moment. His body needed time to recover from what had been forced upon it.

Yet she knew time was the one thing they did not have. As much as she hated to admit it, the services of the caster were paramount to their getting out of this alive.

They needed to continue moving.

"Very well," she said. "But can we at least take it slow for a while?"

Sordaak nodded his agreement. "That we can," he said, bowing his head to the paladin in difference to his leadership. "Assuming the boss man here is in agreement."

Thrinndor nodded his head. There was certainly something going on between these two. Just what was it? He had no idea.

"It's not like we can go very fast with Thumbs over there inspecting every brick!" The caster jerked his thumb over his shoulder in the general direction of the rogue and grinned.

"I resemble that remark!" groused the thief from up the passage. "I can go faster if you like, but I don't want to hear any complaints if I miss something."

"No," said the paladin. "Take whatever time you need."

"Speak for yourself, pretty boy," said the barbarian good-naturedly. "I can practically smell that dragon!"

Cyrillis grimaced at the dwarf. "I hope this encounter with the dragon will be everything you expect it to be." Her voice dripped with sarcasm.

Unfazed, Vorgath looked at the cleric with a smile on his lips—a smile that did not touch his eyes. "Me too."

Chapter Twenty-Two

Working it Out

The moving wall had revealed yet another passage that continued straight for perhaps fifty feet. There it ended abruptly in another "T" branch.

Or so it seemed.

Savinhand had found no more traps as he approached the intersection.

Once there a thorough inspection kept that vein. No traps.

He waved for the rest of the party to join him. He wanted them to witness what he had found.

Another operating mechanism identical to the one they had just left behind—except this one was in an alcove in the left side of the passage, with an opening across from it.

"Two and three," mused the mage as he studied the markings on the floor beneath the valve handle. He then turned to look for the matching markings on the floor near the walls. He found them immediately. The wall at the end of the passage down which they had come had three marks on the floor and the passage across from the alcove had two. "Here we go again," he murmured as he let out a sigh. He looked over at the paladin. "Which way, boss?"

"As in Dragma's Keep," Thrinndor replied, eyeing the markings on the floor, "I do not like leaving any doors unopened."

"You sure you want to open that?" asked the healer. "The last time that did not go so well."

The big fighter hesitated. "They said they were 'The Keepers of the Maze.' How many of those can there be?"

Sordaak's eyes opened wide. "I'm not sure how sound that logic is, but damned if I can poke holes in the theory."

"Anyone else?" queried the paladin. He got shakes of the head or blank stares from everyone. "Very well. Breunne, are you able to fight if need be?"

"Yes," replied the ranger instantly as he stood erect, retrieved his bow and notched an arrow. He threw a sidelong glance at the cleric. "Thanks to our healer here, I'm almost as good as a newly minted coin!"

"I do not know about that," Cyrillis said, her cheeks tainted red. "You clearly have wondrous recuperative powers."

"Strong constitution," agreed the ranger with a wink. "However, a strong constitution cannot remove a drow death arrow on its own!"

"Just the same," replied the cleric, "in the future please try to avoid such activity." Breunne smiled in return. "Yes ma'am."

Vorgath had moved over to the valve. "Are we ready yet?"

Thrinndor looked around at the positioning of the group. He hesitated. "We shall try this one a little differently," he said. "Cyrillis and Sordaak behind Vorgath at the valve." He turned to the ranger. "Breunne between them, bow at the ready." The ranger nodded.

"Savin to the right at the entrance to the alcove and I will be at the left." The thief also nodded. "Vorgath, after you operate the valve, step to the middle here, ready to fight."

"Middle," repeated the barbarian, cracking a smile. "Ready to fight. Got it."

As the group went to their assigned posts, Thrinndor spoke. "As before, take out any healers and casters first. Sordaak, preserve energy as best you can. Wands and scrolls if you have them. The party will reimburse any expenses incurred from use of said wands, scrolls and potions." He looked over to where the healer stood ready.

Cyrillis started to protest, but changed her mind and nodded also.

"Ready?" asked the dwarf, sarcasm dripping from his voice.

"I'll take out any wiggle-fingers with this," the ranger said as he lifted the bow, "if you'll but point them out to me." Again, the healer and mage nodded.

The paladin looked around at their positioning and bobbed his head at the dwarf.

Immediately the barbarian heaved on the valve. This time he got the direction right. The mechanism squealed lightly as it began to move, but the sound was quickly overcome by the sound of water flowing beneath their feet.

They did not have long to wait. After a few seconds the wall began to shift. Slowly at first and then with increasing speed until it came to a rest blocking the passage across from the alcove with a thud. The companions waited.

Breunne could feel the blood pulsing in his back where the arrow had done so much damage. He muttered a word, releasing some healing energy of his own, and the pain subsided somewhat.

Once again they did not have long to wait. Footsteps could be heard in the silence that held the air after the wall had shifted. The steps again came from both directions.

Sordaak spat a curse as his right hand dove into the folds of his tunic, emerging with a scroll. This he quickly tore open and read the words printed therein.

Quickly, a thick fog appeared in the passage in front of the opening for the alcove. The footsteps slowed as they entered the fog. One of the enemy stepped ahead of the group, sword in hand. "We are The Keepers of the Maze. For your intrusion, you must die."

"Damn," muttered the ranger over the sound of the approaching drow, "didn't we just leave this party?" He loosed an arrow at this supposed leader as he came into his line of sight, barely visible through the roiling fog.

His aim was true, and the drow fell back with the feathers of Breunne's arrow visible just below his larynx. His backward step caused him to crash into the fighter just behind him. This fighter tried to disentangle himself from his leader as the rogue's shortsword flashed and this second fighter's neck erupted in a gout of blood as his head toppled over, severed from its body.

"Damn!" shouted the rogue into the din of battle that erupted. "I love this sword!"

Thrinndor barely had time to grin as the second group rounded the corner and waded into the fog. His own flaming blade flashed in the dim light as he parried several thrusts with shield and sword.

Vorgath howled to build his rage as he stepped out into the passage to give himself room to swing Flinthgoor. He did not have to go far to encounter his first drow fighter—much to that fighter's dismay. The barbarian whipped his blade around in a devastating arc that almost cut the male drow in two at the waist.

The barbarian jerked his blade free of the lifeless body and spun to confront another dark elf trying to sneak into the alcove.

Some innate sense must have warned the elf, because he tumbled quickly to his right, causing the flashing greataxe to only graze him as he went down.

Unbelievably quick, the dark elf surged back to his feet and leapt at the dwarf who was way off balance due to essentially missing with his intended blow.

Vorgath yelped more in surprise than in pain as the drow's rapier penetrated deep in a sliver of an opening between the shoulder of his breastplate and the leather gauntlet that covered his upper arm.

A second flash from the drow and the dagger he had in his left hand drew blood from the unprotected flesh on the dwarf's neck. A quick recovery by the barbarian kept that to not much more than a surface wound, however.

Vorgath bellowed as he whipped the head of his blade back around in an arc that should have ended his battle with this pesky foe. This time, however, his blade slashed through nothing but the fog where the elf had been crouched only a moment before.

"What the—?" snarled the dwarf. He spotted the drow again attacking from his left in time to parry the lunge of the rapier with the haft of his greataxe. "Now, stand still, damn you!" He followed the parry with a thrust of his own.

However nimble he was with the huge axe, the dwarf was unable to make contact with what he was beginning to suspect was a drow thief. After several slashes and parries, Vorgath found himself bleeding from several cuts. Although each individual cut was not of itself serious, the loss of blood and exhausted barbarian rage was combining to drain him far faster than he could remember having happened before.

"Ugh," said the dwarf, grunting as he half-blocked yet another thrust of the rapier. As quick as blinking he had still another deep gash in his left arm.

Desperate, the barbarian tried a new tactic. He dropped the head of his axe to the hard stone floor, leaned heavily on it and then stumbled away from the rogue.

Vorgath snuck a peek under his arm as he dropped to one knee. It worked. Confident of the kill, the drow stepped after the dwarf with both blades poised for action.

Mustering every ounce of strength he had left, the barbarian lunged to his feet and whipped his blade around in a vicious arc.

Vorgath watched as the eyes of the drow widened in surprise and the thief tried in vain to spin out of the path of the flashing blade.

Flinthgoor bit deep in the upper thigh of the rogue, nearly severing the limb. Vorgath smiled weakly as he followed his blade in, ripping it free of the drow as the rogue stumbled back a step.

Suddenly the dwarf felt better and a surge of energy revitalized his movement. Cyrillis had sensed his plight and applied some healing even though she could not see him through the fog. Bless that girl!

With a new spring in his step, he leapt after the falling dark elf and again swung his greataxe.

Vorgath could see in the drow's eyes that he knew death was flashing toward him in the form of the dwarf's axe. Still, he tried to block the blow with an arm as he fell backward—unable to stand upright on his severely damaged leg.

Flinthgoor severed the rogue's hand just above the wrist, and the greataxe continued its inexorable path and buried itself in the elf's chest. The drow's eyes widened in surprise and he nodded in deference to the dwarf, acknowledging defeat. He died with his eyes open.

"Damn!" the barbarian said. "What a pain in the ass!"

The dwarf turned to see if he could find any more drow to kill just as he saw a ball of fire flash past his ear into the alcove, where it exploded with a deafening blast.

Vorgath was able to dive under most of the explosion, but he knew those at the back of the alcove must have taken full brunt of it.

As he jumped to his feet, looking right and left for the source of the spell, he heard Sordaak say "Ow."

At least the caster yet lives thought the barbarian as he charged down the path the ball had come from, his axe held high.

He had taken only two steps when he heard a thwip, thwip, thwip as three arrows whipped past his ear, also following the path of the ball of fire.

Vorgath heard at least two of them hit home with a thud not far ahead of him. "Damn ranger!" he cursed as he spotted a drow—presumably the caster—slumping to the ground with not two but three arrows protruding from his chest, his eyes wide in surprise.

He buried Flinthgoor deep in the drow's chest next to an arrow with a satisfying thud. "Two!" he shouted. His eyes had been open, and he had yet to fall to the ground, after all.

"I think not!" said the voice of the paladin from just over the dwarf's left shoulder.

Vorgath spun to see his friend materialize out of the mist.

"He yet lived when I got here!" protested the dwarf as he yanked his axe free of the dark elf.

"Doubtful," responded the paladin, clucking his tongue and shaking his head. "Trying to steal kills—I never thought I would see the day!"

"You haven't!" argued the barbarian. "The damned drow was still alive when I got here!"

"Whatever!" replied the paladin still shaking his head.

As the fog cleared the two stopped arguing and counted the bodies.

Ten. Again ten.

Back in the alcove, Cyrillis leaned over Sordaak, concern on her face. She looked up as the barbarian and paladin walked in. "He took the full force of that fireball," she said.

"I'll live," said the caster. His face was a bright red from the heat of the spell, and his eyebrows were gone.

"Yes, you will," the healer said. "However, your face is badly burned." Her hands searched one of the several sacks tied to her waist, finally emerging with a jar. "Now hold still."

Savinhand searched the bodies of the fallen elves as the rest of the party dealt with injuries. He had again emerged unscathed. Maybe I'm getting better at this combat thing, he mused quietly. He smiled. No, he reminded himself, I've just been lucky to this point. He dumped what he had collected onto the floor of the alcove just as Cyrillis finished administering to the mage.

"How do I look?" Sordaak asked as he turned his attention to the pile on the floor.

Savinhand did a poor job of stifling a chuckle as he saw the caster's face for the first time.

"What?" asked the sorcerer. He tried unsuccessfully to knit his eyebrows together. There were no eyebrows!

Thrinndor answered for him as he too tried to maintain a straight face. "Hmmm, no eyebrows, skin as red as a ripe tomato and white cream resembling a jester's makeup." He was even less successful in stifling a chuckle. "Normal." He shrugged, a big smile still on his face.

Angrily, Sordaak grabbed a rag and started to wipe the cream off.

"Do not!" commanded the healer.

The mage stopped with the rag halfway to his face. Disgusted, he threw it to the ground and started rummaging through the pile the thief had recently deposited.

"Look on the bright side," said the barbarian, a wide grin on his face. "There's a good chance you'll scare off any monsters we might encounter from this point forward!"

Sordaak glared at the dwarf. "Very funny," he said as he allowed his eyes to linger on the barbarian's own burnt face. "Have you looked in a mirror, lately?" The blank stare he got from the dwarf told him his answer. "I didn't think so. I wouldn't either, were I you. Let's see, bright red skin, check. No eyebrows, check. Moustache three-quarters gone and what's left of a once proud beard badly charred." He stopped smiling. "Check and check."

Vorgath puffed out his chest to speak, but again Sordaak beat him to it.

"I'm not worried I'll scare away any of your precious monsters," the caster said. "They'll never make it past you at point!"

The barbarian's eyes widened as he looked down at what once had been a glorious beard. "Whatever!" he snapped as he stomped off to investigate an imagined something over by the far wall.

The caster's eyes followed the dwarf, tempted to say more. However, knowing the fierce pride of the dwarven race, he decided he had pushed far enough. He climbed wearily to his feet. "If we are done with the jocularity for the moment, maybe we can get a move on?" He turned to fix his stare on the paladin.

Thrinndor was silent for a moment as he tried to gauge the status of each in the party. Finally he turned to face the cleric. "What is your spell capacity status?"

Cyrillis hesitated as she got a worried look on her face. "Not good."

The paladin waited for more. He needed to know.

"I am at maybe 25 percent," the healer said, allowing her shoulders to droop. "Vorgath needs more healing—"

"I'm fine," protested the barbarian.

"The hell you are," snapped the cleric. "However, you are as good as you are going to get for the time being, I am afraid."

Her eyes looked went to Sordaak and then to Breunne. "The three of us took injury from that fireball spell," she continued, "with Sordaak taking the brunt of it."

"I'm fine," said the caster, not wanting to let on just how badly he had been hurt.

"Horseshit!" snapped the cleric. There was no getting anything past her when it came to injuries. "However, you also will have to go on as you are until we have an opportunity to rest."

"So what do we do?" asked the ranger. He too was still hurting, but nowhere near as bad as before.

"We move on," said the caster, having pocketed a wand and a couple of scroll tubes he'd dug out of the pile. "Staying here only drains my reserves further still." He looked over at Cyrillis. "And that will in the end put more of a drain on our healer."

"Very well," replied the paladin.

"All is not lost," said the healer, hope edging her tone. "I have tapped the resources of my staff very little, and I have several potions of healing and a wand that has multiple uses available, as well."

"That is good," agreed the paladin. "Allow me to suggest that you use only your spell energy to heal during the course of a battle. And use the other items as necessary in between." Cyrillis made to reply, but he added quickly, "I am certain it is what you have been doing all along. However, just let me do this leader thing. OK?"

Cyrillis exhaled slowly, smiled and nodded.

Thrinndor went on. "Very good. Are there any who might need some of that healing before we continue?"

The cleric hesitated, but her need to heal got the better of her as her hand reached up under her breastplate and pulled out a long, thin, rather plain-looking rod. "Yes," she said and stepped over to confront the dwarf.

"I'm fine," he groused, but not very loudly.

"The hell you are!" she said for a second time. Then she grinned. "Stand still. This will not hurt a bit!"

Again the barbarian started to protest, but he stifled it knowing it would do no good at this point. Besides, he reasoned his strength was needed as a front linesman.

The healer waved the wand at him once and then a second time. She started to do a third but changed her mind. "That will have to do," she said as she stepped over to the caster.

Her eyes pleaded with him not to argue as she raised the wand.

He didn't. He knew that another fireball blast such as the recent one might mean his demise. Wisely, he kept his mouth shut.

Again the healer waved the wand. Once. Twice. She raised it a third time but again hesitated.

Sordaak put a hand on her arm and looked into her eyes. "Thank you," he said softly, his eyes not leaving hers. "That will be fine." He turned and headed out of the alcove.

Cyrillis' eyes followed the mage. She knew he could use more, but she hesitated because she knew the body's natural healing process should be able to take it from this point.

Should be able to.

"Now what?" asked the rogue. He had scooped up anything remaining of value and kicked the rest—mostly small bucklers and useless weapons—over to the wall of the alcove.

"Now we see where this passage leads us," replied the paladin, peering down the hall as he spoke. It went at least another fifty feet, but he could not tell beyond that or see anything remarkable about it.

When no one spoke, he said, "Marching formation."

Savinhand obediently moved ahead of the group, searching as he went. Everyone else stood fast as he continued his search.

Cyrillis raised her hand to cast the aid spell on him, but Thrinndor stopped her. "In light of your reduced capacity, perhaps we should see if he can do without the help."

The rogue looked back at the two but said nothing.

Silently the cleric nodded and lowered her hand.

Savinhand shrugged and continued his search. He didn't want to suggest otherwise, but it had certainly been nice to have the aid.

About thirty feet into the passage the rogue held up a hand for the party to remain where they were as he studied another discrepancy, this time in the floor.

"Need my help?" asked Sordaak from his new place near the front of the party.

"Not yet," said the rogue. There! Another spot in the floor identical to the one he had already identified. Now he was able to discern a pattern developing. He began his search for the disarming mechanism.

Carefully, he studied the walls on both sides of the passage, working his way back toward the party as he did.

There it is! A tricky little bastard, he thought as he removed his tool pouch and unrolled it on the stone floor.

A few pokes and prods with his selected wire later he heard a definitive click as the mechanism disarmed.

"OK," he said. "It's safe to come up now."

"What was it this time?" asked the dwarf as he approached where the thief was standing.

In response, Savin went over and pointed to the noted irregularities he had seen in the stonework of the floor. "Spikes; probably sharpened." He grimaced. "We call them cast-iron butt-piercers." He grinned.

"Ouch," muttered the dwarf. "Some of us have lower butts than others, I might point out."

Thrinndor grinned. "I doubt they had dwarves in mind when they designed these traps."

Vorgath's eyes narrowed as he considered a reply.

"This passage is different," said the mage before the dwarf could think of anything.

"How so?" asked the paladin.

"There's no alcove," replied the mage. "Although the passage ends in the usual split, this one appears to have passages going both directions."

All eyes followed the sorcerer's finger.

Sordaak looked down at the map he had been working on. "I hope this does not go much further."

"That goes without saying," responded the paladin. "But you said that for a reason. Please explain."

"Look at my map," said the caster as he held it out for all to see.

Savinhand, who had come trudging back to join the party when he overheard the mage's proclamation, was first to speak. "Not much there," he said as he pointed to a large blank area next to the lines Sordaak had drawn indicating where they had already been.

"Exactly," the caster said, tapping the parchment with finger. "But look at what is there!"

"I don't get it," said the rogue as he turned his head to get a different viewpoint.

Sordaak rolled his eyes. "There's a surprise!"

"Hey!" replied the rogue.

"See this?" the mage said before Savin could complain further. He pointed at the passages he had mapped. "They are going in pretty much a straight line—at least after that first right turn, anyway."

"So?" Cyrillis said, her eyes glued to the map.

"Well," replied the spellcaster as he took in a deep breath, "the few mazes I have encountered—and they are very few, mind you—have been symmetrical from the entrance." He waited. He was not disappointed.

"What does that have to do with this maze?" asked the ranger. His eyes, too, were locked on the map.

"If the maze is symmetrical from the entrance," replied the maze as if he were giving a lecture, "then there will be passages to the left of where we came in that will require investigating as these did." He let that soak in.

"Shit," said the ranger.

"Exactly," replied the sorcerer. He again pointed to the map. "Not only that, all of this area in between is probably going to require further investigation as well."

"Shit," agreed the cleric.

"Not you, too!" bemoaned the caster.

"What?" she said.

"Please allow those of us—and by that I mean 'us non-clerical types'—steeped in the tradition of cursing as necessary to display our not-so-superior intellect," lectured the caster sternly, "to do so without feeling guilty for having influenced the chaste and devoted in the party by their advocating such behavior by joining in!"

Before the cleric could say anything, Sordaak's eyes traveled from the cleric to the paladin. "That goes for you as well!"

Thrinndor bit off several words he had picked up over the years during his sojourns with the heathen type. Instead, he grinned widely and said, "Very well said." He winked at the cleric, who was not so inclined to let the caster off so easily. "We will endeavor to restrict our wordage to a more appropriate manner."

"Thank you," replied the mage. He deliberately turned away from the cleric, hoping she would let the matter rest.

Her face was red—whether in anger or embarrassment was not immediately known. She said nothing.

Sordaak sighed in relief. "I have a theory," said the caster quickly as he turned back to face the group.

"Do tell," replied the barbarian. His tone said that he was amused by the previous conversation.

Sordaak was fairly certain he was being made fun of, but he chose to ignore the quip. "If I read the markings correctly, the first alcove and door we came to were on position one when we first laid eyes on them." He had their attention. "We shifted that door to position two and that led us to the most recent mechanism." He pointed at the valve by which Vorgath and Breunne were still standing. "That mechanism—valve—was in position two and we shifted it to position three. Again, assuming I am reading the markings correctly."

"I'm with you so far," said the barbarian. "Where's this going?"

"If you'll but shut your face," snapped the mage, "I'm in the process of explaining." He felt the need to get moving; he was losing precious energy while they stood here.

Vorgath folded is arms across his massive chest and said no more. But his demeanor said this had better be good.

"My theory is that we will be able to bypass a significant portion of this maze if we put all doors we encounter in position two and follow that path," Sordaak said as he tucked the map away into a fold in his robe.

"On what do you base this theory?" asked the paladin.

The mage looked up at the big fighter—now their leader—and took a deep breath to reply. He held that breath for a moment and then released it noisily. "On a hunch."

"What?" exploded the barbarian.

"No, wait," said the paladin quickly. "Let us hear him out."

The caster's eyes said "thank you" to the paladin. "Our illustrious leader prefers to go right at all available options," the mage said. "We have come across two doors, each with the number 'two' in it." His gaze took in each of his companions. "I say we put the doors in position two and go that way."

"That makes no sense!" bellowed the dwarf.

"Do you have anything better?" asked the paladin.

"Yes," said the dwarf. "We continue as we have, fighting our way through to the end." He was clearly blustering. "We have no time for theories!"

"But—" began the paladin.

"Allow me," interrupted the mage. Thrinndor nodded.

The magicuser turned to face the barbarian. "We don't have time to do as you suggest," he began solemnly. "While you fighter-types are performing admirably against the enemy drow, a couple more fights like the last two—three at most—will drain our available spell resources. At which point I'll be rendered useless and our healer will be reduced to swinging that big stick of hers as her only way to help." He took in a deep breath. The energy drain was weighing heavily on his mind, but he needed them to understand. "We will perish in this puzzle before we complete even half of it."

"Bah," spat the dwarf as he shook Flinthgoor at the mage. "We can fight our way through this!" However, that statement sounded hollow, even to him.

"No we can't," said the mage. "These side trips are meant to merely be distractions to those who hold the journal, but death to those who do not."

"How do you know this?" asked the cleric.

"Think about it," responded the mage. "We knew there was going to be a maze in here—and a lot of traps." He got a nod from Savinhand. "Anyone else—say some wandering adventurers that happened upon the cabin and chose to investigate—would wander aimlessly into first the traps and then into the maze. Without massive spell power and many strong arms to do battle with, those adventurers would be doomed within these walls."

He went on, firm in the conviction that he'd stoked the proper fires of passion with his speech. "Only with the knowledge that there must be an easier way can there be any hope to exit this maze by a means other than the unwanted journey to the afterlife!"

Silence pervaded the group until the paladin finally spoke. "What is it you propose?"

The spellcaster breathed a sigh of relief. "We go back to that last door, change it back to position two and follow that passage."

"Seems reasonable enough," the ranger said softly.

Sordaak took in another breath. "I have another theory."

"What now?" griped the barbarian. "Can't we just have one of those at a time, please?"

"I'll explain as we retrace our path," said the caster as he turned to look the way they had come. "We need to get moving. This energy drain is making clear thought difficult."

"Very well," said the paladin, concerned for his friend. "Trap search formation. Savinhand, if you please." He bowed slightly and waved a massive arm back the way they had come.

"But of course!" replied the thief.

Instantly Sordaak felt the energy drain stop. He actually smiled for a moment with the relief. Then the smile vanished in a flash.

Quickly they got back to the intersection.

Sordaak looked around as he went through the door. "As I suspected," he said, turning his attention to the alcove.

Thrinndor looked around. Seeing nothing he turned his attention to the caster. "Care to enlighten us?"

The mage looked up at the paladin and shook his head in mock sadness. "It's a wonder you guys ever survived without me!"

"What?" Thrinndor asked.

"Never mind," said the caster with another shake of his head. "Bodies." He waved his hand in the direction of the alcove. "Where are the bodies?"

"What?" asked the barbarian as he joined the conversation.

The spellcaster rolled his eyes. "We killed ten dark elves here," he said impatiently. "Where are the bodies?"

Vorgath's eyes widened. "They were right there," he said as he pointed to where he had stacked most of the enemy against the wall just outside of the alcove.

"Right," said the caster as he folded his arms on his chest matter-of-factly.

The paladin turned his attention back to the caster. "So, what is this second theory?"

"It's two-fold," the magicuser said. "First, whenever we open a door—or shift a wall, as this situation may be—we will encounter a group of ten drow elves claiming to be the 'Keepers of the Maze.'" He paused for effect. "And second, they will be the same ten as before!"

"What?" exploded the dwarf. "Make some sense, man!"

"Think about it," responded the mage. "Both encounters were with ten drow. In both encounters they said the same phrase: 'We are the Keepers of the Maze. For your intrusion you must die.'" Again Sordaak paused, and a smug expression moved across his burnt face. "But the most telling indicator of all is that in both encounters the cleric was a female and the remainder of the party was male!"

The barbarian took in a breath to again profess doubt, but sudden realization caused him to pause. The mage was right! The cleric had been female on both occasions. How had he missed that?

"How is that possible?" Breunne asked.

"Finally," replied the caster, "a good question." He looked at the paladin and shrugged. "One that I don't have an answer for. However, I do have a couple of—"

"Theories?" interrupted the dwarf, his ego still smarting from not making the female cleric connection.

Sordaak glared at the barbarian. "Yes, theories." He waited for the dwarf to say more. When he did not, the mage went on. "One theory," he spat the word in the general direction of the dwarf, "is that the drow are mere illusions."

"That was no illusion I planted my axe in not long ago!" Vorgath said crossly.

"I healed a lot of injury done by those illusions, as well," added the cleric.

"I didn't say it was a good theory!" snapped the caster. "However, a person can be slain by an illusion if one believes he or she has been slain by that illusion." He looked at each person in the party, daring a contradiction. No one spoke.

Thrinndor coughed lightly. "Second?" he said.

Sordaak folded his arms across his chest. "The only other possibility I can come up with—unless they are not the same drow each time—is that someone or something is resurrecting them between each encounter."

"Preposterous!" blasted the barbarian.

"You know," said the magician, "you are beginning to piss me off!" Sordaak's eyes bored into the barbarian. "Either put forth better ideas, or keep your big mouth shut!"

The barbarian attempted to match stares with the caster, but abruptly looked down at his feet and crossed his arms on his chest. He said nothing.

"As I thought!" snapped the spellcaster. "If you want to compare theories, please do so! Otherwise at least allow me to do my theorizing without interruption! We don't have time for that!"

The barbarian again made eye contact with the caster, intent on regaining some sense of composure but changed his mind. He looked down and mutely nodded his agreement.

Sordaak exhaled noisily. "Thank you," he said.

"Resurrecting an entire party of ten would require enormous energy," the cleric said slowly, not wanting to incur the ire of the mage. "Doing so a second time..." Her voice trailed off.

"Agreed," Sordaak said as he turned to face her. "Again, I didn't say it was a good theory." He smiled. "But I don't have much to work with." He turned back to the paladin. "That's it, three possibilities as I see them. One: We're seeing a different group every time. Two: We're activating an illusion every time. Three: Someone is resurrecting the drow and they are there for us at each valve." He looked over at the barbarian. "Unless you have a theory I have missed?"

Vorgath found somewhere else for his eyes to be and remained silent.

"There is one more," began the healer.

Sordaak looked at her, his non-eyebrow raised inquisitively.

"Automatons," she said as if that explained all. When no one else said anything, she explained. "Automatons are a combination of the illusion you spoke of and, for the lack of a better word, flesh."

"I've heard of those," Breunne said thoughtfully.

"Now that you mention it," said the caster, rubbing his chin in thought. That hurt the burned skin on his face, so he quickly stopped. "I have, as well." His eyes went from the ranger back to the cleric. "But I haven't heard of that spell being used for centuries. But that might explain all that we have seen even better. That's a high level cleric ability, correct?"

"Yes," Cyrillis said. "Very high."

"Still," said the mage deep in thought, "that would certainly explain what we have seen the same number in the parties. Same gender and class." His eyes met those of the cleric. "Interesting."

"OK," said the paladin. "It really does not matter as I see it." He looked from the mage to the cleric and back at the mage. "Somehow we are essentially battling the same party every time we open a door panel, right?"

"Yes," Sordaak said. Feeling the energy drain again tug at his reserves, the mage continued quickly. "We must keep moving." He looked back at the paladin. "If my first theory is correct—and it had better be—we need to shift this wall back to position two."

Thrinndor looked dubiously at the valve in the alcove. "You think we will again be attacked following the shift?"

Sordaak took in a deep breath and let it out slowly. "I can't say for this wall since we have already shifted it once." He looked at the blank wall behind which he hoped there to be the passage they needed to traverse. "But, just the same, we should be prepared in the event we will."

The paladin's eyes searched those of the caster. "Very well. Same positions as before. Sordaak, if you could drop the fog spell again, that was most helpful."

The spellcaster nodded as he took up his position behind the valve.

"I believe I have a spell that will aid us as well," Cyrillis said.

The paladin looked at her with a questioning expression. "Do you have the energy to spend on such a spell?"

"Yes. The energy spent on that one spell will be far off-set by that saved in not having to heal you meat-shields." She smiled.

Thrinndor smiled in return. "Very well. Make it so."

As the party took up positions, Cyrillis said, "I will be casting Barricade of Blades. If you all will please stay inside of the ring of blades that forms, it will maximize the effect." She smiled. "Some of them will recognize it was I that cast the spell and will thus try to attack me."

"We will keep them off of you," promised the barbarian as he slapped the haft of his greataxe.

Cyrillis smiled at the barbarian.

"Vorgath," said the paladin, "if you will." He nodded at the valve sticking up out of the hole in the stone floor.

The barbarian leaned Flinthgoor against the nearby wall, placed his hands on the wheel and turned it.

Cyrillis and Sordaak both went to work on their spells. They were again surrounded by a wall of fog and the faint sound of the grinding blades from the cleric's spell.

Soon thereafter, they heard the sound of approaching footsteps, followed by a male voice that said, "We are The Keepers of the Maze. For your intrusion, you must die."

"Whatever," said the barbarian as he retrieved his axe.

The companions waited.

First one unseen group attempted to enter the alcove and then the other. The fog masked the blades, and thus they came as a surprise. Mass confusion ensued. Several screams ripped through the air as three of the drow parted the mists at once and entered the alcove. They were met by Vorgath, Savinhand and Thrinndor's blades and were immediately cut down without a sound.

The second wave followed the first more tentatively. Again they were set upon by the blades. This time Breunne loosed a volley of arrows at the first to appear, causing the barbarians axe to bite nothing but air as the drow warrior fell back into the mist.

"Not fair!" howled the barbarian as he stepped after the falling drow. He was too late. The drow warrior stared with unseeing eyes at the dwarf as he hovered over him with his axe poised to strike. "Damn rangers!" he complained as he looked up just in time for another drow to appear out of the mists.

The wizard! No matter. Flinthgoor sent him to make amends with his friends in the afterlife with one terrible slash. He looked around for others—he could hear but not see them as the remaining drow met similar fates at the hands of his companions.

Again as quickly as it started, the battle was over. Sordaak and Cyrillis released their spells, the mists cleared, and the sound of the blades vanished.

Quickly Thrinndor assessed the situation. "Anyone hurt?" he said. In response he got several head shakes. "Good. Savin, take a look and ensure there are none feigning death."

After a cursory search, it was apparent to the rogue that the barricade had wreaked severe damage among the drow. Not much effort had been required on the companions' part to finish the job. "Not unless they can feign missing arms and heads," Savin said with a shake of his head. "They look pretty dead to me!"

Chapter Twenty-Three

Through!

S ordaak's theory proved correct, so after only three more door operations the party found itself back in the cabin. The new tactics employed enabled the group to speed through all three without taking further damage.

In all, their mood was certainly heightened as they gathered to assess the situation.

Only Sordaak was his normal doom and gloom. In response to Thrinndor's question about energy levels, the mage replied, "Less than 25 percent." He shook his head morosely. "And dropping."

Cyrillis' euphoria at escaping the maze without having to use her healing powers rapidly deflated, as well. "About the same," she said, her eyes concerned. When she looked at her staff, she too shook her head sorrowfully. "Less than half strength on Kurril." She shifted her eyes to search those of her leader. "We are getting dangerously low on energy." She let the thought die on the floor for all to see.

"I know," replied the paladin. He looked forlornly at the caster. "We must push on."

Sordaak nodded and adjusted his sacks and bags. He sorely needed a rest period but dared not sit down.

"Very well," Thrinndor said. "Everyone grab something to munch on." The rustling of bags and sacks could be heard as he continued. "Savin, your turn." At the confused look from the rogue, he added, "You pick the next door."

"Why me?" replied the thief, his biscuit halfway to his mouth.

"Because it's your damn adventure!" said the dwarf, spitting dried bread-crumbs all over the floor as he did.

Thrinndor started to say something to ease the harsh remarks of his barbarian friend but instead shrugged. "What he said."

"OK," Savinhand said between bites. "That one." He pointed to the door in front of him.

"Why that door?" Cyrillis asked.

"Why not?" said the rogue. Stupid question, he thought to himself. This quest was wearing thin on his nerves, too. "If I remember correctly, we decided the selection process was random, so I picked the door I was already facing." He finished his biscuit and washed it down with a mouthful of water from the skin at his belt and moved up to inspect the door without being asked.

After a cursory inspection, Savin turned to the paladin. "Clean," he said and moved aside.

Thrinndor stepped to the door, grasped the operating mechanism, and tensed to pull.

"Wait!" called out the caster.

The big fighter released the mechanism and turned to face the mage inquisitively, the obvious question dying on his lips.

"I know we decided the doors were random," Sordaak began.

"At your behest," Breunne reminded.

The spellcaster shot the ranger a nasty look. Breunne stared back impassively.

"But take a look at the markings on the doors," Sordaak said, pointing at the door the paladin had been about to open.

The emblem affixed to the door was a skull with emblazoned eyes.

Startled, Thrinndor backed up a step. How had he missed that? Quickly he looked at the other doors.

A chimera.

A hydra.

He sucked in a noisy breath. A dragon.

Silence pervaded the small room. "Now what?" asked Savinhand.

Sordaak hesitated. "Assuming the symbols on the doors now depict what is behind them," he said as he pointed to the door with the hydra, "we've been through that door." He then pointed to the chimera, "And that one."

"The chimera?" queried the paladin. "How so?"

"The chimera," explained the mage impatiently, "is a creature created by a supposedly crazed sorcerer."

"That's a bit of a stretch, do you not think?" Cyrillis said, her eyes still locked on the symbol for the dragon.

"Legend has it," continued the spellcaster as if he had not been interrupted, "the sorcerer was crazed from having spent several years in a maze."

"Oh," said the cleric, still not looking away from the dragon.

"Still a bit of a stretch," groused the barbarian.

"Do you have any better theories?" the mage asked.

"We stick with the 'doors are random' theory," Vorgath said stubbornly.

"That theory, while valid at the time, is now outdated," Sordaak said.

"Whatever!" said the barbarian, again finding someplace else for his eyes to be.

"So," Thrinndor said, "the dragon it is, then."

"Unless you want to see what awaits us behind the door with the skull," agreed the mage.

"That is assuming you really want to face this dragon." Breunne voiced what most were thinking.

All except for Vorgath, of course. Abruptly he stepped forward, grasped the operating mechanism for the door with the dragon and pulled.

"Hey!" said a startled rogue as the door creaked open ominously.

The dwarf looked over at the thief. "What?"

"What if that was trapped?" asked Savinhand.

"Then I'd be in a world of shit, huh?" the barbarian said over his shoulder as he stepped through the door, Flinthgoor at the ready.

Savin grinned as he quickly moved to get ahead of the dwarf, who had stopped after going through. "Yup," he said as he brushed past the recalcitrant barbarian.

"I guess that decision is made," said the paladin, more to himself than anyone else. He then called out for the others to hear, "Trap search formation!"

Again the chamber they stepped into was sheathed in mist. When Breunne—the last through—entered, the door shut behind him. Sordaak cringed, waiting for the voice.

He was not disappointed.

"You have chosen…" The voice paused, and each party member found themselves holding their breath as they waited for it to continue. Finally, it did. "Wisely."

A collective sigh escaped six sets of lips at once.

Bolstered that they had finally chosen the correct door, Savin again started to move forward as the mists dissipated.

The chamber was large—much bigger than any previous.

"All right, people," began the paladin. "If our illustrious healer is correct, we should be on the lookout for a dragon." He looked around at the expanse of the chamber. "This place is certainly large enough to accommodate one."

Savinhand cleared his throat. "Not exactly," he said as he approached the group, journal in hand.

"What?" Vorgath's head snapped around

"Calm yourself, old one," replied the thief. "If a dragon is what awaits us for the final test, you will get your dragon!" He waited for the dwarf to say something. When he didn't, Thumbs continued. "But first we have some more tests."

"I thought we were through that?" asked the mage.

"Yes," said the rogue leader, "and no."

"More riddles?" Breunne's voice was forlorn. "I grow weary of the riddles."

"You and me both!" agreed the sorcerer.

"That vestibule was just for the initial weeding out of the weak and undesirable who are not supposed to get this far. Now it gets nasty."

Sordaak allowed his shoulders to slump. "Cyrillis," he said tiredly, "how are you on energy?"

"Same as before," she said. "About 25 to 30 percent."

"I'm slightly less than that," the mage said, turning to face the rogue. "How nasty?"

Savin shrugged. "Nasty enough to provide adequate testing for the potential guild leader and his chosen companions."

"Shit," said the caster.

"Wait," said the paladin. "Are you feeling the energy drain in this place?"

Sordaak quickly glanced at his appointed leader, hope suddenly taking the place of despair. He closed his eyes and looked inward. Opening them, his shoulders again slumped. "Yes," he said quietly.

The paladin nodded. "Very well," he said, "we need to get moving."

The spellcaster nodded his agreement and assumed his place in line. "Just so you know, I'm on wands and scrolls in a support mode until we find a place to rest."

"Same for me," said Cyrillis. Inability to rest and communicate with Valdaar had left her drained as well. "Should we consider turning back?" All eyes turned to her. She licked her lips. "I mean, we now know what the symbols on the door mean. We could go back, rest and start over."

"It doesn't work that way," replied the rogue. He had paused on his way to take point for the party. "First of all, there is no guarantee the doors would have the same symbols—in fact, it is doubtful they would." He turned to look back the way they had come, confirming a suspicion. "Second, there is no door to go back through!"

The rest of the party turned to see for themselves. None was surprised.

"Damn," muttered the caster. "But it's not like we were going to turn back anyway."

"But it would have been nice to have an option," agreed the ranger.

"Once in," said the rogue leader, "there is only one way out."

"What a cheerful bunch!" griped the dwarf. "Certainly you don't want our tale to tell that the barbarian had to raise the spirits of the group so they could continue, do you?"

"Heavens no!" The cleric smiled. "We will be fine," she said, her resilient spirit returning. "If you meat shields would refrain from taking damage, I am certain we will have no further troubles!"

"Ha!" Vorgath snorted as he waved an arm in the direction of the other fighter types. "You just worry about keeping those pretty boys alive. "I'll be fine!"

"Fine?" she blurted out. "Vorgath, remember our agreement?"

The barbarian's face colored a light pink as he thought about continuing this path. Reason won out, however. "Yes, ma'am."

"All right then," said the party leader. "Our destiny awaits." He swept an arm down the path worn in the stone beneath their feet. "Savin, if you please?"

"Certainly," the rogue leader said formally with a smile. He then turned and led off down the path, his senses back on high alert.

Without a word the others took up their places in line. The cavern, if indeed a cavern this place was, loomed much bigger than any previous. The ever-present mist filtered the light overhead, making it appear as if they were outdoors under a cloudy sky. But all knew they were not.

On a whim, Sordaak sent the quasit into the mist to see if they could determine just how high the ceiling was. It might prove important, he reasoned.

Fahlred soared high over their heads and disappeared into the mists. Sordaak immediately felt his familiar's unease, which quickly turned to disorientation. He could no longer tell which way he was going, and even lost track of which way was up, or, more important, down.

Feeling disoriented himself, the caster stumbled, and only the quick reflexes of the paladin kept him from falling to his knees.

"What is it?" asked Thrinndor.

The paladin's steadying hand may have prevented the spellcaster's tumble to the ground, but such was his disorientation that even standing still he was weaving in all directions at once.

Cyrillis approached, arriving just in time to catch the mage's other arm as his knees buckled. "What is going on?" she said.

"He sent his quasit up to investigate the mists overhead, and then…this," replied the fighter.

"Sordaak," the healer said sharply, "snap out of it!" She reached out with her percipience but could sense nothing wrong with the magicuser. No response. "Sordaak!" she cried.

The caster turned his head toward the sound of her voice, but his glazed-over, unfocused eyes showed no sign that he recognized her.

"Sordaak!" This time the cleric shouted his name, her face only inches from his.

Abruptly the mage scrunched his eyes closed. Within the single beat of the heart, Fahlred appeared on the caster's shoulder.

Both the sorcerer and his familiar swayed to and fro, but color quickly came back to Sordaak's cheeks and he stood upright on his own. The mage's eyes opened, and he peered into those of the quasit. Slowly the weaving subsided and Sordaak shook his head.

"What was it?" asked Cyrillis.

The caster's eyes turned upon the cleric, and his gaze regained its focus. He then looked up at the mists over their head. "We won't be going out that way!" he said emphatically.

"What?" queried the ranger as he approached the three now standing together.

"I don't know what's up there," replied the mage as he turned to acknowledge Breunne, "but those 'mists' are not penetrable."

A confused ranger said, "But, we cannot fly, anyway."

"I know that!" the caster snapped. "However it is good practice to know all possible avenues of escape." When he got no reply, he added, "Besides, I just wanted to know whether we are in a big cavern or out of doors."

"Cavern," the barbarian said. "We are still very deep below the surface. You could have asked!"

Sordaak looked at the dwarf and smiled. "I guess I could have, at that!" He again looked at the clouds over their head. "Still, I was curious about those mists…"

"Were you able to find out anything?" Thrinndor asked.

"No," replied the caster as he searched around for the rogue. "Other than we're not going through them." Now, he thought, where had that thief wandered off to? "Where's Savin?"

"What?" said the paladin. He spun to point where the rogue had been only moments before. "He is right there—" Of course he was not. Thrinndor's eyes searched the rocky slope ahead in vain.

"Where could he have gone?" asked the cleric.

"Savin!" the paladin called, raising his voice. No response. "Savin!"

Still nothing.

Worried, the party's leader looked around in all directions. The rogue could be sneaky when the situation called for it, but he usually returned when called. He seldom wandered far ahead.

The cavern at this point had good visibility in all directions—even back to the wall of rock though which they had come, now some two or three hundred feet behind them. The rock to either side was not far, perhaps half that distance.

Ahead of them they had a clear view for a seemingly unlimited distance. There were no outcroppings of rock. No fissures. Nothing where their party member could have wandered off to or into.

"Savin!" Thrinndor bellowed at the top of his lungs, startling the mage.

"Dammit!" said the caster. "Warn me before you do that next time!" He rubbed his right ear, the one closest to the paladin.

Thrinndor glared at the magicuser but said nothing.

"I don't like this," said the ranger with a shake of his head. "There is no place for him to have gone in so short a time."

"Agreed," said the paladin. "Spread out. But stay within sight of one another. No more than fifty or sixty feet apart." He waved an arm in the direction they had been going. "We will sweep ahead—he should be out there, somewhere." Again his eyes searched the immediate area. "Sordaak, you stay here on the path. Breunne, you go about fifty feet to his right, and Vorgath, you go fifty feet beyond that. Cyrillis, you move to fifty feet on Sordaak's left, and I will go fifty beyond that." He got nods from everyone. As they moved out to take their appointed positions, Thrinndor said, "Remember, stay within sight of one another." He paused for a moment. "Make sure you watch where you are going but periodically look to the person on either side of you. Call out if you see anything."

As such, they again resumed their march in a more or less straight line.

They had gone no more than a hundred feet when Sordaak called out, "Breunne!"

Everyone stopped and turned to look at the caster.

"Where is he?" shouted the paladin, fear gripping his heart in its icy tendrils.

"I don't know," came the reply from the caster. He pointed to his right. "He was right there only a moment ago!" He started to go to where he had last seen the ranger.

"Stop!" commanded the paladin. "Stay where you are! All of you!" He ran the short distance to the sorcerer, passing the healer as he did.

The caster held his position, his eyes searching the surrounding terrain for anything out of the ordinary. He found nothing.

Thrinndor asked, "Where was he when you last saw him?"

"Right there," the caster said as he pointed to a spot almost midway between the barbarian and where he himself stood.

Seeing nothing, the paladin said. "All right, I will move about twenty feet to the right. Once there, we will go to that spot." He looked up at the barbarian and the healer. "You two stay where you are." They nodded.

Sordaak nodded his agreement and waited for his friend to get into position. Once there, they slowly moved toward the indicated point.

As they approached where he had last seen the ranger, Sordaak said, "It was right here, somewhere." His eyes nervously searched the area.

"Do you see anything?" asked Thrinndor.

"No," replied the mage. "But this was—" He abruptly disappeared.

"Sordaak!" the paladin shouted.

"Shit!" said the barbarian from where he had been watching the whole process. He started to run back toward his friend.

"Stop!" again commanded the leader.

Vorgath obediently skidded to a halt, Flinthgoor poised for attack. Attack what? He didn't know.

"Walk far around that point there and come to me," Thrinndor said, pointing at the spot he had seen the mage disappear from. "Cyrillis, join me here."

When both had done as directed, he took an iron spike from his bag and tossed it over to where Sordaak had vanished. It bounced noisily a couple of times and came to a rest right where he had expected it to.

"Damn," muttered the barbarian.

The paladin decided to see if something heavier might provide different results and tossed his shield after the spike. Same result.

"Damn," repeated the dwarf. "Now what?"

Thrinndor did not immediately say anything. Instead, he took his time and looked around. In the distance he could see a wall rise up out of the bedrock, similar to the one through which they had come.

"We have a choice," he said. He pointed to the wall of rock ahead. "One, we follow the path as before to see what awaits us at that wall. Or two, we follow the others."

"Where?" The barbarian asked the obvious question.

"I know not," replied the paladin.

"I say we stay with the known," Vorgath said stubbornly. "We head for that wall and see what awaits us."

"We should stay together," Cyrillis said, unable to take her eyes off of the spike and shield as they lay motionless fifteen or twenty feet away. She had a growing bad feeling about this.

"I agree," said the paladin, his eyes also locked in on the shield. "We came in together, we leave together."

The dwarf set his jaw, and Thrinndor was certain he was going to argue. He was wrong.

"Aw, what the hell!" the barbarian said as he hefted his greataxe and stomped over to the shield.

The paladin briefly considered stopping his friend so they could first develop a plan, but he decided that would be counterproductive. He looked over at the cleric, smiled, shrugged and moved to follow his friend. Cyrillis fell in step behind him.

Chapter Twenty-Four

Separation Anxiety

*O*orgath arrived at the shield, Cyrillis and Thrinndor close on his heels. Once there, he stopped and looked around at his friends, a confused look on his face.

The paladin stopped near the dwarf. "Perhaps my aim was off," he said, his voice dubious as he picked up his shield and retrieved the spike. "All right, we stay together and we will walk in ever expanding circles from this point." He held out his hands. "We will also hold hands."

The barbarian eyed his friend. Finally he shifted Flinthgoor to his right hand and reached out with his left. "Just don't get any funny ideas, pretty boy!"

The paladin grinned in return. Cyrillis took his other hand with a smile and together they started walking.

After two complete circuits, Thrinndor stopped. He released the hands of his companions and absently rubbed his chin. "It appears we are meant to continue separately."

"Yup," agreed the dwarf.

"I hope they do not encounter opposition," the cleric said. When the two fighters looked at her questioningly she added, "They have no healing."

Thrinndor said, "As a ranger, Breunne has limited ability in that regard."

"Very limited," replied the healer with a shake of her head.

"And I believe Sordaak is carrying a few healing potions," continued the big fighter. "That will have to keep them."

Cyrillis searched the eyes of the paladin for signs she was being placated. Finding none, she said, "Yes, that will have to keep them." She raised her hands toward the mists far overhead. "That, and prayer."

Thrinndor also raised his.

"Hear me, O Valdaar," she began. "We your faithful servants in this land wrought with unbelievers, who are trying to return your presence to that land, have become separated. While the other group is strong in wile and cunning, they now lack the services of a healer. Protect them my Lord until such a time as I can continue my service to you by performing such tasks in your name. Guide them back to us so that we may continue our quest to return you to this land where your presence is so needed. This I ask of you, O Valdaar." She dropped her hands to her side and lowered her head as a single tear wound its way along the crease of her nose to hang precariously from her upper lip.

Vorgath shifted his feet and cleared his throat. "Now what?"

Thrinndor took in a deep breath and let it out slowly before answering. "Now we go find our companions."

"I have a suggestion," the healer said quietly.

Their leader turned to her and waited, saying nothing.

"Without Sordaak, we may now rest." Her voice grew stronger as she spoke. "Perhaps we should remain here, resting a short while in the event they are returned to us."

The paladin appeared to consider her suggestion and then shook his head. "While this idea holds merit, it is my thought that we must keep moving." He again turned his attention to the distant wall. "I feel our companions will not be returned to us, rather that we must retrieve them if we are to be reunited."

"Finally we agree on something," said the barbarian, although his usual jovial tone was subdued by the gravity of the moment.

A second tear followed the track of the first, yet the cleric nodded as she tightened her grip on her staff and threw her shoulders back. "Very well," she said, wiping the tears from her eyes with her free hand. "We should be moving then."

Thrinndor watched the cleric strain to pull herself together with mixed emotions. While he felt her concern for the absent companions was certainly justified, he also felt there was something more.

The paladin shook his head to clear it, turned his weary body toward the distant wall and began walking, the missing party members weighing heavily on his mind.

Without a discussion, the trio took up formation with the paladin side-by-side with the barbarian at the front of the party and the cleric following behind a short distance. As such, they reached the looming wall in a few minutes.

Thrinndor called the diminished party to a halt fifty feet from the wall that rose up before them, effectively blocking their path. From this vantage point, the wall appeared solid and impenetrable. Stretching from the wall on their left to the one on the right and reaching up into the mists over their heads, there was no break, fissure or opening to be seen.

The barbarian took in a breath to speak, but Thrinndor cut him off with a stern look. "Say nothing, old one, unless you have an idea worthy of the situation."

Vorgath thought about it, crossed his arms on his chest and shook his head. He said nothing as he released the breath in a huff.

"Does anyone see anything that resembles a passage?" the paladin asked, knowing the answer before he spoke.

A shake of their heads was all he got for an answer.

"Right," Thrinndor said. "Well, for some reason the slight path we have been following ends there." He pointed to a spot less than ten feet away from where they had stopped.

Vorgath looked at the rock beneath his feet to discover that what his friend said was indeed true. The rock had been worn slightly from the passage of previous adventurers. But that ended up ahead. Going forward there was no sign of previous passage.

"But that makes no sense," Cyrillis said. "Any that came this far certainly must have continued to the wall." She looked at her leader, perplexed. "For what reason would they stop here?"

"I believe stopped would not be the correct assessment of the situation," the paladin responded as he continued to search the path ahead for anything out of place.

"Explain, please," the healer begged.

"I see a couple of possibilities," their leader began. "First, at this point previous parties either split up—thereby diminishing any further trail—or they went different directions, effectively accomplishing the same thing." He took in a deep breath. "Or second, they were prevented from continuing on the path."

"Prevented by what?" Cyrillis asked.

"Or by whom," the paladin responded. "I do not know." Maintaining his distance, he inspected the end of the path as best he could. He shook his head.

"There's one way to find out," said the dwarf, hefting his greataxe in his right hand and shaking it menacingly.

"Patience, o venerable one," Thrinndor urged with a smile.

Vorgath growled deep within his chest. "You have a better idea?"

"Better?" asked the big fighter as his hand emerged from his pack again holding a spike. "I cannot answer that from here." He grinned as he tossed the spike underhand to where the trail ended.

The spike clanged noisily a couple of times and came to rest just past the end of the barely visible path.

Vorgath noted the paladin's lifted brow. "You expected different?"

Thrinndor's eyes did not leave the spike. "No. And yes."

"Make some sense, man!" griped the dwarf.

In response, the paladin pulled his sword from its sheath and stepped forward. "Stay close."

"Now we're talking," said the barbarian as he took up station to his friend's immediate right, a little behind.

Cyrillis took the left, her stance apprehensive. "Is there a reason we do not take a different path?"

Their leader stopped two paces short of where the path ended. "No." Abruptly he turned to his right and stepped off the path.

In formation they circled the point where the path ended, all the while keeping at least two full paces between them and where the spike lay.

Back where they started, Thrinndor rubbed the stubble on his chin with the back of his hand. He then shrugged, took a step forward, extended the sword in his hand toward the spike and nudged it with the blade. The spike skittered a few inches and again came to a rest. The paladin shrugged again, sheathed his sword, stepped forward and picked up the spike. He flipped it up into the air a couple of times as he eyed the now forty or so feet to the wall of rock.

Vorgath could tell his friend was thinking, and the barbarian wisely decided to keep his thoughts to himself. He amused himself by also studying the open space to the wall.

Cyrillis rested the heel of her staff on the hard stone with a clink, unsure just what to think or do at this point.

Thrinndor caught the iron spike, then impulsively reared back and sent it spinning at the wall. To his surprise, the spike passed right through only to clang noisily some distance past where he had surmised it would.

The barbarian looked up at his long-time friend. "How did you know?"

"Know?" answered the paladin. "I knew nothing. It was but one of several possibilities.

"OK, smart-ass," said the dwarf, "what made you even think that was a possibility?"

Thrinndor grinned. "I tried to figure out why the path would end here and could not—not without some magic portal or some such nonsense, anyway." The barbarian crossed his arms, waiting for the answer the paladin was deliberately withholding. "So I surmised the wall had moved."

"What?" said the dwarf. "I think you took too many knocks on the head!"

"Have I?" queried the paladin, a wry smile on his lips. "Clearly the wall is but an illusion." He turned to look where the spike he threw should have hit the wall. "The only real question now is: Why was it moved?"

"I do not see that it matters," Cyrillis said suddenly. That she was tired was plain on her face.

Thrinndor looked at her quizzically but remained silent.

"Unless we are to turn back," she said as she pointed to where the spike had gone through, "that is where we must go."

The paladin followed where she pointed, allowed his shoulders to drop and signed. "You are of course correct."

"Yup," agreed the dwarf. "Can we get on with it, then?"

The big fighter looked over at his old friend, a tired reply about patience on his lips, but he too decided trading barbs would do them no good at this point. "Very well," he said finally. "Stay together—close together."

Thrinndor drew his sword as his companions stepped close—close enough he could detect the pungent aroma of jerked meat from the barbarian and the faint scent of potions and oils on the cleric.

Sensing they were ready, or at least determined, the paladin took a tentative step forward. Nothing happened, so he took another. Now they were where the faint trail ended. He did not hesitate, instead continuing toward the wall now only forty feet or so away.

Abruptly the wall vanished. Actually, everything vanished as he was suddenly thrust into darkness. He halted immediately and called out to his companions. "Cyrillis? Vorgath?"

"Here," replied the barbarian.

"Me too," said the cleric, her voice tense.

Thrinndor thought quickly as his eyes tried to adjust to the inky darkness that engulfed them. Nothing. He could see nothing.

"Vorgath," he said after a moment, "a torch please." He heard a rustle behind him and to his left.

"On it," replied the dwarf. More rustling as his friend removed the wrap from the oiled end of a torch. Then there was the sharp sound as the barbarian struck metal to his flint.

There was a bright flash as a spark illuminated briefly, then faded. More striking, more sparks. Finally one landed on the oil wrapped rags affixed to the business end of the torch and caught.

Thrinndor heard Cyrillis breathe a sigh of relief as the illuminated area grew to engulf her. "Thank Valdaar," she said.

Vorgath held the torch as high as he could and retrieved Flinthgoor. He looked from one to the other, trying to figure out how to wield both.

Seeing his quandary, the cleric held out her free hand. "I will take that."

"Thank you," the barbarian responded politely with a short bow.

The healer returned the bow but remained silent as she held the torch as high as she could, attempting to illuminate as much of their surroundings as possible.

It was to no avail. If there was anything over their heads, it remained out of the reach of the feeble light of their torch. Nor were any walls visible. The dark stone beneath their feet reflected little light and was of no help.

"Where are we?" she said after she had determined there was nothing to see.

"Good question," answered the paladin. "Hey!" he said loudly, startling both the cleric and the dwarf.

"Was that necessary?" said the healer, her tone acidic.

"Yes," Thrinndor said. "From that I was able to determine we are in a large chamber, strangely similar to where we were."

"How do you know that?"

"Sound reflects off of walls and/or objects," explained the dwarf. "From a noise such as pretty boy here just made, I was able to tell that there is a wall—probably rock, as rock reflects sound better—just ahead of us. There are also walls to our left and right, but further away." He hesitated. "I'm less sure about what I heard from behind, but I believe there to be a wall back there, too. But if so, it's much further away."

"Agreed," said the paladin. "It is similar to how a bat 'sees' in complete darkness."

"OK," said the cleric. She had heard such things but never experienced such firsthand.

"The question now is whether or not we were teleported somewhere," continued the big fighter, "or did someone just douse the lights?"

Cyrillis again held the torch high over her head, its reach now slightly further as the flames had ignited remainder of the rags. Still she could see nothing overhead and she was fairly certain she should be able to do so.

"My guess would be teleported," she said. "I cannot see the mists that were over our head, and I do not believe they were that far up."

The paladin also looked up. He too saw nothing. "Allow me," he said, reaching for the torch. Cyrillis handed it over.

The paladin lowered it toward the ground and then in a sudden movement flipped it high into the air, spinning as it went. As it spun back down, he deftly caught the still flaming brand by the non-burning end and said. "Agreed. The mists would have certainly been visible just then."

Next he knelt and studied the ground, casting about side to side with the torch. He quickly regained his feet and turned to hand the torch back to the healer. "We are most definitely somewhere else. Not only is the rock beneath our feet a slightly different hue, it is smooth as if polished. Certainly this is not a natural cavern."

Thrinndor turned to face the barbarian. "Can you tell which direction we are facing?"

"No," Vorgath replied. "I need a point of reference for my direction sense to function." He looked around slowly. "However, from what I know of teleportation we should come out of it facing the same direction as when we stepped into the portal. If so, that is the direction we were headed." He pointed slightly left of where they were facing.

"Very well," responded the paladin. "We will have to go with that. We must also assume we want to continue in that direction. Let us remain close." He stepped forward, and his companions quickly moved to follow.

Hearing something, a slight rustle in the otherwise completely still surroundings, Thrinndor made a low whistle.

That was followed by two short chirps from behind. Vorgath had received and understood the signal. There were others in the chamber with them and it was understood they were probably not here as a welcoming committee.

"What?" began the cleric, but she appropriately went silent when their leader held up his hand—sword still at the ready, silently asking for her to remain quiet.

Thrinndor waved his shield, motioning for the barbarian to take up station to his right and the healer behind the two of them.

Still, they slowly moved forward.

Abruptly the silence was shredded by the roar of an animal—a big animal if the volume of the roar meant anything. That first roar was immediately followed by another, different roar. First one and then another figure flashed into the ring of light surrounding the torch.

"Rakshasas!" shouted the paladin as he brought his shield up to ward off the attack of the one that had leapt at him from his left. He whipped his flaming sword around in a quick strike but missed badly as the big cat rebounded off of his shield and dove beneath the blade.

The rakshasa circled warily to his right away from the paladin, looking for an opening. The hulking figure was wary now that surprise was no longer in its favor.

Only two? That bothered the paladin as he followed the monster with both his sword and shield. The rakshasa was the long-ago mutation of a tiger head on a humanoid body. Sometimes the animal had paws and claws, others human hands. This one was of the paws and claws variety. Not only did these very intelligent creatures usually travel in larger numbers, they were also known to associate with huge razor-clawed tigers.

There! His battle-tuned hearing heard another creature approaching from behind. "Cyrillis! Ward yourself! Behind you!" he shouted just as the rakshasa before him charged.

Ready for it this time, he used the shield like a bludgeon, knocking the creature aside as he whipped his blade around in a counterthrust that this time hit home. The beast shrieked in pain and leapt back, favoring a gash in its upper torso.

Thrinndor couldn't tell if the creature was slowed as the beast immediately jumped back into the fray. While the paladin was ready for the attack, the speed of it caught him by surprise and his upper shield-arm was raked by the beast's claws in passing.

He gritted his teeth against the pain and swung wildly with his sword in an attempt at counterattack, again missing badly. This was not going well; he could not afford to trade blows with this monster.

Abruptly he dropped his shield and feigned the damaged done to his arm to be more than it really was. He groaned as he looked down at the bleeding caused by the creature's ultra-sharp claws.

The rakshasa fell for it! Sensing an opening, it again leapt at the paladin. Ready for such a move, Thrinndor grasped the pommel of his sword with both hands and whipped it around with all his might.

Incredibly agile, the beast tried to check his attack, but the big fighter's sword stuck home, resulting in another deep gash in the creature's side. Again it shrieked in pain and pawed at the paladin as it jumped back out of reach of the sword, seriously wounded this time.

Seeing a gout of flame out of the corner of his eye, Thrinndor took a chance and glanced over his shoulder to see how his companions were doing. Vorgath was having little trouble with his rakshasa. The beast was bleeding from several wounds and two or three of those looked serious.

Cyrillis was bleeding from a nasty wound along her upper left shoulder and another on her right leg. The tiger was crouched for another attack, several patches of fur smoldering from the recent blast from the cleric's staff. She was holding her own, Thrinndor determined. Her wounds were not serious, but she was probably going to need help from one of the fighters, and soon.

He swiveled his head back just in time as the rakshasa—deep pain burning in its eyes—leapt at him again. The creature was slowed by the pain and possibly by the loss of blood, so Thrinndor was easily able to get his sword around.

Seriously hampered by its wounds, the beast was unable to check its attack and impaled itself on the paladin's sword. The rakshasa's eyes widened in pain and it released yet another shriek.

Thrinndor looked on as the hatred in the monster's eyes turned to sorrow as the creature realized it had failed.

The paladin thrust the blade deeper with all his might, forcing the tip out through the skin of the beast's back. The creature's eyes rolled back in its head and it sagged to the ground.

Quickly, the paladin planted his foot on the torso of the rakshasa and withdrew his blade. He spun to see Vorgath swat his rakshasa to the cold hard floor with the flat of his blade. The beast did not move. To be sure, the barbarian brought Flinthgoor crashing down on the exposed neck of the beast, severing the head in one fell swing.

Cyrillis had fared not as well, however. She was bleeding from at least two more places from when he had last checked, and the tiger was crouched for yet another attack.

"Drop and roll to your left," the paladin shouted as he surged into action just as the tiger leapt at her.

The events almost appeared to have been coordinated, because as the exhausted cleric dove hard to the stone, the tiger flew by where the healer had been only a moment before only to meet the flaming blade from the paladin mid-flight.

The massive beast opened its mouth to roar at the unexpected turn of events, only to have the blade slice through the back of the jaws and deep into its brain. The tiger's eyes flared in fury and pain, then went lifeless as the brainstem was severed. Landing with a thud and rolling to a stop, it did not move again.

"Thank you," breathed the cleric as she climbed unsteadily to her feet. Thrinndor held out a hand but she ignored it, using her staff instead.

The paladin lifted an eyebrow and said, "Status report?"

Vorgath was the first to reply. "A couple of minor scratches and some damaged armor plate," he said as he looked distastefully at a gash in the plate covering his upper left chest. He looked up at the healer. "And yes," he said poignantly, "only minor scratches!"

Cyrillis briefly considered her usual reply but found she didn't have the energy for it. Instead, she checked for her own wounds and found several.

"I fear I have not fared as well," the cleric said as she leaned heavily on Kurril. She brushed back a recalcitrant lock of hair that had escaped the binding at the nape of her neck.

"My wounds are also minor," said the paladin. "Nothing that cannot be fixed with a wrap." His mien changed when he saw just how distressed the healer was. "You, however, must apply some healing to yourself. Immediately."

She started to protest, but her health sense told her that he was correct. Cyrillis bowed her head and mouthed the words to a prayer of healing and felt the power course through her hands as she applied that energy to the most severe of her wounds. Most had been minor, but at least three she would have classified as severe were they on someone else. However, even the minor cuts she had suffered during the tiger's attack allowed precious blood to escape her body.

Those she covered and tied in the more traditional way. Satisfied she would live, Cyrillis turned her attention to her remaining companions. Vorgath indeed showed little sign of having been in a scrape. However, she noted that Thrinndor had a bad series of claw marks where his left arm connected to his shoulder. The healer immediately raised her hands in preparation to do what she was here to do, but she was stopped by the paladin.

"Do not," he said with a stern shake of his head. "I have a small amount of energy remaining." The pain in his eyes belied his words. "That and a bandage will have to do at this juncture."

Cyrillis looked again at his wound and doubt clouded her eyes. The rake marks were deep! As she watched, Thrinndor too bowed his head and mumbled the familiar words to his spell of minor healing. The skin knitted somewhat together as she watched, but it stopped short of healing completely. Blood still seeped from where the gashes remained open.

The paladin removed his breastplate to inspect what remained, shook his head and tore strips from cloth he had brought along for the purpose. He wadded up another piece of the cloth and held it against the wound. He fumbled around with the strips until Cyrillis stepped in.

"Here," she said. "Give me that!" She snatched the strips from his hand. "Allow me to do what I am here to do."

Thrinndor nodded gratefully as she deftly tied the strips in place and tested them to make sure they were not too tight. Then she stepped back to admire her handiwork as the paladin flexed his arm approvingly. At least the blood had stopped flowing.

As their leader reaffixed his breastplate she said, "Without the aid of my healing power, that is all I can do at this point."

"It will do," the big fighter replied. "Thank you." He bowed.

"You should of course rest to allow that to better knit," the healer said.

Thrinndor smiled and looked around. "I doubt rest is in our immediate future," he said with a sardonic smile.

Cyrillis allowed her shoulders to slump slightly and she nodded. "We must rest soon or my healing abilities will soon be rendered completely useless." Her eyes flared, "I do still have the staff!" She hammered Kurril's heel to the stone in frustration. The sound of metal on stone rang out briefly and echoed off of the walls. She cringed and mumbled, "Sorry."

Vorgath grinned. "No worries. The wall ahead of us must barely be outside the range of the torch."

Satisfied with his armor, the paladin walked over to the rakshasa he had slain and knelt beside it for a look. He shook his head. "Rakshasas are magical in nature, and if I remember correctly they have several spells at their command."

Vorgath walked up behind him, and Cyrillis followed with the torch, as well.

"So?" the barbarian said as he watched his friend search the body.

"Why did they not use them?" the big fighter replied without looking up. When he got no response, he went on. "They certainly had the advantage of surprise on us. Why did they not attack with spells first?"

"Perhaps they did," Cyrillis said. The paladin turned to look at her, the unspoken question in her eyes. "Perhaps the teleportation was not a trap as we had surmised, but done by them to separate us from our companions and they had used all of their spell energy thus."

Thrinndor's eyes narrowed as he considered this. Finally he nodded and said, "Perhaps." He appeared to not be convinced.

"The last time we ran into these bad old kitties," the barbarian said, "there were several more in a group if I remember right."

"You do," said a still worried Thrinndor. "We encountered six or seven that time. And they are reported to travel in groups of more than that."

"So," Cyrillis licked her lips nervously, "where are the rest?"

Silence permeated the air for a few heartbeats before Vorgath said, "I think we'll have to assume any others in their party are currently keeping our companions company."

"That is a logical assumption, I believe," the paladin said. "We need to find the others—and quickly—as these creatures have an inherent resistance to magic that may cause our spell-slinging friend some difficulty."

"Oh no!" said the cleric with a moan. "We must find them!"

Finding nothing useful on the big cat-human hybrid, Thrinndor grabbed the shield he had set aside and surged back to his feet in a rush. "Agreed." He turned the way they had been moving, toward the nearest wall, and moved out, assuming his companions would take up proper station.

They did.

After only a few steps, they could see the wall looming out of the darkness before them. In the wall was a set of double doors made of what appeared to be bound iron.

Thrinndor halted a few feet from the doors, sheathed his sword and reached back for the torch. With that in hand, he took a couple of steps to either side of the opening, holding the torch as high as he could, and tried to discern any other openings in the wall. He could not.

Again standing before the doors, he handed the torch back to the cleric and drew his sword.

"Allow me," said the dwarf gruffly as he shouldered the paladin aside.

Thrinndor lifted a brow inquisitively.

"Recent traps have been sized for you bigger folk," Vorgath said. "Let's hope that trend continues." He grasped the pull ring in the right door. "I'd give me some room."

Both the paladin and the healer stepped back a couple of paces.

The muscles in the dwarf's neck bulged as he set his feet and pulled. The metal of the hinges protested loudly as the door inched slowly open.

The door was incredibly heavy, and Vorgath had to plant his left foot on the opposite door to gain leverage. Eventually, however, he was able to get the right door open far enough for them to be able to get through.

The barbarian released the ring, and it fell back to the door with a clang as he reached back for the torch. He could see light coming from the other side of the door, but he wanted to be sure he had some control over light from their side.

With the torch held in front of him, he poked his head through the opening.

Chapter Twenty-Five

Rakshasas, Part Two

Sordaak muttered a curse as he and Fahlred landed together in a heap onto a hard surface. The caster came down awkwardly, twisting his ankle as he did so. The area was illuminated by a torch not far off held by the ranger. Next to him was Savinhand.

"Nice of you to join us," said the rogue amiably.

"Where are we?" said the sorcerer through gritted teeth as he regained his feet, wincing in the process. It didn't help that his familiar clutched nervously to his shoulder, his tail wound around the mage's neck.

"Good question," replied the ranger. "We had just started to explore when you dropped in."

"Dropped is the key word," moaned the caster as he tried to put weight on his rapidly swelling right angle.

"Is it broken?" queried the thief as he approached.

"No," answered Sordaak. "I don't think so." He put a hand on Savin's shoulder for support when he was close enough. "Still, I'm certainly going to be hobbled for a bit."

"Not good," said the ranger as he bent to get a closer look at the ankle. "It is my fear we were separated from the others to make us easier to deal with."

"That is sound reasoning," agreed the mage through clenched teeth. "Maybe we can splint the ankle for support." His voice trailed off, indicating even he doubted that would help much.

"I have limited ability to heal," Breunne said as he pressed his thumb into the already swelling ankle, attempting to determine whether it was broken.

"Ouch!" snapped the caster as he jerked his ankle away. Fahlred hissed menacingly at the ranger.

"Take it easy," soothed the fighter as he reached for the foot. "I won't press again. I just needed to determine how much damage was done."

Sordaak allowed the ranger to again grasp his foot. "I have kept back a couple of healing potions," the sorcerer said helpfully.

"Save them," responded the ranger. "My spells are very limited and my energy too has been drained by the same force that stole yours. I have enough remaining for one, maybe two, heals." With that, he whispered the words to the spell and made a gesture with his free hand as he squeezed lightly on the ankle.

Instantly the swelling diminished and the pain subsided somewhat. Breunne released the ankle, and Sordaak tried to put weight on it. He found that while the ankle was still sore, he would be able to walk—and possibly more important, he reasoned, run.

"Thank you," Sordaak said. "That will do for now."

"I do have enough energy for one more spell," the ranger said tentatively.

"No, save it." The mage smiled. "I think I can run, if necessary."

"It might be necessary sooner rather than later," said the rogue, his voice tense with concern.

"What? Why?" asked the spellcaster, attempting to see what the thief saw. He could see nothing in the direction his friend was looking.

"Shhhh!" Savinhand waved his hand for silence. He got it.

Instantly, Fahlred winked out of sight as the caster sent him to investigate. He warned his familiar to be careful.

Savin held his finger to his lips and pointed in the direction his eyes were attempting to penetrate the darkness. He held up first three, then four fingers and then he too evaporated into the darkness.

"Damn," said the caster again. "I don't have the energy for a big battle."

"I doubt it will be big," said the ranger as he abruptly reared back and threw the torch in the direction the rogue had pointed. He too had heard something, so he took and educated guess as to how far to throw it. Unfortunately, it was not really all that far. "Move from where you were!" he hissed at the caster. "Any direction!"

As he heard the whisper of leather on stone of the ranger moving quickly to his left, Sordaak obediently sprinted a few paces in the opposite direction just as the vision came into his head what his familiar was seeing.

The torch landed with a splatter and slid to a halt not far from their assailants, causing them to scatter.

Rakshasas! Shit! That calls for a change in plans, the mage thought quickly. Those guys have a built-in resistance to many of his spells. That, and they have spells of their own! "Rakshasas!" he whispered as loudly as he dared, hoping his companions heard.

"Shit," he heard from the direction of the ranger, barely audible. He'd heard.

Thrum, thrum, thrum. Three arrows were loosed in quick succession, each striking one of the creatures before they got away from the light of the torch.

Screams of pain rent the air as one of the rakshasas pitched forward onto its face and lay still.

Quickly, the ranger loosed three more arrows, but he was now firing where he thought one of the creatures might be. Another scream ripped across the distance. At least one of the arrows had found its mark.

An idea occurred to Sordaak, and he began waving his arms in preparation for a spell. He hoped this worked, because he hadn't energy to waste.

Sordaak released the energy and an unseen cloud formed around him. It wasn't the hiding characteristics of the cloud he was looking for but what the cloud caused when it contacted flesh. The mists of the cloud were formed from pure, vaporous acid. He was pretty sure the rakshasas were not resistant to acid.

Finished with the spell, silently the caster recalled his familiar and waited. He needed Fahlred's eyes, which could penetrate any darkness.

There was unnerving silence for several heartbeats. Then Sordaak heard one of the cats again scream in pain. This time he was fairly certain his friend Savin was responsible. Next he heard the whisper of steel against leather as the ranger drew a weapon more suitable for close-in contact.

Another idea occurred to the caster. He withdrew a wand from a pouch sewn into the inside of his cloak. Quickly he aimed it high over their heads. "Eyes!" he shouted, and released the wands energy with the trigger word.

Instantly the chamber was lit by a brilliant orb of light that hung suspended far over their heads.

In a flash Sordaak saw two down creatures, the ranger hurriedly switching back to his bow and two more rakshasas spread out with their hands/paws covering their eyes. The rogue was nowhere to be seen.

A roar came from behind the mage, and he spun quickly and threw up his hands in what he knew was going to be a futile effort to ward off the attack of a leaping tiger. Only his acid spell had given him any warning. Not going to be of much good, he thought. Suddenly first one arrow, and then a second imbedded itself into the massive chest of the tiger as it flew through the air toward the caster.

Still the beast flew on and slammed into Sordaak, raking its hind claws down his relatively unprotected torso—a robe and a cloak is not much in the way of protection after all.

Sordaak screamed as he was bowled over by the sheer mass of the beast. Damn! The backside of those arrows hurt too, he thought as darkness once again overtook him.

*

Sordaak felt the white hot pain as he was drug unmercifully from the solace of oblivion.

Why? There was supposed to be no pain in the afterlife.

"Sordaak!" A voice was calling his name. "Sordaak!" More insistent this time. It was Breunne. A rough hand slapped him none too gently on his left cheek. "Sordaak!"

"Wha—?" he croaked through pain-wracked lips.

"Drink this!" He felt an arm reach beneath his shoulders and lift him roughly to a sitting position. "Hurry!" The voice was certainly urgent.

A vial was pressed to his lips, his head was unceremoniously tilted back, and he felt a thick, sickly sweet elixir fill his mouth. He started to gag and cough, but his mouth was slammed shut by some unknown force. It was swallow or explode.

He swallowed. Instantly, he felt healing magic race its way through his veins. He opened his mouth for a curse, but the vial was again thrust through his lips, and he again had no choice but to drink.

This time the mage did not object. Again the magic coursed through him and the pain stabbing its way along the front of his body subsided to an almost tolerable level. He opened his eyes to see Breunne kneeling over him. His hands were tearing at the seal from another of the healing elixirs. Sordaak thought to refuse but decided that would be wasted effort.

When the small flask was handed to him, the sorcerer put it to his mouth and downed the entire contents in one swallow. Once again, Sordaak felt the healing magic race through his body and he began to feel better—almost human, even.

"Thanks," he said brusquely, his voice coarse from the potion.

"Glad to have you back with us," replied the ranger.

"Back with you is a relative term, I fear," Sordaak said as he examined the claw marks in his robes. He reached out with his senses and verified the magic those robes imbued—a certain amount of fire resistance—was still active. It was.

"Please explain," Breunne said.

"I don't know how long I was out," said the caster ruefully, "but it was certainly long enough to remove the remainder of my spell energy."

"All of it?" Savinhand was understandably concerned.

"All of it," said the caster as he used Breunne's shoulder to pull himself shakily to his feet. "And if we don't get moving, whatever has been sucking out my energy won't stop there."

Breunne and Savin waited patiently for the caster to continue. They were not disappointed. Apparently the caster's brush with death made him a bit chatty.

"We need to keep moving." The spellcaster looked around to get his bearings. However, he had nothing with which to compare where they were with where they wanted to be. He looked into the ranger's eyes. "Have you searched the area?"

"Very little," admitted the fighter.

"I got here first," said the rogue. "Initially I searched in complete darkness not wanting to alert anyone, or anything." He turned to look off to his right. "I found I had to move too slowly to get much done, so decided I had to chance some light and lit a torch."

Savin pointed in the direction he was looking. "There is a wall in that direction; a wall with a pair of double doors." He turned back to face his companions. "About the time I discovered that, Breunne dropped in. Shortly after that you arrived."

"The double doors it is, then." Sordaak stepped past the rogue, his legs still a bit wobbly. The sheer act of being in motion bolstered his mood, however, and he continued his discussion. "As a sorcerer, I've become spell energy incarnate. My very being exists as a focal point for that energy." Sordaak stopped talking as he approached the doors.

Savinhand pushed his way past the caster and began his inspection.

"Our skirmish with the rakshasas left me dangerously low on energy," Sordaak continued as he watched the thief work. "My new master warned me to never allow my energy become nonexistent." He shook his head. "Such levels leave me vulnerable."

Savinhand turned to face his companions. "No traps." He shrugged. "I can't find any locking mechanism, either." He looked back at the doors. "They appear to not have been opened in…in centuries."

"Whatever it is that drained my spell energy," Sordaak went on as if he had not heard the rogue, "has started taking my life force." His eyes locked with those of the ranger. "If we don't keep moving, in time it will kill me."

An uneasy silence settled on the companions.

"Open the door," Savinhand said. "We must keep moving."

Breunne shoved his way past the caster, placed both hands on the pull ring, set his feet and pulled. The door did not budge.

"Help me here," said the ranger as he moved slightly to allow Savin room to step in and also grasp the ring. Both men pulled, with the ranger planting a foot on the opposite door for leverage. Still the door did not budge.

"Perhaps they open the other way," said the caster as he stepped in for a closer look.

Both men ceased their effort, each releasing a loud gasp of air.

"What?" the ranger asked between gulps.

"You heard me," said the mage, his attention on the door frame not wavering. "Perhaps the doors open the other way." He leaned forward and pushed on the door.

Initially nothing happened. Slowly, however, the door began to inch away, its hinges protesting loudly at being disturbed.

Breunne and Savin changed tactics, placed their hands on the door and pushed. The added exertion forced the door open ever wider.

Once it was open wide enough to pass through, Sordaak could hear voices from the other side. As he was about to ask for the torch, one was thrust through the opening.

"About damn time," the mage said as he dropped to his knees. His eyes rolled back in his head and he pitched forward onto his face and did not move.

"Sordaak!" Cyrillis screamed as she shoved her way past the barbarian to kneel down beside the mage. "Oh, no! I have very little healing left." She turned her face up to look at Breunne. "What happened to him?" Her eyes went back to his claw shredded raiment, believing she knew the answer already.

"Rakshasa," replied the rogue. "However, his wounds have been healed—"

"Mostly healed," interrupted the ranger. "However his wounds are not what ail him." His eyes were grave as he continued.

Cyrillis' eyes locked with those of the ranger. "What then?"

"He was unconscious following the attack by the rakshasa," Breunne said. "We revived him as quickly as we could, but his energy level had been depleted during the attack." He hesitated. "The resulting rest period drained any that remained." He nodded at the healer's unspoken question. "Yes, he has zero spell energy and he says that whatever has been draining that energy is now draining his life-energy every time we stop."

"You mean?" her eyes welled up as she spoke.

"Yes," replied the ranger. "He is dying."

"No, he is not!" shouted the cleric. "Pick him up! We must get moving! I will work on him as we continue." Hesitation kept the companions from moving as they looked at one another. "Now!" she shouted.

Thrinndor stepped forward. "It does not work that way," he said quietly.

A bewildered healer stared at the paladin through tear shrouded eyes.

"In effect he is resting," the big fighter said, trying to calm the healer. "It is his spell energy we must restore."

Realization dawned on the cleric in a rush. She flung back her cloak and jerked the ties on the potion bag at her belt. "I can fix that," she said as her hand dove inside the bag and emerged with a pair of small flasks in her grasp. "But first he must be conscious." She bit her lip in trepidation.

Without hesitation she set the flasks aside and placed her left palm on the caster's forehead and her right over his heart. Then she bowed her tear-streaked face before raising it to the ceiling. Her prayer was quick and to the point as she released the healing energy from her most powerful spell into him.

The mage's body appeared to jolt under the force of the spell and any vestiges of injuries—including scars—disappeared instantly.

Sordaak's eyes fluttered and then sprang wide open. He sat bolt upright and said, "What the hell was that?"

Cyrillis shoved a vial in his face, having already removed the seal. "Shut up and drink this."

"What is—?" he began.

An insistent healer cut him off. "Drink!" she shouted, causing him to jump.

Breunne and Thrinndor exchanged looks as the mage obediently took the proffered vial and emptied the contents into his mouth. Realization came instantly as the fluid trickled down his throat.

He did not hesitate in the slightest when Cyrillis offered him the second vial. It went the way of the first in short order.

"Thank you," the caster breathed aloud.

"No time for that," said the paladin with a smile as he reached down and grasped the sorcerer under his arms and lifted him to his feet. "We must be moving else we waste the generous efforts of our magnanimous healer."

"Right," said the caster. "I feel much better now!" He looked around with a huge grin. "Anyone have any idea where we go from here?"

"Yes," said the paladin as he spun the caster away from the door they had just worked so hard to open. "That way." He pointed and started off in the indicated direction.

Sordaak followed eagerly, turning to the ranger as he did. "Didn't we just come this way?"

"Yes," Breunne responded with a shrug as he moved to his place in the formation. "But we didn't know where we were at the time."

"We do now?" answered the mage as he fell in step.

"Not a clue," said the ranger.

"We do, too," said the paladin. He jerked a thumb over his shoulder. "We have already been that way, and now we are going this way." He pointed to where the group was now headed.

"But we have already been this way!" Sordaak looked at the thief for confirmation.

"Agreed," said the rogue, "but we didn't know where we were then."

"At the risk of repeating myself," the spellcaster said, "we do now?"

The paladin and the rogue answered simultaneously. "Yes!"

"No," argued Savinhand.

Sordaak looked from one to the other. "Morons! I left that wonderful party at Shardmoor for this?" He shook his head in mock despair.

"I am glad you are feeling better," Thrinndor said, shaking his head but with a smile on his face.

Sordaak bobbed his head amicably and turned to again thank the cleric. However, the stern look on her face forbade that. Her mouth was a straight line, lips pressed together. Her brow was deeply furrowed, and she looked neither right nor left as she marched, the heels of her boots clicking loudly on the stone floor.

Wisely the mage kept his mouth shut as the healer pushed past him. Sordaak slowed his walk, waiting for the ranger to catch up.

"What's with her?" he whispered to the ranger, his eyes never leaving the squared shoulders of the healer, who was now several steps ahead.

Breunne started to speak, then checked himself. When he finally did speak, he also did so in a whisper. "I don't know for sure." He shook his head. "However, I think it might be wise if you didn't mention the party at Shardmoor again."

"What?" the caster hissed, but the ranger was already past him and his demeanor indicated there would be no more conversation.

Shaking his head, Sordaak hurried back to his position in the formation next to the healer. He stole a look askance at her but could see that she was not in the mood for discussion.

The spellcaster was still muttering under his breath when Thrinndor called the formation to a halt by raising his right hand. "Now what?" Sordaak grumbled.

The paladin waited for the company to collapse around him before answering. As Cyrillis and Sordaak approached with the torches, he said, "We have traversed back into the non-man-made cavern."

The sorcerer shook his head to clear it of recent conversations and looked skeptically at their leader. "How can you tell?"

"The stone beneath our feet is no longer hewn smooth." However, the paladin was not looking at his feet. Instead his eyes were casting about for the rogue.

Not seeing him, Thrinndor called out, "Savin."

Momentarily the rogue appeared at the paladin's shoulder. "Yes, boss?"

Thrinndor had expected that so he was able to contain his surprise. "Does that book of yours stay anything about these chambers?"

"What do you mean by these chambers?" Savinhand asked.

"I believe this chamber and the one we just left are identical," Thrinndor replied, "separated by those double doors we just passed through." He stalled before continuing, knowing he was going to raise eyebrows. "It is possible we are headed back the way we came in."

"Told you!" said the caster. There was no small amount of satisfaction apparent in his voice.

The paladin ignored the mage as Savinhand reached beneath his leather tunic and removed the bound journal stored there for safekeeping. The rogue untied the leather strips holding the covering in place and carefully removed the wrapper.

"I don't know for sure," said the thief as he thumbed through the book, looking for a specific page. Finding it, he held up the document for all to see. "But what you describe may be what is drawn here."

Sordaak, Thrinndor and Vorgath crowded around the open journal, all trying to see what was depicted. The mage held the torch closer, mindful to ensure he did not get it too close.

What he saw was a drawing that had two rectangular objects sharing one short side. On each end opposite the shared sides were elven runes. The shared side had an unusual symbol bisecting it as well.

"Like much in this journal, I've not been able to figure this drawing out." Savin turned the book to view it from another direction.

"Hold it still, dammit!" the caster griped as he tried to turn his head to match what the thief had done with the book.

"What is it that makes you think this matches our situation?" asked the paladin.

"Well," Savin began, "if what you believe is correct—that we are in one of two identical chambers—then these could be those chambers." He finger traced first one and then the other rectangle. "Separated by this 'wall' here." His finger indicated the common side.

"Hmmm," the caster said. He pointed to the shared side of the rectangle. "This symbol here could be the elven rune for balance." His tone indicated his uncertainty.

Thrinndor pointed to one end of the drawing. "Is this not the rune for knowledge?"

"Hidden knowledge," corrected the magicuser.

"And this one means blood, doesn't it?" asked Vorgath, pointing to the opposite end of the drawing.

Sordaak took in a sharp breath. "Or birth." His right eyebrow inched higher. "Or beginning."

"I knew it!" said a jubilant Savinhand. "Now it makes sense!" His finger went to the last symbol. "If this is the 'beginning,' this is 'balance' and this is knowledge—we're almost there!"

A grim Thrinndor threw cold water on his enthusiasm. "The problem is that we could be here." He tapped the rectangle next to the rune for knowledge. "Or here." He tapped the side nearest the rune for birth.

Savinhand's jubilation deflated like a balloon. One could almost hear the pop. "Shit," he said, his eyes going from one side to the other.

"Shit," agreed the magician.

"Man," said the barbarian, "you sure know how to rain on a parade, pretty boy."

"Someone has to point out the obvious," the paladin said with a shrug.

"So," Breunne said, looking over the caster's shoulder at the drawing, "what are we talking about here?" His eyes went from the paladin to the rogue. "Spell it out for me."

Thrinndor looked to the rogue. "Go ahead. It is your journal, after all."

"Very well," Savin said with a sigh. "If this map matches up with where we believe we are and the runes indicate what we think they do…" He took a deep breath before looking into the eyes of the ranger. "Then these chambers will be identical, with identical doors at each end." Again he paused. "One door will lead to the Library. The other will lead back to where we started this adventure."

The silence was complete for several moments. Savinhand was certain he could hear his own heart beating.

"So?" said the barbarian. "If the door we open goes back out to the entry, we close it and go to the other door."

The rogue hung his head and spoke softly. "It won't work that way."

"What do you mean?" Cyrillis said.

Savin looked deep into the eyes of the healer. "If we open the door that takes us back to the entry chamber, then it is my belief we will have to start over."

Cyrillis held the eyes of the rogue leader. "I do not understand the problem," she said. "If we have to start over, we will be able to rest and will have foreknowledge as to which doors to open."

"It doesn't work that way," replied Savinhand. "If we leave to rest, the doors will reset. Doors will change. Rooms will change. We will be starting over."

Vorgath rattled of a string of curses that would have caused a weathered sailor to blush.

"Feel better?" asked the paladin, somewhat embarrassed for the cleric in the group. He needn't have been. Cyrillis looked to be ready to spit a curse or two of her own.

Sordaak took in a breath to speak, but the ranger silenced him. "Shhh!" Breunne hissed. The companions went silent and turned to look at the ranger. The fighter raised his hand, palm outward to preclude questions.

Silently, Savin shoved the journal back into his shirt and melded back into the shadows.

"We have company," Breunne said.

Chapter Twenty-Six

No Easy Path

"Can you tell what and how many?" asked the party leader as he pulled his sword from its sheath.

"I hear many almost silent footpads—at least ten," said the ranger as he too stepped back into the shadows. "I don't know for sure, but if I had to guess I would say more rakshasas." He cocked his head to one side. "And more tigers."

Thrinndor muffled a curse. They were too exposed! He made a snap decision. "Follow me!" He took off running at what he figured to be the nearest wall. They needed a tenable position.

"But—" began the caster, who had already started to get his spell components together.

"Now!" shouted the paladin. "Savin, stay close!" He ran, not knowing whether the rogue heard him.

Startled into action, Sordaak sprinted after the rapidly receding figure of the paladin, Cyrillis right behind him.

As the wall of rock loomed out of the darkness, Thrinndor pointed right and left. "Caster and cleric against the rock. Vorgath, Breunne and I will form a semi-circle with them behind us." He paused to consider but knew time was short. "Nothing must be allowed to penetrate our barrier." He left no room for argument.

The ranger and barbarian nodded and moved to where they had been told. Thrinndor took up position in the middle.

"Status?" the paladin directed at the two behind him.

"Cyrillis' two potions boosted my energy to about 25 percent," Sordaak said between heavy breaths. "I also have at my disposal several wands and a scroll or two."

"Great," responded the leader. "Spare no energy. We need to finish this."

Sordaak nodded as he shifted his scepter to his left hand and removed a wand from the folds of his robes with his right.

"Cyrillis?" continued the paladin.

The healer hesitated. "I am at less than 10 percent," she said, her lip trembling in trepidation. "Kurril is exhausted as far as energy goes."

"Do you have any more of those energy potions?" Thrinndor asked, his attention drawn to the darkness beyond the light of the torches.

"One," the healer said.

"Use it."

"But—" Cyrillis started.

"We do not have time!" the paladin hissed. "Use it!" His tone was harsher than he intended. But the cleric got the point.

Quickly her hand dove into her bag and emerged with the vial. She wasted no time in opening and downing the small amount of fluid contained within.

"I also have a few charges left on this wand of healing," she said as she cast aside the vial and pulled a wand from behind her belt. "I have been holding it in reserve for just such."

"Good girl," said the paladin, grateful she bore him no ill will for his harsh words. "Do what you must to keep us alive." His eyes sparkled in true pleasure.

Cyrillis grinned. "Rest assured, Son of Valdaar, none will die on my watch!"

Thrinndor bowed lightly and stepped out of the fire light. He was certain they were as ready as they could be.

"When I shout eyes," Sordaak hissed, "shield your eyes for a heartbeat."

"It shall be so," the caster heard Thrinndor's words from deep in the shadows.

In an instant, the battle was on them.

It started with the scream of what sounded like a cat in pain—a very big cat. One must have wandered too close to the hidden thief, Thrinndor surmised, knowing Savin preferred to attack the rear of any enemy once combat lines had been drawn. Not be the first to attack.

Then the paladin heard the rush of padded feet just outside the reach of the torches.

"Eyes!" Sordaak warned.

Bad timing, the paladin thought, knowing the enemy was close. He shielded his eyes anyway.

Two orbs exploded in a flash of light high over their heads, engulfing the huge cavern in dazzling brilliance.

With the hybrid cats momentarily stunned, Breunne used the opportunity to release a volley of arrows at the approaching creatures. He even had time for a second and third volley before the beasts were in too close for his ranged weapons. He cast aside his bow and drew his sword, smiling with the knowledge he had downed two cats and wounded at least two more.

Her spell energy bolstered and not immediately having anything to do, Cyrillis took a chance and set up a Barricade of Blades in front of each of the two gaps between the fighters. That was going to have to do, she thought as she finished the second because the remainder of her energy must be conserved for healing. She felt better about her energy, now being slightly above 20 percent after the use of the vial.

Seeing the blades, Sordaak made a quick decision and used a wand to conceal them in banks of fog. He smiled in satisfaction as screams of more than one animal in pain emanated from the vicinity of both fog banks.

Thrinndor found himself between the blade-laden fog banks and two of the rakshasas charging at him, a tiger close behind. Lucky me, he thought briefly as he set his feet and readied his sword and shield.

"Watch for spellcasters and healers!" he said to Sordaak over his shoulder as the first rakshasa attacked.

"They're all spellcasters!" the mage shouted back. Under his breath he added, "What bothers me is why they haven't used those abilities." He didn't have time to ponder that turn of events further as one of the big tigers came flying out of the fog bank to his right. It was bleeding badly from several places on its torso, and one of its eyes was missing.

And it was pissed! Seeing Cyrillis first, the rakshasa leapt at her. Cyrillis barely fended off the attack with Kurril, striking the big cat hard with the head of the staff.

Sordaak knew from experience these creatures were resistant to fire and probably electricity. He loosed a volley of force darts, figuring force energy spells had the best chance of success.

He was correct. The already badly hurt cat spun on the caster to confront this new pain. But the cleric used the opportunity to end the cat's life when the heel of her staff fractured its skull in a vicious strike.

Cyrillis saw the paladin reinjure his shoulder when he used his shield to slam one rakshasa into another, creating confusion. But the effort tore open the previous wound and soon his left side was bathed in blood. Saving her energy, she threw two charges from the healing wand at the big fighter. Instantly, Thrinndor's wounds closed and he was able to stand without favoring his left side.

She sensed his gratitude, but she was unable to acknowledge him as the barbarian was taking heavy damage from one of the big cats and its master—a rakshasa of enormous size. Vorgath was flailing away with Flinthgoor, but the combined creatures were just too quick for the two-handed weapon. The creature's attacks were orchestrated—while one distracted the dwarf, the other was attacking from a different side. He was bleeding from several wounds, a couple of which appeared serious.

Sensing the barbarian was slowing due to his injuries, Cyrillis eschewed the wand, instead immediately going to her most powerful healing spell.

She saw the dwarf's back stiffen and with renewed energy he tumbled to the hard stone beneath his feet, narrowly avoiding the razor claws of the tiger in the process. When the barbarian again regained his feet, Flinthgoor was already in motion. The blade bit deep into the back of the tiger, severing its spine and rendering the big cat useless.

Vorgath then turned his attention to the suddenly wary rakshasa, now staying well out of reach of the dwarf's blade.

Seeing that the barbarian had his situation well in hand for the moment, Cyrillis checked on the other flank, where Breunne was dealing with a similar situation—one of the cats and its master. The ranger's blades were much quicker, however, so he seemed to be doing all right. His wounds were slight—really only a few scratches—but she used the wand on him anyway, not wanting to wait until his situation became dire.

Her attention again shifted to the paladin. Thrinndor was struggling with the three-on-one approach. The big cat kept trying it get behind him, and every time he fended off that attack, one of the rakshasas was able to strike an unprotected side. He was again bleeding from several cuts. Cyrillis used a mid-range heal spell on him, judging that the most powerful one she had available would have been overkill.

Sordaak used more of his force darts on the cat trying to get behind Thrinndor, hoping to distract it so the paladin could concentrate on the two rakshasas. His plan worked, sort of. The tiger took notice of the caster, all right, and tried to sneak past the fighter to deal with this pesky threat. Thrinndor had to spin to deal with the cat, leaving himself exposed on his left flank. He tried to protect that side with his shield, but the rakshasa was able to dodge the shield and rake the paladin's left shoulder—again—with its claws.

The paladin screamed as he hacked away at the cat whose attention was elsewhere, dealing it a fatal blow to the neck from behind. But now both rakshasas attacked as one, both able to do severe damage to the fighter. In pain, he dropped to one knee and brought both his shield and sword back around for defense.

Sensing victory, both rakshasas pressed their attack. Cyrillis hurriedly shouted the words to her most powerful heal spell and sent its energy to the paladin. But his wounds were severe. The spell certainly kept body and spirit together—for now, but unless something changed, it would not do so for long.

Knowing she was unable to cast that spell again quickly, the cleric raised the wand to use it instead. But it was used up! She cast it aside and gripped Kurril with both hands as she rushed to the side of the paladin. As she did, she mouthed the words to her mid-range healing spell and used direct touch to thereby dispense more of the healing energy into him.

"Cyrillis, NO!" Thrinndor shouted as she rushed past him. But he was too late. Her staff raised high, the cleric pivoted deftly on a toe to get more momentum into her swing.

Caught by surprise as the cleric came at them from out of the mists, the heel of Kurril stove in the right side of the head of the first rakshasa to get in her way. The animal collapsed into a heap and remained still.

The second rakshasa was much quicker to respond, however. It raked her exposed back with its razor-sharp claws before she could recover to defend herself. Cyrillis screamed in pain as she whirled to meet this other threat but was too late as the cat-creature raked her left arm as well. Seriously wounded, she fell back, hoping to apply some of her healing magic to herself. But in so doing, she tripped over the previously downed tiger and tumbled to the floor just beyond the beast.

Thrinndor struggled to regain his feet, but his right Achilles' tendon had been cut somewhere along the way and he was unable to stand. From his knees, he prepared to meet the attack of the remaining rakshasa, prepared to lunge from his knees, if necessary.

Sensing his opponent's weakness, the hybrid cat ignored the paladin, instead going for the kill on the prone cleric. Cyrillis tried to regain her feet as the creature approached but was unable to do so. As the rakshasa poised for attack, she raised Kurril weakly with her right arm, determined not to give in, but also realizing the futility of the move.

The creature raised its claw for one final attack and the cleric took in a breath to scream. Just as she was about to do so, a brilliant flash of light sizzled past her to hit the rakshasa square in the chest, knocking it back a step.

Cyrillis was unaware she had closed her eyes. When she opened them, she saw a different sort of flash as Savinhand's blade caught the light from the slowly descending orbs when it slashed cleanly through the neck of the rakshasa, beheading it.

As quickly as he had materialized, the rogue disappeared. As he did, he flashed the cleric a smile and suddenly she felt better. Cyrillis used some of her remaining energy to heal herself, knowing that if she went down, others would soon follow.

Feeling stronger, she turned her attention to the paladin, who had managed to stand but was leaning heavily on his sword, which was now being pressed into service as a crutch. She took a step in his direction, kneeled and put out a hand to his damaged heel, again releasing her most powerful healing spell into him by direct contact.

Thrinndor nodded at her gratefully, again able to stand erect without use of the sword. He turned to meet any further attack. "Back to the wall, please," he ordered her gently.

Knowing he meant no ill intent, Cyrillis did as she was told. Once there she checked on the other two fighters. Both were still standing, having dispatched the creatures before them. Both were also bleeding from various cuts and scratches, but her health sense told her that none was serious.

As she got back in position, she noted that the blade barricades had timed out and were gone. The fog spell was also dissipating, showing the damage both spells had wreaked on the attackers.

What she saw both appalled her and buoyed her confidence. There were at least five dead rakshasa where the blades had been. They looked as if they had gone through a meat grinder. In all, she counted four of the tigers, and thirteen of their masters that had fallen to the companions during the melee. She shook her head at the wasted life but said a silent prayer of thanks to Valdaar that the loss of life had not included one of their own.

"Status?" barked their leader, using his eyes to roam the surrounding area for further threats.

"Alive and well," Breunne responded quickly. "Thanks in no small part to the superb healing skills of our cleric."

Cyrillis blushed slightly at the compliment but said nothing.

"Ditto," said the barbarian. He was leaning on Flinthgoor, his breathing coming in gasps from the recent exertion.

"No damage here," said the mage, "and I used less than ten percent of my energy—still more than that in reserve."

"Good," said the paladin. He turned his eyes to the cleric and lifted his right eyebrow.

"I will yet live," she said with a wry smile. "Although I fared less well on spell energy." She shook her head. "My wand is dry and I have somewhat less than ten percent available."

"Let us pray that will prove adequate," said their leader. "I hope we are near the end."

Savinhand materialized a few steps from the paladin. "Yes and no." He looked back over his shoulder. Shadows were lengthening as the luminous orbs were nearing the end of their useful life. "Second wave is not far off."

Thrinndor's head snapped around. "Second wave?"

"You have got to be kidding!" Sordaak complained.

"No," replied the rogue. He looked back over at the paladin. "They just came through the double doors between the chambers." He looked in that direction. That part of the chamber was enshrouded in darkness. "Similar in size and make-up to this group." He waved an arm to encompass the dead surrounding their position.

Sordaak spat a curse.

Their leader looked around at their position. It looked much different in the light. Farther down the chamber, the wall showed an indent—an alcove of sorts.

"All right," Thrinndor said. "We need to move." He pointed over to the opening he had spotted. "We will set up there, quickly!"

Amid much grumbling the group moved.

"How much time do we have?" Thrinndor asked Savinhand.

"They're in no hurry," Savin responded. "They seem to be of the opinion we aren't going anywhere."

"They'd be right!" Vorgath slapped the haft of Flinthgoor.

"Sordaak and Cyrillis, as far back into that alcove as possible," Thrinndor said. His eyes locked with those of the cleric. "And stay there this time," he added sternly. The paladin smiled to show he meant no harm with the comment.

Cyrillis blushed slightly at the rebuke. She nodded and said nothing.

"Sordaak," the group leader continued, "can you cast those orbs further out?"

The mage nodded, not sure where his boss was going with this.

"Good," Thrinndor said. He turned and pointed far out into the chamber, now getting much darker as the previous orbs were getting dim; they had settled such that they were only a few feet off of the floor of the cavern. "What I am looking for is for us to be able to see them, but I want them to have to search for us in the darker shadows."

The magicuser nodded again. "I can do that."

"Second," the paladin said as he studied the entrance to the alcove, which was really almost a shallow cave. "Is there any way you can force them to approach from further out front? I do not want them to be able to sneak up on us from either side."

Sordaak pondered this. "Yes, I think so." He walked out and looked at the landscape. He pointed to the edge of the alcove. "I can extend Force Walls from here straight out from both sides of the entrance. That will require them to be visible for at least twenty feet."

"That should do nicely," said their leader. "Please do both the walls and orbs as discussed prior to their attack." He looked out into the chamber. "Orbs first. I want to be able to range attack them as they approach." He looked over at Vorgath. "That is assuming the old one has a ranged weapon."

"Of course I do, pretty boy," the dwarf responded testily. He removed a bag from his belt. "I don't have one of those dainty bows, just some of these bad-ass throwing axes." He smiled as he dumped twenty or so of the weapons onto the floor of the alcove and began hanging them on his belt for ease of access.

Thrinndor smiled. "That will have to do, I suppose." He turned to find the rogue. "How much longer?"

Savinhand had been watching the approach of the monsters the entire time. "They've seen the carnage we left behind and have stopped to discuss it."

"Maybe they'll change their minds and just go away," said the caster without much conviction.

"Have they spotted us?" asked the cleric. She had been busy selecting where she was going to make her stand.

"They've known where we have been all along," replied the rogue. "They seem to be in no hurry. Wait!" He stood erect, his eyes on the enemy. "They're spreading out and moving this way." Savin stepped back into the shadows and vanished.

"There's something about this that doesn't make sense," Sordaak said as he studied the walls of the alcove.

Thrinndor followed the mage's movement with his eyes. "Please explain."

The caster did not stop his search. "These creatures are incredibly intelligent. It makes no sense that they would walk into this knowing we wiped out an earlier party of their peers of approximately the same size."

Thrinndor looked out at the oncoming rakshasas to gauge how much time they had. Not much. He spun to confront the mage. "We have no time. Please put up the walls and orbs."

"Right," said the caster. "Then I'll get back to this. I'm beginning to think we were herded into this place."

"Hurry!"

With a shake of his head, Sordaak removed the correct wand from its pocket in his robe, walked out a few paces into the cavern, pointed the wand to the indicated point and released the energy with the trigger word. Twice. And after a moment of thought, a third time.

He then put the wand back in its pocket, removed the correct spell components and put up both walls.

"Thank you," Thrinndor said. "Ranged weapons if you please, gentlemen," he said to the other fighters as he pulled his bow from a backpack and set his quiver where he had easy access to the arrows within.

Sordaak replaced the spell components as he walked back to his place in the alcove when an idea came to him. He pulled the components back out and stopped short of entering the alcove.

"What is wrong?" Cyrillis asked.

Sordaak ignored her as he continued his search from where he stood. He, too, felt there was no time for discussion.

There has to be an opening here, he decided as his eyes studied the back of the alcove. No other place makes sense—not that much about this whole adventure made sense, he thought with a shake of the head.

Sordaak readied the components, made the appropriate gesture releasing the energy, and waited. He heard the action picking up behind him, but his eyes never strayed from the back of the alcove.

There! The back wall is moving! It's a trap! Sordaak turned to alert the others, but they had switched to hand-to-hand and were too busy to be of any help. He was going to have to handle whoever—or whatever—tried to come through that opening all by himself.

He was ready.

He hoped.

The wall continued to shift, now wide enough to be used as an entrance. Still nothing came, or tried to come, through. Wider still it opened, completely silent. The mage wondered briefly what form of magic was being used. There! He could now see several rakshasas and their trained tigers, waiting for the signal to attack.

When the rock wall was wide enough, Sordaak again raised the components and made the gesture. This time he put the force wall several feet behind where the rakshasas were massed.

Finally one of them noticed the mage standing and watching them. Sordaak waved and smiled. The monsters leapt at him, but they bounced hard off of the first force wall the mage had established.

Now the caster removed other components from his pouch. His smile broadened as he drew an arcane symbol in the air in front of him.

In the midst of the rakshasas a wall of fire leapt into being. Now there was frenetic action from the creatures as they turned to run back into the cave only to hit the force wall Sordaak had put in place behind them.

Panic set in as the monsters tried their best to distance themselves from the flaming wall.

Sordaak smiled and waved as he cast yet another wall of fire, this time farther back from the first.

Their fur smoldering, the rakshasas now rushed the wall closest to Sordaak. He waved and made the gesture again. A third flaming wall leapt into being where they were standing.

Now true panic set in as there was no place to go. The area between the force walls was one big mass of flames. The rakshasas and their tigers were roasting in the flames.

Sordaak briefly hoped that their deaths would not take too long. His wall of fire spell did not last all that long, and he was again running low on energy. As he watched the first wall wink out of existence, he was forced to replace it with another.

Now the creatures clawed at one another in an attempt to escape. The second wall disappeared, and Sordaak replaced it, too. Two of the creatures tried to climb over the front wall, one clawing his way over the top of the other.

The third wall went out and the caster replaced it. Now he was again dangerously low on energy—that was going to have to be the last one. He was no longer smiling. The death he was inflicting on the creatures was not one he would wish on anyone. Not even these enemies.

He did not have to worry. Both of the two cats trying to escape by climbing fell back into the flames before they got close to the top of the force wall. The monsters were all dead, charred far beyond recognition before the walls of flames again died out.

Sordaak turned back to see how his friends had fared, trying to erase what he had witnessed from his mind.

The companions had fared pretty well, too. It was obvious to Sordaak that the attacking rakshasas had expected the help from the back of the alcove at some point but were committed to the attack nonetheless.

Several—perhaps as many as five or six—of the monsters had fallen to the ranged attacks. More still died in the initial onslaught. In the end, the companions had had to rush out to finish the job, chasing down the rakshasas and their pets wherever they caught up with them.

The party's injuries were mostly minor. A few claw marks and yet another Achilles' injury, this time to Vorgath.

Cyrillis, as of yet unaware of the carnage that had taken place behind her, was making the rounds using spell energy where necessary and more mundane bandages and wraps where those would suffice.

The companions checked bodies to ensure they would not be bothered by these monsters again and gathered to discuss their situation.

Sordaak walked up on the gathering as Vorgath was saying "I got seven kills between the two battles."

Breunne responded with, "I got at least ten—maybe more. Hard to tell." He turned to the caster as he approached. "How about you, Sordaak?"

The mage, his stomach upside down from the stench of the burnt flesh and having to watch the creatures fry before his eyes, just shook his head and stood waiting.

"None?" spat the dwarf. "That figures!"

Sordaak grabbed the arm of the paladin and said quietly, "I need to speak with you in private."

"What's going on?" asked the ranger.

The magicuser whirled and snapped, "Gimme a minute with Thrinndor please!"

The sorcerer's expression was enough for Breunne. He held up both hands and said, "Sure thing."

"What was that about?" asked the cleric as the mage led the paladin off a few paces where they spoke quietly.

"No idea," replied the rogue. "They'll tell us in time, I suppose."

After a few moments, the paladin motioned the group over.

Silently, they complied. "Sordaak has something to show us," Thrinndor said, his tone somber. The mage's eyes remained on his feet. "He says it is quite gruesome." The paladin's eyes went to those of the healer. "You should wait for us here, I think."

The cleric's eyes flared and she lifted her chin in defiance. "I will not!"

Sordaak looked up finally, his eyes searching for those of the cleric. "I wish you would," he said.

The healer shook her head.

"Very well," said the party leader. "This way." He turned and headed into the alcove.

Vorgath noted the lack of spring in his step and wondered what was going on.

Before they entered the opening, the caster stopped the group. "I recommend you cover your noses," he said as he pulled a piece of cloth from his belt, tied it around his neck and pulled it up over his nose.

"Why?" asked the barbarian.

Sordaak just stared at the dwarf until Vorgath shifted uncomfortably. Still he made no move to cover his nose.

"Suit yourself," the mage said. He then turned and entered the alcove. Everyone followed uneasily, all but the barbarian covering their noses as requested.

The stench reached their noses through the coverings even before it became apparent what it was the horrible odor came from.

"What is that smell?" Cyrillis asked, her eyes watering.

Breunne was pretty sure he knew, but he remained silent as he followed the mage.

As they rounded the corner, the smoldering bodies of the rakshasas and their pets came into view, barely recognizable from the burns inflicted.

The group stopped a few steps shy of the wall opening in the back of the alcove.

"What in the Seven Hells happened here?" asked the rogue, his voice muffled by the rag tied across his face.

Sordaak told them.

When he finished, the men heard gagging noises coming from their cleric, but she held her place defiantly. Her normally fair complexion above her mask was tainted green. However she did not move.

"What did you want us to see?" asked the dwarf, his tone subdued.

The caster pointed. "There's an opening back there. I'm not sure how far back it goes."

Chapter Twenty-Seven

Lair of Tigers

"We must investigate," Thrinndor said around his face mask. He did not move. Vorgath stepped around the mage, who was between him and the carnage, grabbed the leg of the first burnt figure he came across and pulled the creature off to one side. Once there he dumped the body and moved to get a second.

Breunne, Thrinndor and Savinhand all stepped in to help clear a path through to the rear opening. Sordaak stood unmoving, unable to take his eyes off what he had done.

When the badly charred skin slid off of one of the tigers the barbarian was moving, the men could hear the gagging sounds from the cleric as she rushed back out of the alcove.

None of the guys said anything. They all were too close to following the cleric.

When the path was clear, Cyrillis rejoined the men, her face above the mask a few shades greener than before. There were also tear tracks down both cheeks, and the mask was wet below those tracks. Her eyes were puffy and red.

The men cleaned their hands as best they could with water from their skins and rags.

Cyrillis swallowed and said, "Try wine. It will cut through the smell." She sounded better.

Vorgath looked at her and muttered under his breath. "Not sure how we will be able to tell. This place reeks!" But he did as directed.

"Ready?" Thrinndor asked the gathered party. He got nods from all, some less vigorous than others. "Were do we stand on energy?" he asked Sordaak and Cyrillis.

"I have enough in reserve for maybe one or two crowd-control spells," answered the caster. "That's it."

"I have even less," replied the cleric. "Maybe enough for one minor heal spell. No more."

Their leader nodded grimly as he checked the status of his fighting force. They were all tired. He was pretty sure they had been moving for well into the second day, now. None were without bandages in at least one place, and most had more than one.

"Very well," Thrinndor said. "We will have to use extreme caution. We cannot rely on our usually reliable healer for support."

Cyrillis nodded. Her skin color was returning to normal. "I will support with this," she said as she shook Kurril defiantly. Her voice also sounded stronger.

The paladin smiled at her through his mask. "All right, battle formation. Savin, you are out front looking for traps."

The rogue nodded as he stepped around his leader and made his way through the path previously cleared. The rest of the group followed in the requested formation.

The opening in the back wall was maybe a little wider than ten feet, and it bent to the right not far back into the rock. The passage narrowed a bit and became more and more smooth the deeper in they went. Savin was certain the cavern—at least this far back—was not natural. It had been hewn from the surrounding rock. And, from the look of it, hewn thousands of years ago. Lit sconces were set at regular intervals all along the passage.

Thrinndor and the rest of the party caught up to the rogue as he inspected a large door he had come to forty or fifty feet after the bend at the beginning.

After a few moments the rogue stepped back. "This door is not trapped. I'm certain they wouldn't have had time." He turned to face the paladin. "Nor is it locked."

The paladin nodded. "Vorgath," he said. "If you please."

Without a word the barbarian stepped past the thief, grasped the pull-ring and pulled. The door opened easily, and the dwarf stepped back, wary.

Nothing happened.

On the other side of the door, the passage continued as on this side, again lit by the same type of sconces at the same regular interval.

At a nod from his leader, Savin stepped through the opening and ducked into the shadows, vanishing to those behind him.

"Move out," said the paladin after he had given the rogue a chance to get an appropriate distance ahead of them.

The party met no further resistance. There was no one left to oppose them. What they found was a complete miniature rakshasa civilization. Sleeping quarters for several dozen, a temple, storage units laden with food, training grounds and more.

But they found no living creature. Nothing.

The companions searched all over, finding little of interest. After they had searched several rooms, they were becoming anxious to get out of there, but Thrinndor wanted to leave nothing behind that had not been searched, sorted and categorized.

"It's people like you that require each new administrator of the Library to create a new location for it and change up the entry requirements," Savin complained good-naturedly.

The paladin was too tired to return the smile, however. Believing they had finally rid themselves of the rakshasas and their pets, he decided to split the party up into three groups to speed the search—Vorgath with Cyrillis, Breunne with Sordaak, and Savinhand with him. They were to meet back at the entrance door in no more than one hour. A signal was to be given in the event any trouble was encountered.

They encountered none.

Even before the hour had passed, the party was again standing at the door to the city. Vorgath and Cyrillis were the last to arrive. The other two groups were comparing notes on what each had found; which was essentially nothing.

A group of fifty or so rakshasas and their pets had lived here for...how long? It made no sense.

Just as the companions were about to enter into a third round of sharp discussions on the matter, Sordaak held up his hand wearily, demanding attention. He got it. After a few moments the side conversations died.

"I have a theory," he started, knowing he would be interrupted.

"There's a surprise!" grumbled the dwarf. "Do we have to hear it?"

"No," replied the caster. He was not smiling. "But we do have to get moving—I can't stand here any longer." He turned and started walking, five pairs of eyes following him toward the door. "Normally I'd spell it out for you as we walked, but I am too tired to do so, so the discussion will have to wait until I—we—have rested."

"Makes sense," their leader said, weariness apparent in his voice as well. "If we do not find the entrance to this Library soon, we will have to consider alternatives. We must rest."

"Right now," said the caster as he pushed the door to the outside chamber open, "I don't care which door we open. If we get to the Library, we can finally rest. If we open the door and we are back outside, we can finally rest. We'll just have to start over." He was too tired to argue. He stepped through the door, the others falling in step behind him.

"Agreed," said the paladin. "However, we do not need to get careless now that we have made it this far. Trap search formation, please."

The companions stretched sore muscles and tired legs as they got into position, scrambling to catch up to the sorcerer.

In silence the companions made their way back to the rear of the alcove, each holding his or her breath and keeping eyes averted until the death bin was cleared.

Once again torches had to be lit; Sordaak and Cyrillis were again elected to carry them.

Without speaking, Thrinndor lead the party back toward the middle of the cavern, bearing slightly to the right. Once there, they continued their march along the faint path they had been following when they had been beset by the rakshasas. Their usual banter was subdued, and even the barbarian was silent as they each were required to watch were they stepped, as the floor was uneven here. Intermittent rocks and sandy spots littered the path before them.

After tripping for a third time, Sordaak muttered, "I have had enough of this!" He pulled a wand out of his pocket and aimed it at the ceiling over their heads and said the trigger word. A small ball of blue light energy shot from the end of the wand and went high above their heads. There it exploded into the brilliant ball of light they had become accustomed to during their recent battles. It illuminated the path ahead much better than even ten torches could have.

It also illuminated their objective: A set of ornate double doors stood in the rock wall less than a hundred feet away.

"Thank you," said the paladin. While he was indeed grateful, he would have preferred to have been consulted on the wisdom of such a light. Bah! You are just grouchy, he thought

When the companions got to the doors, they found the rogue already there inspecting them. After a few moments Savin turned to acknowledge his companions.

"Yes, they're trapped," he said. "Yes, I can remove the traps, but this might take a while." He turned back to studying the doors.

Vorgath flopped to the ground. "Wake me when it's over." He pulled his helm over his eyes and was snoring in seconds.

Thrinndor shook his head and unslung his pack from his shoulder. "Perhaps we should take this opportunity to eat something."

Sordaak turned away from the doors and started walking back the way they had come.

The paladin called after him. "Sordaak?"

The mage spun and jabbed a finger at his leader. "I can't!" He was almost shouting. He corrected himself. "Actually," he said, quieter this time, "I can. Eat, that is. But I can't stop walking. No rest, remember?"

"Yes, I remember," replied the paladin, his tone placating. He pulled a biscuit from his bag, unwrapped it and took a bite. "I'll walk with you."

"That's not necessary," said the caster, continuing to walk away.

"I know," Thrinndor said. "But I want to anyway."

"Suit yourself," the mage said with a shrug. He, too, pulled a biscuit from his bag and began munching. As Thrinndor caught up with him, the sorcerer gagged on the second bite and quickly washed it down with some water.

The paladin thumped him on the back a couple of times. "Easy there, wiggle-finger," he said.

Sordaak looked up at the big fighter, tears from the choking in his eyes. "Thanks," he said, his voice hoarse from the bread crumbs. "Biscuits are getting a bit dry."

"Yes, they are," agreed the paladin as he also tipped his head back and took a deep pull from his water skin. "Something bothering you?"

Sordaak choked again and spat out some bread crumbs. "Bothering me?" His tone was incredulous. "Lack of sleep. No spell energy. Used as a chew-toy by a ginormous tiger. Roasted several tigers alive to make up for it." He grinned. "And that's just for starters. What could possibly be bothering me?" He shook his head at the question.

Thrinndor chuckled. "You seem a little tense."

"A little tense?" Sordaak shook his head again. "A little tense would mean I'm feeling better. I'm a LOT tense!" He smiled at his friend.

The paladin returned the smile. "Good. As long as you stay away from the ledge." Thrinndor's eyes twinkled. He had really grown to like this sorcerer.

"No worries there," replied the magicuser. "I don't like heights!"

Both got a good laugh out of that one.

"How about you?" asked the caster. "How are you holding up under the rigors of leadership?"

The paladin cast a sidelong glance at his friend. "You know it is what I was born and trained to do, right?"

Sordaak nodded. "Of course. That's the reason I passed the reins to you in the first place. That doesn't mean it's easy!"

"You certainly have that right!" said the big fighter with a shake of his head. "Between you, the disappearing thief and that meathead dwarf, you all make certain to keep me guessing."

"I suppose we do, at that," said the mage with a chuckle. "You seem to handle it well."

"It is all that training." Thrinndor grinned in return.

Both turned at a yell from the ranger. They were being waved back. Thrinndor looked up at the diminishing light from the orb—only a few minutes of that remaining, and neither he nor the caster had brought a torch.

Thrinndor returned the wave and he and Sordaak turned to go back. They made the return trip in silence. As they approached the others they could see Savinhand standing off to one side talking with the ranger, a biscuit in hand.

"Got it, boss," the rogue said with a smile. "There was actually a series of three traps, each progressively harder to find, and each progressively harder to disarm." He grinned. "But I got them. Kind of helped that I knew they were there." His eyes glistened. "That and the old codger showed me how to do these traps years ago!"

As they got closer the paladin could see that the rogue had been sweating. "Very good," Thrinndor said. "Were the doors locked as well?"

"Of course," the thief said with a shrug. "And they were of a mechanism I had not encountered before. But I figured them out. It just took longer than expected."

Thrinndor looked around. Vorgath was still snoring, oblivious to all going on around him. The paladin considered briefly rousing him in the usual abrupt manner but decided against it. "Get up, old one," he said loudly. "We must finish this."

The barbarian reached up and moved the helm back, exposing his bloodshot eyes. "I told you not to call me that!" He said nothing more as he rolled to his feet and retrieved Flinthgoor. "Let's go."

The remaining companions got to their feet, not without some complaining, however. Without being asked, Vorgath shouldered his way up to the doors. He didn't even look around to see if everyone was ready.

"Are we ready to see what is on the other side?" asked the cleric before the barbarian could open the door.

"I don't see that we have an option," said the caster. "I cannot stand here any longer. If our assumptions are correct, on the other side of that door will be either the cabin with four doors, or the entrance to the Library—one or the other. Either way, we go through."

"Agreed," said the paladin. "We must enter either way."

"I doubt we'll have a choice," said the rogue, quietly. All eyes turned to him, even the barbarian. "If our past experiences with the doors in here are to be of any indication, which room it is won't be revealed to us until we get inside."

The companions nodded. Some in agreement, others because they were resigned to whatever was to be revealed on the other side at this point. It didn't matter. They were going to get some rest.

Vorgath shrugged and grasped the operating mechanism, which he turned and pulled. The right door opened easily, the left following suit without a finger being set on it.

"Interesting," said the thief. "I'm not sure I've seen that before."

Further comment was stifled by what was revealed inside the two doors. It was a room that had three other visible doors, one each in the other walls.

It was the cabin.

"Shit," said the paladin, as his shoulders sagged in defeat.

"I thought we agreed you would leave the cursing to those of us who did it best?" griped the dwarf. His eyes went back to the chamber before him. "Shit."

"You sure we cannot just turn and go back to investigate the doors in the other chamber?" asked the cleric.

Savinhand hesitated before answering. "Sure? No. But allowing us to change our minds at this point would seem to run against the lessons we have learned in here, to date."

"Which are?" said the barbarian, still holding the door.

"Stick with whatever choice you made, for good or ill," Sordaak said before the rogue could reply.

"Just the same," Breunne said, "shouldn't we at least check?"

"No," Thrinndor said. "As best we can tell with the information we have available to us—tracks, directions, et cetera—this set of doors should be the ones opposite where we entered the chamber."

"Should be," the ranger repeated, not convinced. He shrugged, however, conceding the point to his leader.

Thrinndor took in a breath to continue the conversation but changed his mind. He let the breath out noisily and pushed his way past the barbarian, who had not moved.

The paladin entered the chamber, the others dejectedly following. When they all got inside, Vorgath being last, the doors closed on their own.

"There's a surprise," said the rogue, sarcasm echoing in his tone. "Doors closing on their own."

"Want me to try to stop them?" asked the barbarian as he took a step in their direction.

"No," responded the paladin. "We will stick by our choice." He looked knowingly at the caster, who nodded.

"Doubtful you could do anything about them, anyway," said the rogue.

"Whatever!" said the dwarf as he watched the doors close.

The left door closed first, the right just a second behind. When the right door boomed shut, the lights went out.

There was a sharp intake of breath by several in the party, but they didn't have time to act on it before the light came back up.

The room around them had changed dramatically. The chamber seemed to have gotten larger—at least double the original twenty by twenty.

Now they appeared to be in some sort of antechamber. Well lit and comfortable. There were couches, beds, tables and chairs. And there were shelves laden with supplies. There were rows of casks, presumably with various libations inside.

"Ummm," began the rogue, "I think it's safe to say we're not in the cabin anymore."

"I believe that would be a correct assumption," agreed the paladin, his right eyebrow melding with his hairline.

"It appears we are meant to rest here," said the cleric.

All eyes focused on the sorcerer.

Sordaak was looking over the foodstuffs on one of the shelves. "This food appears fresh." The sorcerer turned to face his friends. He made them wait. "And the energy drain is not affecting me here."

"Damn, that's good news," said the barbarian. He walked over and inspected the casks. He selected one, picked it up, snatched a tap from a nearby shelf and carried both over to one of the tables and set it down with a thud. He then walked to the shelf with various tableware implements, selected the biggest flagon, grabbed a slab of bread from another shelf and straddled a chair. He pried the stopper out, took a big whiff of the contents and said, "Ah...smells to be of a very good week," and hammered the tap into place with the flagon.

The barbarian then set the cask upright and filled his new flagon to the brim. He had just quaffed half the cup and bitten off a large chunk of bread when Sordaak spoke again.

"Anyone—besides me, that is—notice there is only one door?"

Vorgath stopped chewing long enough to say "nope." He ripped off another chunk of the bread and washed it down with more of the wine. He then gave a long belch. "However, how many doors do we need?"

The sorcerer tilted his head to the right, lifted a brow as he thought about it and said, "Well said."

"Besides," said the rogue, "I believe you missed this door over here." He pointed to a small entrance in the corner opposite the obvious set of double doors.

"No," said the caster as he selected a flagon from the shelf and sat down opposite the dwarf. "That door is obviously there to allow us to freshen up in private."

"What?" said Savinhand.

Sordaak rolled his eyes. "The moon on the door." Same blank stare from the thief. "Oh for heaven's sake, have you never noticed a moon on the necessary chamber door?"

"Of course I have," Savin said. He looked again at the door. "I just didn't notice this moon!" He shook his head. "Damn I'm tired." He then walked to the door in question, opened it and stepped inside.

The companions heard him slide the bolt home and returned their focus to the laden shelves.

"This stuff is fresh!" Cyrillis said as she picked up a loaf of the bread. She selected a wheel of cheese, picked up a knife and joined the barbarian and the caster at the table.

Silence was the order of the moment as each selected different meats, cheeses and breads to their taste.

When the door opened, Savinhand reappeared and said, "Wow! That is one well-appointed necessary room! There is a tub, a shower, a sink, the standard necessary chamber, towels, fine soaps and—best of all—a vat of hot, steaming water piped into all the basins!"

"Nice," said the cleric around a mouthful of bread.

"I'm next," said the caster. "I won't be long. I will be asleep in ten minutes." He opened the door. "Or less."

One by one the companions used the facilities and took care of their ablutions. Cyrillis asked to go last; she wanted to soak in the tub. She got no arguments.

*

"Good morning," Savinhand said amicably to Thrinndor as the paladin sauntered up to the small cook stove and poured himself a cup of coffee.

"Good morning," the paladin responded good-naturedly. "Although I do not believe it is currently morning back in Hargstead." He grinned.

The thief nodded. "Probably not," he said as he turned over the breakfast meat he was frying. He was not exactly sure what animal the sausage was from, but it certainly smelled good.

After he had fried up the sausage, he crumbled some into the pan, added flour and milk (where the milk came from he really wanted to know, but it was cool and fresh) and made up a thick, savory gravy. He then fried up the two dozen eggs he had found and called his friends over to breakfast.

"Come and get it before I throw it to the dogs!" he said with a smile.

"What dogs?" said the dwarf, as he looked around the chamber, making sure he had not missed the animals.

"Just a saying, old great wise one!" replied the rogue.

"You certainly do not know him very well," said the paladin as he filled his plate. "Although you got the 'old' part right." He grinned at the barbarian.

"There you go," replied the dwarf as he ladled several spoonful's of gravy onto the eggs, biscuits and sausage already on his plate. "Talking trash even before the day begins. I guess I'll have to learn you some manners once I take care of this breakfast!"

"Good luck!" Sordaak said. The caster was the last to make his way to the table, scratching his head and rubbing his eyes. "I've worked on his manners now for three or four months and you can see where that has gotten me!"

Thrinndor chuckled as he sat down at the table. "So that is how it is going to be?" he said. "Teaming up against me?" His eyes sparkled as he continued. "Very well, I will allow a few minutes to straighten out you both after I finish this most excellent repast!"

"Whatever!" said the barbarian around a mouthful of biscuits and gravy.

"Whatever!" echoed the caster as he filled his plate.

"Could we please go through a morning meal without you blowhards trotting out all that crap?" Cyrillis asked as she sat down at the table with her plate.

"What?" asked the barbarian innocently.

"Who, me?" said the paladin.

"Whatever!" the caster repeated himself on purpose.

"Men!" the healer said with a shake of her head. She was smiling but trying not to show it. "You know," she said as she looked up at the paladin, "I learned more of those exercises that will help you guys stretch out in the morning without the loss of teeth." She grinned at the barbarian.

"Ha!" Vorgath snorted as he shoveled a fork laden with eggs into his mouth.

"They are called calisthenics. We will work on them after you finish eating, if you like," the cleric added.

"OK," replied the barbarian. "You stretch, I'll watch."

"In your dreams, old man!" Cyrillis replied.

"Now you're getting the idea," Vorgath replied with a smile of his own. He held up his coffee in salute.

"You know," the healer said, returning his smile and his salute with her coffee, "it is a good thing I know you are not serious, or else a curse might be invoked that could affect your manhood!"

The dwarf put down his coffee with a thud. "Just exactly how are these calisthenics done?" The companions broke out in laughter.

"Relax, o venerable one," said the healer as she wiped mirth from her eyes, "we will have time after you finish your breakfast!"

The barbarian looked over at the paladin. "I'm starting to like this girl," he said while working yet another mouthful of gravy-covered biscuit.

"That is good," replied Thrinndor, "because I believe we might be stuck with her!"

"Damn straight!" Cyrillis said with a wink.

Chapter Twenty-Eight

Preparations

"What do you mean?" Cyrillis asked.

"Look at them," replied Sordaak. "There are no operating mechanisms. No locking mechanisms. No keyholes. Not even any hinges that I can tell."

"Really?" Vorgath asked. He walked over to inspect the doors for himself.

"Really," said the caster.

"That's because they don't open that way," Savinhand said. He had started cleaning up after breakfast but stopped now and stared at the doors with the others.

Sordaak turned his head slowly to focus on the thief. "Do tell."

"If I'm correct," said the rogue, "I believe on the other side of those doors will be our final test."

"The dragon!" Vorgath stood too fast, sending the chair he had been sitting in skittering across the floor.

"So?" The caster's eyes never left those of the thief.

"Remember what I said about the final test?" Savinhand asked.

Sordaak tried to read the rogue's mind by the mirror in his eyes. He could not. "No. Refresh my memory, please."

"The doors to the final test will be password-protected," Savinhand said, his eyes leaving those of the sorcerer and moving back to the doors.

"And you do not know the password," said the dwarf.

"Nope," replied the thief, the reverie broken. He pulled the journal from its pocket beneath his leathers. "Nor is there anything in here about it, either—not that I can find, anyway." He paused and slid to book over to the magicuser. "Maybe another set of eyes will help."

"I thought no one else could touch the journal," said the sorcerer as he licked his lips.

"Nah," interrupted the ranger. "I made that up to keep unwanted eyes from having a go at it." He shrugged. "I've held it for the last couple of years, after all." Breunne smiled at the caster. "Although I've never opened it."

Sordaak considered lambasting the ranger for the lie, but his need to investigate overrode that desire for now. He licked his lips again as his hands caressed the tome. "I'll comb through this." He then looked up at his friend the rogue, and then shifted eyes to the cleric. "You two need to sit and think about any and all conversations you had with your mentors. See if you can remember anything he might have said to you concerning this library, and these doors in particular." He looked from one to the other. "Anything!"

Then the caster allowed his shoulders to droop as he turned to the paladin. "Sorry, boss," he said. "Habit."

"No problem," Thrinndor responded with a smile. "My brawn and charisma make a good leadership choice most of the time." He bowed deeply at the waist. "But in times such as this, I will gladly defer to your intellect."

Sordaak bobbed his head, returning the bow as best he could while remaining seated.

Savin looked over at the cleric. "Perhaps it would be to our advantage to work together. Compare notes, so to speak."

Cyrillis nodded, her eyes still lingering on the magicuser. She got up and moved to a remote table. Savinhand followed her.

Thrinndor turned to first Breunne and then Vorgath. "We will sit over there," he said, pointing to a table in the opposite corner of the room from Cyrillis and Savinhand. "We need to work on a strategy based on what we know already."

The barbarian briefly considered arguing that his strategy was ready but decided against it. Instead he shrugged, picked up Flinthgoor and ambled over to the indicated table.

There, the dwarf leaned his greataxe against the wall, scratched his belly and belched loudly. Second thoughts entered his head, and he sauntered back to the main table and scooped up his flagon and the cask of wine. He shook the cask, determined it was lacking in contents and made his way over to the rack that held similar containers.

Thrinndor watched his friend with amusement. "Take care with that, old man. You certainly will want your entire wits about you when we face the dragon."

Vorgath, about to pick up a cask of wine, hesitated. His hands moved instead to one clearly marked Ale. "You are, of course, correct," the barbarian said as he brought the mini-keg of ale back to the table, pried out the cork and tilted it to pour it directly into his flagon.

Most of the drink made it, though some missed and spilled onto the table. "Damn," muttered the dwarf, "that's ale abuse." He smiled and shook his head at the humor.

He sat the keg back on the table, picked up his flagon and quaffed half its contents in a single swig. He set it down with a thud and again belched loudly. He then turned to look at the paladin and ranger as they took a seat at the table across from him. "Perfect accompaniment to that magnificent repast prepared by our superb chef!" He picked up his flagon and held it up to salute to the rogue across the room.

Savinhand, deep in conversation with the healer, did not notice.

Vorgath didn't notice the rogue not noticing. He put the flagon to his lips and took another deep pull. "Damn, that's good," he said as he wiped the foam from his lips. "They must have a dwarf for a brewmaster." He narrowed his brows, daring his companions to say otherwise.

Neither did.

Breunne sat the cask he had selected onto the table—one marked Water— and pried out the cork. He poured himself some and sipped at the contents. "Ah, mountain stream water," he said as he took a longer drink and winked at the dwarf in the process.

"Mine, too," Vorgath said, returning the wink.

Both laughed briefly before again taking a pull from their respective cups.

"What's the plan?" asked the barbarian as he set his empty cup down. He considered refilling it, but decided with no small regret the paladin was correct; he was going to need his full senses for the task at hand. He stole a look at the rogue and cleric as they huddled together in the far corner.

"Plan?" said the paladin with a shake of his head. "That is what the three of us must determine."

"Well," began the barbarian, "my plan is kill me one dragon." He smiled, again eyeing the cask of ale in front of him. Once again he showed great restraint and passed.

"Good plan," conceded the paladin. "But I am fairly certain that dragon, should we indeed be about to face one, will not just lie down and allow you to end its life without a struggle."

"Good god, I certainly hope not!" spat the dwarf. "I want to be able to tell the tale of an epic battle for many years to come!"

"Then we must plan." The leader in the paladin was speaking now. "What do we know about this dragon?"

Breunne took another sip of the water. "It is of the green variety. Meaning we'll have to prepare for poison gas."

"Correct," agreed the paladin. "We can have our casters provide resistance to the poison part of the attack." He looked from one to the other. "What else?"

Vorgath hesitated. "It's a she."

"Also correct," agreed the leader. "Although I doubt we will be able to find an advantage with that." Again he looked around. "Anything else?"

"Well," said the ranger with a sidelong glance at the healer, who was still deep in conversation with the rogue, "we know that the dragon—if it's indeed the dragon we face—is known by, and possibly even friendly with, our healer."

Thrinndor nodded. "That may useful to us. Although just how so eludes me at the moment."

"Maybe we can have her distract the dragon," said the ranger, "while some of us circle in behind."

"Perhaps," said the paladin. "Although I doubt the dragon will allow that."

"Agreed," said the barbarian. "I say we go in swinging and let the chips fall where they will."

Again the paladin was not quite convinced. "I doubt the dragon will stand still for that, either." After a few uncomfortable moments he tried again. "What do we know about dragons in general that might be of use to us?"

"They're big," said the ranger with a smile.

"And ugly." Vorgath returned the smile.

"Something of a little more use, please," Thrinndor said sternly. He smiled to remove any perceived rebuke.

"They can fly," said the ranger. "Although I doubt that will come into play down here." He looked at the ceiling over their heads. "Wherever here might be."

"We must not take for granted what we expect to find on the other side of those doors," cautioned the paladin. "For all we know they could lead out into the open air."

"For that matter," agreed the ranger, "some of these caverns we have encountered are large enough for her flight to become a factor."

"Also true," Thrinndor agreed. "We must prepare for the eventuality this dragon will attempt to use her flight to her advantage. What else?"

"Some of the older, more intelligent dragons are known to be able to cast spells as a sorcerer." Breunne got to his feet and poured himself another cup of coffee.

"And this particular dragon is not only old enough for that," Thrinndor said solemnly, "she has been under the tutelage of a proficient caster."

"But the caster in question here is a cleric," said the barbarian. He was unsure whether that was important.

"Good point," mused the paladin. "However, as we have seen, clerics have some potent offensive spells at their command, as well."

"That is certainly true," said the ranger. "We should keep Sordaak on the lookout to nullify any such spells."

Thrinndor looked over at the caster, who had his nose deep in the journal. "I will certainly make a point to remind him as such when the time comes." He turned back to the barbarian. "Anything else?"

"Well," said the ranger as he scratched his head, "we shouldn't ignore her teeth and claws."

"Good point," said the paladin. "If that dragon is allowed to get close enough, those are certainly formidable weapons."

"Oh," Vorgath said knowingly, "she'll be close enough!" He considered retrieving Flinthgoor to emphasize his point but decided these guys knew what he meant.

"Well," Thrinndor said as he cast a dubious eye on his friend, "if you plan on going toe-to-toe with a dragon, it might be in your best interest to don the rest of that armor." He looked at the dwarf's bare arms and his unprotected legs.

"Bah!" spat the dwarf. "I don't need no stinkin' armor!" He glanced down at his breastplate then with a mischievous smile and corrected himself. "No more stinkin' armor."

"While your prowess in battle is certainly not in question," said a smirking Breunne, "you must not allow yourself to be caught in the claws and/or maw of the dragon." His tone turned serious. "Our cleric—as good as she is—would not be able to heal you fast enough to prevent that dragon from ripping into you like you did those biscuits!"

"Good one," said the paladin. But he quickly erased the smile from his face. "Breunne's point is well made. If Cyrillis is forced to focus all her attention on keeping your body and soul together, she doubtless would be hard-pressed to keep an eye on the rest of us."

"Whatever!" Vorgath said. "If she keeps me alive, I will make certain the dragon does not get through to lay a claw on any of you!" He stuck out his chin defiantly. This was a plan he liked.

"While that certainly is an option we may consider," the party leader said diplomatically, "we must also consider other options before we commit to such a plan."

The barbarian took in a breath to argue but changed his mind. He clamped his mouth shut and crossed his massive arms on his chest, glowering at both of his companions at once.

Breunne was first to break the uncomfortable silence that followed. "Mayhap we could combine the tactics mentioned thus far," he said.

Vorgath raised an eyebrow but said nothing.

"Go on," said the paladin, thankful to the ranger for easing the tension of the moment.

"Well," said the ranger as he collected his thoughts, "first we let Cyrillis see if she can invoke any memories with the dragon, thereby distracting it." He pointed at the barbarian. "While she's busy doing that, you go in swinging." Vorgath's glowering eased somewhat. "Meanwhile, Savin does his thing and attempts to get behind her." He sat back in his chair, obviously pretty proud of his plan as well. "After you get her attention, Thrinndor and I will go in to do what damage we can from both sides at once."

Thrinndor nodded as he looked for holes in the plan. "Sordaak can work from a distance to do what damage he may. Meanwhile the cleric is left to focus her healing on the three of us." He stroked his chin as he looked over at his friend.

Vorgath nodded slowly, as well. This was more like it.

Seeing an opportunity, the paladin again pushed his earlier suggestion. "However, if you are going to go in and be the chew toy, you should do so with maximum protection."

The paladin held his breath. Before the dwarf could say anything, however, the ranger said, "Agreed."

It was the push the barbarian needed. He nodded as he leaned forward to put his ham-like fists on the table. "I like it. Very well, I'll dig through my bag and see if I can find the armbands and gauntlets that go with this breastplate." His face turned reflective. "I don't think I threw them away." He smiled mischievously.

"I've got your covered in the event you can't find them," said the ranger. "I have an extra set."

"Thanks just the same," replied the dwarf with a shake of his head, "but—no offense intended—any armguards that fit those skinny arms"—he pointed at the well-formed biceps of the ranger—"won't be near big enough for these massive babies!" He flexed his arms and patted the muscles there for emphasis.

"They are enchanted," the ranger said smugly. "They would fit even a giant."

"Why didn't you say so in the first place?" Vorgath asked.

"I wasn't given the opportunity!" the ranger snapped.

Sordaak came into the conversation unnoticed. He tossed the journal onto the table between the three seated there, drawing their eyes to him.

"Nothing in there I can find of any use," the caster said. "Although I recommend another set of eyes verify that." He flopped into a chair next to the barbarian and poured himself a flagon of ale.

The mage lifted the cup to his lips and took a healthy swig. He screwed up his face in distaste, turned and spoke over his shoulder. "It would be better if it were cold!" he said.

Breunne lifted a brow in his best Thrinndor fashion and said, "Who are you talking to?"

"Whoever it was that provided this food and drink," replied the caster, somewhat irritated.

"What?" asked the paladin.

Sordaak rolled his eyes. "It was one of the things I meant to bring up earlier," he said. "Someone—or something—put this repast out for us. Fresh." He looked around, searching yet again for another door, and again finding none. He locked eyes with the paladin across from him. "Not only that, but I am fairly certain those eggs were not here last evening."

"What?" cried the paladin. "Are you sure?"

"No!" barked the caster. "I'm sure of nothing!" He surged to his feet, knocking his chair over. "However, something is certainly going on here! I have yet to be able figure out just what that something is, though!" He scowled at the kitchen area, not knowing what it was that made him so irritable.

Thrinndor glanced quickly at the table where the rogue and cleric were working. Sure enough, they were looking this way, too. Damn! He looked over at the caster, who was now pacing.

"What is wrong with you?" asked an exasperated paladin.

"I don't know!" the mage snarled. "If I did, I probably wouldn't be so antsy." He went back to pacing.

When Savinhand and Cyrillis came slowly walking up to join the group, Sordaak looked at them and muttered. "Sorry, I didn't mean to disturb you."

"It's all right," replied the thief. "We were getting nowhere on our own." As he approached the paladin he whispered, "What's up with him?"

"I'm not deaf!" snapped the caster.

"I am not certain," Thrinndor said, also whispering. "He has been like this since he gave up on your journal."

Sordaak spun and jabbed a finger at the paladin. "I didn't give up!" said the sorcerer, his voice almost a shout. Suddenly the magicuser realized how he was acting and he fell into a chair. He leaned forward, put his elbows on the table and his face in his hands. "I'm sorry," he mumbled again.

The remaining companions looked around at one another. A couple of them shrugged and rolled their eyes. Vorgath circled his ear with a finger in the universal sign telling what he though of the spellcaster's antics.

Cyrillis looked at the mage, her concern apparent on her face. She was about to say something when Sordaak looked up and said, "Did you guys get anywhere?"

The healer looked at Savin, who shrugged. She turned back to the caster. "No," she said demurely. "Neither of us could remember anything that might be of use here." When the mage again put his head in his hands, she added, "I am sorry."

"No," came the muffled reply, "it's not that." Sordaak looked up, his face twisted. "Hell, I don't know what it is!" He looked around, his face now haunted. "Doesn't anyone but me wonder how we're going to get out of here?" His words came in a rush.

"Excuse me?" said the paladin. "We will be going out through those doors." He pointed at the double doors.

"Oh," the caster said sarcastically, "those doors we can't figure out how to open?" His irritation grew visibly. "Those doors?" He pointed at the offending portals." The only doors into or out of this place?" He was almost shouting when he finished the sentence.

His companions again looked at one another. "Ah," said the paladin, relieved, "so that is it!" He got nods from the others.

"What?" asked the sorcerer as he looked from one to another of his companions. "What are you talking about?"

Thrinndor hesitated and then pushed ahead. "Do you feel trapped?" His eyes never left those of Sordaak.

"No!" snapped the mage. Realization dawned on him in a rush. "Yes," he said, much calmer now. "Claustrophobia. Of course!" He stood and looked at the doors. "We've got to get out of here!"

"We will!" Cyrillis said soothingly. "I have no doubt we will find the way soon."

Sordaak's irritation lessened noticeably. He found he was able to master his fears now that he knew what they were. "Perhaps we should all sit down at the table and compare notes."

"Sounds like a reasonable next step," Thrinndor agreed. He breathed a sigh of relief to see his friend back on a semi-even keel. Especially a sorcerer friend—those guys could get crazy!

The companions made their way back to their seats around the main table and sat. Silence held the moment as each looked around uncomfortably.

"OK," said the spellcaster, "I'm over that, for now." He made eye contact with each of his companions. "So let's figure out how to get out of this place before I have another episode."

Suddenly everyone was talking at once.

Thrinndor held up his hands for silence. "While you guys were working in your separate groups Vorgath, Breunne and I worked on a plan for what comes once we get the doors open." He had everyone's attention. "We used the tried and true method of first determine what needs to be done, and then we each came up with a solution or solutions."

"Perhaps we could use that approach for the doors," Cyrillis said.

"I believe that to be a good idea." Thrinndor smiled at the cleric.

"Great," said the rogue. "Should I write this down?"

"Not necessary," replied the paladin, ignoring Savin's sarcasm. "We will not have long lists." He straightened in his chair. "First we will discuss what we know. I will start by stating the obvious. We have a set of double doors that we know through which we must pass." He looked around the group. "What else do we know?"

"We know they will not open by normal means," said the cleric.

"Very good," said the paladin, eliciting a smile from the healer. "Anyone else?"

The table was quiet for a moment. Finally Savinhand said, "There are not any of the usual things associated with doors: handles, hinges or locks." He shrugged and smiled.

"They are between us and where we need to be," Vorgath growled.

Thrinndor rolled his eyes but said nothing. He was glad to have any input from his friend at this point.

"We know we haven't actually tried to open them yet," said the ranger, warming up to the process.

Taken aback by the comment, the paladin realized Breunne was correct. They had not tried the doors.

"Should we?" asked the caster.

"Why not?" said the barbarian as he pushed himself to his feet. "Anything's better than sitting around talking about it!"

"Wait!" said the paladin as he, too, got to his feet and joined the dwarf at the doors. "Perhaps we should let our trapsmith take a look at them first."

"Already did," Savinhand said, coming up behind the two standing at the doors. "No traps, no keyhole, no lock and no operating mechanism."

"And no way to get a hand-hold on them," griped the barbarian as he got closer to the doors. "They might as well be a wall!"

An idea struck Thrinndor. "Sordaak," he said, "what about your spell for opening doors?"

The caster scratched his head idly and stood to go inspect the doors. "I don't know," he said. "Theoretically it should be possible."

"I doubt that will work," said the thief. "Certainly those that built this place would have thought to ward against such an attempt."

"We will not know unless we try," answered the paladin.

"Right," said the sorcerer as he loosened the tie that held his spell component bag at his side. "The energy used for that spell is minimal." Once free, he shook out the required items, retied the bag and set his feet for the spell.

The companions stepped back to give the caster room, and a hush fell over group.

Sordaak closed his eyes and held first one hand out—the one with the components—and then the second as he began to chant softly. When nothing happened, his voice deepened and got louder as he strained against the doors.

Still nothing happened. A bead of sweat broke out on the mage's forehead, and all could see him straining against whatever binds were keeping the doors from opening.

Still nothing. Now Sordaak's hands were shaking. Suddenly his eyes flashed open, allowing all to see the strain he was enduring. He took an involuntary step toward the doors.

Still he did not release the spell. Yet the doors did not show any sign they were being coerced.

Sordaak released his breath in a gasp as he fell to his knees, the spell broken. His breathing came in ragged gasps.

Cyrillis rushed to his side. "Are you injured?" she asked quickly. She could sense no harm; however, he was obviously having difficulty.

"No," he said through clenched teeth. "I'll be fine." He struggled to his feet with the healer's help. He staggered to one side as his eyes once again focused on the doors. "Well," he said, leaning on the cleric, "they're not going to open that way." He shook his head as he stood erect. "What's the next bright idea?"

"This!" shouted the barbarian as he switched weapons to a maul. He sprinted forward and swung a mighty blow at the door on the left.

"Wait!" Savinhand shouted.

He was too late. There was a deafening clang as metal slammed into metal followed by what could only be described as an explosion.

In reflex, everyone in the room clapped hands to ears. Vorgath was launched backward, flying the entire forty or so feet to the wall and crashed into the food shelves there. Bread, casks, meats and shelving flew every which direction as the dwarf hit and then slid to the stone floor, where he did not move.

Cyrillis was the first to recover. She rushed to the barbarian's side to find him alive but unconscious. Her percipience told her he was uninjured, except for his hands, which were burnt where they had held the metal haft of his hammer.

Thank the dwarven constitution, she thought as she applied some healing salve to his hands, shaking her head at the foolhardiness of the barbarian. Knowing he would need those hands soon, she also said a quick prayer of healing. Instantly, his hands looked as good as new.

"Will he live?" asked the paladin, who had come over to check on the situation.

Cyrillis barely heard him through the ringing in her ears. Knowing they all would be afflicted that way, she nodded to answer.

The healer disentangled the dwarf from the shelves that were lying on him and pulled him away from the mess. Vorgath began to groan, and his eyes popped open.

"What in the seven hells happened?" he moaned as he sat up, rubbing the back of his head where a small knot had already formed.

Savinhand was standing over him by this point. "I tried to warn you," he said, "but you were way past warning." He shook his head. "Those doors are warded! There is no way to muscle your way through them—even a giant wouldn't be able break through."

Vorgath's eyes fixed on the rogue. "You didn't think that would've been good information before I tried to beat them down!"

"I tried!" Savinhand shot back.

"Try harder!" griped the barbarian as he climbed to his feet. He spotted a cask of ale that had shattered, spilling its contents in a widening puddle on the floor. "Oh no!" he said as he lurched toward the mess.

"Damn," muttered the healer. She looked up at the paladin. "Yes, he will be fine!" She shook her head as he helped her to her feet.

"All right," said the party leader as he, too, shook his head. "What is left? Have we exhausted all possibilities?" He got mute stares from everyone except the dwarf; he was still in mourning over the spilt ale.

Savinhand walked over to the doors. "We need the password or passphrase."

The paladin was starting to get concerned but dared not show it. These doors were the only way out of here. At least they had food and drink for a long stay.

"All right," said the paladin, "we can approach that the same way."

"What?" Savin said, turning to look at his leader. The ringing in his ears had subsided somewhat, but he wanted to make sure he had heard correctly.

"We can use the same approach and discuss what we know—or think—about what the password should be related to." Thrinndor was thinking out loud and knew that probably sounded hokey.

Sordaak shrugged. "What else do we have?" When no one said anything, he added, "Then let's get on with it."

Slowly the party reassembled at the table. Most were dragging their feet because they feared what it meant to fail at this point.

Vorgath was still shaking his head to clear the ringing in his ears, hence the flagon of ale in his left hand. "For medicinal purposes," he said when he got a questioning look from the healer.

"Whatever!" she muttered as she took her seat.

Savinhand led off the discussion. "I've already tried anything I can think of related to either the Library and/or the Guild—and all combinations thereof."

"I have tried name combinations with both Phinskyr and Ytharra," Cyrillis said, her tone indicating it was all she had.

The group again fell silent. The futility of the situation was weighing heavily in the air.

"We've got to be missing something!" Sordaak's agitation was returning. He fought to keep it under control. "We would not have been sent here and made it this far without the required knowledge of how to complete the task!" Talking seemed to calm him somewhat.

The sorcerer stood and resumed pacing. The rest of the group watched. He looked up and faced the cleric and the rogue. "There must be something he told one of you, possibly something obscure. He was a guardian! He lived hundreds of years to pass along information to each of you. He would not have died without passing this tidbit. Think!" The mage almost shouted the last word, causing Cyrillis and Savin to jump slightly.

The thief was irritated, and he let it show. "I have done little else since I became aware I was to be the next curator!" His face was shading toward red. "Do not assume I have not!" He raised his voice to match that of the caster.

"All I'm saying," Sordaak said, lowering his voice slightly, "is that one of you two has the required word—or words—in your head!" He glared at both. "You just have to figure out when and where he gave it to you and apply it!" Again the mage's voice rose as he spoke and was now even louder than before.

"Listen," the rogue leader stood as he spoke, his voice matching that of the caster, "I have racked my brain from one end to the other and back again!" He was seething. "If it's there, I don't know how to find it!" He waved his hands in frustration and was now shouting at the caster.

Sordaak did not back down. Instead, he put both hands on the table and jutted his face close enough to the rogue that Savin could smell what the mage ate for breakfast. "I don't care!" He spat each word. "Do it again!"

Savinhand also didn't back down. His face got even redder as he put his face to within inches of the magicuser. "You have no idea what you are talking about," he shouted. "I've known that old man for more than ten years!" He was certain he was spitting on the caster but didn't care. "We had conversations that went on for days! And I have played them back in my head, over and over again." He matched stares with his friend. "It's not there!"

Thrinndor cleared his throat uneasily. "Gentlemen," he began.

"What?" both Savin and Sordaak shouted at once as they turned to face this interruption.

Nonplussed, the paladin continued. "You must calm yourselves," he said. "Fighting will not get us the answer."

"But it will certainly make me feel better," said the rogue through clenched teeth.

"Me, too," agreed the sorcerer.

"Stop it!" shouted the cleric. Everyone at the table turned to face her. Something in her tone got their attention, even more than her raised voice.

"You have something to say?" Sordaak said.

"Yes," she said, her voice now barely above a whisper. She got to her feet and walked over to face the doors. She bowed her head, and Thrinndor thought he saw a tear course its way down her cheek.

"Melundiir," she whispered without raising her head.

A loud boom could be heard deep beneath their feet, and the doors began to inch open.

Chapter Twenty-Nine

Conflict of Interest

"Shit!" Sordaak leapt from his chair, grabbed his pack and shouldered it in one motion.

"Battle formation, now!" shouted the paladin, knocking his chair against the wall as he launched into action.

The fighters frantically threw on discarded armor pieces, hastily drew weapons and moved to stand before the doors. It was a good thing they were so slow in opening.

The magicuser finished tying his robe at his neck as he got into position behind the gathering fighter types. "Have you known that name all along?" he hissed. "Or did you just remember it?"

Cyrillis spun and glared at the caster until he cringed. "I did not even remember that I knew her name until just then!" She ground out each word.

"Dreadfully sorry!" the mage said, sarcasm edging his voice.

Thrinndor craned around so he could view both of them at once. "Knock it off!" His eyes flashed. "Prepare yourselves."

Savinhand leaned over toward the cleric. "Nicely done," he said. "However, do you think it would have been too much to ask to have given us a little warning?" He tried to keep his tone light.

Cyrillis turned her glare on the rogue but said nothing.

By now the doors were open far enough to see into what was beyond. Not that that helped much. Unlike the room they were in, the way ahead was dark.

"Sordaak," said the paladin, not taking his eyes off of the darkness, "how many charges do you have in that light grenade wand?"

"Plenty," said the caster. "I even have a backup, should it become necessary."

"Good," Thrinndor said. "When I ask for light, give me one at maximum distance. We will see what that shows and decide at that time whether more are indicated."

"Got it," replied the caster.

The doors stopped moving once they were slightly past full open.

"Savinhand," continued the paladin, "I am going to step into the chamber first. That will outline me for anyone or anything watching the doorway. Once I am inside, do your thing and see if you can find out what we are facing."

"Understood," the thief responded. He then stepped over and stood next to the door on the left and hunched over, making himself as small as he could.

"Boss man," said the caster. "Would you like me to send Fahlred in for a look-see?"

"Good idea," replied the paladin. "Make it so."

The sorcerer rolled his eyes. Must the big oaf be so formal all the time? He called his familiar to him and communicated what he wanted done. But before he was finished, the room in front of them suddenly became brilliantly lit.

And brilliant described more than the room. Once the companions' eyes adjusted to the light, they were able to see mounds of coins, piles of gems, weapons, jewelry, various pieces of armor and much, much more—all in a room that dwarfed anything they had encountered so far. As far as the eye could see, they saw treasure!

However, closer to the party they saw the figure of a woman, and she was walking toward them!

"Welcome," the woman said in a melodious voice, one that sounded like it should be accompanied by chimes.

"Hold your positions," Thrinndor hissed as quietly as he could and still hope to be heard.

As the woman drew closer they could see that she was beautiful! She was resplendent in a flowing green gown that flattered her mature figure. She appeared to be of an indeterminate age, and yet somehow she conveyed an enormous wisdom by merely walking.

"I trust you have enjoyed your stay." Somehow she made her words not seem like a question.

Finding his voice at last, the paladin said, "It was you that provided us comfort and food?"

She nodded gracefully as she got closer. "Of course."

Thrinndor, unsure as to what to do, bowed deeply at the waist. "Then we are most certainly in your debt." He rose back to his full height and allowed his guard to drop. "Your courtesy and kindness gave us succor in a time of need. Thank you, my lady." He again bowed deeply.

"The pleasure was mine to give." She nodded her head slightly, acknowledging the bow. She stopped walking about twenty feet from the paladin and appeared to be waiting. "It was the least I could do for those who have come so far to slay me."

Thrinndor again stood to his full height as a stunned silence gripped the companions.

"A pity such a fine troupe will be sent to the afterlife with empty hands and failure on their hearts." She shook her head slowly in what appeared to be true sorrow.

"Melundiir?" Cyrillis asked hesitantly as she moved to stand beside the paladin.

"Cyrillis?" the woman said. The musical notes in her voice shifted subtly to alarm and then to sorrow. "I had always known we would again meet, and it is with true regret that it must be in this way." She again shook her head slowly. "Step forward, my dear, so that I may refresh my memory of you."

The cleric took a step forward. Thrinndor attempted to grab her arm, but Cyrillis shook him off and took another step. And then another.

"Is it really you, Melundiir?" Doubt clouded the healer's voice.

"It is," replied the woman.

Abruptly Cyrillis broke into a run and threw her arms around the neck of the woman and hugged her tightly. The companions could hear her sobbing.

After a few moments of this, the woman gently pushed the cleric back. "There, there my dear, it is good to see you, as well. You have grown to be such a beautiful young woman. And I can see that Ytharra has indeed taught you well."

Cyrillis took a halting step back. "I know I was but a girl," she stammered, "but this is not how I remember you."

"I know." The woman looked on the healer with deep regret burning in her eyes. A tear made an appearance and wound its way down her cheek. "Perhaps this will be closer to what you recall."

As she stopped speaking her form began to change. Slowly at first, then with ever increasing speed, her face took on a reptilian look and she began to grow.

"Damn," Thrinndor muttered. "Spread out! Sordaak, resistance to poison all around. Hurry!"

"I can't," the mage whispered back. "That's a clerical spell."

"Shit!" spat the paladin.

"Wait!" hissed the caster as his hand dove beneath his robe. When it emerged, he was holding a crooked-looking wand. "I have this," he whispered. "It won't be as effective as her spell, but it should help."

"It will have to do!" agreed the paladin as he watched the woman continue her transformation into a dragon. A huge dragon!

"No, Melundiir!" Cyrillis moaned. "They are going to kill you!"

"No," the dragon responded, her voice much deeper now, "you all are going to try to kill me." She emitted an evil laugh as she grew ever larger. "Now be a good little cleric and go help your puny friends." More laughter. "They are going to need it."

The cleric did not move, instead standing her ground. "It does not have to be this way," she said, now having to crane her neck back to look into the face of her once friend. "You can leave and you will yet live. Certainly you must know that Ytharra sent us, and Savinhand is destined to become curator of the Library!"

"It doesn't work that way," replied the dragon as she continued to grow.

Cyrillis was certain she could see a tear in her friend's eye.

"Any that walk through that door must perish," the dragon continued, "or I myself must be slain." The dragon shook her head. "There is no other way!"

"There is always another way," the cleric argued stubbornly.

"No," the dragon's eyes flashed. "Return to your people or I will slay you where you stand!"

Melundiir, now at full size, roared an ugly roar that hurt the cleric's ears. Then she spread and beat her wings. The resulting wind buffeted the cleric until she was forced to retreat. Cyrillis put her hands up to protect her face from the debris that came with the wind.

The cleric stumbled as she took the last couple of steps back. Thrinndor caught her arm or she would have fallen. "Take your place," he said sternly, not taking his eyes off of the dragon.

"We must not," the healer said, her eyes moist with tears.

"We now have no choice," replied the paladin, his tone iron. "There is no other way out of here, except through the Library." He paused as he released her arm and reaffirmed his grip on his shield. "Now, take your place."

Thrinndor was deeply concerned that his healer would not perform her duties as required. When she did not move, he shouted, "Cyrillis!" The shout forced her to look at him. "Remember why we are here!" Still she gave him a blank stare. "Valdaar!" He shouted as the buffeting from the dragon's wings increased. "We are here to gain information to return our lord to us!" He shook her for good measure.

Cyrillis blinked and said, "But—"

"No!" shouted the paladin as he jutted his face close to hers. "There are no buts!" He shook her again and pressed his face closer. "Now get to your position." He pushed her that direction, hoping that necessity would bring her back to them. He had no time to discuss the matter further. The dragon was advancing.

"Vorgath," he shouted above the wind beating at his face. "Go!"

Vorgath screamed his battle cry, raised his axe and charged in swinging. At the same time, Breunne loosed a volley of arrows specially selected for this purpose. He had gotten them from a vendor who claimed they had special powers against dragons. Whether true or not, he'd probably never know, but when the arrows struck true in the chest of the dragon, she leapt into the air, her wings creating a windstorm in the chamber.

Thrinndor fought the wind as he, too, charged in, both his sword and shield held high against attack.

The barbarian got to the dragon just as she went airborne, cursing at the top of his lungs as he swung Flinthgoor in a mighty arc that clanged harmlessly off of the scales on the underbelly of the monstrous beast.

Vorgath screamed in rage as he reared back and flung his axe at the retreating dragon. "Get back here, you coward!"

To no avail. The dragon gained height and banked as she fled off toward the other end of the chamber. His aim was off, and the barbarian had to scramble about fifty feet to retrieve his weapon.

Breunne loosed another volley—his third—after her, unsure whether this last grouping hit the monster. He was certain his previous six arrows had found their mark, but he remained unsure just how much damage he had managed to do.

Vorgath came stumping up to the paladin thoroughly disgusted by the recent turn of events. Before he could say anything the paladin said, "She will return." Thrinndor's eyes tried to find the dragon, but he had lost her. "She must. Either we must die, or she. There are no other options." He looked at his friend to see what effect his words had.

Still held by his rage, Vorgath appeared to not have heard any of it. His eyes were fixed on the opposite end of the room and his jaw worked silently

Savin appeared out of nowhere. "I'm thinking she wants us to follow her."

"Precisely why we will remain here," said the paladin. "I do not want to get caught out in the open floor." He turned to find the cleric. "This will also give us time to better prepare." His eyes strayed back to the open area. "We must not assume she will tarry long."

As the companions gathered once again, Thrinndor turned to their cleric. She had not moved and stared blankly after the vanished dragon. "Cyrillis," the paladin said, trying to get her attention. Nothing. "CYRILLIS!" He shook his head and turned to the mage. "You talk to her; you seem to have some sway over her." Thrinndor turned to talk to the other fighters.

"Why me?" Sordaak griped. But he knew the answer. "Cyrillis," he said, snapping his fingers in front of her eyes. Nothing. He put his mouth closer to her ear. "Cyrillis!" Still nothing. He got in front of her, gripped her shoulders and again shouted, "CYRILLIS! Snap out of it!" She continued to stare ahead. "Damn," he muttered. Gripping her shoulders tightly, he suddenly leaned forward and kissed her full on the mouth.

Abruptly her eyes focused on those of the caster. She threw back her hand, pushed herself away and slapped him with all her might. The force of her blow knocked Sordaak back a couple of steps.

"Ow!" he said, rubbing his stinging cheek with his right hand. "What the hell was that for?"

"Why did you kiss me?"

"Why did you hit me?"

"Why did you kiss me?"

Sordaak continued to rub his cheek. "You had checked out on us, and it was all I could think of." After a brief moment of thought he added quickly, "To bring you back, I mean."

"Well," she said, confusion blocking her normal train of thought, "I will thank you to keep you lips to yourself."

"You've got it, sister," replied the sorcerer as turned to address the paladin. "Next time you snap her out of it." He was still rubbing his cheek as he stepped past the fighters, mumbling.

The discussion was interrupted by the screech of the dragon in the distance.

"She will return soon," said the party leader as he stared to where the dragon had disappeared. "We should take the time to better prepare."

"Too late!" The next dragon scream came from high over their heads. They all looked up to see the dragon diving on them. The companions scattered as the dragon opened her tooth-laden maw to spew forth a green vapor that quickly engulfed the party.

"Cyrillis!" Thrinndor shouted as he dove to the ground and rolled to gain separation, "Poison Neutralization, now!"

The healer coughed as she covered her mouth with a rag. "On it," she said as she cast the requisite spell on each of them, starting with herself. She would be of no use if poisoned.

"Spread out," commanded the paladin. "Try to surround her when she comes down. Sordaak, see if you can bring her to us."

The barbarian, recovered from his rage, scanned the chamber. "Without her breath weapon, she's nothing but a big bag of flying teeth and claws." He slapped the haft of his axe for emphasis.

"Wrong again, midget!" The dragon swooped down from above and clamped her claws onto the shoulders of the dwarf and beat her wings hard to lift him high off of the stone floor.

"Let me go, you big windbag!" shouted the dwarf as his friends receded from view.

"As you wish, o diminutive one!" the dragon said with an evil laugh.

"Shit!" said the dwarf. "Not now!"

The dragon banked hard and flung the dwarf back in the direction of his companions. As she released him, Melundiir said an elfish word, again laughing as she did.

Vorgath landed hard on the backside of one of the mounds of coins, which cushioned his fall somewhat. He was adept in tumbling and knew how to best protect himself from long falls.

Still, he hit the coins hard with a splash and rolled down the backside of the mound. He lost his wind upon impact and became disoriented.

Thrinndor, who saw the whole episode, rushed to his friend's side, Cyrillis and Breunne right behind him.

"Are you alright?" the paladin said as he skidded to a halt amid a flurry of coins.

Vorgath jumped to his feet with a crazed look in his eye. He searched around and found his greataxe, which he had lost during his roll down the mound. He took the two steps necessary to get to it, picked it up and swung the massive head of the axe around in an arc intended to decapitate the paladin.

Thrinndor had hung back a step, wondering just what was going on with his friend, which probably saved his life. He had enough warning to get his shield up and duck at the same time. This action deflected the flashing blade harmlessly over his head.

"What the—?" He didn't have time to complete the thought as the dwarf spun around and again brought his weapon back into play for another attack on the paladin.

"Shit!" screamed the paladin as he dove hard and to his right to avoid the blade of the barbarian. "VORGATH!" he shouted as he rolled to his feet only to again have to use his shield to deflect Flinthgoor away from his neck. He didn't know why, but he could hear the dragon laughing loudly as she approached for another round. The paladin didn't have time to worry about the dragon, however, because his best friend was busy trying to kill him.

The ranger also heard the dragon coming and tore his eyes away from the scene playing out before him to confront the monster. Instead of trying to release several arrows in a volley, Breunne elected to take his time and make each arrow count. He aimed for the head.

"Sordaak!" shouted the paladin as he again barely countered a slicing blow from the barbarian, this time with the blade of his sword. "Vorgath is under a spell. Can you remove it?" He ducked under the dwarf's axe and rolled hard several times to put some distance between him and the raging lunatic.

"I can try," said the caster. "Depends on what rank that damn dragon cast her spell at."

Flinthgoor kicked up coins as its head buried itself into a mound next to the paladin, a narrow miss. "HURRY!" bellowed Thrinndor as he again rolled hard to his right.

The sorcerer mumbled the words to a spell, pointed an index finger at the barbarian, who was poised to strike again at the paladin, and spoke the word of release.

Vorgath hesitated and then turned to look around, obviously confused. Thrinndor was on one knee, his sword and shield held high to ward himself from the next blow. "What the hell is going on?" the barbarian said.

"The dragon had you under her spell," said the paladin as he climbed back to his feet.

"You mean..." the barbarian rumbled deep from within his chest. Angrily he turned to locate his adversary.

"Hey guys!" shouted the ranger. "If you are done with social hour, I could use some help over here!" Breunne had succeeded in getting the attention of the dragon when one of his arrows had entered the beast's open mouth and penetrated deep into the soft tissue of her upper jaw.

The dragon screamed and dove hard at the ranger. Only spinning hard to his left at the last possible second kept Breunne from being crushed under the massive weight of the monster as she crashed hard into a pile of coins where he had been.

The ranger rolled back to his feet, sword in hand, as the dragon again opened her massive jaws and blew another cloud of green noxious gas at the offending human.

Melundiir leapt suddenly at the ranger, who this time was too slow to dodge. The massive talons on her front legs raked across his back as he twisted out of the dragon's grasp. He howled in pain as he twirled, slashing with his sword as he did.

The ranger's blade bit deep into the lightly scaled skin just above the dragon's right front paw.

That's when he asked for help, the paladin and barbarian quickly responding. Sordaak pointed a finger and released a bolt of lightning that hit the dragon in the back of the head. He knew the creature had resistance to most magic and would probably brush aside some of the spell's energy, but not all of it.

The bolt must have done more damage than he thought, because the dragon howled in rage and/or pain and spun to seek out this new adversary. Instantly, she also released a bolt of lightning, hitting the surprised caster square in the chest and knocking him to the ground.

Cyrillis heard Breunne's cry for help and quickly rushed to his side and didn't see the caster go down. While the ranger's injury was surely painful, it was mostly superficial and required minimal care.

Breunne thanked her as he returned to the fray. Thrinndor and Vorgath had taken the opportunity of the dragon being distracted by the mage to hammer at her from an unprotected flank. Both the barbarian's greataxe and the paladin's flaming bastard sword bit deep into her right side just under her wing.

Unbelievably quick for a creature of that size, the dragon whirled and with her injured right paw knocked Thrinndor to the ground. Her swing just missed the barbarian as that same paw passed harmlessly over his head.

Savinhand, silent to this point because the fast-moving dragon evaded him on every occasion he had attempted, finally was able to join in. He jumped unseen onto the back of the monster, his vorpal sword in his right hand and a specially enchanted dagger in his left.

The rogue's quick eyes scanned for a separation in the dragon's scales. Finding only one such as she flexed to slap aside the paladin, the rogue plunged both weapons to the hilt into the opening.

Melundiir screamed in pain, craning her neck to fix her eyes on this new hurt. Her head lunged at him, with her vast jaws snapping shut where the thief had been only a split-second before.

Savin tumbled as soon as his eyes locked with those of the dragon, knowing she was not going sit idle while he worked his pain on her back. As he regained his feet, his eyes again scanned for a point where he could again deploy his weapons.

While all this occurred within the blink of an eye, it was not quick enough. The dragon flicked her tail, and the barbed end of that tail hit the rogue squarely between the shoulders and sent him sprawling into the coins at the monster's feet.

Having tended to the ranger, Cyrillis turned her attention to the remainder of her companions. She stretched out her percipience. Thrinndor was unharmed as of yet, and Vorgath had minor scratches where the claws of the dragon had picked him up and some scrapes and bruises from when he had come crashing back to the stone floor. Savinhand was yet undamaged as well, she sensed, but that was certainly not going to last. The healer shook her head as she spotted him on the creature's back.

Where was Sordaak? Quickly she scanned the area where she had seen him last. He was not there! The cleric could not find him anywhere! "Sordaak!" she shouted, suddenly worried. No response. She ran in the direction she had last seen him, her heart pounding in her throat.

Sordaak heard her, but for the moment was unable to answer. The force of the dragon's lightning bolt had not only knocked him down, it had taken his wind. His bruised lungs gasped for air, which in turn hurt his bruised chest.

The caster struggled to sit up just as Cyrillis topped a mound of coins and spotted him. "Oh, no!" she exclaimed as she slid to a halt by his side. "How bad?" Her voice shook with concern.

Unable to answer, he accepted her help to rise to a sitting position, shaking his head in an effort to clear the cobwebs. The healer hesitated only slightly, pouring her most potent healing spell into him through direct contact with both hands.

Instantly, the mage felt better as the cleric's healing energy surged into him. "Thanks," he wheezed through clenched teeth. While the spell restored his flesh and bone, his lungs still craved the oxygen they had been deprived of. "Damn, that hurt!"

Back over where the fighters were struggling, Thrinndor got painfully to his feet just in time to see the rogue go flying by to land with a thud at the base of a pile of gems. A quick glance showed that Vorgath had the dragon's attention and the barbarian was holding his own for the moment.

The paladin ran the few steps to Savin's side to see that two of the barbs from the dragon's tail were lodged in the thief's back. He moaned as he struggled to rise.

"Hold," the paladin said sternly. The rogue stiffened but moved no further. As the fighter grabbed one of the barbs, he said, "This might sting a little." He yanked first one and then the other barb free of the thief's back. Savin gritted his teeth against the pain but did not cry out. Thrinndor closed his eyes and sent one of his inherent healing energy uses—he could do this twice a day, now—into the sitting rogue.

In seconds, the wounds stopped bleeding and the skin knitted together. Savinhand rolled over and opened his eyes, no longer tainted with pain. "Thank you," he said as he climbed shakily to his feet.

The paladin also stood, retrieving his sword and shield as he did.

Vorgath was no longer giving as good as he got. The dragon overpowered him by sheer size and strength. She pressed her advantage, continually forcing the barbarian to retreat. Now they were separated from the rest of the companions by more than fifty feet.

The dwarf slashed left, right, high and low with Flinthgoor, but the dragon was able to dodge or parry all but a few of the attacks. Vorgath had not been so fortunate. He bled from several open wounds, including one deep gash on his forehead that threatened to blind him as the blood ran into his eyes.

Thrinndor tilted his shield and released the one bolt from his crossbow, hoping to distract the creature.

The dragon showed no sign of even noticing as the bolt glanced harmlessly off the shielding on her back. Instead she lashed out with both of her front claws at once at the puny creature crouching before her.

The barbarian was only able to block one, although in doing so his greataxe cut deep into one of the monster's forearms. The other paw raked the dwarf along his left thigh and side. The talons gouged deep, and the force of the blow knocked Vorgath several feet to the right where he collapsed in a heap.

While the wounds were not mortal, the combined damage and loss of blood were slowing the proud barbarian. Still he struggled to his feet, leaning heavily on Flinthgoor.

The dragon, sensing victory with this particular pain in her side, coiled her muscles for the attack that would finish him.

Sordaak pointed his finger and launched a ball of fire at the back of the dragon's head. The ball exploded right on target, causing the monster to flinch, just as two arrows from the ranger struck her in the neck, penetrating some unseen niche in her scales.

Melundiir screamed as her head jutted skyward. She turned her massive bulk and spread her wings just as Breunne, who had joined the paladin and rogue, let loose with another volley. The wind generated by the dragon's enormous wings caused the arrows to fly off track and they passed harmlessly over her head. Another gust buffeted the paladin and ranger, knocking them back a few steps. The fighters had to cover up as coins were picked up by the merciless blasts, becoming flying debris that hurt when they hit. Savinhand had again vanished.

Deciding defensive spells might help his side the most, the sorcerer waved his arms and conjured up a cloud to obscure—and, he hoped, slow down—the dragon.

Unfortunately for the companions, Sordaak didn't take into account the wind factor of the wings. The fog spell came into being around the dragon but quickly got blown into the faces of the ranger and paladin.

Cyrillis, sensing the barbarian was out of range and in serious trouble, took a circuitous path around the dragon to get to him.

Vorgath saw the dragon turn aside, and he stumbled into action. He knew his time was running out, but he wanted to do what damage he could before succumbing to his injuries. Avoiding the flapping wings, he got behind the monster and wound up his axe for one final blow.

As the barbarian started his swing, Cyrillis got within range and cast her most powerful healing spell at him, infusing him with additional energy. His blade whipped through the air and cut completely through the dragon's tail, severing it just a few feet from where it extended from the body, leaving only a stub.

A horrendous scream ripped the air as Melundiir spun and with a wing knocked the barbarian onto his back. She pounced on him and tried to bring her rear claws to bear when the paladin jabbed his flaming sword through a gap in the scales on the beast's thigh, shoving it in until the hand-guard stopped. He jerked it free as the dragon screamed again and whirled to face this new threat. Her movements are slowing, the paladin thought.

Sordaak launched yet another ball of fire, accurately hitting the monster in the mouth as she opened it to strike at the paladin. The explosion jolted the dragon, and her eyes lost focus as she thrashed about, knocking the paladin from his feet.

Breunne continued to pour arrows into any opening he saw as fast as he could reload. He was now sure his constant peppering was beginning to have an effect. He was out of the special dragon arrows, but he had plenty made by his own hand that were specially crafted to cause additional damage.

Cyrillis reached the barbarian's side and immediately assessed that he was badly hurt. He was bleeding from several serious gashes, and his eyes were glazed over. Instantly she poured her healing energy into the dwarf and watched as her magic did as directed. Wounds closed, bleeding stopped, and color came back into his cheeks. The healer could see he still bled from several places, and she suspected internal damage as well, so she released another spell into the prone dwarf for good measure.

Now his wounds were all closed and his breathing had eased, but his skin still had no luster. He had lost a lot of blood. She could hear the dragon fighting behind her and suspected the barbarian would be needed by the companions, so she closed her eyes and cast a restorative spell on him.

The barbarian's eyes fluttered briefly, and he smiled at her. "Thank you," he said as he pushed himself back to his feet, "but all that wasn't really necessary."

"Why you!" Cyrillis halted as she saw him wink. "Get back in there and finish this!" she said with a smile of her own.

Vorgath startled her when he bellowed one of his raging battle cries and raised his greataxe above his head, charging back into the melee which had shifted twenty or so feet away.

Sordaak was now alternating between balls of fire, cold cones and bolts of lightning, trying to see which did the most damage. It didn't seem to matter, he decided, and thus continued the rotation, content in the knowledge that damage was being done.

Savinhand appeared behind the dragon as he again leapt onto her back. This time he spun and tumbled his way ever higher up between her shoulders. His last jump saw him doing a somersault as he drew his weapons, one for each hand. As he landed, he swung the sword with all his might at the neck of the monster, hoping for a soft spot in her scales.

The point of entry didn't seem to matter. As the blade made contact with the scales, the sword flashed a bright light and began to vibrate in his hand. There was not enough force to push the blade clear through, but it went far enough.

The dragon screamed one last time and collapsed into a pile on the stone floor, her neck nearly severed.

Chapter Thirty

The Library of Antiquity

The air in the chamber grew deathly quiet—quiet enough to hear the labored breathing of the companions.

"Well," said the barbarian between gasps as he leaned on Flinthgoor, "that was easy!"

Cyrillis was silent as she approached the dragon and her companions. Only she saw that the sides of her old friend continued to rise and fall weakly. She made her way around to the head of the beast and bowed her head.

Thrinndor could see tears flowing down the cleric's cheeks. He held up his hands to silence the companions and signaled for them to stop where they stood. As one, they complied.

"Do not weep for me, my dear." The deep, raspy voice came from the head of the dragon.

Vorgath started to raise Flinthgoor for further action, but the paladin stopped him. "Do not!" he whispered sharply.

Cyrillis' head snapped up and she opened her eyes just as the eyes of the dragon fluttered open. "Thank you for releasing me from my life of servitude." The dragon moaned and coughed up some green blood before she was able to continue. "Only one of us was going to be able to walk away from this, and I am glad it is to be you." The beast's eyes again closed, and the healer thought she had passed.

However, they opened once again, but only halfway this time. "Ytharra was a good master," she said, her voice more of a hiss. "He has trained you well, and you have been proper in your selection of companions." More coughing, more green blood. "I pray as I pass that you find that for which you so desperately search." The dragon's eyes closed again.

Cyrillis wiped away tears as the dragon opened her eyes just a slit. "Thank you," she whispered. Her breath left her one final time in a rush as her lungs collapsed.

Cyrillis again bowed her head, and her shoulders shook as she sobbed quietly.

Her companions stirred uncomfortably, none wanting to break the silence. The sorcerer was the only one to move. Sordaak walked up quietly to stand beside the cleric. He reached out and tapped her on the shoulder. The healer looked up with red eyes and threw her arms around the caster's neck and hugged him tightly, her shoulders continued to shake.

Finally, her sobbing subsided and she pushed herself back from the shoulder she had been leaning on. "Thank you," the cleric said, using the palm of her left hand to brush away her tears.

"You are welcome," Sordaak replied with a smile.

Abruptly, Cyrillis' left hand shot out and she gave the magicuser a stinging slap to the face that caused his head to turn. "You kissed me!"

"You needed it!" protested the mage as he rubbed his suddenly red cheek.

"Yeah, well," the healer said as she turned to look at the paladin, "do not do it again." She walked way, her back stiff.

"Yes, ma'am," Sordaak said, his eyes following her as she walked away. "As you wish, your highness!" He too turned and walked stiffly in the opposite direction.

Thrinndor's head bounced back and forth between the two, unsure what he was supposed to do next. He cleared his throat noisily. Both had stopped not far off, but neither turned around. They ignored him.

"Look," the paladin said, "we are near our destination and must move on." Still no reaction. He shrugged as he looked over at his old friend. "How about you, Vorgath? Are you ready to see what awaits us?"

"Of course," replied the barbarian. "Unless you'd like to count our spoils from the dragon first?"

"No," said the paladin. "This chamber can wait." He turned to look down toward the far end. "I must know what awaits us in the Library of Antiquity."

"Very well," said the barbarian. "I suppose I can wait to know how much my additional ten percent will tally up to." He smiled mischievously at his friend as he started walking.

Thrinndor followed a couple of steps behind. "Your ten percent?" he said. "If my count is correct, I have you by three."

"Three? Bah!" spat the dwarf. "My count has me by four!"

Breunne and Savinhand fell in behind them. "Savin," said the dwarf as he turned to look at the rogue, "settle this, please. Who finished ahead in kill count?"

"Let me see," the thief said as he pulled a piece of parchment from behind his sash. "The kill on the dragon goes to whom? Oh, that's right." He smiled. "The dragon kill goes to yours truly."

"You aren't part of the bet," argued the dwarf. "Who won?"

Savinhand made a show of counting, using his fingers as he went. "Ummm," he said hesitantly, "the companion with the most kills is..." He paused for effect. "Breunne!"

"Not fair!" protested the barbarian. "He's not part of this!"

"He asked to be included," replied the paladin.

"Yeah, but his use of ranged weapons makes him ineligible!" Vorgath said. However, even the dwarf didn't sound convinced.

"I didn't protest your throwing of that oversized wood chopper," the ranger said with a smile.

"Very funny," answered the barbarian. But he knew he was fighting uphill on this one. "Damn, I can see I'm going to have to work on my bow use." He shook his head in disgust at the prospect.

Sordaak caught up with them. "What are you guys talking about?" he asked. He looked over his shoulder to see the cleric also following, but at a distance.

"Kill count," Breunne said with a smile.

"Oh, yeah?" the mage said. "Who won?"

"Damn cheating ranger!" griped the barbarian.

"Vorgy is a bit grouchy that Breunne bested him in our little wager," Thrinndor said with a wink.

"Bested you, too," said the dwarf, trying to hide his smile. Good thing I like these guys, he thought. Most dwarfs don't take kindly to being kidded.

The idle banter stopped as the group approached a single door in the wall ahead. The door was not overly large—smaller, in fact, than the ornate double doors they had recently come through—and it appeared to be made of simple wood, although it had several gilded markings on its surface.

The companions stopped a few feet from the door, allowing the cleric to catch up.

Savinhand took a tentative step forward and placed his hand on the operating mechanism. Before he moved it, he turned to face his friends. This was hard.

"Ladies and gentlemen," he said formally, "herein lies the culmination of an arduous journey." He closed his eyes as he gathered himself, and then he opened them again. He spoke slowly, his voice low. "To pass through this door, you must promise here and now not to remove anything from inside."

Vorgath started to protest, but Thrinndor held up his hand to silence him.

When nothing was said, the rogue leader repeated. "Again, in order to enter, you must promise to exit the Library with nothing in your possession that you did not have with you when you entered."

The thief's eyes took on a hard look. "I will first open the door, and then each of you must make that promise to me before being allowed to enter." He paused. "If you cannot make that promise, you will not be permitted inside—you must wait for us here."

Without waiting for a reply, Savinhand turned and opened the door. The silence was broken by a voice. "Hail Savinhand! Leader of Guild Shardmoor! The new Administrator! And now keeper of the secrets of the Library of Antiquity!"

Sordaak looked around briefly for the mouth that made the voice, but not seeing one, he shrugged as he gave up. It did not matter. He was too anxious to get inside the Library.

Thrinndor's lips were a thin line as he stepped up to be first to enter.

"You sure?" Savinhand asked, his eyes locked on those of the paladin.

"Yes," the fighter said. "I have thought of little else since you spoke of the possibility that Valdaar's Fist could be inside these hallowed walls." He lips turned up for a thin smile. "I have come to the conclusion that it cannot be so."

The rogue leader's right eyebrow shot up. "Please explain."

"Phinskyr—Ytharra—was not only the previous administrator," Thrinndor said. "He was a guardian." He paused to let that sink in. "As such, he was bound to keep a bloodline open that would lead to the return of our Lord. He would have also known that returning our Lord would have been impossible without his sword." His smile grew broad. "Therefore the blade cannot be inside."

"Well said," responded the thief. He nodded and then his voice got solemn. "Very well. Do you, Thrinndor, promise that you will not remove anything from within these walls that you did not enter with?"

The smile left the paladin's face. "Yes, I do."

Savinhand stepped aside and motioned for the fighter to enter.

As Thrinndor entered, Sordaak elbowed aside the barbarian, who also tried to step up to be next. "Move over, midget! Let those who actually know how to read get first crack!" He winked at the surprised dwarf.

Vorgath stepped aside and made a show of bowing deep, waving the mage forward. "After you, egghead!"

"Thank you, o diminutive one," the caster said formally as he stepped up to stand before the rogue.

Savinhand smiled at his friend. "Do you, Sordaak, promise that you will not remove anything from within these walls that you did not enter with?"

"I do," answered the caster.

As the mage started to push his way past the rogue, Savinhand stopped him with a raised hand. "Perhaps you should check that special bag of yours here at the door?"

A startled Sordaak started to protest but noticed the big grin on his friend's face. "I don't think so!" The mage returned the grin as he pushed his way inside. He said over his shoulder as he passed, "Remember, I promised, too!"

In like manner, the remainder of the party was admitted to the Library only after the oath was taken.

Savinhand was the last to enter, following Breunne after he had sworn not to remove anything. He got inside to find the rest of the companions gathered around a table in the center of the room.

The Library was really a large study, Savin decided. The room itself was not large—perhaps forty or fifty feet square. There were shelves covering most of the walls with a

few jutting out into the room at semi-regular intervals. All shelves appeared to be laden
with books, tomes and stacks of parchment. There were tables and stands interspersed
all along the walls and some open cabinets in places. Some held more books, others
held the occasional artifact—a sword here, a helm there, some jewelry over on that
table and a staff and scepter leaning against the wall in the far corner.

There was a large fireplace centered in the opposite wall with a cozy fire
burning cheerily within. There were several comfortable-looking chairs in a
semi-circle out in front of the hearth and more weaponry mounted on the wall
above and to the side of it.

Savin walked up on his friends, his footsteps silent on the deep pile carpet that
covered the entire floor, save that immediately in front of the fireplace. "What gives?"

Cyrillis turned to address the rogue. "We are awaiting our turn with the catalogue," she answered. Sordaak was seated at the table, turning the pages on an
immense, ancient-looking tome in the center.

"Not me," said the dwarf as he threw his hands up, weary of standing
around with so much to see all around him. He turned and walked quickly in the
direction of the fireplace and its apparent plethora of weapons.

"How does it work?" asked the paladin. He was standing behind the mage
and looking over his shoulder.

"Good question," said the mage. "From what I can tell, everything appears
to be categorized by type and then in alphabetical order." He hid the fact well
that he was somewhat annoyed with the paladin for being back there.

"Correct," said Shardmoor's leader. "From what I was told, to enter a new
manuscript or artifact, the curator must simply put the information required on
the first page, close the book, and the entry is placed in the proper category, in
the proper order."

"Nice," said the mage, nodding as he turned another page.

"I can see you are going to be a while," Thrinndor said. "I am going to go
see what has the dwarf so excited."

Everyone turned or looked up to see what the paladin was talking about.
Indeed, Vorgath was jumping around excitedly, apparently looking for something.

"May I help you, old one?" Thrinndor asked when he got close.

"No!" blurted the barbarian as he spotted what he was looking for over in
a corner—a ladder. Hurrying over to it, he rolled it into place to allow him to
reach above the fireplace.

An amused paladin stood back and watched with folded arms as his friend
climbed the ladder. He idly wondered which of the weapons the dwarf was so
excited about.

Vorgath climbed past he pole-axe and continued up past the staff that was
hung above it. When he reached out and put a hand on a two-handed broad-
sword, Thrinndor shook his head and said, "Figures."

What he didn't figure was the dwarf underestimating the weight of the sword. When in his exuberance he lifted the sword from the hooks that held it, he lost his balance and teetered precariously on the ladder before toppling over, heading unceremoniously for the floor.

Only proximity and quick action by his friend prevented him from landing hard on the stone floor of the hearth. Thrinndor caught his friend and said, "You should work on your dexterity during your next training session, old one."

"Bah!" spluttered the dwarf. "Put me down!" The paladin did so and ignored his friend as he held up the blade in his hands for closer inspection. "Florashiim." Vorgath breathed the name, his voice reverent.

"Florashiim?" repeated the paladin, craning his neck to get a better look. "You are certain?"

Vorgath gave his friend his best of-course-I-am-sure look, and then went back to studying the sword.

"What's a Florashiim?" asked Breunne as he walked up. He too wanted know what the hubbub was about.

The paladin turned to acknowledge the ranger as he stopped to also peer over the shoulder of the dwarf at the massive sword he held. "Florashiim is the sword of Praxaar," replied the paladin. "It was given to his Paladinhood for safe-keeping should he return to the mortal plane and require its use."

"Praxaar's blade?" Breunne said, trying to get a better look. "Are you sure?"

Vorgath turned the same look on the ranger. This time he chose to elaborate. "Of course I'm sure. The dwarves of Tithgaard forged this blade more than two millennia ago." His eyes went back to the blade. "I would know it anywhere."

"How did it come to be in here, then?" asked the ranger, his curiosity piqued.

"Now there's a good question," replied the dwarf. He looked up at his friends. "Give me room."

As Thrinndor stepped back with the ranger, he said, "If we can get the magicuser away from the catalogue, perhaps the answer will be within its pages." He glanced over at the table to verify that Sordaak was still seated there. He was.

When Vorgath decided his companions had given him enough space, he began to swing the blade, testing its balance. After a couple of slashes, the barbarian stopped to again look in admiration upon the blade.

He then spread his feet wider and began to wield the blade in earnest. The barbarian twirled it over his head, behind his back and with full extension of his massive arms. All the while he stepped, spun and leapt in unison with the blade. When he stopped, he was breathing hard from the exertion. He again held the blade up so he could gaze upon it. "Now this is a sword!"

"May I see it?" asked Thrinndor as he and the ranger stepped back in to surround the dwarf.

Reluctantly Vorgath handed it over. "Be careful with that," he said.

"I will not break it, I assure you," replied the paladin as he took the sword from the dwarf. After a brief inspection he handed it back. "We must check the catalogue." He turned and headed back toward the table.

When Thrinndor got close enough, he said simply, "Get up."

Annoyed, Sordaak merely glanced at him and went back to copying something from the catalogue onto a piece of parchment stacked on the table for the purpose. "I'm not finished."

"Yes, you are." The paladin moved to stand menacingly behind the caster but made no other overt gesture.

The mage bit off a nasty reply as he looked up and saw Vorgath with the sword. Abruptly his tone changed. "Is that Florashiim?"

"Yes," Thrinndor said. He folded his arms across his chest.

"I'm finished," said the caster as he stood and picked up the parchments he had been writing on. "For now." He moved away from the table, allowing the paladin room to sit.

"Thank you," the big fighter said as he sat and began thumbing through the book. Finding the section devoted to weapons and then to swords, he flipped to that page. He turned a few more pages before stopping at a page marked 'Florashiim.'

His finger traced the words written on the page as he read.

"What does it say?" asked the barbarian as Thrinndor got to the bottom of the page.

The paladin looked up, processing what he had just read. "It says," he started slowly, "that the sword was lost when the Praxaar's Paladinhood broke into warring factions following the god's departure from this realm." He looked back down at the page before him. "It passed from leader to leader over the years until the ruling faction was overrun by an army led by paladin's claiming to—get this—be wielding Valdaar's Fist."

"What?" came several voices at once.

"When was that?" The calm in Sordaak's tone belied the turmoil he suddenly felt in the pit of his stomach.

Thrinndor looked again down at the open page to make sure before he spoke. "Four hundred years ago."

"Where?" asked the mage, still unwilling to leave the table.

"It does not say," replied the paladin.

"Valdaar's sword was free in the land a mere four hundred years past?" asked Cyrillis. "Can it be so?"

The paladin looked at the cleric. When he spoke there was an unfamiliar tremble in his voice. "This catalogue only records the events leading to the addition of the artifact in question being inducted into the Library."

A stunned silence fell over the companions.

Finally, the cleric spoke again. "Is there any mention of our Lord's blade in that catalogue?"

Thrinndor turned to stare at the cleric. Without answering, he turned his attention back to the catalogue and began leafing through the pages. Abruptly, he slammed shut the cover. "There is nothing in the weapons section concerning it!" An idea occurred to him suddenly. "Wait," he said as he reopened the book and began scanning the contents page. Next he flipped through to another section and began rifling through the pages. Finally he spread out a page. "Damn!" His finger again traced down the page.

"What?" Cyrillis was unable to contain herself.

Without answering, Thrinndor reached out and pulled the stack of blank parchment papers over to him, removed the quill pen from the ink well that held it and began scribbling on the papers.

"WHAT?"

The paladin finished what he had been writing before looking at her. "There is a tome here titled 'Valdaar's Fist.'" He looked again at the page he held open. "It says here that it is a work in progress—not yet complete."

Thrinndor brusquely shoved back the chair, grasped the parchment on which he had made his notes and began to walk away.

"One last thing," Savinhand said, stopping Thrinndor in his tracks. Annoyed, the paladin waited for what was to come. "It's a good thing. If at some point you find something in a book, tome or other written work that you require a copy of, you have but to call out for a scribe."

Sordaak, who had started away, stopped and raised an eyebrow.

"The scribe will appear," the rogue leader continued, "and you can point out to him or her what it is you require and they will make you an exact copy of it while you continue other searches."

Sordaak nodded. "Nice." He wandered off to find the documents associated with the locations he had written on the parchments in his hand.

"And there are multiple scribes available," Savin continued as he watched the back of the retreating sorcerer.

"Nice," Sordaak repeated as he disappeared behind a bookshelf extending toward them into the middle of the room.

Thrinndor nodded as he also turned and headed toward the section indicated on the scrap of parchment he held.

With reluctance, Vorgath headed back over to the area of the fireplace to return the sword to its rightful spot above the mantle.

Savinhand began to look over the shelves to his immediate left to see just what it was he had inherited.

Breunne and the cleric turned to look at one another, as they were the only two remaining at the table. Cyrillis bit her lip and said, "You first." She feared not finding in the catalogue the information she so desperately needed.

The ranger shrugged. "I have no particular need of any knowledge this library might provide." He smiled. "Thus, I will be glad to help you in the search for your family."

Cyrillis released her lip and lifted her chin. "Thank you," she said with a nervous smile of her own.

"My pleasure," the ranger said. He held the chair for the cleric, indicating she should sit, which she did.

Their search began slowly, as they didn't know what documents might hold the information she needed. As they progressed, they occasionally heard the caster and/or the paladin call for the services of a scribe. One would instantly appear and tend to whoever called.

After a half-hour or so, the cleric and ranger had enough written down to warrant investigation. They decided to split up, agreeing to call the other should they find anything of interest.

In this way the companions passed the next several hours.

Vorgath wandered seemingly aimlessly, touching and handling every weapon he could get his hands on. While there were several that were interesting, none had the attention holding power of Florashiim. Still, he had plenty to keep him busy.

Thrinndor researched any and all scraps of information related to Valdaar's Fist. After he had exhausted that, he joined Breunne and Cyrillis in the search to find from whence the cleric came.

Savinhand at first just wandered aimlessly, stopping only when he found something that interested him. After a bit, he decided to research just how it was that he was supposed to protect this amazing piece of history. Coincidentally he found a tome for that. The tome explained in detail how the Library had been protected over the years. He began to formulate a plan on how he wanted to do so.

Breunne and Cyrillis—and Thrinndor when he joined them—got off to a rough start. While there was a section in the catalogue that was set aside for family trees and heritage, they had no names with which to begin their search. However, by the time the paladin joined them, they had managed to slim it down to a few possibilities. The three of them were able to narrow it further when Breunne made the big breakthrough.

He called for the cleric and paladin after he had double-checked what he had found, not wanting to falsely raise hopes. When Thrinndor and Cyrillis came over, he showed them what he had found.

Amid growing excitement, both the paladin and cleric also double-checked the data.

Finally, Thrinndor locked eyes with the cleric, who was smiling broadly. She nodded and the paladin called out for a scribe.

A female drow elf appeared at his elbow in the blink of an eye, and the three of them described to her what they needed. Without a word the elf nodded and left with the scraps of parchment and a stack of tomes to carry out their instructions.

Thrinndor leaned back in his chair and rubbed his eyes. He decided to go see what the others were up to. He left the cleric and the ranger in quiet conversation as he walked away.

The paladin heard the barbarian before he saw him. He was snoring peacefully in a corner behind a bookshelf. He discovered Sordaak making notes from an enormous document he was holding open with his left forearm as the mage wrote feverishly with his right hand.

"Are you about finished?" asked the paladin as he approached. His appearance startled the mage, and his pen scratched across the parchment he had been writing on when he jumped.

"Don't do that!" hissed the magicuser, his heart pounding.

"Sorry," replied the paladin, trying to hide a smile.

"And no," said the sorcerer continued, his heart rate returning to normal, "I'm not 'about finished'! I'm never going to be finished!" He bent back over the book from which he had been working.

"Explain, please," requested the paladin, not moving.

Sordaak sighed heavily before looking up from his work. "To a sorcerer," he began as if explaining to a child, "knowledge is power." He waved the pen at the shelves all around him. "This place is teeming with knowledge." His eyes bored into those of the paladin. "I am never leaving!" He again bent back over the book and began scribbling on the parchment beside him.

Taken aback, Thrinndor did not move. He was not sure how to answer that. "You know I cannot allow that."

Sordaak closed his eyes and lowered his head as if praying. Without looking up he said, "Yes, I know you cannot allow that." He paused, during which the paladin thought he might be done. "But if you don't go away and leave me alone for the time I do have," he looked up to stare at the paladin, "I'm going to turn you into a toad!"

The two locked eyes and thus began the usual stare down. Finally Thrinndor turned and began to walk away. "Very well, I will come get you when the rest of us are ready to leave."

The sorcerer watched the receding back of the fighter. "Just a warning," he said, seeing his friend's shoulders stiffen. "You will have to drag me out of here kicking and screaming." He turned his attention back to his work and called, "Scribe!"

Thrinndor smiled but did not turn. "So be it."

Unable to find the rogue, he headed back to where he left the cleric and the ranger. They were still talking quietly.

While waiting for them to finish, Savinhand walked up. Seeing him approach, Breunne and Cyrillis halted their conversation.

"If you have reached a stopping point," began the guild leader, "we have accommodations prepared for us just outside the door. The scribes will finish the work requested while we rest."

Thrinndor suddenly realized just how tired he was. First escaping the rest chamber and then fighting and defeating the dragon. Finally, several—how many, it was unclear—hours of research in the library.

The paladin nodded. "Show them. I will go get the barbarian."

Breunne got up and stretched. They had been sitting for quite some time, and his legs were stiff. Cyrillis also stood, steadying herself by holding on to the table as circulation returned to her legs, as well.

Thrinndor walked quietly over to where he left the dwarf. Vorgath was still snoring. The paladin smiled as he decided against waking his friend. Instead, he reached down and grasped the barbarian by his breastplate, lifted his torso and began dragging him back the way he had come.

The barbarian's eyes fluttered open, and he began to wave his arms, unsure what was going on. "Hey!" he shouted. "Put me down!"

"Shhh!" hissed the paladin. Then he whispered intently, "We are in a library!" He didn't let the dwarf go as he continued to head for the door.

"Thank you!" came the disembodied voice of the magicuser from somewhere behind them.

Vorgath shrugged and promptly fell back to sleep, snoring loudly.

Thrinndor smiled and shook his head. Damn barbarian could sleep anywhere, anytime!

"They have prepared accommodations for us outside the library," the paladin called over his shoulder.

"Enjoy!" returned the caster from across the room. "I'll have plenty of time to sleep when I'm dead!"

Thrinndor shook his head as he continued to make his exit. Damn caster would probably remain up the entire night and then some.

The paladin dragged the barbarian through the door out into the open area beyond. Thrinndor looked around and spotted Savinhand waving at him through a previously unnoticed doorway to his right. He turned and headed that direction, Vorgath still in tow and still snoring.

When he got to the door, he passed through into a smallish chamber set up as a common area with a large table, several chairs and many shelves laden with food and supplies. There were also several doors that led out of the chamber at various points along the walls, presumably sleeping quarters. Cyrillis and Breunne were seated at the table, some bread and a flagon of some drink on the table in front of them.

Thrinndor pointed with his free hand at the dwarf and raised an eyebrow.

Savin pointed to the closest door and shrugged. "Any of the open doors will do."

The fighter went through the indicated door. Finding a bunk on the other side, he hefted his friend up and deposited him unceremoniously in it. He flexed his hand and arm as he turned to exit. Damn, that dwarf was heavy! Thrinndor shook his head. On his way back out, he kicked the door shut behind him.

The paladin then headed for a shelf laden with casks. He selected a flagon and poured himself a tall one from the keg already tapped. He then picked up a plate, piled some bread, meats and cheeses on it and turned to join his companions at the table.

As the paladin plopped down into a chair next to the ranger, the door he had so recently closed reopened. "Did I hear someone say food?" the barbarian said from the doorway.

Vorgath rubbed his eyes as he made his way over first to the shelf with the beverages. He essentially followed in the footsteps of the paladin, dropping his bulk instead into the chair next to the cleric.

"You lazy dog!" accused the paladin with a shake of his head.

"Hey," responded the barbarian defensively, "it was you who so rudely interrupted my nap to drag me in here—literally." He smiled at his own play on words. "I told you to put me down!"

The companions were silent for a while as they enjoyed the fresh food and good drink. They got up only to refill their flagons or get something else to eat. After his second such trip, Vorgath bought the cask back to the table.

"I am certain we have a lot to discuss," said the paladin without preamble. "However, may I suggest that we do so only after we have rested?"

"Sounds good to me," responded the ranger with a nod.

"What about the wiggle-finger?" asked the barbarian around a mouthful of bread, crumbs spewing from his mouth all over the table.

"He is occupied," Thrinndor said. "He asked me to come and get him when we are ready to leave." He smiled as he shrugged.

The party leader stood and stretched. He reached for his flagon and finished off what remained. "That is it for me. We will discuss what is next in the morning." After thinking about it for a moment, he corrected himself. "Or whenever it is that we arise."

The others nodded and raised their flagons in tribute as he headed for an open door.

Chapter Thirty-One

Decisions

Thrinndor stumbled out to the common area when he felt he could lie in bed no longer. Truth be told, he had not slept well. What must still be done played out in his head with several variations on the original. He had tossed and turned most of the night.

As he was the first to rise, he began the unfamiliar task of making a pot of coffee. There was a small cook stove that, thankfully, already had a small fire going in it. He guessed at the amount of coffee to put in the basket, filled the pot with water and edged it up to what he hoped was the correct point on the cook top. For added measure, he pushed a piece of wood from the pile next to the stove into the coals.

He shrugged, scratched the unruly mop of hair on his head and stumbled over to door with the moon on it and relieved himself. After washing up, he made his way back to the table and sat down. He put his head in his hands, closed his eyes and waited.

He might even have dozed off; he wasn't sure. After what seemed to be only a few moments Thrinndor looked up to see Sordaak standing at the stove pouring a cup of coffee.

"Good morning," the paladin said sleepily.

The caster turned to look at the paladin. "Is it?" he said. "Morning, I mean?" He put the cup to his mouth and took a sip. Instantly, he pulled the cup away from his lips. "Damn, that's hot!" He blew on the liquid in the cup to cool it.

As he turned to leave the room, Sordaak stopped suddenly and looked into the cup first and then at the paladin. "You make this?" The paladin nodded. "Well, don't do it again! Leave the coffee making to those that know how." He picked up a loaf of bread and headed for the door. "Damn sure should keep me awake, though!" he grumbled as he left for the Library.

Thrinndor scratched his head as he watched the mage pass out of sight around the corner. Whatever, he thought as he got to his feet and walked the short distance back to the stove. He poured himself a cup of the steaming black liquid and returned to his seat.

After a few minutes, the other companions began to make their appearance. Vorgath was first to arrive. He made his way to the stove and poured himself a cup of the viscous black fluid. He took one look at the contents of his cup and raised an eyebrow as he looked over at the paladin.

Thrinndor shrugged as he put his cup to his lips and tested the contents. Both eyebrows shot up as he looked into his cup.

Breunne was next, followed immediately by Cyrillis from a door opposite everyone else. Both made their way to the stove, collected a cup and poured themselves some coffee.

"Be careful with that," said the barbarian as he sat in the chair across from Thrinndor. "It should carry with it a warning."

"Silence, old one," barked the paladin as he took another taste, screwing up his face involuntarily as he set it down.

Both the cleric and the ranger looked at the black fluid in their cups. Breunne shrugged as he sat, and then grimaced as he sampled the fluid inside. Cyrillis made a side trip over to the casks and added some water to hers before making her way over to the table.

Another of the doors opened and Savinhand emerged yawning and rubbing his eyes. By comparison he looked dapper and ready to face the day. The only one of the companions to look so.

"Don't bother that with nasty stuff on the stove," Breunne said. "Discard it immediately and start over, please." He took another sip from his cup. "Please!"

"Very funny," said the paladin. He held his cup to his lips but couldn't bring himself to drink.

Savin took the lid off of the pot and peered inside. He looked over at the companions seated around the table. His eyes settled on the paladin. "You did this?"

"How did you know?" Thrinndor asked defensively.

"Just a lucky guess," the rogue said as he turned back to the stove. "Perhaps you should leave the coffee making to those that know how."

"You are the second to tell me that," said the paladin.

"Well," said the barbarian, "That's because the rest of us are too polite!"

The light talk continued while Savin prepared breakfast. There was a definite reluctance to talk about events from the previous day—or at least to open the conversation.

Thus breakfast was only a memory; dishes piled in a tub and everyone seated back at the table with a second (or third) cup of coffee before conversation moved that direction.

The companions were all seated and the small talk finally died out when Savinhand decided he would get the ball rolling. "I took the liberty of having some of the denizens of this place count and place into piles the coins, gems and pieces of jewelry from the dragon's lair out in the main chamber." He got several lifted eyebrows for his efforts. "The weapons, scrolls, wands and other magical items I asked them to put in a separate pile for us to go through to determine usability."

"Very helpful," said the paladin. "Thank you."

"Wait," the cleric held up her hand. "You mean to tell me we get to keep that stuff?"

"Yes," the rogue leader replied, figuring out what she meant. "The spoils of the dragon are not part of the Library."

"What I want to know," Thrinndor said, "is just how the dragon got 'spoils' in the first place?"

"Huh?" replied the barbarian. "She was a dragon. Dragons have spoils. What are you missing?"

The paladin rolled his eyes. "She has been trapped down here since Phinskyr/Ytharra made her the final test, right? So how did she gather these spoils? From what I saw, there are a lot of these spoils."

Vorgath continued that train of thought. "It also seems likely that a dragon that active would have drawn a lot of attention." His gaze shifted from the paladin to the thief and back. "I have heard of no such activity—and I have people looking for people looking for dragons! I think I would have heard!"

Savinhand's eyes traveled back and forth between the two fighters. "Both valid questions," he said at last. "But you must bear in mind that we don't have any idea where we are!" He leaned back in his chair, a cup of coffee cradled carefully in his left hand. "The entrance to this complex is—was—two days north of Shardmoor. From there we were teleported to I have no idea where!"

"Teleportation has its limits—distance-wise, anyway." Breunne decided to join the conversation with something he knew well.

"Standard teleportation has those limits," Savin responded. "I don't think those limits apply to whatever these rakshasas—if they were indeed the spell power behind this entire complex—were capable of with their combined might. We could be in a totally different land, or at the very least some remote part of our own."

The three fighters—the cleric too, for that matter—worked that over in their minds. After a few minutes, one by one they nodded in reluctant agreement.

"Look," the thief continued, "we are just surmising all of this. What we know is this: We have a dragon, she ransacked quite a bit, she was not disturbed, except by us, and she was the final test for the Library of Antiquity. That's it. We could be anywhere!" He sat back up. "Except in an area where she could have been noticed by one of us!"

After some thinking, Thrinndor shook his head in frustration. "All right. This is just a riddle we will have to list as unsolved and get on with what we are down here for—wherever here is."

The ranger nodded. "However, do we want to get into what we have learned right now? With our caster not present? Or should we maybe take a distraction and go see what the dragon left us?"

Vorgath stood up. "I know which one I vote for!"

Thrinndor hesitated. He wanted to get to the information gathered from the evening before. All eyes were on him. "All right, we will go through our spoils. However, I want everyone back in here within the hour. We have much to discuss."

He got nods from them all as they got to their feet.

"What about Sordaak?" asked Cyrillis.

"The mage told me I would have to drag him kicking and screaming from the Library when we were ready to go," the paladin said with a smile. "I doubt his research will factor much into where it is we need to go next, so we will let him continue his studies until our path is set. He will come along."

The cleric nodded. "Understood," she said as she turned to follow the ranger out toward the main chamber.

"Besides," continued the paladin, "Once we get him away from here, I am certain he will then have an input."

Cyrillis nodded again and continued walking.

The companions minus their magicuser made their way through the main door, past the entrance to the Library and out into the huge chamber the dragon had used as a lair.

Vorgath had stopped and was staring at one of the several large piles of coins not far into the chamber. "All of this is mine?"

"Ahem," the ranger had come up behind the barbarian. "Actually, I think ten percent of that belongs to me."

Savinhand snickered as he walked by.

"Shut it, trap-boy!" grumbled the barbarian.

"While this pocket change is nice," said the paladin as he pushed his way past the three, "I am certain the dragon's other wares are far more interesting."

"That would be correct," said the thief. "This way." He side-stepped a couple more piles of the coins and made his way beyond to several items laid out on a makeshift table.

The companions spread out and gathered around the table.

Breunne sucked in a deep breath and held it. His hand was shaking as he reached out to grasp an ornately carved bow that was covered in runes. "Could it be?" he whispered. His voice was also shaking.

The other companions were staring at him. "Could it be what?" Vorgath asked the obvious question.

As his hand grasped the grip of the bow, the ranger slowly looked up at the others. "This is Xenotath." His voice was a reverent whisper. "Bow of the First Ranger, Kregolarr."

"Are you sure?" asked the rogue leader.

"I wasn't," Breunne said, "until I touched it." His eyes drifted back to the bow, which he now held in his left hand, his right caressing it gently. "This is the bow of the First Ranger!" He shook his head slowly, his eyes never leaving Xenotath. "I don't expect you to understand." He pulled back the string. "But as you know to take in the next breath so you may live, I know this is that bow." Tears were now running down his cheeks.

"Yeah, well," said the barbarian, "let's see what else is here that might actually be of some use!" He looked over at the ranger to see what effect his words had, but he might as well have been talking to a wall. Breunne had turned away and was looking for a place to sit down.

"Whatever," muttered the dwarf as he pushed items around on the table, looking for something that might be of use. Savinhand and Cyrillis did the same.

The healer separated several wands into two piles: ones she could use and those she could not. She assumed those other wands would be able to be used by Sordaak.

There were two rings that she knew to be enchanted, but she was unable to determine what their purpose was. There were other pieces of jewelry, also enchanted, but again handling them told her nothing.

Savinhand selected a pair of daggers he said were so sharp that they must be kept in the special sheaths they were found with or risk losing fingers and even a belt. He demonstrated this by placing the edge of one of the blades against a piece of thick leather. Without pressing on it, he pulled it back with only two fingers, and the blade cut through the leather with ease.

He claimed those as his own, of course.

There was a belt, old by any standard. It was made from a strange metal alloy and covered in runes.

There were several other items: bracers, a circlet, a pair of boots, a pair of spectacles, an ornate robe, a musty old cloak and a breastplate. Try as they might, they could glean nothing from any of them.

"We're wasting time here," said the paladin. "We need Sordaak to tell us if any of this is useful."

"You gonna go get him?" the barbarian asked. "Because I'm not!"

"No," Thrinndor said. "I value my life more than that." He smiled at the dwarf. "We will pack this stuff up and have him check it over once we are well away from here."

"Sounds reasonable," Vorgath agreed. He found a pile of bags nearby and raked everything on the table into one.

"What about all this coin?" the barbarian said when he had cleared the table. "There's no way we can carry all that out of here!"

"Agreed," said the rogue. "I have a solution, but it's going to cost you." He expected a nasty reaction but was disappointed.

"Go on," said the paladin.

Savin cleared his throat. "Those same drow that separated these piles have agreed to deliver it to a place of your choosing for a price." When no one asked, he added, "Ten percent."

Vorgath waved a negligent hand. "Done."

Thrinndor nodded, as did Breunne.

Cyrillis bit her lip as she looked at the pile designated for her. It was far more than she had ever had in her life. Clerics, in general, have little use for coin. However, setting some aside for the future seemed like something that needed to be done. Of course, a large portion of it would go to further Valdaar's service.

"Very well, I will send around the Drow Elder and you may make arrangements with him as you please." He thought briefly and then turned to Thrinndor. "Do you think Sordaak will try to squeeze his pile into that 'portable hole' of his? Or will he want it shipped?"

"Shipped, I am sure," replied the paladin. "He said the artifact's storage was limited." He eyed the large pile set aside for the caster. "I doubt he will want that rattling around in there."

Savin nodded agreement. "Very well, I'll make the arrangements."

Thrinndor hesitated as he considered the next move. He sighed heavily and allowed his shoulders to droop. It was time to discuss what was next for the companions. He feared there would be some disagreement on the matter, hence his trepidation.

He watched as the others made the necessary arrangements with the Elder, waiting his turn. When the drow of indeterminate age approached, he arranged for his portion to be delivered to his mother's keep, Khavhall.

Complete, he turned to the others. "Let us go back inside and discuss what we are to do next."

Without a word, the companions started back toward the rest chamber.

Almost there, Savin turned and pulled the paladin aside. "You sure you don't want Sordaak involved in this discussion?" When Thrinndor did not immediately reply, he went on. "Because I can say visiting hours are over." He smiled. "I need to begin preparations for setting up my defenses, anyway."

Thrinndor considered the offer briefly. "Very well," he said. "But only if you can do so without drawing too much of the caster's ire." He returned the smile. "He will not be pleased."

"Understood," said the rogue. "Allow me to worry about him."

The smile the thief displayed worried the paladin somewhat. But he was unable to continue the conversation as Savin turned and walked away, whistling as he went.

Thrinndor went inside to join his companions, only to discover that the requested documents had been delivered. There was a stack on the table marked for each of them—Vorgath excepted, of course.

The stack marked for the magicuser was actually three stacks. And as the paladin watched, a hurried scribe, hair in disarray, added more parchment sheets to one of the stacks and ran back out of the room.

I hope they are well compensated, the paladin thought with a smile. He looked briefly though his small stack and was pleased to see all was as he had asked. When he looked up, he noted that the others were waiting on him to begin. Thrinndor cleared his throat. "We will begin shortly. Sordaak has had a change of heart and will join us."

As if on cue, an obviously disgruntled mage stepped through the door, immediately followed by the rogue. At a glance from the paladin, Savin shrugged and circled his right ear with his right index finger and pointed at the caster.

Sordaak stormed over to the stove and poured himself a cup of coffee and sat down in front of his stacks of parchment papers. When he noticed everyone staring at him, he gave a curt, "What?"

Suddenly everyone had somewhere else to look. All except Thrinndor. "We must discuss what we are to do next." Seeing the mage's bloodshot eyes, he added, "And you must rest."

Sordaak turned his attention to the stacks on the table in front of him. "I'll have plenty of time for sleep when I'm dead." A drow rushed in and set another sheaf of papers on one of the stacks in front of the mage. Sordaak glared at her. "Where's the rest of it?"

"Coming, my lord." The young woman bowed deeply and left as fast as she could.

"See that you do!" he shouted after her.

An uncomfortable silence settled over the companions, finally broken by the paladin. He began tentatively. "Sordaak…"

"Yes?" the mage replied, not looking up from the handful of papers he had in his left hand.

"We must talk about what we have learned and what we are to do next." Thrinndor's voice gathered confidence as he spoke.

The sorcerer let out a breath in a huff, tossed the papers he was holding onto a stack, folded his arms on his chest and leaned back in this chair. "All right!" he said. After a few seconds his hand shot out and retrieved his coffee cup. His eyes shifted to the paladin. "Today!"

"Yes…well," stammered the paladin. He looked over at the cleric. "First, we will talk about what we have learned from the Library. Cyrillis has an announcement." His eyes implored her to please begin the proceedings.

The cleric shifted nervously in her chair. "Well," she began, her eyes shifting from the caster to the paladin and back, "after much research and lots of help from Breunne and Thrinndor, I was able to determine that I am indeed of the lineage of Angra-Khan."

"Very nice," muttered the caster. He took a sip from the mug in his hand and scrunched up his face in distaste. "But we already surmised that." He glared at the paladin. "Please tell me there is more."

Thrinndor shifted his weight to his other foot. This was not going as planned. "Vorgath found Florashiim, and we were able to discern how it came to be in the Library."

"Old news," said the caster with an air of aloofness. "Next?"

Now the paladin was sweating profusely. He looked over at the ranger who still held the bow in his hands, unable to set it down. "Breunne found Xenotath, Bow of the Frist Ranger in the lair of the dragon."

"Now that's news!" The caster leaned forward. "May I see it?" He extended his right hand toward the ranger.

Breunne reluctantly handed the bow over.

Sordaak rubbed his hands over it reverently. He eyed, and presumably read, the runes inscribed across its many surfaces. When he looked up, his eyes shone with excitement. "This is truly amazing!" He handed the bow back to the ranger. "We must make you some arrows worthy of such an artifact!"

Not sure what to say, the ranger merely nodded.

"Anything else?" the mage asked the paladin. "Presumably you have saved the best for last?"

"Umm…yes," replied the paladin. He straightened his tunic and stood to his full height. "I was able to discern the last known location of Valdaar's Fist."

"What?" Sordaak leaned forward, spilling half of his coffee in the process. He ignored that. "You've found the sword?"

"No," corrected the paladin. "I have found where it was seen last."

The mage rolled his eyes. "Are you going to make me beg for the information?"

"No," exclaimed the paladin. "Valdaar's Fist was last seen 400 years ago in Ice Homme."

Sordaak sprayed coffee for several feet when he launched the small amount of the black fluid he had sipped from his cup. "Ice Homme? Minion stronghold Ice Homme?"

"That's the place," Vorgath said, tired of the verbal dancing going on around him. "So, that's where we're going next?"

"Obviously," said the caster as he began shuffling through one of the stacks in front of him. "With a side trip, of course."

"Of course," said the paladin. "Side trip?"

The female scribe came in again, another sheaf of papers in her hand. She was about to put them on the stack when the mage exploded. "Could we get some privacy, please?" He snatched the papers from her. She spun and scurried out of the door. "Savin?" the mage turned to the thief. "Can we lock that door, please?"

"Yes," replied the thief. "But why?

The mage glared at the rogue. "We have some discussions to do about where we are going next," he said. "The damn minions have spies everywhere!" When Savinhand didn't move, he added bitingly, "I trust no one!"

Savinhand went to the door and obligingly locked it. For good measure he slid a shelf unit over to block it.

"I'm not sure that was necessary," the mage said dryly. "How much do you trust these drow?"

"They counted your coins and will deliver them for you—and the rest of the party as well," replied the thief. "I trust them."

"That makes me feel better," the sorcerer looked at the ceiling. "The thief leader trusts them!"

"Listen," said the rogue guild leader, "you asked and I answered. They have been here for many hundreds of years and have been tasked with tending to the needs of any that visit the Library." He glared back at the caster. "I trust them."

Sordaak looked away. "Very well," he said. "You trust them. Now I trust them." He looked back at the rogue. "Keep the door locked."

Savinhand rolled his eyes. "Yes, master!"

"No need to get snippy," said the caster. "We are all part of a secret quest. What we are about and where we do it must not be allowed to become the topic of discussion, even among people you trust."

Silence again fell upon the companions.

"So what is this side trip?" Vorgath grew tired of waiting.

"If we must go to Ice Homme," the mage answered, "then there is a stop I'd like to make not far from there."

Silence.

"I'll bite," said the ranger. "Where? And why?"

"Mioria, realm of the Storm Giants," the caster said matter of factly. Now a stunned silence fell on the companions.

"What?" said the rogue.

"On purpose?" chipped in the ranger.

"Hear me out," said the magicuser. "I was able to unearth a little-known truth. Storm Giants possess spell ability that allows them to call storms and call lightning, among others. But those are the ones I'm after."

"How so?" asked the barbarian. "And why do we need to go seek them out?"

"I'm glad you asked," answered the mage. Indeed, he had been waiting for someone to ask. "I was able to dig up a tale that says that if the cloak is removed from a living Storm Giant, then the spell powers associated with Storm Giants are bestowed on the wearer of that cloak."

"Interesting," said the cleric. "But from what I remember of Storm Giant lore, their cloaks are fixed around the necks of the giants from the time they are but children. The band that binds the cloak is an unbroken piece of Mithryl and it is not removable."

"Very good," said the caster. "You have done your research." He looked from the healer to the parchment sheet in his hand. "This is instructions, including the spell required, that makes it possible to remove that band from a living Storm Giant!"

"What does that have to do with me?" asked the barbarian, bored.

"I kind of forgot to mention that one of the attributes the cloak bestows upon the wearer is the strength of a Storm Giant!"

Vorgath leaned forward and put his hands on the table. "You're sure of this?"

Sordaak nodded. "I researched it from three different angles. It is so."

"Damn," whispered the dwarf. "The strength of a Storm Giant." He looked over at the paladin. "That would be a worthwhile goal."

"Agreed," said the paladin. "But what does that have to do with Ice Homme?"

The sorcerer grinned knowingly. "I thought you would never ask," he said. "Storm Giants migrate to the cliffs of Mioria just before winter sets in."

"The cliffs of Mioria?" Breunne asked. "They're only a week or so hard travel north of Farreach."

"Precisely," said the sorcerer. "Practically on our way!"

Thrinndor looked over at the rogue. "Assuming we are able to leave this place where we came in?"

Savinhand's face took on a surprised look. "Yes," he said. "That is your only option." He glanced at each of them. "Once you exit, the portal will disappear, to reappear only at a place of my choosing."

"Once 'you' exit," Cyrillis said. When everyone looked at her, she repeated, "He said 'once you exit'. As if he will not be exiting with us."

All eyes shifted back to the rogue. "That's correct, I won't," he said.

The companions began to speak all at once, and the rogue leader raised his hand for quiet. When the murmur had died down, he said, "I will have to join you at your next destination." He paused, trying to figure how to tell them what they needed to know without saying too much. "I must tend to my duties as curator/administrator of the Library of Antiquities." He took in a deep breath. "For reasons I'm sure you understand after seeing what was inside, I must ensure it is not only protected from those who would plunder its resources, but also ensure there is a connected path to its riches should my time as curator/administrator come to an abrupt end."

Savin got nods from the paladin and sorcerer. He smiled. "After all, hanging around with you guys can certainly be considered hazardous to one's health!"

The room went silent for a few heartbeats.

"How long?" The party leader was the first to break the silence. Savin had become an integral part of their plans. Besides, there was the geas and his oath to consider.

Savin's face got longer when he faced the paladin. "I know what it is I must do, and I have a plan on how to accomplish it." He hesitated. "I know I have sworn to serve you and your quest—and I have no intention of breaking that oath—but this is something I must do." His eyes were pleading with Thrinndor to understand.

The companion leader did. "How long?" he repeated. He still needed to know how long they would be without the services of a rogue.

"A week, ten days, tops!" promised the thief. "There is a lot to do."

"A week then," said the paladin.

Savin rushed ahead with the thought. "You all must traverse the distance to the cliffs of Mioria. That will take you at least three days." He was thinking fast. "The way I see it is we have a couple of choices." The smile returned to his face, although more tentatively. "One, you can do your assault on the Storm Giants without me and I'll meet you in Ice Homme in a week." He took in another deep breath. "Or two, you can delay your assault by taking care of training, outfitting for the trip and/or other items of interest until I finish my duties here."

Thrinndor's face took on a stern look. "Travel to and from our trainers—not to mention the training time—would far exceed the weeks' time frame." He glowered at the thief. "That is not an option! We must continue our quest posthaste."

"Then you must take on the Storm Giants without me," the thief said as he shrugged.

"I, for one," Sordaak said, "do not care for that option."

"Me, either," said the barbarian. When everyone turned to look at him, Vorgath explained. "Without our almost competent trapsmith, I would have to open the doors!"

Thrinndor nodded. "Well said."

"I have another possible option," Savinhand said hesitantly.

The paladin lifted a brow. The rogue certainly had their attention.

"The drow that serve this place asked me to make it known that they have trainers available in each of the disciplines we might need." He surveyed the room to see what they were thinking. "While they will not take the place of each of your personal trainers, they are well versed in the appropriate doctrines that would allow each of you—us—access to a trainer without traveling back to your homes." Vorgath started to speak, but changed his mind. Savinhand smiled. "Yes, there is even a high-ranking barbarian available."

A silence settled on the group while each pondered the merits of the offer. Training without a trip home was an obvious advantage.

The paladin stepped forward. "May we each speak with the proposed trainer before we make a decision?"

"Of course," Savin said. He started toward the door, but stopped short. He turned and smiled at the caster. "Training here would have another benefit." Sordaak raised an eyebrow. "You would have access to The Library of Anti—"

The mage cut him off. "I vote we remain and train here."

"I thought that might sway you," replied the thief. "However, I will only be able to make that available until I need to move the entrance."

"When will that be?" The sorcerer was suspicious.

"Four, maybe five days." Savin was apprehensive.

"Sold!" Sordaak said. "Can I start now?"

"You should rest," said the healer. She immediately regretted having opened her mouth.

The mage glared at her. "I can sleep…"

"…when you are dead," she finished for him. "I know." She returned his glare. "However, a tired sorcerer is one apt to make errors." She folded her arms across her chest.

Sordaak appeared to consider her request. "How long have I been awake?"

"Without a sun to go—" Cyrillis started.

"Thirty-six hours," said the barbarian. "Plus or minus an hour or two." He grinned.

"Well," said the caster as he pondered, "I just drank a cup of coffee. That will keep me going for another four hours." He looked over at the cleric. "I will get some sleep after that, promise." It was his turn to smile. "Will that do?"

Cyrillis turned slightly red. She lifted her chin. "That will have to do," she said. "But see that you do."

"Yes, ma'am." As the rogue opened the door leading to the main chamber, Sordaak was almost running to get back to the Library.

"Just make sure you avail yourself of a trainer," the paladin called after him.

"Yes, sir," came the reply from well outside the room.

Savinhand followed the caster out into the main chamber, returning after a few minutes with a bevy of drow elves. He made introductions all around and left his companions with their new trainers.

An elderly drow waited patiently while this process was completed and then left with the thief when he stepped back out into the main room. Obviously the trainer for the magicuser, Vorgath thought.

*

Four days later, the companions were all gathered back in the common area at the request of the rogue leader.

"It's time, I'm afraid," he said.

"Nooooo!" Sordaak protested. He was smiling.

"Yes," said the thief, returning the smile. "We all knew this day was coming. It is time for me to close the entrance as you know it and move it to its new location."

"How about you drop me off there?" Sordaak was in a jesting mood.

"You know I cannot," Savinhand said, shaking his head. The caster nodded sheepishly. "The denizens of this place have arranged for some horses and pack animals—loaded out for a month trek for all of us—to be waiting for you when you exit.

"You will leave from there to begin your journey to the Cliffs of Mioria. After I complete the move and get as much of the defenses set up as I can, I've made arrangements to be teleported to just outside of Shardmoor. Once there, I will take care of some Guild business, including a chain of command for my continued extended absence."

He took in a deep breath. "Finally, when I am finished there, I have given Sordaak a token that will notify him when I am ready, and he can then remote teleport me to your current location. If all goes as I have planned, that will occur about the time you get to the Cliffs."

Savinhand looked around at his companions, realizing this was good-bye. He was not good at good-byes. This was hard. He choked up. "Are there any questions?"

Forthcoming in 2015…
The Valdaar's Fist Saga Continues!

Valdaar's Fist Book One – *Dragma's Keep*

Valdaar's Fist Book Two – *The Library of Antiquity*

Valdaar's Fist Book Three – *Ice Homme*

Valdaar's Fist Book Four – *The Platinum Dragon*

Acknowledgements

Thank you to the following for their contribution to this book:

Again to my wife, Lisa Pumphrey, who has allowed me the time to put everything else on hold as I worked to get this second book complete and ready for print. Her patience and understanding has helped keep me on an even keel during all this drama. Thank you and I love you!

Thank you to my friends and family for your patience in waiting for this book to become a reality. I appreciate your enthusiasm for *Dragma's Keep*, and your none-to-gentle pushes to get on with Book Two! While Book One will always have a place in my heart as being my first, *The Library of Antiquity* is even better. This book moves faster and has more content. I truly hope each of you—as well as the others who pick these books up to read—enjoy reading this austere tome as much as I enjoyed writing it.

About the Author

Vance Pumphrey traces the evolution of his high fantasy novels from his Nuclear Engineering career in the U.S. Navy—not an obvious leap. He started playing Dungeons and Dragons while in the Navy, though, and the inspiration for the Valdaar's Fist series was born.

The Library of Antiquity is the second book in the Valdaar's Fist quartet. A third book in the series follows soon.

Retired from the Navy, Vance lives in Seattle with his wife of thirty-plus years.

To find out when the next Valdaar's Fist book will be released, check out VancePumphrey.com.

Made in the USA
Charleston, SC
05 September 2015